DEAD SHOT!

The Rucker careened around the pinnacle. One
of the leading mules was holding back. Bright
blood ripped from its gaping mouth. One of the
front wheels struck a rock, bounced up, and
shattered. The ambulance tilted sideways and
went over with a crash. The mules dragged it
a short distance and then halted. The driver
had been catapulted from his seat. His head
had struck the hard ground and his neck was
twisted awkwardly. The upper wheels kept
spinning. The woman clambered out of the
wreckage, still holding her carbine.

The three Apaches rounded the pinnacle,
shouting in triumph. They did not see Alec fifty
yards from them. The repeater cracked flatly
three times. . . .

THE

GHOST

DANC

NCERS

Gordon D. Shirreffs

FAWCETT GOLD MEDAL • NEW YORK

A Fawcett Gold Medal Book
Published by Ballantine Books
Copyright © 1986 by Gordon D. Shirreffs

Library of Congress Catalog Card Number: 85-91234

ISBN 0-449-12783-4

Manufactured in the United States of America

First Edition: February 1986

To the Sutphen Boys: Dale L. Walker—
"The Decatur Kid,"
"Lobo" Loren Estleman, "Rio Bob" Randisi,
"Bad River Tim,"
Champlin and "Tze-go-juni" Louisa Rudeen.

The Chiricahuas need no legends; their truths are legend. Their history was written by their enemies.

CHAPTER 1

THE THIN SMOKE ROSE STRING-STRAIGHT INTO THE DAWN sky, almost like an admonishing finger to anyone within sight of it. Several dark dots, like scraps of charred paper rising in an updraft, circled slowly around the smoke. The origin of the smoke had to be the old long-abandoned rancho sited at the ancient springs once called Los Ojos de Prieta, The Springs of Dark Water, but now more commonly called Los Ojos de Muerte, or simply Death Springs. The place had an evil reputation; it was said to be haunted by the spirits of those who had died violently there. It was hardly the place for one to die peacefully. This was Chiricahua Apache country and deadly dangerous. It was mostly the Chiricahuas who had given the springs their unsavory reputation. They no longer visited the springs. The spirits of the vengeful dead were too many now, and haunted the area at least in the superstitious minds of the Chiricahuas. Few Americans ever stopped there. Mexicans did so only of dire necessity in that arid country. No one unless drunk or not in his right mind would stay there overnight.

Brevet Major, First Lieutenant Alexander Kershaw held up his right arm to halt his half-platoon of Apache Scouts as he reined in his tired dun. The trail dust drifted off. Sergeant Mickey Free trotted his gray up from the rear of the column and stopped beside Alec. His eyes too were on that ominous smoke. The patrol was south of the border on the Sonoran side and had been for several days. They had been on patrol for almost a month and were a week overdue to return to Fort Bowie. Their strict orders had been to patrol the area—Sulphur Springs Valley, Swisshelm and Pedregosa Mountains *southwest* of the Chiricahuas. Standing orders were explicit that no American troops or Apache Scouts were to cross the border *at any time*. It was a court-martial offense to do so. Now they were well beyond the border and due south of the

Chiricahuas. Alec Kershaw had struck Apache sign just north of the border. That had been the very day they should have returned north to Bowie. The patrol was out of rations and low on water. The horses were worn out, underfed, and badly in need of water as well. The Scouts were ready to return. They knew Mexican troops and civilians shot first and asked questions later when it concerned Apaches. They watched Alec out of the corners of their eyes as he uncased his field glasses.

The German field glasses, eight-power, made by that master of his craft, Vollmer of Jena, picked out the black dots circling lower and lower around the smoke column. The clear lenses resolved the dots into *zopilotes*, the great Sonoran black vultures. They were hanging on seemingly motionless dirty-white patched wings, riding the dawn wind that had begun to drift the smoke southward. Something, or someone, was dead or dying down at the springs.

Mickey dismounted. "*Zopilotes*," he said. "Best scouts in the sky." He grinned. "If you're looking for someone dead, that is."

Mickey Free was a half-breed. His mother was Mexican, a *captiva* of the Pinaleno Apaches. His father had been a Pinaleno warrior. Mickey's left eye had been marked at birth. It was cocked and covered with a whitish-gray film. The defect gave him a sinister appearance. He was invaluable as a scout and manhunter. He was trilingual, speaking fluent English, Spanish, and a number of Apache dialects. Mickey was a dark-minded man, a killer, and highly successful in his line of work—manhunting. He was distrusted and feared. Alec knew his value in the field and had enlisted him as sergeant. Alec Kershaw always did have an affinity for the outlyers, the loners, and those who went their own way. Such a preference had hurt his military career, but he would have it no other way. Mickey had appreciated Alec's evaluation of him. They had become a good team, and beyond that they were friends.

Alec lowered the glasses. "We've located the raiding party, Mick."

Mickey shrugged. "Or where they've been. They'd be

long gone by now if it was them. Seems like they left something dead behind too.''

Muerte Springs were situated in a large shallow bowl opening to the south like a horseshoe, with a broad panoramic view of barren rolling desert terrain, somewhat like dun-colored waves frozen into position. The bowl was encircled within the arms of a black malpais formation of low hills that extended north for some miles, beyond which was more semi-desert-type of terrain. A narrow, twisting pass cut between springs and desert. In the far distance rose the dim, hazy trace of the Chiricahua Mountains, like an island from the sea.

Alec looked to the north. ''I'd say they either went north or south. South to get into the Sierra Madre, or north to the Chiricahuas. Either way, we've likely lost them. We can't backtrail into Mexico if they did head for the Sierra Madre. If they've headed for their stronghold in the Chiricahuas, we'll never be able to catch up with them. Once they're in there, no one can follow them.''

Southeast Arizona Territory and Northern Sonora had been aflame in the six years following the Civil War. Apache hit-and-run raids were almost weekly occurrences from the Stein's Peak country just over the New Mexico Territory line, west to and beyond Tucson, then south to the Mexican border and beyond Magdalena in Sonora, then east again to the New Mexico line. It was thousands of square miles of desert, hill country, deep canyons, and rugged mountain ranges. The raiders swept down unseen from their mountain strongholds, the Chiricahuas, Dos Cabezas, Dragoons, Whetstones, Rincons, and Santa Ritas. They came too from the Atascosas, Patagonias, Huachucas, and other mountain ranges. Ranches were raided, mines attacked, and the miners slain or forced to flee. Wagon trains, army supply wagons, stagecoaches, and stage stations were attacked regularly. Horses, cattle, and mules were driven off. The stock stolen in Mexico was driven north and sold in the United States; that stolen in the States was driven south and sold in Mexico. All of the various tribal divisions of the Apaches were involved—Chiricahuas, Mimbrenos, Arivaipas, White Mountain, Tontos, Pinalenos, Mansos, and others. It was almost as though they had joined together in a vast conspiracy to knock Americans and Mexicans off balance and keep them that way until they were either slaughtered or driven forever from Apacheria, the Land of the Apaches.

Mexican troops were too few in number and almost helpless in the face of the constant raiding. American troops, always in short supply due to a parsimonious Congress, and usually too slow in pursuit and too inexperienced to catch their elusive, wily, and highly mobile foes, accomplished little or nothing. Many remote posts were held only by the range of the garrison's rifles. Ennui, sickness, alcoholism, and desertion weakened the few troops in the newly formed Department of Arizona. Only the recently formed Apache Scouts managed to have some success in tracking down the hostile Apaches. They knew the country as no white man could ever know it, and better than that, *they knew their own people*. A current saying in army command circles was: "It takes an Apache to catch an Apache." *Or to kill them off;* that was the thought of Alec Kershaw.

"The scouts should be back by now," Alec said. The patrol had force-marched the night before while the trail was still hot. An hour before dawn he had sent out five of his best men—The Thin One, Jackrabbit, Bear, Antelope, and The Limper. They had fanned out in a semicircle miles in extent, trotting tirelessly through the darkness, their senses acute to razor sharpness.

Mickey covertly studied Alec. When he had first met him, he had taken an immediate liking to him, a rare occurrence for Mickey. It had developed into respect and trust for this tall, rangy six-foot-plus Regular Army officer with the weather-tanned features and hard, gray, sun-tightened eyes. Alec's face was lean, the jawline strong, the nose hawklike. There was a whitish scar at the corner of his left eye extending down toward the jawline, a memento of a Navajo knife slash. His sun-darkened hair was a reddish-blond of the type called sandy by the Scots. His dragoon mustache and beard were coppery-red. He was wide of shoulder, with a slim horseman's waist. His body was trim and muscular. His walk was catlike. On patrol with his Scouts he wore their distinguishing mark, a red flannel headband. He had on an enlisted man's shirt with no insignia of rank on the shoulders. His breeches were faded blue with the one-eighth-inch-wide yellow officer's stripe. While on patrol he wore Apache desert footgear, the *n'deh b'keh,* which were thigh-length, thick-soled, and button-toed. He wore them folded below the knee and tied with a leather thong. When he was around superior officers or on a military installation, he wore the regulation blouse, field boots, and a faded campaign hat. Now the blouse was rolled around the boots and stuffed into his cantle roll. Alec's field supply of powerful Mexican Baconora brandy was in leather flasks inside the boots. He might forget rations on the trail. He could go almost as long as an Apache without water. He went nowhere without his Baconora.

Alexander Kershaw was the living embodiment of the scout officer described by General MacDowell, Commander of the Department of the Pacific: "They must be active, zealous officers. They must wish to really accomplish something, and be able to endure fatigue and be willing to undergo great *personal privations.*" General Crook, newly appointed commander of the Department of Arizona, under whom Kershaw had served during the Civil War, had added his opinion to that of MacDowell. "I require extraordinary white men to lead Apaches as Chief of Scouts. We need the Apaches to beat their own people. Therefore, the Indian Scout officer must be that 'rare' man." George Crook knew soldiers in large bodies with excessive baggage were only a hindrance in fighting Apaches, who put a premium on mobility and endurance. Alec Kershaw was that "rare" man to General Crook. He held perfect control over his Scouts because he never lied to them.

Alec focused his field glasses on a moving dot crossing the barren ground between him and the distant springs. The dot was resolved into his best tracker—Nonithian, The Limper. He was moving at his awkward but ground-gaining trot. When he had been a child, a mountain lion had seized him by the leg and dragged him off. An arrow from his grandfather's bow had killed the lion. The Limper had grown up and passed his novitiate to be a warrior despite his handicap.

His experience with the mountain lion had given him a
"power" derived from the powers of the lion itself. He had
gained the ability to track man or animal with an uncanny skill
bordering on the miraculous. Most Apaches had power of one
kind or another. Some had good tracking ability. None of
them had it as much as The Limper. His companions said of
him, "He can track man or animal on solid rock on a pitch-
black night in a male rainstorm." Exaggeration certainly, but
his tracking did seem like something of a miracle.

The Limper halted and signaled for the others to join him.

Something was wrong at the springs. The Scouts knew it.
They were nervous and skittish. They had been out too long.
They didn't like being in Mexico. They hated Mexicans with
a consuming passion. Further, Muerte Springs had an evil
reputation among the Apaches.

The Limper was a small man with a gnomelike face and
huge, expressive eyes. He pointed toward the springs.
"Smugglers, Nan-tan," he reported in his own tongue.
"Seven of them. *Nakai-yes*. Mexicans."

Alec usually spoke in Chiricahua dialect to his Scouts. It
sounded like Chinese spoken through a mouthful of saliva.
"Are they alive?"

The Limper shook his head. "They have crossed the canyon."

"How did they die?" Mickey asked.

"Shot in the back. Scalped," replied the scout.

Mickey looked at Alec. Apaches rarely scalped to let out
the slain person's spirit. They would crush the skull instead.
They might take one scalp for a victory ceremony, but it was
always discarded after use.

"Chiricahuas? Those we trailed?" Alec asked.

The Limper shook his head. "They must have come by
here but didn't stop. They bypassed the malpais and rode
north toward the Big Mountain. Fast, like this." He made the
hand sign for a bird in flight, the Apache symbol for swift-
ness.

"Then who killed the *Nakai-yes*?" Mickey asked quietly.

"*Pinda-lick-o-ye* or *Nakai-yes*," The Limper replied.

Americans or Mexicans. "How do you know?" Alec asked.

The scout turned and pointed. "There are two trails beyond the malpais. One is that of the Chiricahuas who did not stop at the springs. They rode fast for the Big Mountain."

"And the other?" Mickey asked.

"Come and see for yourself. It would be better if the others stayed away from the springs," The Limper replied.

The smoke had dwindled to a thin thread. The wind-borne *zopilotes* had swung lower, and some of them did not rise again. More of them were winging in from the south.

Alec halted the platoon half a mile from the springs. He did not have to tell them of the death there. They knew. Seven more corpses would have added that number of vengeful spirits hovering around the springs. There were others there from the past. Muerte Springs had been haunted by the dead for many years.

The Limper led the way, fingering the four-stranded medicine cord hanging around his thin neck. It was a fearful journey for him, made worse by the fact that he knew specifically what was waiting there. Still, he would do anything for the Nan-tan.

The springs welled up at the foot of a rocky hummock. The shallow bowl in which they were situated was surrounded by scrub trees and thick brush. To the north the low malpais hills were wrinkled like elephant hide. To the south the view was open to infinity.

Alec's dun shied and blew repeatedly as they neared the bowl. Alec dismounted and led him closer, then turned him over to The Limper.

Mickey drew his Sharps rifle from its saddle scabbard and opened the breech to check the load.

"Afraid of the dead, Mick?" Alec asked with a crooked grin.

Mickey closed the breech. "You bet! And the living too! This Sharps is the best insurance in this country, Major."

Alec withdrew his Winchester '66 "Yellow Boy" rifle from its saddle scabbard and levered a round into its chamber.

They left The Limper with the horses. The Nan-tan was wise

in the ways of The People. He would not order any of them to go into such a place of horror as the springs were that day.

Alec and Mickey topped the rim of the bowl and looked down into it. The smoke had emanated from what had been a tumbledown group of shacks and adobes that had once been, long ago, the ranch of a Mexican who had more courage than brains. The burning roofs had fallen within the structures to form a thick bed of smoking ashes.

Mickey quickly turned his head to one side. "Jesus!" he spat out.

The sprawled bodies were almost impossible to see because of the crowding, pushing, grunting vultures that fought for better positions to tear at the bloated flesh with their iron-hard beaks. Thin dust rose from the clawed scraping of the big carrion-eaters. Their repulsive red necks thrust in and out like striking snakes as they ate, gulping voraciously. A persistent cloud of bluebottle flies, disturbed at their feast, buzzed angrily overhead.

Alec pulled his bandanna up around his nose and mouth. He went down the slope followed by Mickey. They waded in among the repulsive birds, striking out with the butts of their rifles, driving them back. The vultures raised and lowered their wings, grunting horribly as they stubbornly retreated. One of them flopped around with a broken wing, while another lay in the dust with a broken leg. The instant Alec and Mickey turned away, the vultures closed in again.

"Goddamn!" Alec shouted. He yanked out his Remington .44 revolver and fired it into the midst of the birds until the hammer clicked on an empty shell. The living were scattered, the dead and dying left behind. Those able to take wing flew beyond the rim of the bowl, leaving wreathing dust and drifting feathers to mark their passage.

Mickey spat. "Waste of good ammunition. For Christ's sake, Major, they were only doing their duty." He grinned crookedly.

They set to their gruesome task. The seven corpses had been shot in the back, their skulls crushed in, stripped to the skin, and neatly scalped. The work had been thorough, including the ears. The face skin had sagged into grotesque caricatures of human features.

Mickey picked up one of the empty bottles scattered on the ground. "Tequila," he reported. "A lot."

The water in the large shallow rock tank fed by the springs was covered with a film of greenish scum. Several kegs sat beside the tank with bandannas stretched over the bungholes so that water could be strained into them, eliminating most of the objectionable substances.

Mickey picked up a dust-covered Mexican silver dollar. "Fresh-minted 'dobe dollar," he said. He pointed out several others scattered under nearby brush. A few more glinted at the bottom of the rock tank.

"Well, Mick?" Alex asked.

"Smugglers. Come up from Sonora. Magdalena most likely. Camped here sometime late yesterday afternoon. Got heavy into the tequila, mebbe to get the taste of the water out of their mouths or mebbe because they didn't like this place and needed a little tequila courage to stay here. Someone Indianed up on 'em. Shot them in the back. Killed the lot. Stripped and scalped them. Crushed in the skulls to let out the vengeful spirit so's to make it look like 'Paches done it. Took the smuggling money, horses, mules, clothes, guns, and scalps and left during the night."

Alec nodded. "It's also possible the killers were known by those they murdered here. It isn't likely these smugglers would be stupid enought to camp here without setting up a guard." He fished a full bottle of tequila out of the tank. He opened it and sniffed the contents. "You ever smell tequila like that?" he asked as he handed the bottle to Mickey.

Mickey sniffed it. He nodded. "You remember those friendly Opatas camped over in the Patagonias? Scalped just like these poor bastards. They had been given poisoned tequila by someone."

"What do you think, Mick?" Alec asked. He was really seeking confirmation of his own suspicion.

"*Gambrusinos?*" Mickey asked.

Gambrusinos—Mexican nationals for the most part, with a leavening of half-breeds and outlaw Americans. The literal translation meant "moonlighters"—adventurers and fortune hunters by night and seemingly honest citizens by day. Their specialty was waylaying travelers who believed it was safest to travel at night in that Apache-infested country. There were many such bands. Some were of minor consequence. Others had more stature. The largest and by far the worst was the one led by Chico Diaz. He was said to be part Mexican, part Yaqui and part American. One might add, *and all bad.* His band operated freely on both sides of the border. There was no crime they would not commit. Material gain was their only interest in life. They were robbers, rapists, murderers, smugglers of stolen goods, and perhaps worst of all was their method of scalp hunting. The Mexican states of Sonora and Chihuahua paid good bounties for Apache scalps. The rate was one hundred pesos for a mature male, fifty for a female, and twenty-five for a child of either sex. No questions were asked about the source of the hair. Recently, because of the increased depredations of the Apaches, the ante for a male scalp had been upped to two hundred pesos. The peso was about the same value as the American dollar. The scalps, many times with the ears still attached, were delivered in reeking bales. Cash was paid over the counter. Chico Diaz's men sometimes disguised themselves as Apaches and attacked small out of the way *placitas,* isolated ranches, wagon trains, mines, and even waylaid small military patrols. After scalping their victims and turning in the scalps, they would then sally forth to track down the supposed Apache raiders.

"Clever bastards," Mickey said. "They likely knew Chiricahuas were operating in this area again. They killed this bunch, then made it look like Apache work. They forgot one thing—no Apache in his right mind would ever come here for any reason, unless maybe he was nigh to dying of thirst, and then he'd stay just long enought to drink and then split ass out of here."

"Which reminds me. Go back to The Limper. Tell him to bring my horse and his for water. Then you go back to the platoon and bring down the rest of the horses for watering and the scouts' canteens for filling."

The Limper brought the two horses. He looked nervously

toward the corpses and then up at the *zopilotes* circling patiently high overhead.

After watering their mounts, Alec and The Limper led them toward the south for half a mile. There the trail forked. A small group of horses had been ridden due south. A larger group had split off toward the east. Alec and the scout followed the trail of the larger group until they were beyond the eastern edge of the malpais hills where it then trended northeast toward the San Bernardino Valley.

"How many men, do you think?" Alec asked.

The Limper pointed south. "Five men, I think. They had pack mules with them." He pointed northeast. "Fifteen, maybe twenty or more, leading maybe ten pack mules or horses."

The Limper looked to the southwest. "Dust, Nan-tan. Many horsemen coming this way."

"Follow the trail to the northeast," Alec ordered. "If they cross the border, report back to me at once."

The sound of distant gunfire came on the wind from the southwest as Alec returned to the springs. He rode down into the bowl and dismounted. He yanked his rifle from its scabbard and ran up the west slope of the bowl. The first thing he saw was Mickey Free riding at full gallop toward the springs. There was a large group of horsemen halted two hundred yards behind him. The sun glinted from polished metal. A bright-colored guidon snapped in the fresh breeze. There was no doubt but that they were Mexican soldiers.

Mickey drew up his horse. It flung off with forehooves thrashing. He hit the ground running with his Sharps rifle in hand. He led the gray down into the bowl, then slogged back up to where Alec was studying the Mexicans through his field glasses.

A bugle sounded. The Mexican troopers dismounted and spread out into a skirmish line as the horseholders trotted to the rear, each leading four mounts. An officer stood up in his stirrups and looked toward the springs.

Mickey lay down beside Alec and thrust his rifle forward. "Regulars," he said. "They stampeded the platoon. God alone knows where the scouts are now. Mebbe halfway to the border already." He half-cocked his Sharps.

"Hold it, Mick," Alec said. He stood up and waved his arms. "American *soldados!*" he shouted.

The officer focused his field glasses on Alec. He lowered them, then spoke to another officer on foot. The skirmish line fanned farther out to the right and left and halted. There were a lot of them.

"Mebbe we'd better pull foot, Major," Mickey suggested.

Alec shook his head. "We can't outfight them and we can't outrun them. We'll have to bullshit our way out of this mess."

"You know I ain't too popular on this side of the line. They've got a price on my head."

"You can run if you like. You should have run with the platoon when you had the chance."

Mickey shook his head. "This is my place of duty," he said simply.

Alec stood up again. "I'll have to go out and parley. I don't want them to find out we're all alone here." He raised his arms and walked toward the Mexicans before Mickey could protest.

The Mexican officer was resplendent in gold-braided blouse and kepi. He cantered his horse toward Alec. "Captain Ramon Gonzalez, Regiment Fronteras Fusilieros, on detached duty with the Tenth Cavalry," he said, casually hand-saluting. "I recognized you, Major Kershaw, despite your rather, shall we say, unusual garb for a United States Regular officer of cavalry? You may recall our last meeting along the border."

Alec nodded. Gonzalez was a typical *godo gachupin*, and an arrogant sonofabitch. "It was *you* who was then on the wrong side of the border."

Gonzalez smiled a little. "So you firmly reminded me at the time. You realize, of course, that due to your present position, I can arrest you and your band of savages without any recourse from your government. I'm afraid I would have to detain your 'command' and have them escorted to the border and turned over to your authorities. You know the standing orders from both governments, Major. May I ask why you crossed the border this time?"

Alec shrugged. "We were dangerously low on water," he

lied. "Muerte Springs was the closest source of water, so we came here. . . ." He saw the obvious disbelief on the Mexican's face.

Gonzalez leaned forward on his pommel and studied him. "There is water north of the border at your abandoned Camp Farrar. I know your savages can go as long as a camel without water. It would have been simpler and certainly more convenient for you to go to Camp Farrar. Is that not so?"

Alec shrugged. "You forgot about *me* and the horses, Captain."

Gonzalez smiled. "Since when have these Apache animals worried about riding a horse to death? And I have it on good authority that you yourself have been practicing the way of the bushy-haired devils. It is rumored you have almost taken on the physical attributes of an Apache."

"Not quite, Captain, although I do try."

"Disgusting!" Gonzalez snapped.

"A matter of opinion," Alec said.

"Why have you really come here? I know no Apache in his right mind would come near Los Ojos de Muerte except in dire necessity."

Alec decided to make a clean breast of it. "We saw the smoke rising from the area of the springs and decided to investigate. We had been trailing Chiricahua raiders. The trail was hot. We didn't think they would stop here, but by that time we needed water."

"And *did* they stop here, Major?" Gonzalez asked dryly.

Alec shook his head. He pointed up at the *zopilotes* still making lazy circles over the springs. "No, Captain, but someone else did. Would you like to see what happened to seven of your citizens? I can promise you safe conduct."

Gonzalez signaled back to his command. A young officer rode to him. "Wait here, Teniente Lopez," the captain instructed. "If I'm not back in fifteen minutes, move in on the springs."

As Alec and Gonzalez passed Mickey Free, the Mexican glanced sideways at him. "I don't trust that one-eyed killer," he said nervously.

Alec shrugged. "Who does? I might be the only exception, and sometimes I'm not too sure myself."

Gonzalez turned away in disgust as he saw the scene of bloody violence. "Apaches," the Mexican said. He pinched his nostrils together and covered his mouth with the palm of his hand.

"You said yourself no Apache in his right mind would come here," Alec reminded him.

They walked together upwind. Gonzalez opened his cigar case and held it out to Alec. They lighted up to get some of the stench out of their nostrils.

"If not Apaches, then who?" Gonzalez asked.

"*Gambrusinos* possibly. Scalp hunters certainly."

"You are certain of this?"

Alec nodded. "They left a trail heading south. They had loaded pack mules with them. They're likely heading back to collect their fourteen hundred pesos for the scalps." He would not tell the Mexican of the other, larger party heading northeast into the United States. They would be Alec's prey, and his alone. "You'd better get a move on, Captain," he added. "That is, if you intend to round up those killers and their fresh hair."

"We still have you to dispose of, Major," Gonzalez reminded him. "Well, in any case, we can take you along with us on the trail of the scalp hunters and return you to the United States later."

"How loyal are your men?" Alec asked casually.

The Mexican shrugged. "As loyal as can be expected. I . . ." His voice died away as he found himself looking into the muzzle of a full-cocked revolver.

Alec smiled grimly. "In that case, Captain, they won't want to see you get your brains blown out all over Muerte Springs. Now all I want is for my sergeant and myself to be allowed to ride away from here."

Gonzalez thought quickly. "Certainly, Major! After all, your arrest is not important. We can forward the complaint against you to your commanding officer. So you are free to leave." Once Kershaw and his half-breed sergeant were in the open on wornout horses it would be a simple matter to run them down and bring them back. There was another possibility. If they resisted arrest, one might apply *ley del fuego*—the law of fire. They would be killed while resisting arrest.

Alec walked the Mexican up to the rim of the bowl. "Now," he said quietly, "tell your *teniente* to bring your horse here. Tell him we're going to take a little ride as far as the border, where you'll be freed, providing you act like a good little muchacho. Don't try to escape. If you do, my friend, it's a lonely grave out on the desert. Is that clear?"

Alec and Mickey rode north with Gonzalez, skirting the western edge of the malpais hills. Five miles from the border Alec dismounted and ordered the Mexican to do the same.

"Your government will hear of this," warned Gonzalez.

Alec took the reins of the Mexican's fine bay. "Start walking," he ordered.

Gonzalez's face darkened with anger. "But you said nothing of taking my horse!"

Alec smiled. "I promised your *teniente* we'd take a little ride to the border, where you'd be set free. I didn't say your horse would be set free with you."

"Damn you to hell!" Gonzalez shouted.

Alec pointed to the south. "*Vamos!*" he said.

When Gonzalez was fifty yards from the two Americans, he turned and yelled, "Wait until you find out what happened to your four scouts last night, gringo bastard! I stand to collect eight hundred pesos for their scalps!" He plunged down a slope and ran with his head down.

Mickey raised his rifle. Alec shook his head. "We're in enough trouble as it is."

They rode hard to the north. Gunfire crackled behind them. In an hour the pursuit was over. They halted to rest the horses. Alec rooted through the Mexican's saddlebags and found a packet of cigars and a bottle of brandy. They lighted up, squatted in the shade of the horses, and passed the bottle back and forth.

Mickey drank, wiped his mouth, and handed the brandy to Alec. "Now what? We've lost four good men, maybe five if they catch The Limper. We're long overdue from patrol. We crossed the border against strict orders. We escaped from the greasers, and you had to cap the whole goddamned mess by stealing Gonzalez's horse." He rolled his one eye upward.

Alec scratched inside his shirt and hoped he wasn't getting lousy. "And my reputation with some of my superior officers hasn't been the best lately," he added.

"You'd better head back to Fort Bowie, Major. On the way you'd better think of some damned good excuses. You ain't got any other choice, seems to me." Mickey looked sideways at Alec. "Or is there something else on your mind?"

"There is," Alec replied.

"Like followin' the trail of those *gambrusinos* who headed up the San Bernardino Valley."

"You always were good at reading minds."

"Why go? We can't catch up with them now."

"Maybe not, but as long as they keep heading north into U.S. territory, there's a chance they can be caught," Alec said.

"*If* they keep on. Where could they be heading?"

"Up the San Bernardino Valley to the San Simon Valley." Mickey nodded. "Then what?"

Alec drank and passed the bottle. "The Butterfield Trail road from New Mexico to Tucson. When General Crook took command, he ordered large supplies of rifles, repeating carbines, revolvers, and cartridges to be brought along it from the supply depot at Fort Union in New Mexico Territory. That was over two months ago. They hadn't reached Arizona when we left Fort Bowie. Knowing our supply system, which moves glacially at best, there's a strong possibility they may be en route now."

Mickey was puzzled. "What's glacially?"

Alec shook his head. "Slow, man, slow, and I mean *slow*. . . ."

"So what's the connection?"

Alec stood up. "Supposing someone in Tucson got wind of that shipment from some drunken soldier from Fort Lowell, Crook's headquarters. Those weapons and cartridges would be worth their weight in gold to an Apache or a Mexican outlaw, and even to some Americans who aren't too fussy about where their guns come from. Supposing this informant tips off someone who might be interested in stealing those weapons. If they knew the shipment was about due, it would be a simple thing to send an agent into New Mexico to find out when it was coming.''

"Someone like Chico Diaz?''

"You're very bright,'' Alec observed dryly.

He looked back toward the springs area. "That horror back there is some of the most conclusive evidence we've found yet of those *gambrusinos*. Mickey, this is a chance I can't bypass. I've got to tail them to see where they're heading, and maybe get a chance to stop them from whatever deviltry they've got in mind.''

"Such as hitting the government supply train.''

Alec nodded.

"Then we'd better get started.''

Alec shook his head. "I'm going alone; maybe with The Limper as tracker, if I can find him.''

"You're taking one hell of a risk, not only with your career but with your life as well.''

Alec looked to the northeast and the San Bernadino Valley. "That's why we're here, Mick.'' He slapped the scout on the back. "Round up the platoon if you can. Take them back to Fort Bowie.''

"And what do I tell your commanding officer?'' Mickey asked sarcastically.

"Lie like hell. You're top dog at it. Try to get them to send out a strong patrol along the Butterfield Trail. Maybe I'll meet them out there if I make it myself. *Maybe . . .*''

Alec slapped the bay on the rump and started him back to his master.

"Well, anyway, they can't charge you with horse-thieving,'' Mickey said with a crooked grin.

He watched Alec ride off. "*Vaya con Dios!*'' he shouted. "*Acaso*,'' he added under his breath. "Go with God! *Maybe . . .*''

Alec looked toward the springs. The dots in the sky had thickened and were soaring lower and lower. The *zopilotes* would soon clean up the corruption there. By dusk the bones would be stripped.

He rode on. After an hour he looked back and noticed several of the huge vultures circling high overhead in the eye of the sun, away from the feast at Muerte Springs. It seemed to Alec that they were watching him, in anticipation. Perhaps it was just his imagination. . . .

CHAPTER 2

ALEC AND THE LIMPER WERE A GOOD TEAM WITH AN AL-most uncanny rapport in tracking. The Limper had patiently waited for Alec on the San Simon Valley Trail, then they had gone ahead into the gathering twilight. They had come over forty miles from Muerte Springs in three days, losing the trail now and again only to have The Limper find it with that in-stinctive ability of his. For hours after the gibbous moon had risen on the night of the third day, Alec could see The Limper a quarter of a mile ahead of him, questing back and forth like a hunting lobo.

The Chiricahua range, called by the Apaches the Big Mountain, loomed to the left, rising high from the dry valley of the San Simon, a swelling line of lofty forested domes and pine-edged ridges against the pale moonlit sky. It was a vast citadel, a literal stronghold of the most ruthless and warlike Indians in North America, the Chiricahua Apaches. The par-ticular band that held the stronghold were the real rim-rock variety, the *Nedahe,* or Wild Ones. Their leader was *Bais-han,* or Knife. The Mexicans had dubbed him *Cuchillo Roja,* Red Knife, because his knife was always dyed red with the blood of Mexicans and Americans. There was no greater war leader among the Chiricahuas. The Mexicans and Americans had no greater nor more implacable enemy than he.

An hour before moonset, The Limper had far outdistanced Alec, who was afoot leading his weary dun, striding along tirelessly and seemingly alone in a vast and uninhabited world. There was no sight or sound of any other living thing on that huge expanse of plain and mountain.

The dun began to limp. Alec halted. He poured half the

contents of one of his canteens into his campaign hat and watered the horse. When he was done, Alec let him drift awhile and graze. Alec walked up a rise and looked to the north. The Limper was not in sight. He focused his field glasses on a distant ridge faintly seen in the waning moonlight. He thought he saw the tips of trees rising from beyond the ridge, a possible indication that there was water there. Maybe The Limper was waiting there for him.

The moon was about to set when Alec started off on foot again, leading the dun. He was a mile away from the ridge when he heard a gunshot from beyond it. The echo rolled along the plain and then died away. He dropped the reins, jerked his Winchester from its scabbard, ran sideways fifty feet while levering a round into the chamber, and hit the dirt behind a low hummock.

It was silent again except for the faint whisper of the night wind rustling the dry grasses.

The moon had all but disappeared behind the Chiricahuas when Alec moved on again. He led the dun up the long slope of the ridge. He was almost at the crest when the breeze shifted a little. The dun shied and blew hard, dancing sideways and tugging at the reins. Alec ground-reined him and went up to the crest. He lay flat and looked down into a wide swale holding a *bosquecito* of timber, indicating a sure source of water. The timber was dark with shadows.

He crouched and ran down the slope and into the edge of the timber. He entered it noiselessly, testing the night with eyes, ears, nose, and that indefinable sixth sense a frontiersman and Indian fighter must have or pay the penalty of sudden and violent death.

The faintest of odors came to him. There was no sound other than the faint rustling of the leaves in the wind. He waited.

Minutes ticked past.

Alec moved forward. He could smell the water, but there was another odor mingled with it. His left foot struck something heavy and soft. The odor was now sweetish and cloying. He knelt and blindly examined the body in front of him. He felt about the torso and chest, then up the neck to the head and scalp.

His hand encountered a thick stickiness. The smell of blood was fresh. He held his hand up in front of his face. The palm was dyed dark with blood. Alec instantly retreated into the depths of the *bosquecito*.

The woods were empty of life. The waterhole was nothing but an expanse of mud imprinted thickly with hoof- and foot-prints.

Alec returned to the body. He thumb-snapped a lucifer and cupped the tiny flame in his big hand. The faint light revealed The Limper, scalped, ears and all. Alec searched for a wound. He rolled the body over. The Chiricahua had been shot in the back. His Spencer carbine and cartridge belt were gone. His horse was not in the *bosquecito*.

Alec went back for the dun. He took his camp spade from his saddle and began to dig in the center of the waterhole. He was puzzled. The party The Limper had tailed had passed this way at least a day ahead of him, possibly more. Then who had ambushed and killed him? It might have been rim-rock Apaches, or possibly an American or Mexican traveler who figured he needed that fine Spencer repeater and horse more than The Limper. There was also the possibility that whoever the scout was tracking had suspected they were being fol-lowed and either had left someone on guard at the water hole or had sent someone back to ambush him.

Water began to seep slowly into the hole Alec had dug. In an hour he had enough to fill both his canteens and water the dun again. He risked lighting one of Gonzalez's cigars to aid his thinking. He could not backtrack. There would not be enough water for him and the dun to survive. He was closer to the Butterfield Trail than he was to the water at Muerte Springs or Camp Farrar on the other side of the Chiricahuas. If he could not locate the *gambrusinos*, he'd have to round the northern end of the Chiricahua range into Apache Pass and thence to Fort Bowie. He'd have to travel at night. Any traveler by daytime would risk the eagle-eyed surveillance of Baishan's Chiricahua Apaches from the mountain heights. A faint trace of dust would bring them down into the valley like ants after honey.

Alec led the dun on through the darkness, walking in long

and loose mile-eating strides. There had been sporadic thunderstorms over the Chiricahuas in the past few weeks. If he was lucky enough, some of the seasonal waterholes on the eastern slopes of the mountains might have filled with rainwater. If he was lucky enough . . . There was more than plenty of fresh running water in the Chiricahuas, of course, but then, gawdamighty, there were more than aplenty Apaches there too. . . .

CHAPTER 3

THE FAST-MOVING ABBOTT-DOWNING STAGECOACH bound from La Mesilla, New Mexico Territory, to Tucson, escorted by a squad of troopers from Fort Cummings, caught up with the slowly moving quartermaster supply wagon train while it was crossing the San Simon Valley some miles east of the dry bed of the San Simon river. They were twenty-five miles from Apache Pass and Fort Bowie. The Wilson wagons were laden with overdue supplies of Spencer M1867 .56/50 seven-shot carbines and Colt .44 caliber six-shot revolvers converted to cartridge. There were many cases of cartridges for both weapons. A four-mule Rucker ambulance carried Paymaster Gideon Bolster and a metal trunk filled with new currency amounting to many thousands of dollars.

The twenty-man cavalry escort had been patched and stitched together from raw recruits, transferees to the department, and a few would-be deserters being returned to their units, meanwhile pressed into service as part of the escort. The escort was under the command of one aging Captain Pringle, who somehow had managed to serve throughout the Mexican and Civil Wars without achieving a single brevet. After Appomattox he had been shifted westward, ever westward, one jump ahead of the Benzine Board that was bent on washing out surplus and inefficient officers. He was bound now for the Department of the Pacific. If he didn't make it there, he'd have to retire on half pay or blow out his brains. Captain Pringle would not be missed by the army.

Captain Pringle rode with Paymaster Bolster in the dubious and dusty bouncing comfort of the Rucker. Paymaster Bolster never traveled without a case of dark Jamaican rum, bottled lemon water in which to mix the rum, and a hamper of canned oysters and other delicacies. Gideon Bolster was a man who liked his comforts.

The cavalry escort was actually in the charge of Second Lieutenant Orton R. Newfield, United States Cavalry and recent graduate of the Military Academy. The army term "shavetail" designating a brand-new second lieutenant fitted him perfectly. It had originated with the army pack-mule trains. It was the wise custom there to shave off all but a tuft at the end of the trail of a newly acquired mule so that the mule-wallopers could easily recognize them. Lieutenant Newfield was as green as an unripe apple and got no help or advice from Captain Pringle. His noncoms knew he was green and took advantage of it. In short, Mr. Newfield had assumed command of a "J" Company outfit whose assigned commander was a total military failure; the noncoms were weak reeds; the ranks were ramparts of sand.

The convoy had halted to water the animals a few miles east of the San Simon crossing. It was a slow process watering so many of them from the water barrels carried on each side of the freight wagons. The Concord was a brave sight as it came down the long gentle slope of the valley, swaying and bouncing on its great leather thoroughbraces. It was drawn by six mules urged on by the hoarse shouting and cracking whip of the driver. A cloud of fine yellowish dust boiled up behind the vehicle. The escort squad of troopers pounded along on each side of the stagecoach trying to keep out of the dust.

There were four passengers within the coach. The Reverend Henry Walpole had been sent out by his bishop to study Apache reservation conditions. Major Morton A. Sherston was returning to his position as sutler of Fort Yuma. His rank was purely an honorary one, sometimes given to well-established sutlers. Phillip K. Rimbold was a mining engineer representing Eastern copper interests with a view to reopening some of the producing mines that had been shut down because of Apache depredations. Mrs. Anne Murray Sinclair, army widow, was en route to Fort Bowie to meet her fiancé Brevet Colonel, Major Burton Trapnell, recently assigned to the Department of Arizona.

Anne Sinclair was not a beauty in the classic sense, but she had been the reigning military belle at Fort Marcy and Santa Fe when her late husband and later her fiancé had been stationed there. In woman-starved Arizona Territory she would be a positive sensation. She was tall and slender, slim of waist, and rather full in the bust. Her eyes were hazel, lips full, nose a little large, skin clear and fair, with a dusting of tiny freckles. Her reddish hair was almost of that shade known as titian. She wore a quasi-military type bonnet and a dress of cadet gray with jacket to match, replete with tiny brass bell buttons, as her chic traveling costume.

Lieutenant Newfield halted the coach. Stage driver Ab Gleason had served with Bobby Lee in the Army of Northern Virginia. He didn't have much use for army blue. He drew up the coach within inches of the young officer.

"Lieutenant Newfield, driver," Newfield said. "Are you planning to drive through Apache Pass?"

Ab nodded. "Hell yes. Ain't no other way to go."

Newfield flushed. "In that case, you'll have to travel with us for protection."

Major Sherston thrust his red face out a window of the coach. "What's this, Lieutenant? I'm due at Fort Yuma in three days!"

"We've heard rumors from eastbound travelers that Apaches might have been seen beyond the San Simon, sir," Newfield explained. "A mail courier passed us this morning heading east. He warned us about Apaches."

"Jesus Christ!" exploded Sherston. He looked back over his shoulder. "Sorry, Missus Sinclair. These young shavetails see an Apache hiding behind every bush."

"He may be right, Major," Reverend Walpole said hesitantly.

"I'll lose too much time," growled Ab. "I got a schedule to keep."

"Drive on then," Sherston ordered.

Newfield shook his head. "I'll have to check with my commanding officer first." He walked up to the Rucker. Captain Pringle was snoring gently with a silk handkerchief draped over his head and face. Major Bolster was relieving himself on the left rear wheel of the ambulance.

"Major, sir," said Newfield. "Can I awaken the captain? A stagecoach has caught up with us. They want to continue alone despite my warning them about the Apaches. I suggested they travel with us for their own safety. They have declined."

Bolster glanced at Pringle. "I doubt if you can awaken the drunken old fool, Newfield."

"Then as senior officer present can you take the responsibility?"

Bolster shrugged. "Let the damned fools go on."

"There's a woman on the coach, sir."

The paymaster looked over his shoulder with a sly grin. "Is she a looker, eh, Newfield?"

The lieutenant couldn't resist. He pointed. "Here she comes with the rest of the passengers. See for yourself, sir."

Bolster turned. His jaw dropped. He quickly turned away and buttoned up his trousers, softly cursing Newfield all the while. "Pringle!" he roared. "Wake up! We've got female company!"

Anne Sinclair took in the scene. She wasn't embarrassed. She was an army brat. Her father, a colonel of infantry, had been killed at Antietam. Her late husband, a captain of cavalry, had been killed by Comanches on the Staked Plains.

Major Sherston casually saluted Paymaster Bolster. "Are you in command here, sir?" he asked importantly.

Captain Pringle leaned out of the Rucker and focused his bleary eyes on the four passengers. "Captain Bernard Pringle, General Service United States Army at your service." He hiccuped.

"This officer halted us on our through journey to Tucson, Captain," Rimbold explained. "Some warning about Apaches. He said we would have to travel with your convoy for safety. Is that correct?"

Bernard Pringle had managed to have a thirty-year career

in the military without ever making an important decision. One could make mistakes that way. It was best to either evade the issue or to make no decision at all. "Mr. Newfield has taken a great deal of responsibility on himself," he said with a smile. "New young officer, you know."

"You didn't answer my question, sir." Rimbold said impatiently.

"We have our own escort from Fort Cummings, Captain," Major Sherston said. "Should be sufficient protection for the journey."

Sergeant Kort came up from the rear of the convoy in time to hear Sherston. "The escort has left, sir," he reported. "The sergeant in charge said his orders were to escort the stagecoach only as far as he could be assured of their safety. He figured since the lieutenant had said the stagecoach should travel with the convoy that it was all right."

"Go run him down!" Sherston shouted. "He's to return at once!"

Pringle shook his head. "Too late. It's settled. You'll have to travel with us." He had suddenly realized that if he made the decision to let the stagecoach go on alone, and anything happened to it and the passengers, he would be held responsible. At this late stage of his career he could no longer take even the most minor risk. Further, he might even be commended for his action.

An hour later Lieutenant Newfield led his horse to the Rucker. "Orders, Captain? We're finished with the watering."

Pringle hiccuped. "Move out, mister!"

The wagon train made a slow and ponderous movement toward the San Simon, which was now apparent as a line of brush thrusting up from the dry riverbed. Two troopers galloped ahead as point. Lieutenant Newfield took his position riding ahead of the Rucker.

The river bottom was thick with brush taller than man-high. The rutted road was hub-deep in sand and flanked on both sides by a dense wall of the brush. The hoofs and wheels of the convoy raised dust high in the windless air, obscuring the river bottom.

The two point troopers reached the far bank and dismounted to wait for the convoy to catch up. It was Private Danbury who first saw the mounted officer sitting a splendid sorrel horse just west of the riverbank. Danbury rode back to report to Lieutenant Newfield. Both senior officers were dozing. Newfield rode to the west bank and approached the lone officer. The trend of the land put them out of sight of anyone at the river. The point troopers waited below the crest of the riverbank.

The lone officer had the twin silver bars of a captain on his shoulder straps. Newfield reined in his horse and saluted smartly. "Second Lieutenant Orton J. Newfield, sir. Second-in-command of the wagon train escort," he said proudly, then added, "My commanding officer Captain Bernard Pringle is indisposed."

The officer smiled winningly as he responded to the salute. "Captain Milo Chaffin, Mr. Newfield. We're evidently right on time to escort you to Fort Bowie."

Chaffin was handsome in a lean and rakish way. His complexion was somewhat dark, almost Mexican or even Indian-like. He was clean shaven and his hair was a jet black, rather lank, and too long to be regulation. His uniform and equipage was immaculate and of the finest quality. There was something different and vaguely foreign-looking about his blouse. His cap was of the French kepi style worn by many Volunteer Zouave regiments during the Civil War rather than the regulation forage cap. His eyes were a startling light blue, almost like swift-running snow melt under thin ice and about as cold-looking.

Newfield was puzzled. He could see no other troops.

Chaffin studied Newfield. "You didn't expect us, I see. There has been considerable Apache activity hereabouts. Why, just yesterday a mail courier and two miners riding with him were ambushed and killed not two hundred yards from where we are now."

Newfield stared at him. "We heard rumors that Apaches might have been seen beyond the San Simon, sir, but we were not told there would be an escort meeting us here at the river." He looked uncertainly back over his shoulder. "Unless I was just not informed of it by my commanding officer." Chaffin smiled easily. "That's probably the very reason, Newfield. In any case, here we are! At your service, so to speak. Any questions, mister?"

Newfield shook his head. It wouldn't do to disagree with a superior officer. He was learning fast.

Chaffin rode forward a little to peer down into the riverbed. "Is that the paymaster's Rucker I see down there?" he asked.

"Yes, sir," Newfield replied. "We have the westbound stagecoach with us as well. They caught up with us. Captain Pringle deemed it wise to have them travel with us for protection."

Chaffin nodded. "I wondered why we hadn't seen it west of the river."

"There's a lady with the coach, Captain. A Mrs. Anne Sinclair. She's traveling to Tucson to meet her fiancé. You may know him. Colonel Burton Trapnell."

The officer looked a little surprised. "Is that a fact? Yes, I know him well. We had heard Mrs. Sinclair was traveling west this day. Burton Trapnell is a fortunate man. He has everything, so to speak. A great career ahead of him. A great deal of wealth. Powerful political connections. Last, but certainly not least, a beautiful widow with means of her own hastening west to marry him."

"You know the lady, then?" Newfield asked.

Chaffin shook his head. "Not personally. We at Fort Bowie have been looking forward to meeting her. Is she a looker, mister?"

"A beauty, sir!" Newfield cried.

"So I've heard. Well, follow me, mister." Chaffin turned his sorrel and started to ride west.

Newfield stared uncomprehendingly at the empty road stretching straight toward the distant Dos Cabeza Mountains shimmering in the heat haze. He turned to look at Chaffin, who had dropped behind him. "Where is your command, sir?" he asked uneasily. He found himself looking into the muzzle of a revolver and behind it at the satanic grinning face and icy blue eyes of Chaffin. The pistol cracked. The .44 caliber slug hit the young officer squarely in the center of the forehead and blew his brains out of the back of his head.

. Chaffin dismounted and went through the dead man's pockets. He stripped Newfield of his weapons, uniform and boots. He strapped them to the lieutenant's saddle. A spattering of heavy gunfire broke out in the riverbed of the San Simon.

Chaffin stripped off his own uniform and dressed quickly in Apache garb—calico shirt, baggy white trousers tucked into thigh-length moccasins folded and tied just below the knee, a white kiltlike *himper* folded over from his cartridge belt to fall level with the knees, and a calico headband. He quickly applied vertical stripes of vermilion and black paint to his face. When he was done, the icy eyes seemed to be peering through the mask of a devil straight from hell itself. He led the two horses to the riverbank and down it toward the wagon train.

The gunfire had erupted from the thick brush at the sides of the road. The smoke mingled with the rising dust. The attackers opened fire on the convoy at point-blank range. Each target was picked precisely. Troopers were knocked from their saddles and teamsters from their seats. Some troopers panicked and spurred to return to the east bank. Withering gunfire met them from ambushers who rose from the pits they had dug just within cover of the brush. Other troopers crashed into the brush on foot. Most of them were killed or wounded before they could see anyone at whom to shoot.

Bernard Pringle awoke from a drunken sleep to stare into the twin muzzles of a shotgun. His bloated features were blasted away. Gideon Bolster was no coward. Her drew his Colt and aimed at the Apache who had killed Pringle. Before he could fire, a sinewy arm encircled his neck from behind and a knife blade probed into his heart.

Private Kennedy, the ambulance driver, came unscathed through the first volleys. He dropped to the ground and crawled under the ambulance.

Morton Sherston was killed instantly by a large-caliber bullet that came crashing through the wood paneling of the coach.

Phillip Rimbold kicked open a stagecoach door and shoved

Anne through it. "Get into the brush! Hide! I'll cover you," he said as he drew his nickel-plated Colt.

Anne dropped to the ground and crawled into the brush just as the attackers cut the mule traces and led away the mules. The coach was rocked back and forth until with a mighty heave it went over. Rimbold pulled himself up through the upper door. A rifle butt crushed in his skull. He fell heavily atop the Reverend Walpole, pinning him to the bottom side.

Anne drew her double-barreled derringer and crawled directly away from the road, figuring the Apaches would be more intent on looting the wagons than on searching the brush. The river bottom was a hell of crashing gunfire interspersed with the shrieks of the wounded and dying and the hoarse shouting of the combatants. She crawled farther, then veered to her left, heading toward the west bank. She stood up once to get her bearings and saw a tall Apache, whose features were hideously daubed with vermilion and black stripes, running down the bank leading two horses. She faded back behind a bush and peered through the leafy branches.

"Find the woman!" the painted warrior yelled in Spanish.

Anne froze stock-still as the Apache seemed to look directly at her. An eerie feeling poured through her as she saw his light-colored eyes in direct contrast to the paint and his lank black hair. She closed her own eyes. When she opened them, he was gone, but she could still hear him shouting, "Find the woman! Find the goddamned woman!"

Most of the soldiers and teamsters were dead, dying, or wounded by now. The heavy firing died away. Now and then a gun report punctuated a lone cry and silenced it. The dead were scalped and stripped. Knives ripped through the canvas wagon tilts. Cases of guns and cartridges were unloaded from the wagons.

"Pete! Pete! Where the hell are yuh?" a hoarse voice shouted.

"Coming, Chico!" Chaffin called back.

Chico Diaz was short and thickset, with long dirty dark hair. He was powerfully muscled, slope-shouldered, and deep of chest. His arms were gorillalike, seemingly too long for his body. His thick legs were bowed. His black eyes were flat-looking, their intensity added to by the fact that he blinked much less than the average person. His Apache clothing was splashed with fresh blood, almost as though he had wallowed in it. He held a Henry rifle in his left hand and a bloody bowie knife in the other.

"What do you want, Chico?" Chaffin asked.

"You said there was sure to be a woman in that stage-coach. There ain't any, and it don't look like there ever was. Maybe it's the wrong coach, you bastard!" shouted Diaz.

Chaffin threw back the canvas curtain covering the coach boot and pulled out a small leather trunk. He pried off the lock with his sheath knife and threw back the lid. He pulled out a handful of lingerie and waved it triumphantly in Diaz's face. The faint aroma of lilac sachet drifted from the under-things. Diaz needed no further proof.

"Search that goddamned coach!" he roared.

Chaffin opened the door on the upper side of the Concord and looked inside. He saw the contorted face and wide un-seeing eyes of Phillip Rimbold. There was the body of an-other man under him. It moved a little. Chaffin withdrew his head for a moment, then quickly thrust it back in again. This time he saw a white face staring fearfully up at him. Chaffin grinned and winked.

"Well?" Diaz demanded.

Chaffin shook his head. "*Nada,*" he said. "Couple of stiffs, both men."

Chico Diaz cupped his hands about his mouth. "Spread out in the brush! There's a woman hiding out there some-where! Find her!" He turned to look at Chaffin. "By God, I hope she ain't been killed by mistake!"

"She'd better not be, Chico," Chaffin said dryly. "Her fiancé is a very wealthy man. He won't pay good cash for a corpse."

Anne reached the front end of the wagon train and crawled toward the ambulance, hoping she might find a horse on which to escape. Something moved behind the body of Pay-master Bolster. Anne cocked and pointed her derringer right into the homely, frightened face of Private Kennedy, the am-bulance driver. She crawled in beside him.

The Apaches had set fire to some of the emptied wagons. Thick smoke began to fill the river bottom, shrouding the ambulance and the west bank.

"There are none of them near us, Mrs. Sinclair," Kennedy whispered. "If I can get the Rucker up close to the riverbank unseen, I might be able to drive it out of here. It's the only chance we've got. Are you game?"

She nodded. "We have no other choice," she whispered.

He reached up into the wagon and withdrew his Spencer carbine from under the driver's seat. "Can you use this?" he asked.

"Fairly well," she replied.

"Crawl to the bottom of the west bank and then to your left as far as you can go. If I can lead the team off the road there and get through the brush, we might make it far enough away from here so that I can drive it up the bank and then head for Fort Bowie," he said.

She nodded and began to crawl toward the bank.

The ambulance team of four mules was skittish because of the gunfire and the smoke and flames rising above the convoy. Kennedy spoke quietly to the two leaders as he led them slowly from the road and into the thinner brush close under the west bank. Anne met him a hundred yards further along. Kennedy unbuckled Captain Pringle's gunbelt and holstered Colt from his body. He tumbled the corpse over the side. Anne got into the ambulance and knelt down on the rear seat, resting the Spencer on the back of it as Kennedy led the mules farther along the bank. He prayed for the first time since leaving home five years past.

The raiders brought a string of pack mules carrying *aparejos*, large leather cargo sacks, on their backs. The cases of weapons and cartridges were loaded into them. The captured mules and horses had other cases lashed to their backs.

"Let's make it look like Apache work, muchachos!" Chico Diaz shouted.

Five badly wounded men were stripped and bound head-down on the big wheels of freight wagons. Small fires were started a foot below their heads. Their hoarse screams were added to the crackling of the flames and the raucous laughter of the raiders. The naked dead had their skulls crushed in a common Apache practice to let out the vengeful spirits of the dead. Genitals were hacked off and stuffed into their mouths. Arrows were shot into the bodies. All of the wagons were put to the torch. A pall of greasy black smoke rose high above the San Simon.

Chaffin tossed a brand into the door of the stagecoach. He waited awhile, then tossed in another brand. Smoke rose through the door and the windows. There was a short, sharp scream from the Reverend Walpole. Thick white smoke billowed up as the horsehair-stuffed seat pads began to burn. Chaffin grinned. He strolled toward the front of the convoy and the paymaster's ambulance, which he knew would hold thousand of dollars in government funds.

"Did you find that goddamned woman yet?" Diaz roared through the smoke. "How the hell can one lone bitch get away from you bastards?"

Chaffin stared in disbelief. The Rucker was gone. He shouted for Diaz.

"I'll handle this myself, you stupid sonofabitch!" Chico Diaz shouted. "The woman is probably in that Rucker along with those funds! You stay here in command. Get that pack train started for the rendezvous. We'll meet you there."

Diaz and ten of his men still in Apache disguise rode hard along the west bank of the river, where the broken and trampled brush showed the hurried passage of the ambulance. Far ahead of them dust rose thinly from the hooves of the galloping mules and the spinning wheels of the Rucker.

CHAPTER 4

THE SUN WAS SLANTING FAR TO THE WEST. A FAINT POP-ping sound came on the wind. Alec raised his head. *Gunfire!* He shook his canteen. It was half full. He had found the *tinaja* just an hour past. The shallow rock pan was filled with old rainwater, thick and almost gelatinous, filmed with scum upon which rested drowned insects and bird feathers. It was palatable after a fashion. Water skaters glided over its surface, evidence that it wasn't poisoned. He poured the last of a tin cup of water slowly through the bandanna he had tied over the mouth of the canteen for straining purposes. Then he wrung out the bandanna and tied it around his neck, grateful for the dampness.

Alec had let the worn-out dun have his fill before he replenished the canteen. He corked the canteen, hooked it to his belt, and walked to the grazing horse for his field glasses. He trotted up the low ridge beyond which the sound of gunfire had come. He went to ground and bellied up to the crest, placing his head through a small bush, and looked down into the Valley of the San Simon. A plume of dust rose from an old rutted trail—it could hardly be defined as a road—and the powerful glasses picked out a Rucker-pattern army ambulance moving fast with the plunging gallop of a four-mule team. A stabbing tongue of red flame followed by a puff of white smoke came from the rear of the vehicle. The faint report seemed to roll along the plain and die away. The driver was standing up, lashing the team with his whip. Their pace was flagging. Two hundred yards behind the ambulance rode a trio of horsemen, and in the distance was the dust of more horsemen following the leaders. There was no question about their identity—*Apaches!*

The Rucker would have to pass to the right of Alec's position and around a rock pinnacle that would temporarily cut it off from the view of its pursuers. The field glasses revealed a woman riding in the rear of the vehicle holding a carbine in her hands. As he watched she fired back at the pursuers.

Alec plunged down the slope and mounted the dun. He rode toward the rock pinnacle out of view of the ambulance and the Apaches. He unsheathed his Winchester and levered a round of .44 Henry flatnose into the chamber.

The Rucker careened around the pinnacle. One of the leading mules was holding back. Bright blood dripped from its gaping mouth. One of the front wheels struck a rock, bounced up, and shattered. The ambulance tilted sideways and went over with a crash. The mules dragged it a short distance and then halted. The driver had been catapulted from his seat. His head had struck the hard ground and his neck was twisted awkwardly. The upper wheels kept spinning. The woman clambered out of the wreckage still holding her carbine.

The three Apaches rounded the pinnacle shouting in triumph. They did not see Alec fifty yards from them. The repeater cracked flatly three times. The 200-grain bullets slammed into the riders. One warrior went over sideways while another fell forward on his horse's neck. The third buck fell from the saddle with his right foot caught in the stirrup. He was dragged bouncing, turning over and over across the rocky ground.

Alec sheathed his Winchester. He raced toward a riderless roan, caught the reins, and led the horse back to the white-faced woman standing there in the dust and powder smoke with her carbine pointed at him.

"Can you ride?" he shouted as he brought the dun to a hoof-pawing halt in a cloud of dust and flying gravel.

"Try me!" she cried.

"Throw me the carbine," he ordered. "*Now!*" he roared as she hesitated.

She tossed the Spencer to him, bent, and ripped her long gray skirt from hem to mid-thigh, then hooked her left foot into the stirrup and threw a long shapely leg over the saddle. Alec handed her the reins and clouted the carbine barrel over the roan's rump. It buck-jumped up the slope, nearly upsetting the woman.

"Damn you! I told you I can ride!" she yelled angrily.

He couldn't help but grin. He glanced back as they rode up the long easy slope toward the shadowed mouth of a narrow canyon. The rest of the Apaches had rounded the pinnacle and came to a plunging, gravel-scattering stop as their leader held up an arm.

The slope became steeper. The roan's girth broke under the strain. The saddle slid sideways from under the woman.

"Drop that damned saddle!" Alec shouted as he unsheathed his rifle. He fired a few rounds toward the Apaches and turned to look at her.

She flushed beneath the dust and perspiration. "Don't you dare look at my legs!" she cried.

"Damn your legs! Ride! Besides, legs like yours shouldn't be covered up anyway."

She glared at him. "You're no gentleman!"

Alec grinned. "This is one helluva time to remind me of a shortcoming I've been told about by quite a few women over the past years."

They neared the canyon mouth. Alec dismounted and handed the reins to her. "Keep on. Get within the entrance. I'll try to hold them off here if they keep coming. Keep out of sight. If anything happens to me, follow the canyon to the west and then north. It won't be easy, but if you keep on long enough, you might come out on the Fort Bowie road. Hide by day. Move by night."

She nodded, then rode on into the canyon.

Alec fed cartridges into his rifle magazine. He focused his glasses on the ambulance and the raiders. The Apaches were cutting loose the mules. Several of them were stripping their dead comrades and the ambulance driver of weapons and clothing. One man was inside the ambulance. He crawled out with a metal box held in his arms. He looked up the slope to where Alec held his position.

Alec drew out his pistol and placed it handy. He had fifteen rounds in the Winchester for long-range shooting and six rounds in the Remington for close-up work.

He waited. The Apaches were being ordered out as skirmishers to the right and left into the more broken ground on each side of the fan-shaped playa of silt, dirt, and gravel flushed out of the canyon over the centuries during flash floods and spring runoff.

Alec took out his flask of Baconora and took a stiff jolt. "Helluva price they'll pay for one goddamned woman if they keep coming this way," he said aloud. He drank again, waited a few seconds for the reaction, then said, "*Wagh!*"

"Oh, I don't know," she said quietly from behind him. "I've got a few good points besides my legs, you know."

He turned quickly. "We'll look into that later. Now, get the hell back into cover!"

She shrugged and patted the Spencer. "I know how to use this. I got one of them a couple of miles back, at maybe two hundred yards." She grinned prettily. "Slowed them down a bit. Besides, you may be needing all the firepower you can get. Do you have any more of that, whatever it is, in the flask?"

He nodded. "Baconora, the drink of heroes. It isn't for everybody." He held out the flask to her. *"Una copita?"*

With all her bravado and coolness, both of them knew she was badly frightened and had been so ever since the raiders had struck the wagon train. She needed some Dutch courage. She took the proffered flask and drank deeply. Her eyes watered. She gasped. "My God," she said huskily.

Alec grinned. "Wait until it hits bottom."

Suddenly, the warm glow of the silky amber fluid exploded within her and seemed to send a shock wave of power and well-being throughout her body. She felt she could whip the world, or at least make a damned good stab at it. Now she knew why he had called it the drink of heroes.

Some of the flanking Apaches were out of sight at times, now and then bobbing up only to go to ground again. Each time they appeared they were that much closer.

"Range?" Anne asked.

"I make it two fifty."

She shook her head. "I make it closer to two seventy-five."

Alec shrugged. "Suit yourself. I figured on waiting until they get much closer and perhaps try a rush. If they're stupid enough to do that, we should be able to get damned near all of them."

"I've always heard Apaches are the best guerrilla fighters in the world, and rarely, if ever, do they make attacks like this."

Alec nodded. "You're right on both counts, which makes me assured they are *not* Apaches."

Anne stared a him. "What do you mean?"

Alec put his field glasses on the man who had been shouting orders to the others and who had entered the ambulance to remove the small trunk or chest. He was dressed Apache-fashion, even to face paint. He was short and thickset, with powerful shoulders and long arms.

"Well?" Anne asked. "Aren't they Apaches?"

"Tell me what happened."

She quickly told him the story. When she concluded, she covered her face with her hands. "My God, it was horrible," she added after a time. She looked at him. "Now, do you still think they are not Apaches?"

Alec nodded. "I just saw their leader remove what is evidently the paymaster's chest from the ambulance. Apaches have no use for paper money. They don't understand it. I think they are *gambrusinos*—border outlaws, Mexicans, half-breeds, and some Americans. One of their favorite tactics is to dress and act like Apaches to foist off the blame on the real Indians, though God knows the Apaches can kill as brutally as those men down there."

"Why would these *gambrusinos* want me?" she asked quietly.

"I think you already know."

She shuddered. "Shoot straight when they come," she said.

He shrugged. "I always do."

She held him for a moment with her fine eyes. "You won't let them take me alive?" she pleaded.

He shook his head. "But they're not going to get you." He almost added, *As long as I am alive.* He looked sideways at her. "Do you have a hideout gun?" he asked.

She nodded. "My derringer. Why?" She knew the answer without his saying it.

The pseudo-Apaches were working up the slope and onto the more open ground.

"Give them five rounds rapid when I say the word," Alec whispered. "Shoot low. Then move about twenty feet or so to your left and wait for my next command."

The attackers were 150 yards away now, boldly darting in zigzag fashion across the open ground.

"Fire at will," Alec ordered.

The two weapons spat smoke and flame, arousing distant sleeping echoes along the line of hills. A man staggered sideways and fell heavily. Another flung himself to the ground and thrust his rifle forward to fire. A Winchester .44 caught him square in the forehead. Anne crawled to her left while Alec crawled to his right. A moment later bullets began to strike the place they had been. It was accurate shooting, but the birds had flown. The firing died away. It became quiet; an uneasy sort of quiet.

Alec crawled over to Anne. "Reload and get back to the canyon behind us. Stay under cover."

"I'm out of cartridges," she said.

"Damn! Well, they don't know that. Perhaps they won't buck up against us again. They won't likely want to come up against two repeaters in a hurry. They may wait until dark. I'll fire a round now and again to keep them off balance. I'll join you as soon as I can."

Alec watched her as she crawled back toward the canyon. Interesting rump, he thought, but most of them were in one way or another. He was a leg man himself.

Time drifted slowly past. Alec touched off a round whenever he saw a movement. Long shadows began to drift down the slopes. One after another the men retreated cautiously to the ambulance. The dying sunlight reflected from the field glasses of their leader as he studied the situation. Finally, he ordered one of his men up the slope. The man didn't seem anxious for the detail. The leader pointed his pistol at the man's head. There was no further stalling. The man *moved*.

He moved slowly. He was good at taking cover. All Alec could see now and then was a quick showing of rump, head, or an arm or leg, and then it was gone. There was one place the scout would have to cross about fifty feet without cover. Alec figured it was about four hundred yards away. The light was deceptive. He full-cocked the Winchester, adjusted the rear sight, took a deep breath and let out half of it, sighted, tightened his right hand around the small of the stock, and took up the trigger slack. The scout sprinted across the open area. The rifle cracked flatly. The man staggered in full stride, then fell as though struck by a massive invisible fist. He slid down the slope and lay still forever.

Alec worked his way back into the canyon.

Anne stood just within the screen of brush. "That," she said with deep admiration, "was first-class shooting."

"I told you I always shoot straight," he said dryly. He grinned.

CHAPTER 5

THERE WAS A PREMATURE TWILIGHT IN THE CANYON AS the sunlight passed on.

Anne stood guard with Alec's Winchester in her hands. She watched him over her shoulder as he worked. He was cutting up a worn and greasy jacket of thick buckskin to make boots for the horses. He cut long strips from the sleeves to bind the boots about the fetlocks. She studied him. His weathered features were lean and hawklike. A scar was noticeable at the corner of his left eye. It traced a line down into his short beard. His clothing was army regulation, but he had no insignia of rank on the shirt. His gray campaign hat was faded and sweat-stained and had no insignia on it. It was his footgear that held her attention.

"Those are Apache moccasins, are they not?" she asked.

He nodded. "Best footgear for desert and mountain."

"Where did you get them?" she asked quietly.

He looked up at her. "A Chiricahua squaw by the name of Kaw-Tenne. It means Looking Glass. Makes the best *kabuns* in the Territory and is a first-class medicine woman to boot."

She was getting alarmed. *Who was this man?* "Aren't Chiricahuas the enemy?" she ventured.

Alec shrugged. "They weren't at the time. I was with a peace commission that had a meeting with them. Took advantage of it to pick up a few pairs of moccasins. That was months ago, and I've been carrying them around with me ever since." He looked down at her fine English-made boots. "You won't get far in the canyons with those on, Mrs. Sinclair."

She swung the Winchester to cover him. "Just a minute.

Who are you? Where are you taking me? How did you know my name? I'll not go another step farther until you tell me.''

He grinned. "Would you mind pointing that rifle some other way? It's got a fine trigger pull, and you seem nervous.''

"Talk!" she snapped.

"The name is Alexander Kershaw. My permanent rank is first lieutenant, breveted major. First United States Cavalry. Commander of Company D Apache Scouts out of Fort Bowie. My enemies call me That Sonofabitch Kershaw. My friends call me Alec and sometimes, like my enemies, You Sonofabitch Kershaw. My Scouts call me *Nan-tan*, or chief, to my face, and *Na-txe-ce* when referring to me among themselves. It means Never Still, which I might add is a great honor coming from them. I plan to take you to Fort Bowie. I recognized you from a daguerreotype my great friend Major Donald Sinclair used to keep next to his heart during the war.'' He was silent for a moment. He looked up at her. "I've never quite gotten over his death on the Staked Plains.''

A faint shadow of pain crossed her features. There was a suspicion of brightness in her eyes.

"You said you were traveling to Tucson to meet your fiancé, Mrs. Sinclair. May I ask who that fortunate man may be?''

"Brevet Colonel, Major Burton Trapnell, at present on General Service attached to the Inspector-General's Department, recently assigned to duty here in the Department of Arizona. Just before I left Santa Fe he wrote me and said that he had asked to take temporary command of Fort Bowie. I was to stop there on the way to Tucson to see if he had been given that assignment.''

Alec stared at her. "My God," he said quietly. "Burton Trapnell is going to marry a woman like you? That pompous, self-important military ass? I can't believe it!''

Her face grew taut. "Sir!" she snapped.

Burton Trapnell was the most self-seeking officer Alec had known in the service, and that dated back to their days as cadets together at the Military Academy. He was vain, egotistical, and not only disliked by most of his fellow officers, but hated by some.

"Do you know if he has taken command of Fort Bowie?" she asked.

I hope to God not, Alec thought. "He hadn't when I left there some weeks ago," he replied. "We'd better get on the way. It will be dark until the rising of the moon. I don't want those *gambrusinos* coming in here behind us." He unstrapped his cantle roll and removed a beautifully beaded pair of woman's moccasins from it. "Sit down," he said to her. He pulled off her boots and handed her the moccasins. "Pull them up as high as possible, then fold them just below the knee and tie them there as I've done mine."

"Can you do it for me?" she asked.

He looked up into her guileless eyes. He put on the moccasins and pulled them up under her long skirt. He folded the skirt and underskirt up into her lap and tied the moccasins in place. He then took his sheath knife and sawed off her skirt and underskirt to knee length. He handed her the cut-off portions and stood up. As he picked up his rifle he wondered if she was playing a little game. She could have easily put those moccasins on herself.

She stood up and walked about. "Wonderful!" she cried. She turned to look at him. "How did you just *happen* to have a pair of Apache women's moccasins with you?"

Alec tied her boots to his saddle. "They were for a friend of mine. I had them made some time ago, but was unable to deliver them personally. I was planning to take a short leave in Tucson and put them in my cantle roll. Then I was ordered out on an emergency patrol some weeks ago and forgot to take them out."

"Were they for an Apache woman?" she persisted, her curiosity aroused.

He eyed her. "They can make their own."

"Perhaps they were for your wife?"

He sheathed his Winchester and tied the Spencer to the roan's saddle. "I have no wife. Any more questions? If not, we'll get on our way. You lead until it gets dark. I'll take the rear."

Anne led the roan into the canyon proper. She wondered why he disliked Burton so much. Alexander Kershaw—the name had puzzled her some because she couldn't quite recall where she had heard it. Oh, yes—*Kershaw*! It was a name that was legend in New Mexico, due to Quintin Kershaw, mountain man, Indian-fighter, rancher, and soldier in the Mexican and Civil Wars. In short, a living legend. Anne had heard Quintin Kershaw had two sons, one of whom had been killed serving with the Texas Confederates who had invaded New Mexico in 1861–1862, while the other son had served with the Union forces defending the Territory and had lost his left arm in battle. He had two daughters. One of them was named Rafaela and taught in the Catholic orphanage in Santa Fe. Anne had known her slightly. There was another daughter, or so she had been told, who had entered a convent in Mexico City. Anne could not recall her name. She had never heard of an Alexander Kershaw.

She glanced back at Alec's impassive features. There seemed to be a lot of the Indian in him, but that would be an impossibility for a man who had graduated from the Military Academy and gained a commission in the Regular Army. She had noticed the coolness that many officers held toward Burton. Her fiancé had a brilliant Civil War record and had been breveted a colonel. After the war he had risen quickly to the permanent rank of major, an extraordinary feat for one of his age and length of service in a ridiculously small peacetime army slashed to the bone by a parsimonious Congress. Burton had inherited great wealth from one of his grandfathers and could have retired to a life of ease and comfort, but he was still ambitious to achieve his major goal in life, to be a brigadier general of Regulars, and perhaps rise even higher.

"The last I heard of Colonel Trapnell he was stationed at Fort Marcy, serving as head of the Benzine Board," Alec said suddenly.

Anne knew that the board had been established after the Civil War to evaluate and weed out the deadwood from an oversupply of officers, in order to fit the newly established Tables of Organization. Many officers of Volunteers had managed to achieve high rank during the four years of bloody conflict. Regular Army officers too had attained temporary high rank to which they never would have ascended had it not been for the emergency of the war and an inordinately high death rate of officers. Congress had dashed many hopes by their budget-cutting. The unwanted child of this drastic action had been the Benzine Board, so called because of the cleansing properties of that agent. The board had set to work with a vengeance, eliminating the overaged, physically or mentally unfit, the incompetent, and the alcoholic.

Anne looked back at Alec. "When General Crook took over the Department of Arizona, Burton felt that his services would be of greater value here in Arizona Territory. Burton is ambitious, as you probably know. He says, 'My eyes are on the stars,' and I'm sure you know what he means."

Alec grunted. One of the reasons he himself had asked for reassignment to Arizona was because of officers like Trapnell, and Trapnell in particular. Alec had been one of the officers in the campaign to subdue the Navajos right after the war. He had witnessed the proud, bold, and predatory Navajos defeated and forced into the concentration camp at Bosque Redondo near Fort Sumner in New Mexico Territory. Defeatism, apathy, disease, and semi-starvation had eaten like a cancer into the Navajos. It was then he had begun to realize the magnitude of the Indian problem in the Southwest and the hopelessness of the Indian cause. Their future would mean either extermination, total defeat, or the degeneration of reservation life and possible extermination by starvation and disease. Alec had come to loggerheads with his superiors about the matter. His sympathy for the Navajos and his outspoken attack on the authorities had brought about his transfer to Arizona. To many officers and enlisted men such an assignment was considered a punishment. Alec had welcomed it to get away from New Mexico. Realization had come starkly to him, however, when he found himself on another series of campaigns to either exterminate or totally subjugate another proud tribe—the Apaches.

Anne stumbled in the thickening shadows. "It's getting too dark to see the way," she called back. "Can't we stay here for the night?"

Alec shook his head. "They may be back there tailing us." He led his dun past her. "Besides, there's no water in here. We'll have to keep on until we find some."

Anne watched as he took the lead with an easy catlike stride, noiseless, powerful, and ground-gaining. Where had she seen someone, or something, who walked like that? Then it came to her—a ghostlike panther she had once glimpsed on a moonlit night in the mountains of Northern New Mexico. *Leon fantasma* the Spaniards had called it—the phantom lion.

The passage through the dark pre-moon depths of the canyon was like traversing the anteroom of hell. Anne staggered on through the thick thorned brush on the rocky canyon floor. The heat of the day had not dissipated. There was not a breath of wind. Sweat soaked the hair at the back of her neck and dripped from her face. It ran down inside her clothing, soaking her underthings and hose, stinging the broken blisters on the soles of her feet. She itched intolerably. Her clothing was ripped by the sharp hooked thorns. The right side of her skirt and underskirt had been caught firmly, and she had been forced to tear it loose from hem to waist. The backs of her hands were bleeding and swollen from thorn scratches. She was horrified to realize the odor against which she wrinkled her nose was emanating from herself and not from the horse she was leading. My God! Would he never stop? When she pleaded for water, he would allow her only a gamey mouthful, and then he would not let her swallow it, but rather rinse it around her brassy-tasting mouth, then spit it back into the canteen.

The moon rose. The going was no better, but at least there was sufficient light to avoid some of the worst of it. Hours later, when the moon was high, she stumbled and went down hard, bruising her knees and left elbow.

He came back to her. "Get up," he ordered.

She shook her head. "Go on without me," she pleaded brokenly.

"Get up, damn you!" he snapped.

She sat up, looked him in the eye, somewhat intimidated by the coldness of his gray orbs, and said clearly and succinctly, "You go to hell, you would-be Apache sonofabitch!"

He studied her for a moment. "My, my," he murmured. He scratched inside his shirt. He grinned. "All right, little lady. You win. Get some rest." He walked off a little way, then turned. "You win, that is, if the *gambrusinos* don't come up behind us and the Chiricahuas don't come in from the other way." He looked at her expectantly.

She rubbed the backs of her bleeding hands. "Oh, Major Kershaw," she said. "I feel so safe and comfortable in your presence, how can anything like that possibly happen?"

He didn't answer. He took his rifle and vanished up the canyon. For a few awful moments she thought he had left, but then complete exhaustion overcame her and she fell dead asleep. She awoke once to see him high on a slope, watching, always watching and listening. She could have sworn he sniffed the faint rising breeze like a hunting wolf.

Alec shook her awake. "Come on," he said.

They kept on. The moon was far on the wane. The weary roan stumbled and went down. The sharp dry snap of a leg bone could be heard plainly in the graveyard stillness. Anne was almost out on her feet. She leaned against a boulder, feeling her muscles twitch interminably. She passed a trembling hand across her burning eyes. "You'll have to shoot him," she said.

Alec strode past her, tin cup in left hand, whipping out his sheath knife. He wrenched the roan's head to one side, distending the taut throat. He dragged the razor-edged blade deeply across it, then caught the thick gush of dark blood in the cup.

"My God!" she cried in horror. "Couldn't you have shot him?"

His look at her was like a blow across the face. "And maybe alert every goddamned Apache and *gambrusino* as well within earshot? A pistol shot might be heard for miles. This is *Chiricahua* country, lady!"

She looked at the full tin cup. He held it out to her. She shook her head in disgust. She watched him as he sipped at the fluid. The moonlight glistened on his blood-wet lips, and with his tanned hawklike face and almost startlingly light gray eyes, he looked like something out of a medieval painting of a demon.

"Vampire," she said clearly and distinctly.

Alec shrugged. "I've been called worse," he said dryly.

He knelt beside the dead roan and spread out his soiled bandanna. Swiftly he excised the neck meat.

"Why?" she asked incredulously.

He wrapped the meat in the bandanna. "We don't know when we'll get to Bowie. Might be two or three days, maybe longer if the Chiricahuas are around. We'll need food for strength."

"I can't and won't eat that!" she exclaimed.

"You will, or go hungry. It might make the difference between living and starvation. At that, I'd prefer mule meat. It has a sweeter taste. Apaches prefer mule neck meat over any other. A Spanish chronicler of the eighteenth century recorded the fact that when the Apaches can get flesh of horse, mule, or burro, they shun that of all other animals. Now, mount the dun."

He gave her a leg up, tied the bandanna to the pommel, then took the reins and started on the way again. She could feel the warm blood of the horsemeat soaking through the bandanna into her skirt and underskirt and then on to her skin. She closed her eyes, gripped the saddle horn with all her strength, and tried not to get sick.

The moon was almost gone when at last he stopped at the mouth of the canyon overlooking a long slope extending into another canyon almost at right angles to the one they were in. At the bottom of the other canyon were the ruts of a long-disused road with small brush growing between them. A ramshackle conglomeration of adobe and rock structures, shacks and sheds, a large stone-walled corral, and a sagging wooden windmill clustered beside the road. Extending up a gentle slope were the rusted remnants of a narrow-gauge set of rails with a few dumped-over, rusted ore cars.

"Is there water there?" Anne asked hoarsely.

He nodded. "There usually is. It's been abandoned since '67. There were productive mines here in the fifties. A branch stage line ran through here. Ore and freight wagons used the road. It was quite a thriving place. It was protected by Regulars until the war started, and then they were ordered out of the Territory. Then the Chiricahua Apaches took it over again. When the California Volunteer Column came through Arizona on its way to New Mexico, they secured Apache Pass and its water supply by building Fort Bowie. Even then it was too dangerous to reopen the mines. They were reopened in '66 when the Regulars returned. The Chiricahuas were somewhat at peace then. That is, until Mangus Colorado of the Mimbrenos was murdered by soldiers. The Mimbrenos were allies of the Chiricahuas. In '67 the Chiricahuas struck here, massacred the miners, and destroyed as much as they could of the mining operations.'' He pointed to the slope rising behind the abandoned buildings. "See the headboards in the cemetery? There are a lot of them.''

"What do they call this place?'' she asked.

"The Americans called it Oroville. The Spaniards and Mexicans call it Muerte Canyon because of its reputation. No one calls it Oroville anymore.''

"Will we be safe here?'' she queried.

He shrugged. "It's not safe anywhere in this area, Anne. This is *Chiricahua* country. There's no safety beyond the range of your rifles, and precious little within it. Only a few hardcase miners and ranchers like Pete Kitchen down near the border are holding out. Even the forts aren't completely safe. Sentries are murdered at their posts and no one hears or sees a thing until the body is found. Soldiers have been killed at night walking from one building to another. No one goes to the latrines, even if armed, after dusk or before dawn. The Apaches run off grazing horses, ambush patrols, kill mail couriers and travelers almost within gunshot sound of the forts.''

She stared at him incredulously. "They come right on the posts to kill?''

"It's considered a great feat for an Apache. Besides, a fort is usually a good source for a gun and cartridges.''

"It happens even at Fort Bowie?''

He nodded. "Even at Fort Bowie.''

Alec took his rifle, reata, and the pair of canteens. "I'll have to scout the place. Sit tight and don't show yourself. If anything happens to me, wait until dark after the coming day, then follow that road down there. Hope to God you're not heard or seen. The road will eventually take you to Apache Pass and Fort Bowie.'' He drew his Remington revolver and gave it to her with extra cartridges. For a long moment he looked at her, then placed a big dirty callused palm against her face. He smiled a little. "You'll make it," he said quietly. "You've got the guts, lady." He patted her cheek, turned on his heel, and vanished into the brush.

The station was a shambles. A wooden shed had been burned to the ground. Some of the rock-walled buildings had also been burned, their roofs collapsed inside, and the walls blackened. Alec raised the warped wooden cover of the well and dropped in a stone. He was rewarded with a faint splashing sound. He pushed open the sagging door of the main station building and eased inside. His moccasined feet crunched through broken glass and pottery. He thumb-snapped a lucifer into flame and held it up high. The roof sagged dangerously. There was a thick mound of ashes and rusted tin cans in the large beehive fireplace. He looked into the other rooms. There was nothing there but litter and decay.

The false dawn pewtered the eastern sky as he stepped outside with a rusty bucket in his hand. He tied his reata to it and lowered it into the well. He pulled it up brimful and tasted the water. It was silty and a little gamey. He filled the two canteens over the open well so that dripping water would not show on the dry ground.

He checked each of the remaining buildings. The blacksmith shop was still well equipped with charcoal for the forge and with dusty, rusting tools. There was a heavy workbench with a vise. A Peter Wright anvil was set on top of a thick section of cottonwood log. There was a shrinking barrel used to shrink red-hot iron tires on wheel rims by sudden cooling. A tire bender stood against the wall along with a pole drill, bolt bin, tire setter, and horseshoer's box. The forge bellows was still in good condition. Although dust filmed everything, it seemed as though the blacksmith had left fully intending to return. The Apaches would not damage such a shop or even enter it. The had a deeply rooted superstitious fear of blacksmiths, believing they were somehow related to Pesh-Chidin, the Spirit of Iron.

Anne was sound asleep, curled up like a kitten with one arm oustretched, her full bosom rising and falling and her lips slightly parted. Alec smiled. She was a good one. She had fought as well as any man. During the hellish traverse of the canyon, where the going had been tough enough for Alec, she had not complained. He grinned as he recalled her defiance when he had tried to get her to continue the journey. "You go to hell, you would-be Apache sonofabitch!" she had said. At that, she had come closer to the truth than she realized.

He let her sleep. He led the dun down the slope and around into the side canyon beyond the mines. He filled his hat with water from the canteen for his horse, then picketed him far up the branch canyon. There was a long and wide tailings slope of light-colored material descending to the canyon floor from the mines. He checked the mine entrances. One of them had been blocked by fallen timbers and earth. Another had a dangerously sagging ceiling. The best one offered a view directly down the tailings slope to the station. He moved in cautiously, sniffing the astringent-smelling air, noting a cool dampness. He was fifty feet inside the entrance when he heard the faint drip, drip, drip of water. He lighted a long wooden splinter. The flame reflected from the wet glistening surface of the rocky mine wall, illuminating a large shallow pool on the uneven floor. He tasted it and found it good. This would be their temporary stronghold. He cached his saddle and saddlebags there and went to get Anne.

She was still asleep. He slung his rifle and picked her up. She opened her eyes, smiled faintly, rested her head on his shoulder, curled her arm around his neck, and promptly went back to sleep. Alec carried her into the mine. He shook some field mice out of a pile of old ore bags and made a pallet, placing her upon it.

The canyons were beginning to fill with grayish light. He returned to the station and refilled his empty canteen, then located a nopal cactus from which he cut a large plate. He returned up the slope past the little graveyard with its crooked rows of weathered dove-gray and black headboards. The inscriptions were almost obliterated, but he knew what they said—"Tortured and Killed by Apaches"—for the most part. Some of the occupants had been killed or mortally injured in the mines. Probably none of them had died a natural death. Some had no names, just the label *Unidentified;* they had been so shockingly mutilated their own mothers could not have identified them. The graveyard would be avoided by the Chiricahuas. They had that intense fear of the vengeful dead. It might be a deterrent to them, but it was rather poor comfort to Alec.

Anne was half-awake when he entered the cave. She watched him as he chopped the nopal plate into pieces and put them into the water-filled bucket. "Why are you doing that?" she asked.

"The mucilaginous juice will precipitate the silt and any other foreign bodies in the water," he replied.

She studied him. "More Apache lore?"

He nodded. "I learned it from my Scouts."

"And many other things about their life-way, but perhaps not as much as you'd really like to know?"

He looked at her. "You're very observant."

"Where do they live, these feared Chiricahuas?" she asked.

He stood up. "Come here, Anne." He led her to the mine entrance. To the south loomed the great mass of the Big Mountain. He pointed to it. "Up there," he said quietly.

She shuddered. "That close?"

Alec nodded. "It is one of their finest strongholds."

"And this Muerte Canyon is one of the ways they come and go?"

He looked at her again. "I didn't mean to tell you that," he said. "That's one of the reasons they drove the miners from here. They rarely use the same entrance continually. They might not come this way for months. Then again, they might pass through here any day. There have been raiding parties north of here this past month or so, although I don't know if they were from the Big Mountain. They could be from the Dragoons, or the Dos Cabezas, or half a dozen other major or minor strongholds."

"How long must we stay here?" she asked.

He shrugged. "*Quien sabe?* We can't move by daylight. If there's no sign of the Chiricahuas, we could move out of here after dusk today. Are you hungry?"

She smiled. "Famished!"

"Stand guard at the entrance, but don't let yourself be seen."

Alec made a fire of the driest wood he could find and watched the drift of the smoke. It trended toward the rear of the mine rather than toward the entrance, indicating that somewhere far back in the dark interior was another source of air.

He semi-roasted some of the dark horsemeat over the glowing embers. He filled a large rusty can with water and placed it in the embers to boil. The meat was already a little gamey, but the roasting would allay some of the spoiled taste. If he left it raw much longer, it would become inedible, at least to them. An Apache would eat it uncooked no matter how well advanced it was in decay. Food was food. Despite his attempts to live and think as they did, Alec hadn't quite gotten to that stage as yet.

When the roast was done, he cut it in half and placed Anne's portion on the mess tin he used in the field. It was actually half of a canteen split for the purpose. He put his own piece on a fairly clean slab of wood.

She gnawed at the dark greasy meat. "Do you have coffee?" she asked.

He nodded. He took one of his wool socks from a saddlebag and filled it with roasted issue coffee beans. He knotted the top of the sock and then pounded the beans with the butt of his pistol. When he was done, he dropped the sock into the boiling water.

She winced. "My God!"

He grinned. "Arbuckle's! Quickens the spirit and makes the heart lightsome!" he quoted from the Arbuckle's coffee label.

"I wasn't thinking of that! It's the sock!" she cried.

Alec shrugged. "It was clean . . . some . . . anyway. Well, the boiling water should make it antiseptic."

"*Some* . . ." she echoed dryly.

Alec finished eating first. He idly tapped a hardtack biscuit against his belt buckle. He handed it to her after a time and took another for himself, then began the tapping routine again.

"Why do you do that?" she asked.

"Habit. We used to call these biscuits weevil castles during the war. They were usually infested with them."

She smiled. "How you do put a person on."

He held the biscuit out to her. "Look all right to you?"

She nodded.

"Watch," he said. He dipped the hardtack into the hot coffee and held out the cup toward Anne. Tiny little creatures were swimming frantically on the surface while others emerged from within the biscuit. "During the war we used to eat them in the dark so we wouldn't see them. Could taste 'em though—like cold gelatin. Best way to eat them was to soak the hardtack in hot bacon grease and top it with brown sugar. Sort of like a French pastry." He skimmed the weevils from the coffee, then bit into the biscuit with relish.

She handed her hardtack back to him. "I'll pass for now. I've often wondered why men voluntarily become soldiers and put up with such things."

Alec shrugged. "Soldiering is for some men as whoring is for some women. It's as simple as that."

She had no reply, but she could understand up to a point at least. There had been times when she had wondered guiltily how it would have been to be a courtesan. She simply could not think of herself as a common whore, although the two professions were much the same under the skin—perhaps bed sheets would be more apt.

Alec deftly shaped a cigarette from Mexican Lobo Negro tobacco he shook from a small hard leather flask onto tissue-thin scraped corn shucks.

"Can I have one?" she asked.

He shaped another cigarette, placed it between her lips, and then lighted both from a burning splinter. "You've been too long in Santa Fe," he observed. "Does dear Burton know you smoke?"

She shook her head. "And don't you tell him," she warned.

He blew a smoke ring and poked a dirty finger through it. "I wouldn't tell dear Burton a goddamned thing. We never did converse much socially."

"Kershaw is a well-known name in the New Mexico Territory," she said thoughtfully.

He nodded. "It is, but not through my doing."

"Through Quintin Kershaw. But I heard he had only two sons, one of whom was killed fighting for the South at Glorieta Pass, while the other fought for the Union at Valverde and lost his arm."

"That's right. They were half brothers. It was Francisco, or Frank, who was killed. Dave was the one wounded at Valverde. He's running the Kershaw rancho, Querencia, now on the Plains of San Augustine."

"Are you related to them?"

"In a way," he admitted.

"But you knew my husband during the war." She thought for a moment. "He used to write from Virginia and often mentioned his friend, a Lieutenant Alexander Calhoun."

Alec refilled the coffee cups. "That was me," he said quietly. "I changed my last name to Kershaw after the war."

She could tell by his tone of voice that he didn't care to discuss the subject much further. Yet she pressed on. "Donald had mentioned the fact that you were a Kentuckian and had been appointed to the Academy from that state at the same time he was appointed from Ohio."

"We were classmates for four years. When the war started, he was appointed to the First Cavalry, the old First Dragoons. I served in New Mexico until some time in 1862, then requested duty in the East and was assigned to the First."

She nodded. "He told me that. I wondered at the time why you had served in New Mexico instead of in the East when the war started."

"I was partially raised in New Mexico, Anne," he replied. "My mother had inherited a ranch in northeastern New Mexico Territory—the Rio Brioso. You may have heard of it."

"I have," she said quickly. "In fact, I visited there. Wasn't it originally developed by Quintin Kershaw?"

"You've a fine memory," he said dryly. "Yes, it was. He lost it and had left there before the war to settle on the Plains of San Augustine. Before I went to the Academy I spent my summers there on the Rio Brioso and the winters back in Kentucky and Washington, D.C. My mother's father was Senator Alexander Allan, formerly colonel of the First Dragoons. There wasn't much question about my future. It was to be the Regular Army. That was fine with me."

"Donald once told me your father was killed while serving with the Confederacy in New Mexico."

Alec looked away from her. A shadow seemed to pass

across his features. "Colonel Calhoun was severely wounded at Valverde." He could not tell her the true story of how Calhoun had died by his own hand rather than live as an armless cripple the rest of his life. Alec looked at her. "He was not my real father. I was led to believe for years that he was. It wasn't until after his death that I finally knew that he was not." He thoughtfully rolled two more cigarettes and gave one to her. He lighted them both.

"Donald said you were wounded twice, once at Valverde and again at Gettysburg."

Alec nodded. "It's part of the profession. They are considered to be honorable scars. But there are other war scars on my soul about which no one else knows, or cares."

She shook her head. "I don't understand."

Alec didn't know why he was telling her all this. It wasn't his habit to do so. "Perhaps we soldiers see too much violence and horror. The cornfields at Antietam dyed red with blood; the snow-covered fields at Fredericksburg turned blue with the bodies of Union dead; the woods at Chancellorsville ablaze from cannon fire cremating the dead and wounded of both sides alike. The Union Iron Brigade at Gettysburg making a stand against the Rebel advance that first day and being shot to pieces." His voice died away.

After a moment or two she spoke. "And you saw all this?"

He looked at her and she could see the anguish in his fine eyes. "I was there," he said in a strange-sounding voice.

"But you didn't leave the service after the war. After all that horror, why did you stay?"

"I didn't at first. I took a leave of absence and enrolled in medical school. I was allowed to do so on the condition that I return to the service as a surgeon, and if not, as a cavalry officer." He grimaced. "I lasted almost two years, and then came back without the degree. I could not overcome a strange restlessness to get out of the classrooms, lecture halls, and laboratories. Something drew me back to the Southwest and my real profession."

She studied him. "And still there are doubts, aren't there?"

"There are. Ever since the war I've been trying to fit together the tiny pieces of the jigsaw puzzle that is Alexander

Kershaw. I have not succeeded. I'm beginning to doubt that I ever will.''

"But you seem content. You have a great interest in the plight of the Navajos and the Apaches despite the fact that they are your sworn enemies. Isn't that so?''

Alec nodded. "I became interested in the Apaches while a young lad staying at my mother's Rio Brioso rancho. I learned the Jicarilla Apache dialect. During the early days of the war in New Mexico I studied the dialects of the Mescaleros and Mimbrenos at the suggestion of Quint Kershaw. To this I added a study of their culture and life-ways. I've been on duty here in Arizona for three years now. When George Crook took over command of the department, he assigned me to recruit and command Apache Scouts. Crook doesn't burden officers with orders, instructions, and memoranda, but chooses merely to give them an insight into what is expected of them. I believe his intent was to use me as an instructor of other officers in the methods and intricacies of dealing with the Apache Scouts and the Apaches themselves. I have devoted myself to that end.''

"With the catalyst of the Navajo problem in New Mexico spurring you on. Is that it?''

He studied her. She had a natural bent for putting her finger right on the point of any discussion. "You have a 'power,' as the Apaches would say. You are right. That was part of the reason I came here to the Arizona Territory. My part in the Navajo problem brought me nothing but defeat and jeopardization of my army career.'' He smiled grimly. "And now, it seems, that problem has followed me to Arizona in the shape of your fiancé—Burton Trapnell.''

"Perhaps he has changed,'' she suggested.

"Perhaps,'' he admitted. "I doubt it. No matter. I've been thinking for some time of resigning. To that end I've been arranging to take over some ranch property south of Tucson, close to the border. The Soledad Canyon area.''

"If Burton is still against you, why not stay and fight it out? General Crook seems to think highly of you.''

Alec reached for his rifle. "I think you're well aware of the political power Trapnell has. In addition, he is now, as you told me, assigned to the Inspector-General Department. They are powerful men in the service, Anne. They can go over the head of any department commander." He stood up and walked to the mine entrance. He turned. "Douse that fire. Get some sleep. We'll take turns standing guard."

"There is something strange about you, Alexander Kershaw," she said thoughtfully. "It is as if you are two persons intermingled, each of them struggling to take control. Sometimes one is the victor and the other the defeated, and then again, it may be the other way around."

He grinned. "Took you quite a while to deduce that, Mrs. Sinclair. Well, you've got all day long to think about it. Now, get some sleep. If we can, we'll try for Fort Bowie at dusk."

He awoke her after some hours to stand a lonely guard while he slept. She was almost surprised to see that he too needed rest. He seemed to be composed of rawhide and steel. After a few hours sleep he was up and about again, vanishing into the woods, scouting, always scouting the canyons and the road to Fort Bowie.

Alec returned to the cave at dusk after watering the dun and moving him farther up the small branch canyon.

"Can we leave now?" she asked.

"I don't know," he replied. "The area seems deserted except for us, and yet I have an uneasy feeling. We'd best wait awhile. We can't leave once the moon is up, so it will have to be after that. It won't give us enough time to make Fort Bowie during darkness, but we can hide out tomorrow and continue on after dusk."

"Why is it you're so sure we can't leave now?" she asked.

"I said the area *seems* deserted. Apaches are seen only when they want to be. They can kill without being seen. Even a rattlesnake gives warning before it strikes. Apaches never do. There's only one way to survive in this country. Quint Kershaw put it succinctly: 'Eternal vigilance is the price of safety here and one's very life' "

When the sun was gone, Anne woke up to find herself alone in the mine. It had turned chilly. She was sleeping under Alec's thin issue blanket. She wrapped it more tightly around herself.

Alec shook her awake. She hadn't even known she had fallen asleep again. The cave was dark.

"You were shivering in your sleep," he said. "Here, cover yourself with my extra shirt."

She shrugged gratefully into it. When she looked up to thank him, he was gone again.

She slept fitfully. The shirt had the rank odor of a hard-living man compounded of the male smell, tobacco, bay rum, harsh government-issue soap, and sour, stale perspiration. She woke up once more to find herself lying on her belly with something hard, like a smooth stone, pressing against her left breast. She felt around for it then realized it was within the breast pocket of the shirt. She took it out and identified it by feel as a small fabric-covered case. Curiosity got the best of her. She got up and found a block of matches.

She walked back farther in the mine so that the light would not show through the entrance. She ignited one of the matches. The light revealed a photo case covered in stained and worn crushed green velvet. She undid the ornate brass hasp and opened the case. Within it was a daguerreotype of the head and bust of a young woman, hardly more than a girl. Her hair was thick, dark, and glossy. Her immense dark eyes seemed almost too large in proportion to her pale and lovely oval face. She was decidedly Spanish in appearance, obviously of the upper class, the almost aristocratic *gente fina*, common among the great landowners of New Mexico. The match flared out. Anne lighted another. There was faint handwriting within the cover. She could just make it out: *To my cherished and beloved Alexander from your ever-adoring Guadalupe.* It was dated Santa Fe, October 1861.

Something warned her. She seemed to be developing some of Alec's instinctive awareness. She closed the case, slid it into the shirt pocket, and ran noiselessly back to her pallet. Faint moonlight limned the entrance to the mine. She felt rather than heard Alec's noiseless approach. A moment later he whistled softly.

She opened her eyes. He was kneeling close beside her, and for one delicious moment she thought he might have something on his mind other than her comfort.

"Don't panic," he whispered. "There are Apaches far down the road and they are coming this way."

Her guts seemed to be gripped suddenly by an ice cold iron claw, and for a moment she almost thought she was going to embarrass herself.

"They've evidently been raiding," he continued. "Some of them are bandaged. Their extra ponies are loaded with loot. They have some prisoners."

"Soldiers?" she whispered.

"They don't take adult males prisoners. Too dangerous. They take the younger women and the children, those who can't turn against them and harm them. The women become wives or slaves. The young boys become warrior trainees. It's one way the Apaches keep up their dwindling fighting strength."

"Will they stop here in the canyon?"

"I think so. For water at least. They won't spend any more time here than they have to. It has a bad name with them. To them it's haunted by the spirits of those they have slain."

"What can we do?" she asked.

"Sit tight and hope they don't find us. One slight advantage we might have is that the cemetery is between us and them. They usually avoid such places. It's not much, I'll admit."

She closed her eyes. "I'm afraid. God, Alec, I'm scared half to death."

"I'm not feeling too cheery myself," he admitted. "One *never* gets used to them." He drew her close, tilted up her chin, and looked into her eyes. "But you can't give in to panic," he whispered. "Not in this country. It might mean the difference between life and death. Do you understand?"

She nodded, pressing her head close to his chest. She was woman-tough, which is different from the toughness of a man, less obvious, more resilient, and difficult for a man to understand. She could feel the steady beating of his heart. At that moment she realized that this diamond-hard panther of a man, this efficient killing machine had a deep inner core and a tenderness and understanding belied by his stern, forbidding exterior. She wondered how many others knew about this inner being of Alexander Kershaw. Certainly, Guadal-upe, whoever she was, or had been, must have known.

CHAPTER 6

THE CANYON WAS A GHOSTLY LANDSCAPE FROZEN IN SI-lence and bluish moonlight. There was no wind. Nothing moved. The shadows were sharply defined on the light-col-ored earth, as though they had been inked in.

Alec and Anne were concealed at the mine entrance behind a jackstraw pile of old pit props and brush. He handed her his field glasses and pointed down the slope to the right. At first she saw nothing other than the landscape; then a figure ap-peared, moving swiftly and noiselessly, as though it were a phantom conjured from moonlight and shadow.

The scout vanished into the thick brush on the far side of the road about two hundred yards from the station. Minutes passed. Then a form took substance within the brush across the road from the buildings. He vanished again. He reap-peared farther up, crossed the road swiftly, and disappeared behind the stone corral. Soon his head and shoulders ap-peared above the corral wall. He surveyed the heights with his field glasses.

The scout was looking directly at the mine entrance. Anne buried her head within her crossed forearms. Her breathing became erratic. She willed herself to stay calm. *But you can't give in to panic,* Alec had told her.

When she looked again, the scout was at the well. He dropped something into it, evidently to check if there was water. The next moment he was gone. She let out her pent-up breath with a gasp.

Alec nodded. ''No matter how many times I see them, I always get the same feeling.''

She rested her chin on her forearms. ''Is it always like this? The constant danger, hardship, vigilance, fighting, and kill-ing?''

"Most of the time," he replied.

"Why do you keep at it?"

Alec shrugged. "It's the only life I really know. I've been at it since '61 when the war started."

"You could have finished your medical degree."

"That's true, but I would have returned to the service as a surgeon and probably would have been stationed somewhere on the frontier anyway," Alec said. He suddenly pointed down to the road.

A mounted Apache had appeared. He had a heavy cartridge belt around his waist and another on his left shoulder crossing his chest. A repeating rifle rested on his thighs. The shaft of a lance was upthrust behind his left shoulder. The polished blade glistened in the moonlight. The booted hooves of his horse made no sound on the road. The warrior's head moved constantly in the ritual of alertness—looking ahead, then to the right and left, then to the rear and back again to the front.

The foot scout appeared out of the brush and spoke to the mounted warrior. He turned in his saddle and raised his rifle in both hands, thrusting it rapidly up and down.

A mounted group of warriors appeared down the road. Several of them wore bandages. One of them had his left arm in a sling. More mounted warriors followed, then came captives riding with their ankles tied together under the barrels of their horses. Most were young women and girls with a few boys among them. Two warriors formed the rear guard.

The Apaches stopped at the station for water. Some of them stood guard in a perimeter around the buildings while others tended to the watering.

"They won't stay long," Alec whispered to Anne. "Their eyrie is up on the Big Mountain. Apaches are not desert people; they are mountain people. They are nomads in a sense, living in the cool mountains during the summers and descending to the lower levels when Ghost Face, the winter, places his snowy blanket on the heights."

The raiders were soon gone into the shadowed canyon leading to their stronghold as swiftly and noiselessly as they had appeared, almost as though they had been but chimeras of the imagination. The only signs they left of their passing were water droplets splashed on the light-colored earth and a few steaming piles of manure.

Anne woke up. It was just before moonset, hours after the Apaches had left. Alec was gone again. She reached out instinctively for his Remington revolver. "Alec?" she whispered. There was no reply. She crawled to the mine entrance and peered down into the canyon. It was dark with shadows. A hollow thumping sound seemed to come from down at the station. She recognized it as the wooden well cover being moved. Probably Alec getting water, she thought. Then she slowly realized with a sense of fright that they didn't need water from the well, and in any case, he would never have allowed a sound like that.

Gnawing fear ate into her. Maybe Alec had left her. She really couldn't blame him. He could return to Fort Bowie easily without her encumbering him. She looked down into the canyon again. Perhaps it had been he who had accidentally dropped the well cover after all. Or she might have imagined hearing the noise. Yes, that was it!

The thumping sound came again. There was no mistaking it. She crawled back into the cave past the dripping seep water to a place where the tunnel was partially blocked by a fall. She clambered over the rubble and lay down with just her head showing above it. She thrust the heavy pistol forward, resting her right forearm on the mounded earth. It was very quiet in the darkness, broken only by the faint drip, drip, drip of the seep water.

Anne's courage slowly returned. Perhaps it had been her imagination after all. She crawled back over the mound and tiptoed back toward the seep. Something blocked the faint grayish light. Gradually, the unmistakable silhouette of a hatless human figure kneeling beside the water pan came into focus.

Anne took a step forward. "Alec?" she called softly.

The figure straightened up, whirled, and extended a long-bladed knife in his right hand. There was no mistaking the silhouette of an Apache head with its thick mane of hair. Anne raised the pistol, cocked it, and pulled the trigger, almost without thinking. A brilliant flash and ear-splitting report

filled the narrow confines of the tunnel. She clearly saw the
broad painted face and the dark eyes wide with complete surprise. The Apache whirled and ran, staggering in his stride,
to vanish out the mine entrance. Anne recocked the pistol and
ran after him, her fright giving her a sudden surge of courage.
She halted at the entrance. The was a sudden rush of hissing,
sliding gravel as the warrior plunged down the long steep
tailings slope. Slowly, the rushing sound subsided, and then
it was quiet again.

Alec found her barricaded behind a pile of pit props. Her
face was white and taut. "Are you all right?" he asked.
"What happened?"

She buried her face against his chest. He held her close.
"There was an Apache in here," she said tensely. "I fired
at him. He ran down the slope. I didn't see where he went
because of the darkness."

He shook his head. "Jesus! That pistol shot sounded like
a twelve-pounder Napoleon cannon. If the Chiricahuas up on
the heights didn't hear it, we've got more luck than brains."

"Dammit! Where did you go?" she demanded tearfully.

"Along the road. I found a dead horse half a mile from
here. Probably ridden to death. I thought at first it might have
been left by the party that passed through here. Not likely
though. None of their horses looked like that. I had a feeling
there might be a lone Apache around here somewhere. Then
I heard your shot. Sit tight. Stay near the entrance where you
can see anyone approaching."

"Where are you going?" He could hear the fear in her
voice.

"We can't let him loose. If he gets back to his people,
they'll be in here like a swarm of hornets."

"Why can't we leave now?" she demanded.

"There may be others who heard your shot. We've only
got one horse. We'd never outrun them. He's got to be
stopped, I tell you!"

"You'll not leave me alone again," she said determinedly.

He had no choice. He led the way down a deep gully to the
rear of the station buildings and left Anne behind the stone
corral while he crossed it and went to cover behind the barn.

The moon was far to the west. Shadows thickened at the bottom of the canyons. Anne crossed the corral at a crouch without making a sound. He turned and looked at her. "You're learning fast," he whispered. "Give me the pistol." He handed her the Winchester in return.

One of the thick shutters used to close a barn window hung loose. Alec did not recall seeing it that way. He placed his back against the wall and edged to it, cocked pistol held upraised. He heard a faint rustling sound within the barn. He looked quickly around the shutter.

A man's silhouette appeared in the window frame like a deadly jack-in-the-box. A long-bladed knife fanged out toward Alec's throat. The action was so swift and startling Alec squeezed the trigger. The gun flash illuminated the contorted painted face of the young Apache. He fell backward with a savage grunt.

Alec charged around to the front of the barn, kicked open the sagging door, and plunged inside, the Remington describing short arcs from side to side. The dying moonlight coming through shutterless windows and the open doorway revealed the warrior down on his knees, wreathed in powder smoke. His right hand clutched his left bicep. Bright blood leaked between his fingers and ran down his forearm to drip from his fingertips. He instantly released his grip on his left arm and snatched up his knife from beside him.

Alec came up off the floor and kicked out a long leg. The heel caught the buck on the point of the jaw, snapping back his head. The next instant the pistol barrel was slapped with stunning force alongside the Apache's head. He fell backward and lay still. Alec stepped hard on his right wrist and removed the knife from the nerveless fingers.

Anne came through the front doorway. "Is he dead?" she asked.

Alec shook his head. "I haven't killed him, not *yet* anyway."

He held the knife in his right hand. "I don't want any more shooting."

"What are you going to do?" she asked quickly.

His intent was plain on his taut face.

She looked down at the Apache. "He's hardly more than a boy."

Alec pointed to a cord about the Apache's neck. "Drinking tube and head scratcher," he explained. "He's an untried brave. Their first four times on the warpath they can't touch water with the lips nor scratch their heads with the fingers."

It sounded so incongruous, she almost laughed, but she knew he was serious.

"Why did he come up to the mine? I thought they would keep away from the graveyard."

"Looking for water. The war party must have drained the well. There wasn't much in it. Evidently he knew about the seep. He must have been damned desperate to go up there."

Alec frisked the young buck for a hideout knife and removed it from the top of his right moccasin. He held it up to show Anne. "The last resort. Like a Scottish Highlander's *skean dhu*—the black knife." He picked up the buck's legs by the ankles and started to drag him toward the door. "We'll have to get rid of him somewhere else."

She gripped Alec by an arm. "Look at his left arm," she said quietly. "Can't you stop the bleeding at least?"

"Waste of time," he said.

She thought quickly. "You'll leave traces of his blood. They'd be sure to find that, at least."

He looked at her. "You're a caution, you are, lady."

"Alec, please, for my sake?"

He shook his head. "Jesus . . ."

He slit the brave's sleeve up to the shoulder. "My God," he said quietly.

The left forearm was swollen and black-looking. The bicep was wet with blood from the fresh wound. Anne turned quickly away, sickened at the sight and odor of the forearm. She ran outside. The new wound was of the flesh, the bullet having furrowed through the skin. Alec bandaged it. He placed his palm on the youth's forehead. It was hot and dry. His lips were cracked and swollen.

"What is it?" Anne asked timorously from the doorway.

"Gangrene," Alec replied.

"I've heard of it, but know nothing about it."

He looked up at her. "Death of tissue in an area of the body, produced by infection or by the loss of the blood supply and the nourishment and oxygen it provides. Common symptoms are discoloration of the skin, pain in the affected area, and fever.

"Gas gangrene is caused by a bacteria that produces gas under the skin. A toxin is formed that decomposes tissue. In dry gangrene, circulation is gradually reduced in the arms and legs. Tissue shrinks, loses its warmth, and begins to change color until finally it is black."

"Like that?" she asked.

Alec nodded. "See here?" He indicated a hole that oozed a foul-smelling pus. "It's evidently a bullet wound that was sustained some days ago and went untreated. Now infection has set in with a vengeance. Sometimes bullets are rubbed with garlic; they're said to cause such blood poisoning."

The Apache's eyelids began to flutter. Alec swiftly tied his ankles together. He could not tie the warrior's hands behind his back, not with a terribly infected arm like that. He bound the brave's right arm to his body.

"How do you think it happened?" she asked curiously.

"Probably, he was originally with the war party that came through here. Perhaps at the start of the raid he was wounded and separated from the rest of them. In any case, he was likely missing and they had no time to look for him. They continued on their raid. During that time his wound became badly infected. He tried to return to the Big Mountain. That's his horse I found, ridden to death. His thirst and pain must have been intolerable. That's why he came here. This is the end of the war trail for him."

"What do you mean?"

"He'll die an agonizing death within the next few days. That is, unless I kill him."

"Can nothing be done to help him?"

Alec shook his head. "Look here," he said quietly. He wiped away the blood just above the brave's elbow to reveal the faint telltale spots of the spreading infection. "If it gets much higher, that will be the end."

"But there must be something we can do!" she cried.

"He's only a boy! Have there been no survivors of this horrible thing?"

"Only by amputation, and then that's not a certainty. Many more have died from it than the few who have survived. We'd be doing him a favor by killing him before he's fully conscious."

"No! No! No!" she protested.

"Damn you! Will you not listen to reason! Have you ever seen a human being die from this condition? No, you haven't! I have! Too many times! Now, I don't want to stand around and watch the inevitable even if he is a wild Apache and my sworn enemy!" He walked to the door and looked up toward the heights. "Perhaps they could help him up there, but I doubt it. Still, it might make him feel better. But I don't know how he's going to get there." He knew there was no hope.

She came to stand beside him. "What could they do?" she asked.

He shrugged. " A *diyi*, that is, a shaman, or medicine man or woman might give him some comfort. He would call out the Gans, the masked dancers, or Mountain Spirit impersonators. They would perform as Crown Dancers wearing fantastic hooded headdresses made of sotol stalks and painted with mystic symbols. They believe that evil causes sickness and that by ritual dancing and singing it can be extracted and driven away."

She looked up into his face, so set and thoughtful. She knew then that he would not kill the boy. "And if that doesn't work, what then, Alec?"

He did not reply for a moment or two. "The Ghost Dance," he said at last in a low voice. "It's the last resort. It goes on all night. To me, it's more of a death ritual than an attempt to heal. When one sees the Ghost Dance, one knows the end is not far off."

"Then there is no hope for him?"

Alec nodded.

She gripped his arm. "You've had medical training."

"Under antiseptic hospital conditions with the proper instruments and medication, the least of which is chloroform."

"Can't you improvise?"

"You're either simpleminded or you have a macabre sense of humor," he said dryly.

She turned away. "He's awake now, Alec."

Dark, pain-filled eyes fixed Alec with a basilisk stare of utter hatred, the look of an implacable enemy.

Alec rubbed his jaw. "He'll try to kill me the first chance he gets," he warned Anne. "Keep him covered while I get him out of here." He picked up the youth. The Apache struggled but found himself in a steellike grasp. So by the teachings of The People he became *en-thlay-sit-daou—He who abides without moving, one who is calm, clearheaded, and courageous in the face of events.*

Alec carried him into the rock-walled blacksmith shop. "Clear the workbench, Anne," he requested. He placed the youth on it. There was an old lantern hanging from a rafter. He shook it. There was oil in the reservoir. He lighted it.

He took his rifle from Anne and handed her the pistol. "I'm going up to the mine for our things. If he tries to get loose and at you, shoot to kill. Understand? If you don't he'll sure as hell kill you, and then maybe come looking for me."

When Alec left, Anne stood across the shop from the prisoner, never taking her eyes from him. He watched her intently, almost unblinkingly, like a snake mesmerizing a trapped rabbit. She could feel the cold sweat from the palm of her hand greasing the pistol butt.

Alec returned with the saddlebags and a bucket of seep water. He started a fire in the forge. He selected a hacksaw and some files from a tool box, clamped the blade in a vise, and filed it to set fine teeth. The Apache's knife was of very old Mexican make or possibly even Spanish Toledo steel, the finest in the world. Alec touched up its already razor-sharp edge. He set the water to boiling. He found a wagon kingbolt and placed it in the glowing charcoal. He located a half-gallon can of wagon grease and cleaned the dust and dirt from the top.

"They'll know for certain we're here now," Anne said.

Alec nodded. "You may as well understand that there will be no escape for either one of us once we attempt this operation. If he lives through it, we might use him as a hostage to barter with the Chiricahuas."

"And if he dies?"

He shrugged. "I die too. Perhaps not here, or for some time, but assuredly I will die, and it will not be a swift flight into oblivion. They will want me to *know* I will die in time . . . a *long* time. . . ."

She paled. "Perhaps we had better not go ahead with it, then."

"I'm going on with it."

She studied him. "Can you truly tell me why? You were almost adamantly against it at first. What made you change your mind? Alec, tell me the truth."

He glanced at the youth. "For some years I've tried to learn all I can about these remarkable people. I've already discovered a great deal from my association with my Scouts and from Mexicans and Americans who know the Apaches quite well. But that's not the same as knowing the truly wild ones, such as the Chiricahuas. My Scouts are a mixed bunch, half-breeds, Arivaipas, Tontos, White Mountain, and so forth. I've learned something of the Jicarillas of northern New Mexico and the Mescaleros of the central and southern area, and the Mimbrenos of the west and south. It is the Chiricahuas I want to know. They have a custom that if a great favor is done them, then the person doing that favor may be adopted into the tribe. If I can save this boy's life, perhaps I'll be rewarded in that manner, or at least with friendship. They are people of honor, perhaps more so than their deadly enemies, us and the Mexicans. I plan to gamble on that honor."

"Isn't that a rather hopeless gamble?"

"I may never get another opportunity like this. There is still time, perhaps, for you to leave. Take the dun and ride for Fort Bowie. Odds are you won't find any Apaches between here and the fort now. You saw the returning war party. They likely won't be raiding for a time."

Anne hesitated. God, it was tempting, dangerous as it was certain to be. She looked at the earnest man who had saved her life at the risk of his own. He had kept her alive in a country that was naturally as hostile as the Chiricahuas who called it their own. She knew him now for a man with great strength of will and discipline, and perhaps more because under his hardcase exterior and tough ways there was a warm and understanding human being, although she felt he took great pains to conceal it.

"Well?" Alec asked.

She shook her head. "You'll need my help." She smiled a little thinly. "After all, it *was* my idea."

"There will be no going back."

She looked into his eyes. "I know. I've put my trust in you ever since you saved me and I can do no less now. We are together, for better or for worse. What do you want me to do?"

"Cut off strips of your underskirt and boil them for bandages. When I am ready to operate, you must hold his head."

Alec walked over to the youth. He spoke quietly while gently touching the arm, explaining in the tongue of The People what he must do. There was no expression on the youth's face. He evidently had realized there was no other choice.

Alec poured some of the water into a pan, then thoroughly washed and soaped his hands and forearms, rinsing them several times. He poured some of his precious remaining Baconora over the hacksaw blade and the knife. He looked at Anne and nodded. She went to the youth and held his head. He made no movement of resistance. He had conjured himself into *en-thlay-sit-daou*. Come what may, he was as ready as he'd ever be for the medicine of the White-Eye.

Alec laid out his tools. The kingbolt was glowing red. He stepped back a little from the workbench upon which the youth lay. "Raise his head, Anne," he said. She did so. "Look directly at me, boy," he said in the Chiricahua dialect. He moved so fast, Anne hardly saw the big-fisted jab travel about eight inches to strike on the point of the jaw and knock the Apache unconscious.

"You could have killed him!" she cried angrily.

"You damned fool!" he grunted. "The operation is bound to kill him anyway. Hold his head down with all your strength. Look the other way and for Christ's sake, don't faint!"

The finely honed knife opened the arm to the bone. The hacksaw teeth rasped into the bone at the joint. Sweat dripped from Alec's face. In a matter of a few minutes he had amputated the lower arm at the elbow joint. The Apache opened his eyes. They were fixed in agony, but no sound came from his taut lips. Sweat burst out on his forehead and ran down his face, streaking his war paint.

Alec picked up the white-hot wagon kingbolt with pincers and applied it to the raw stump to take up the arteries more swiftly than ligatures could have done. He threw the bolt to the floor and then applied the cool axle grease thickly to the stump. He wrung out the boiled strips of underskirt and skillfully bound the wound. He stepped back, dashed the streaming sweat from his own face, snatched up the flask of Baconora, and stalked outside. Anne turned aside and retched violently.

Alec was leaning against the front wall of the shop when she came out. "He's conscious now. Will he live?" she asked quietly.

Alec looked up at the sky. "Yosen willing."

"Their god?"

"The principal one anyway. They have quite a few minor deities as well to pray to in time of need."

"You may have missed your calling," she suggested.

"I can always go back."

"Ah, but *will* you?"

He handed her the Baconora flask. "Only Yosen may know that, and I'm not sure he does."

A coyote yapped somewhere in the darkness along the road.

"They'll be after the dead horse," Alec said.

"Have you ever thought of serving somewhere else?" she queried.

"If your colonel has his way here as he did back in New Mexico, I may have to, or leave the service altogether. Believe me, I've more than just considered that prospect. It wouldn't take much for me to resign. Maybe it's just as well. There's no promotion and little glory in leading Apache Scouts."

"Isn't it voluntary? Why do you stay with them?"

"Two reasons: Despite it all, I like the service. And in time it will prove to be the only way the Apaches will eventually be subjugated. It will take some years yet, but it will be inevitable if Crook has his way. Half-wild men tracking down their still wild brethren."

She sipped at the warming brandy. "Can we leave now?"

"No. He will need care for a few days. *If* he lives."

Her intense fear of the place and the Apaches had been subdued by the terror and excitement of the operation, but now it was returning tenfold.

"I know how you must feel, Anne," he said quietly. "But when you insisted on my operating, I warned you of what would happen. It's too late to leave now." He smiled thinly. "We've crossed our Rubicon, so to speak."

She gripped his arm. "Perhaps they'll come for him soon. Please, for God's sake, let us leave now!"

Somewhere in the velvety darkness on the heights a wolf howled. In a little while another howled from another direction. There was a pause, then still another howled, this time opposite from where the first wolf had called, from a place overlooking the road where it entered the canyon.

"Are those real wolves, Alec?" Anne asked.

"Possibly."

"Couldn't they be Chiricahuas?"

"Possibly."

"They can't be both," she said.

Alec looked up at the heights. "Yes, they can. Wolves and Chiricahuas, they are one and the same." He reached inside the shop and took the rifle. He vanished into the darkness.

She stepped back into the false security of the shop. The young Apache was conscious, lying still, staring fixedly at the ceiling, sweat streaming down his painted face. He turned his head slowly to look at Anne. He spoke in his own tongue. She shook her head. He nodded his head toward one of the canteens. She filled a tin cup with water and brought it to him. He quickly turned his head away from the cup.

"What's the matter with you?" she cried angrily. "First you want water and now you refuse it! You can go to hell!" She poured the water back into the canteen.

Anne sat down in a corner on a toolbox with the Remington pistol in her lap. Slowly, she began to realize it was her fear of him and his kind that had kindled her anger at his refusal of the water. She concentrated, thinking to herself, he too is one of God's children, despite his barbarism. She didn't know when she fell asleep.

CHAPTER 7

IT WAS VERY QUIET EXCEPT FOR THE SOFT RUSTLE OF THE leaves moved by the night wind. Alec approached the dead horse in the road. Something moved swiftly away from it, into the shelter of trees and brush. A coyote or wolf had already been at the body. He worked in the darkness, not daring to risk a light. He removed the saddle and the saddle blanket. The blanket was stiff and ridged with caked sweat. He found a double-barreled shotgun and cartridges for it. He excised the neck meat of the horse. It would be enough to feed three people for a few days, albeit rather scantily.

Now and again he looked up at the heights darkly silhouetted against the sky. After the first outbreak of wolf howling there had been no more. Wolves usually got at the prey first, keeping the weaker coyotes at a distance until they were done. The residue would be left for the coyotes and the next day the carcass would be picked to the bone by vultures, crows, and long-tailed white-necked ravens. He wasn't sure about the wolf howls. Perhaps they *had* been the real thing, although Apaches could imitate them to perfection, a favorite signal of theirs.

Alec awakened Anne. He fed the forge fire and fashioned a spit for the roast. "How's he been?" he asked her over his shoulder.

"He awoke some time ago and indicated he wanted water. I offered him a cup, but he turned his head away. Why? He was obviously very thirsty."

Alec filled a cup with water and took it to the youth. He held it out to him and pointed at the drinking tube. The youth thrust the tube into the water and greedily emptied the cup. He lay back and studied Alec with enigmatic eyes.

Alec looked at Anne. "As far as he's concerned, he's still on the warpath. As a novice, he can't touch water with his lips."

Alec turned to the young Apache and spoke rapidly while using many gestures. The brave spoke but one word in reply.

"What did you say to him? What did he say?" Anne asked curiously.

"I told him I knew he was a novice and understood the rules by which he must abide during his first four times on the warpath. He's evidently quite surprised at my knowledge of his tongue and culture. I asked him if he was all right now."

"And?"

Alec smiled a little. "He said no."

"Well then, what is wrong?"

"Nothing is wrong," Alec replied. "He's required to use backward speech until he's accepted as a full-fledged warrior. So he said no instead of yes, meaning that he *was* all right. Backward speech is not unusual in some tribes. Probably because of some deep-seated religious reason. You must remember that warfare to many Indian tribes is a spiritual experience."

"He's making a remarkable recovery after that makeshift operation, Alec. Frankly, I did not expect him to survive."

Alec nodded. "His people, by environment and training, are perhaps some of the toughest human organisms ever developed. He's in a sort of limbo right now. He's in the presence of persons, myself in particular, he's been taught to consider as the deadliest of enemies. He knows now I've saved his life. He also knows his people will come for him once they know he's alive. When that time comes, our roles will be reversed. Then, if he so chooses, *he* can save *our* lives."

Alec removed the roast from its spit. "There are no other people on this continent like the Apaches, and among them the Chiricahuas are the most matchless. Their environment is incredibly hard. Plants and animals are armed with spikes, thorns, and spines; fangs, claws, teeth, and poison. Everything must live on something else and every existence has to be bought with another. The Apache's whole life-way is dedicated to tearing a living from nature. This has developed them into the finest type of athlete. They are usually of medium height, built like a deer, with small hands and feet, small bones, thin arms and legs. Their sinews are taut and their bodies are devoid of fat. They have immensely deep chests. The adult Apache warrior is an embodiment of physical endurance, lean, well-proportioned, with sinews like steel. They seem insensible to hunger, fatigue, and pain. You've got a good example of that in our young friend here.''

"You sound like a lecturer, Alec," she said with a smile.

He nodded. "General Crook has had me lecture to other officers and non-commissioned officers on the subject. For some time I've been preparing a manuscript from my observations and notes. General Crook plans to have it published by the government for use here in the Territory."

Anne studied him. "It sounds like a labor of love," she suggested.

Alec shrugged. "Perhaps not of love, but of dire necessity. These people will never be defeated by our present methods. It's impossible. For warfare in their own domain they are without peer. They have cunning, stealthiness, endurance, ruthlessness, fortitude, and fighting skill. They are unexcelled by any other Indians. They have the eye of the hawk; stealthiness of the coyote; the courage and mercilessness of the tiger. Indeed, General Crook has dubbed them the Human Tigers. All outsiders, especially their non-tribal neighbors, are their enemies. They are extremely religious, perhaps not in our Christian sense but in the fulfillment of their own beliefs. The more deviltry they plan, the more religious they become."

The young Apache was studying them with eyes like darkened lights.

Anne looked at him. "He seems almost to understand what you're saying," she said.

Alec glanced at the Apache. "Perhaps he does. If he understands English, you'll never know about it. He was trained early for his trade, that is, for thievery and warfare. Apache youths are not ordered to go on the warpath. That is their own decision. A novice must participate in four war parties. He must eat inferior food. He acts as a servant to the warriors, cooking, and taking care of their horses. He's not allowed to speak except to answer questions or when he is told to speak. He is expected to learn the sacred names of objects used for war. There is a special vocabulary of over one hundred war related items. He must use the backward speech. To the Apaches, war is sacred. Every act on the warpath is ridgidly prescribed.

"A novice's training is hard, rigorous, and sometimes extremely dangerous, even to the point of death. From the first game he kills he must swallow the raw heart whole so as to have good hunting luck thereafter. He cannot eat hot food on the warpath. The horses will founder if he does so. He cannot eat entrails, as that will also give bad luck with the horses. Meat from the head of an animal is forbidden."

"*Na-txe-ce,*" the Apache said quietly.

"What is he saying?" Anne asked.

Alec smiled. "My Apache name. It means Never Still. I was dubbed that by my Scouts, and the Chiricahuas picked it up. I earned it the hard way, chasing after them, or running *away* from them, as the case may be."

"It's a sort of a compliment, isn't it? Praise from an enemy is praise indeed," Anne said.

Alec shrugged. "It wouldn't stop him from sticking his knife into me."

"*Agua,*" the youth said in Spanish.

"Give him water, Anne," Alec said.

The brave sucked up the water through his drinking tube. He allowed a faint smile to cross his features. He pointed to Anne. "*Tze-go-juni,*" he said.

"He's accepted you and has given you a name," Alec explained. "Very nice and fitting too. Tze-go-juni. It means Pretty Mouth. I should have thought of it first. He knows we've saved his life, but doesn't know why, except that it was done." Alec looked at him. "You're free to leave at any time," he said.

The youth shook his head.

"Why won't you go?" Alec asked. "We won't try to stop you, or follow you to kill you. Why should we do that after having saved your life? Only a fool or madman would do such a thing."

"I'm not afraid for myself, Never Still," replied the youth in the Chiricahua dialect. He looked at Anne and then back at Alec. His meaning was clear enough.

"What is all this?" demanded Anne.

"I've offered him his freedom. He has refused. He is not afraid for himself, he says."

"Meaning?"

Alec smiled. "We'll be under his protection when his people come for him."

"How much protection will that be?"

Alec shrugged. "Who knows? They are not always a predictable people." He smiled. "Like us," he added dryly.

"So what will happen now?"

"We can get some sleep."

"Shouldn't one of us stand guard?"

"I doubt if that would be of much value. If you're afraid to stay here, we can go up to the mine."

She nodded. "I'd feel one hundred percent better."

Alec packed the saddlebags. He cut the cooling meat into three equal portions. He pointed to the third portion. "Yours, my brother," he said to the Apache.

"Thank you," the youth said. He hesitated, then pointed to himself. *"Nah-delthy-ah, shee-kizzen."*

Anne looked at Alec.

He smiled. "He's told me his name and called me his brother. It's Nah-delthy-ah, which translates into 'The Runner,' or 'Going to Run.' It's a rare honor for an Apache to tell you his name. It means he has accepted you. Of course, it might not be his real name, or perhaps just *one* of his names. It just might be the one he uses for convenience to identify himself. In any case, it is a great honor. We've made a real friend here, Anne."

"I hope that bond lasts," she said quietly.

"It will as far as he's concerned."

They climbed the hill to the mine. Anne looked back over her shoulder at the faint light of the blacksmith shop. Suddenly, the light blinked out.

Alec drew her close for comfort. "It's in the laps of the gods now, Anne. He may be gone by himself in the night. They may come for him tonight. It's quite possible he may still be here tomorrow. They may come for him then."

They went into the mine. Alec lighted the stub of a candle.

They sat there gnawing at the tough, cooked horsemeat. Anne laughed suddenly.

He looked at her curiously. "What is it?"

"I imagine this is what a caveman and his woman would have lived like. Spending their evenings together, sitting in a dim cave gnawing on tough half-cooked meat."

Alec nodded. "We seem to have reverted back into prehistoric times."

She lay down on the old sacks. "Why really did you operate on him?" she asked.

"Perhaps because of the Hippocratic oath?" Alec grinned slyly.

She shook her head. "Hardly. You haven't answered my question, Alec," she persisted.

"I've already told you."

"You mean the little sermon about saving his life in order to be rewarded by his friendship and perhaps even so far as to be adopted into the tribe? Alec, is that *all*?"

How could he tell her the real reason? That first a suggestion and then an order had been given him by General Crook to learn all he could about the Apaches in order that they might be defeated and subjugated in time. He greatly admired George Crook. He firmly believed that the general, as well as being a feared and powerful enemy of The People, might in time become one of their most powerful friends.

"Alec, is that *all*?" she repeated softly.

Alec stood up and walked outside without speaking.

It was a long time before Anne fell asleep. Once during the night she thought she heard a wolf howl, repeated several times, but she wasn't sure whether it was a dream or not. In any case, reality or dream, they sounded much closer than those she had first heard.

CHAPTER 8

DAWN LIGHT SHOWED AT THE MINE ENTRANCE. ANNE awoke shivering in the morning chill. Alec was not there. She looked down the slope. He was tethering the dun outside the blacksmith shop. He entered the shop. Smoke began to rise from the chimney.

Anne hurried down the slope, feeling as though an unseen myriad of black eyes were watching her from the heights and the canyon woods. She could almost sense the presence of the Chiricahuas.

Alec was operating the forge bellows when she entered the shop. "Dun lost a shoe," he said laconically, "and two others are about worn out."

The Runner sat on the workbench gnawing at some of the cold horse meat. His eyes seemed brighter and more alert than they had been the day before. As Alec had said, "Perhaps some of the toughest human organisms ever developed."

"I've made coffee with the last of the beans, Anne," Alec said. "We've about enough horse meat for another meal."

"And then?" she asked quietly.

"We've got to leave. That's why I'm shoeing the dun. If the worse comes to the worst, you can ride him out of here."

"And what about you?"

"I'll follow you on foot."

She shook her head. "You'll never make it, Alec. We stay here together or leave together."

"You've got guts, or else you're not overly bright," he commented dryly. "I don't know why the Chiricahuas haven't shown up yet. They're out there somewhere. I can *feel* them. Perhaps we could take a chance and ride out of here together. They *might* allow us to leave. . . ."

The Runner finished the meat, then pulled his moccasins down around his ankles. He thoroughly rubbed the grease from his hand over his muscular thighs and calves.

Alec watched him over his shoulder. "One of their customs, Anne. They feel that if fat meat is fed to the stomach the stomach will get fat. So they rub, or feed, their legs with the fat instead in order to be good runners. One time there was a warrior who fed only his belly and never his legs. There came a day when his enemies were chasing him and gaining on him. He pleaded with his legs to run faster. They replied

that he had never fed them and told him to run on his belly."
He grinned. "Makes a lot of sense, doesn't it?"

The Runner looked toward the doorway as though he had
received a silent message.

Alec placed three horseshoes and several bars of iron in the
forge. "No matter what happens from now on, you must not
show fear, Anne. Do you understand? *Do not show fear!*"

The shop grew hot from the glowing coals in the forge.
Alec stripped off his shirt and undershirt, revealing his deep
broad chest and long powerful muscles. There was a puck-
ered bullet hole in his left shoulder and a long ragged scar on
his right forearm. He saw her eyeing the scars. "Left shoulder a minie ball at Valverde. Almost killed me with infection.
Right forearm a bayonet slash from the first day at Gettysburg," he explained.

"And the scar at your left eye?" she asked boldly.

He studied her for a moment, as though reluctant to answer
her question. "From a Navajo," he replied quietly. He poked
at the horseshoes with a pair of tongs. "The poor bastard was
wounded and starving. We had him cornered. I went in after
him to talk him into surrendering. At first I thought he would
do so. When he had his chance, he tried to blind me." His
voice died away.

"And you had to kill him?" she asked.

He shook his head. The memory was alive in his mind as
though it were yesterday. "One of my sergeants did so. He
saved my sight and maybe my life. I've never felt right about
it since." Alec turned back to his work.

She was about to speak again when a shadow darkened the
open doorway. The icy claw gripping her bowels came again.
She looked at Alec. He glanced toward the doorway.

The newcomer was tall for an Apache, with a heavier,
more muscular build than most. His broad face was expressionless. His eyes were dark, but seemed to have a reddish,
almost imperceptible glow within them. His thin-lipped
mouth was shaped like the curved downward slash of a knife.
He looked at The Runner.

The youth stood up and walked awkwardly, weak from his
wound and the amputation, staggering a little due to the loss

of balance from the missing forearm and hand. The two Chiricahuas spoke rapidly, then the newcomer clasped his arms around The Runner and held him close, looking over the youth's shoulder at Alec.

Alec seemed unconcerned. He tonged one of the glowing bars of iron to the Peter Wright anvil and held it there. He raised the hammer and began to pound on the iron with steady, powerful strokes, showering sparks on all sides. He did not look at the two Apaches. They drew back a little, as though avoiding the flying sparks. Awe grew on their dark faces. Sweat dripped from Alec's face and torso. His muscles stood out. The clanging rhythm filled the shop.

Anne suddenly saw an Apache face at one of the windows. In a moment or two every window framed another such face. They stared, putting hands over their mouths in deep awe as they watched Alec. The hammer against the iron began to sound a melody, or so it seemed to Anne. Alec appeared oblivious to anyone or anything but his work.

Minutes ticked past. Then as suddenly and as unexpectedly as they had appeared, the Chiricahuas vanished. Alec quenched the iron bar in a bucket. He walked to the doorway.

"Are they gone?" she asked in a very small voice.

Alec nodded. He whirled and ran to her and caught her as she fainted dead away.

Later, when she had recovered, she watched him shoe the dun. "Why did you work that piece of iron instead of the horseshoes?" she asked.

He looked up. "Apaches have a superstitious fear of blacksmiths and blacksmithing. The call it *Pesh-chidin*, the Spirit of Iron. The blacksmith act was added insurance to saving The Runner's life. The Apache who came to the door is Baishan, which simply means 'knife.' He's the chief of the band living on the Big Mountain. The Mexicans have dubbed him Cuchillo Roja, or Red Knife, supposedly because it is said his knife is always red with the blood of his enemies. He's the grandson of old Intchi-dijin, or Black Wind, who was a famous war chief in his day until a Mexican bullet blinded him many years ago. After that he became a *diyi*, or medicine man, and a very powerful and famous one. It is said that he can see into the future. I suspect The Runner is related to Baishan, perhaps even his younger brother.''

"How do you know all this?"

"Baishan and I have fought against each other, without any definite conclusion, I might add. Know thy enemy, the saying goes. I've made a point of doing just that."

"And so has he most probably," she said.

Alec nodded. "Somehow our paths keep crossing. It's almost as though we're destined to meet someday, when one of us will be victorious over the other." He walked to the doorway and looked up at the Big Mountain. "I went partway up there once. I was with the peace mission I told you about. Of course, we didn't get into the very heart of the stronghold, the citadel, so to speak. It's beautiful up there, Anne. It's like another world, a veritable Eden, an eyrie of safety and beauty for the Chiricahuas."

She studied him. "Did you go up there on a true peace mission, or just to scout it for possible invasion someday?"

"Both, I'm afraid," Alec admitted. "Never fear, no white soldiers could ever take that stronghold. The Chiricahuas know every canyon, summit, mountain, and trail in those hundreds of square miles. They're safe enough, for a time at least. . . ."

"Couldn't soldiers invade it aided by the Apache Scouts?"

He finished shoeing the dun and led it to the door to tether it outside. "It's a possibility, but at present not a probability."

The day drifted past. Alec packed the saddlebags and cleaned his guns. He filled the canteens and watered the dun from the seep pool. Anne managed to get some sleep despite her unsubdued fear of the Chiricahuas. She gave herself a sponge bath out of an old washtub in the privacy of the blacksmith shop. Her clothing was badly in need of a cleaning, but she had no way of achieving that. She ruefully studied the hem-to-waist rip in her skirt and underskirt. She had managed to pin it together using some pieces of wire, but they kept falling out.

Alec came to the shop when the sun was low over the western heights. He watched her trying to pin the skirt together. "Follow me," he said. He led the way to a large century plant partway up the canyon. He took his sheath knife and cut through a stalk a bit, just below one of the murderous-looking thorns. When the cut was almost but not quite through the stalk, he stopped cutting, then grasped the thorn, pulling it outward and then down along the long fleshy stalk, peeling off a long thread of tough fiber. He cut the fiber loose at the bottom of the stalk and handed it to Anne.

She was puzzled. "What am I supposed to do with this?" she asked.

"Apache needle and thread," replied Alec. He took it from her hand and knelt beside her. He pushed the sharp tip of the thorn through the material of the skirt just below the waistband, then through the other side of the rip, and continued down to the hem, neatly stitching the two sides together. He cut off the thorn at the bottom.

He looked up at her. "It'll do until we reach Fort Bowie," he said, standing up. "Just don't tell anyone there who did the seamstress job on your skirt." He grinned.

Back in the shop, he said, "We'll risk leaving at dusk. I don't know if the Chiricahuas will stop us. I doubt it, or they would have returned by now. But we don't know who else might be between us and Fort Bowie. Therefore we'll travel after dark."

A horse nickered sharply from the shadowed road.

Alec placed his Winchester just inside the doorway of the shop. He gave Anne the Remington pistol. "Get in the rear. Don't show the pistol, but keep it handy. Don't shoot unless I do, and then only when you have a clear shot. Shoot to kill. . . ."

Alec walked outside. Baishan sat a blocky claybank. He held the lead ropes of two mares. One was a palomino with four white stockings called *cuatralbo* by the Mexicans, with their sharp definitions for horse coloring. The other mare was a dapple-colored roan with a white star on its forehead, or a *ruano estrello*. They were lovely things of obvious grace and beauty, with flowing manes and long tails. They had small hooves. The roan had a pair of bulging sacks tied together, slung over her back. The palomino had on a small Mexican saddle with silver trimmings.

Baishan dismounted. He had no weapons with him.

"What do you want?" Alec asked.

Baishan studied him for a moment. "You've saved my younger brother's life. We have never heard of anyone saving a life after the black poison has set in. For that you and your woman are free to leave this place. One of the mares is for her to ride. She can choose the one she wants."

Alec smiled. "I thank you," he said.

The Chiricahua shook his head. "It is for me to thank you. You have great powers, my friend. The power to heal the black poison sickness and that of the Spirit of Iron. We already know of you as a great warrior. For all these things you have our respect. You can leave whenever you are ready. You are also welcome to return here as a friend, but not as an enemy."

"And if I am ordered to do so? That is my duty," Alec said.

Baishan shrugged like a Mexican. "I will not kill you myself. That I can never do. But there are others of my people who will kill you on sight. You know the rules of warfare as well as I. It's getting late. Now, let your woman choose the mare she wants."

"What does he say?" Anne whispered from close behind Alec.

Alec kept a fixed smile on his face. "Damn you," he hissed. "Didn't I tell you to stay out of sight?"

"Woman's curiosity," she countered.

"You are to pick one of the mares for yourself."

"My God," she breathed. "They're both so beautiful. I can't make up my mind."

"Dammit!" he snapped. "We can't stand here like two grinning idiots much longer! Choose!"

She frowned thoughtfully. "Oh, well, then let it be the dappled roan with the star on its forehead."

Alec pointed to the roan. "That one, Baishan."

The Chiricahua nodded. He removed the sack from the roan's back and the saddle from the palomino. He saddled the roan. Then he drew his knife, twisted the palomino's head hard to one side, and cut its throat. He jumped back to escape the flow of blood. The roan shied and blew, dancing back-ward until Alec caught and held her steady.

"But why? For God's sake, why?" Anne cried in horror.

Baishan supplied the answer. He spread a square calico cloth on the ground and swiftly excised the neck meat of the mare. He tied the cloth together around the meat and handed it to Alec. "I would have had this prepared for a feast in your honor, my friend, but there is not time. Sometime, when we meet each other again, we'll have an unborn foal cut from its mother's belly and stewed in her own juices. There's nothing better." He wiped his blade on the palomino's mane, sheathed the knife, and mounted his claybank.

"For this we thank you, my friend," Alec said.

Baishan nodded. "If there comes a time, Yosen willing, when you leave your people and come to us as friend and brother, there will be a place for you and your woman on the Big Mountain." He paused and studied Alec. "But remember this, Never Still, it is harder to kill a friend than an enemy."

Alec raised a hand in salute. Baishan touched the claybank with his heels and rode toward the road. He stopped there and turned in his saddle. He raised his right arm in salute and then rode off into the shadows.

"What did he say?" Anne asked.

He would not tell her of the terms laid down by Baishan in order for him to visit the Chiricahuas in their stronghold. That would have to be his secret. He did not want her ever to men-tion, casually or otherwise, that he now held a virtual pass into the stronghold, and possibly membership in the band as long as he did not come as a soldier and an enemy. If he was ordered to go there as a soldier, then of course he was duty bound to go, but that would destroy forever his one great chance to study the Chiricahuas in their home environment and learn everything he could about them.

"Alec?" she asked.

He smiled. "He thanked me for saving his brother's life. We are free to leave the canyon. He said I was a healer and a man of Spirit of Iron and held in great respect by his people."

She studied him. "Is that all? Aren't you holding some-thing back?"

"Nothing," he replied. "These are evidently for you." He pulled two pairs of beautifully made beaded woman's moccasins from the sack Baishan had left. "These are usually worn by young girls during the puberty ceremonies."

She looked at him quickly to see if he might be joking, but could not tell from his expression. "They're beautiful," she said.

There was also a fine deerskin dress in the sack, as well as a pouch of Lobo Negro tobacco and a packet of scraped cornshuck cigarette papers, evidently Mexican loot. There were small bags of salt and pepper and a larger one of flour. Best of all, according to Alec, there was a flask of tequila.

Anne took the deerskin dress behind a partition in the corner of the shop and quickly stripped off her dress and underdress. She slipped into the soft velvety deerskin and stepped outside to whirl about with an expression of delight.

Alec looked at her. Something seemed to rise within him and slowly turn over, and he began to realize how much this woman had come to mean to him in the past few days. She caught his look and stopped, turning to stand still and look steadily at him in return.

Alec broke the tenuous contact. "Shall we eat before we leave?" he asked lamely.

She shook her head. "Let's get out of here while we can!"

Alec placed his saddlebags on the dun and tied the sack behind Anne's saddle. He gave her a leg up into the saddle, then looked up into her face. "Anne, under no condition must you mention our experience with saving The Runner's life, or the aftermath. This could be considered collusion with the enemy. Do you understand?"

She nodded. "You'll have to think of a remarkable story to tell how we managed to find this horse, dress, and moccasins," she said dryly.

He mounted. "I'm good at that."

"You'll have to be. I'm not sure, if I were your commanding officer, whether I'd believe anything but the truth."

They rode from the canyon.

Somewhere behind them a wolf howled once.

Anne looked at Alec. "Chiricahua?" she asked.

"Or a wolf after the dead horse."

They moved on.

"Perhaps Baishan?" she said.

He turned in the saddle and looked back. "Or The Runner."

They rode on through the darkness.

CHAPTER 9

ALEC AND ANNE RESTED THEIR TIRED HORSES AT THE EAST-
ern approach to Apache Pass. It was a dry-looking, sun-baked
tangle of rocky slopes and arroyos covered with thorny vegetation. This was the very heart of Apacheria— the Land of the
Apaches. The pass was a long and narrow saddle separating the
Dos Cabezas Mountains from the Chiricahuas. The Dos Cabezas, or Two Heads, took their name from a pair of stone
domes capping the summit. The face of Bowie Mountain
loomed to the south. Helen's Dome was a curious-looking
landmark, a rocky promontory rising to the southwest. Sheer
mountain walls rose above the pass. The lower areas were
clothed with chaparral, agave, yucca, sotol, beargrass, mountain mahogany, manzanita, and oak trees. In the higher reaches
grew open woodlands of oak, pinon pine, and juniper. There
were sandy drainages of riparian woodland shaded by walnut,
hackberry, ash, oak, and cottonwood trees.

The pass was one of the few feasible routes through the
Southwest to California. It lay along the shortest route between the settlements on the Rio Grande in New Mexico Territory and Tucson. One of its chief advantages was Apache
Springs, issuing from a ravine into the eastern approach to
the pass. It was an always dependable source of good water
in an otherwise arid land.

Alec and Anne rode side by side up into the pass before the
coming of the full moon. "The Spaniards were here over
three hundred years ago," he explained. "They called these
mountains the 'Sierra de Chiguicagui' and this pass the
'Puerto del Dado,' meaning a die, the singular of dice, which

meant that one took a gamble with his life by entering it. The Spaniards have a classic talent for such names.''

Anne kneed her roan closer to Alec's dun. ''Why is it so dangerous now?'' she asked.

He swung an arm to indicate the scope of the area. ''Cochise and his Chiricahuas watched increasing numbers of travelers cross the pass. This was and still is one of the main southern transcontinental routes. In 1857 James Birch started his San Antonio–San Diego Mail, the so-called 'Jackass Mail' on this route. A year later the Butterfield Overland Mail supplanted it. The coaches made the trip from Tipton, Missouri, to San Francisco, about 2,500 miles, in the amazing time of twenty-five days. West of Apache Springs there is an open basin. A stone stage station was built there. The Chiricahuas kept on friendly terms with the Butterfield agent who paid them to supply the station with firewood.''

''I thought the Chiricahuas were always hostile to the white man,'' Anne said.

''There were intervals of comparative peace. At that time they were raiding mostly in Mexico. The Apache life-way, then as now, is warfare for the prime purpose of loot.

''In 1861 Cochise was living just north of here. He had a confrontation with a Lieutenant Bascomb about some stolen horses and oxen Bascomb accused him of taking. Cochise managed to escape, but left behind as captives his brother, two nephews, and a woman with two small children. He retaliated by capturing one of the men at the station and held him for a hostage. Later, he ambushed a wagon train just entering the pass. Eight Mexican teamsters were tied to the wagon wheels and the wagons set afire.''

Anne shuddered. ''My God,'' she said softly.

''Things went from bad to worse. Cochise was reenforced by Mangus Colorado and his Mimbrenos. The station manager and some other white men were riddled with lance holes and mutilated beyond recognition. The soldiers hung six Apaches at the pass summit. That was the start of the war that has been going on for a decade. Two months after the hanging the Civil War started. Federal troops abandoned all military posts in Arizona. They went east to the war. The

Apaches, knowing nothing of the Civil War, assumed that
they had driven the soldiers from Arizona.''

"Look," Anne said quietly. She pointed to small white-
painted crosses at one side of the road.

Alec reached out and gripped her hand. "Apache victims,
Anne. There are a lot of them scattered through the pass. They
were buried where they fell." He did not release her hand as
they rode on.

"There are a lot of ghosts in here," he continued. "After
the Federal troops left, the Overland Mail was discontinued.
Confederates occupied Tucson in February of '62. A column
of California Volunteers marched through the Pass on their
way to reenforce Union troops in the New Mexico Territory.
They took Tucson in July of '62. Cochise with his Chiricahuas and Mangus Colorado with his Mimbrenos lay in ambush here, but were defeated by the Californians. Mangus
was wounded. He was killed later trying to escape. Fort
Bowie was established here to guard the springs, and escort
travelers, mail couriers, and supply trains.

"The death of Mangus confirmed Cochise in his bitter-
ness. From then on he spared no Americans or Mexicans. Arizona begged for more troops, but there were none to be had.
There were times when Fort Bowie, with less than a hundred
men and sometimes as low as fifty, stood almost alone against
the Apaches. The fort was moved and enlarged in '68. Some
units of the First Cavalry were assigned to the Territory. I
served with them and fought against Cochise a number of
times. He's a great warrior. . . ." Alec's voice died away.

The moon was rising as they neared the pass summit.
Faintly, very faintly, as though it were an elfin horn, they
heard the Call to Quarters from the trumpet at Fort Bowie.

Anne reined in her roan. "I think there's a stone stuck in
her left hind hoof," she said as she dismounted. She inspected the hoof.

Alec looked down at her. There wasn't any shoe on the
hoof. The Chiricahuas had hardened the hoof by a method
they and Mexicans used.

"Did you find the stone?" he asked dryly.

"Let me have your knife," she said. She took it and

worked busily as though removing the stone. "*There,*" she said in satisfaction.

Alec dismounted. "You've evidently done this before?"

Anne nodded. "Oh, yes! I learned how on the family farm. We bred horses, you know."

Alec began to realize that in addition to her other attributes and qualities, she had some talent as an actress.

She turned toward him, so close they were almost touching. Impulsively, she raised her arms and slid them around his neck, drawing his head downward so that their lips met. They came together like two teenagers experimenting with their first sexual encounter. She pushed her body close to his. Her breathing was hard and erratic. He could feel the pressure of her unhampered breasts through the soft deerskin of her dress. They parted momentarily, then came together again, even more passionately than at first. Alec felt her body and began to pull at her dress.

"No!" Anne whispered.

He looked down at her. "Isn't that what you want?"

She had no immediate answer. She couldn't say yes, and yet she didn't want to refuse him for fear she might lose him.

He gave her a leg up into her saddle. He looked up at her. The growing moonlight was soft on her face. He knew he would have to have her someday, then felt that it was an impossibility. Once they reached Fort Bowie she would be gone forever. "Why here and now?" he asked.

She hesitated. "I wanted to do that before now. I owe you my life."

"You owe me nothing. It was my duty." He felt like a damned noble fool after speaking.

She studied him. "Is that all?"

He turned away and mounted his dun. "Not at all. You know that as well as I."

"Perhaps if it had been a more convenient place?" she asked.

He nodded. "But there's no possibility of that now."

They rode on, two people thrown together by a queer trick of fate in about as hopeless a situation as one might imagine. If Alec had been an Apache, he would have thought of it as a practical joke perpetrated by the master trickster Coyote, the combination Puck and Loki of The People. Not only was Anne the widow of one of his best friends, she was now the fiancée of a man he considered one of his worst enemies.

Alec reined in the dun as they neared the fort. "By the way, Anne, did I ever tell you the method Mexicans and Apaches use to harden horses' hooves? They mix the liver of a deer with ashes or lime and form a paste. It's applied to a hoof and allowed to dry. Then another layer is applied, and so on, until a thick crust is formed. The coating becomes rock-hard and keeps the horses from getting sore feet. Then rawhide is cut into pieces just big enough to fit around the hooves and tied on with thongs. Crude, but effective."

"Damn you," she said. "You just couldn't resist that, could you?"

He grinned. "I'll ride on first. These posts have a notorious habit of shooting first and asking questions afterward."

Alec reined in again a hundred yards from the gate and cupped his hands around his mouth. "Hello, the guard!" he shouted.

The challenge rang out instantly. "Halt! Who goes there!"

"Major Alexander Kershaw! Company D, Apache Scouts!" Alec replied.

There was a moment's hesitation.

He rode closer. "What the hell is wrong now?" he called out.

"Sorr, if that's really you, I ain't too sure just *what* to say. We heard yez had been kilt by the 'Paches!'"

"Is that you, O'Reilly?" Alec shouted.

"It is, sorr! Are ye sure you're not a ghost?"

Alec nearly broke up. "Call the Corporal of the Guard, you Irish idiot! I've a lady out here with me waiting to get on the post!"

There were a few more seconds of silence. "Now, sorr, beggin' your pardon, but where in bloody hell wud yez be gettin' a lady out thayer in that hellhole av a country?" O'Reilly shouted back.

Alec grinned. "It's Mrs. Sinclair, Colonel Trapnell's fiancée."

"Bejasus, Major! Is *she* a ghost too? We heard her body was never found!"

"I found her," Alec replied. "She's very much alive. Now, get the Corporal of the Guard and let us on the post."

Alec rode back to Anne. "They think you're a ghost."

She smiled. "I heard."

They could hear O'Reilly shouting, "Corporal Schmidt! It's Major Kershaw and Missus Sinclair! Ye can go tell the colonel his lady ain't been kilt by the 'Paches at all!"

Fort Bowie was a parody of a military post. The fort was a rectangle, with a row of officer's quarters, enlisted men's barracks, a headquarters building, and a guardhouse forming the four sides. Beyond them was a hospital, quartermaster and commissary warehouses, the sutler, or post trader's store, the bakery, and the blacksmith's shop. There were cavalry stables, a large stone-walled corral, a wagon yard, and a small butcher's corral.

Anne and Alec could hear men shouting as they poured from the barracks. "It's Major Kershaw come back from the dead! He's brought the colonel's lady with him!"

Anne looked sideways at Alec. "You seem very popular," she said.

"Maybe with the enlisted men. I won't say the same about their new commanding officer."

Colonel Burton Trapnell was in his office carefully editing his detailed report on the, to him at least, deplorable conditions at Fort Bowie—the slackness of the officers and the slovenly attitude of the enlisted men. Although a cavalry officer, he had been temporarily assigned to the Inspector-General Department at his own request. General Crook had demurred accepting him in the Department of Arizona, but Trapnell had gone over his head to get the assignment. The fact that one of his uncles was prominent on the Military Affairs Committee had helped immeasurably of course. His reception by General Crook had not been too cordial. Crook knew of Trapnell's record during the war, which looked good on paper but was rather a hollow shell. There had been rumors of cowardice at Valverde and later at Gettysburg, but there had been no specific proof of it. Officers of the First

Cavalry were remarkably close-mouthed about other officers in the regiment. The First believed in washing its own dirty linen. They had a way of dealing with their own. That was one of the reasons Burton Trapnell had always sought assignments taking him away from the regiment in the field.

General Crook had been particularly reluctant in agreeing to let Trapnell take over temporary command of Fort Bowie, but there wasn't much else he could do. Major Bernard, the post commander, was on sick leave. Captain Dennis Sullivan, who should have been assigned to take command, was now confined to quarters for drunkenness on duty. Trapnell had made the charges against him. The next ranking officer in line for the post command had been Brevet Major, First Lieutenant Alexander Kershaw, at present assigned to command the Apache Scouts. The current position of all three of those officers had been to the advantage of Trapnell. That fact, although purely coincidental, had been another reason for him to believe in predestination, and the ultimate attainment of his ultimate goal—brigadier general. However, if there was one officer in the entire United States Army who could put a stain on Trapnell's glistening escutcheon of military service, as he privately thought of it, that officer was Alexander Kershaw. Kershaw was the only officer in the First Cavalry who had been present at both Valverde and Gettysburg and could conceivably, if he so desired, confirm the charges of cowardice against Trapnell.

Sergeant-Major Loomis knocked on the door of Trapnell's office. "Colonel, sir! Major Kershaw has just returned."

"Good! Tell him to report to me at once!"

Loomis hesitated. "Sir, he's got a lady with him. A Missus Sinclair. They say he rescued her from the Apaches. He did it singlehanded, sir! By God, Colonel, there's only *one* Major Kershaw!"

Burton stood up. "That's enough!" he snapped. "You forget yourself. Where are the Major and Mrs. Sinclair?"

"Out on the parade ground, Colonel. The whole damned garrison including Captain Sullivan are out there with them."

It was beyond Burton Trapnell's ability to run out onto the parade ground in front of the whole garrison to see Anne at last. He snugged his blouse down around his hips, placed his forage cap on his head, looked in the mirror, and tilted the cap just slightly at the right angle. More than one person had told him that he bore a striking resemblance to Napoleon III, the victor of Magenta and Solferino. He buckled on his swordbelt and hooked up his Tiffany presentation sword.

He could hear the voices out on the moonlit parade ground as he left his office and paused under the ramada shade built over the porch. Trapnell had excellent timing as a rule. Any time he appeared in public, or before his command, he made sure he had an audience. Tonight he would be disappointed. All eyes were on the pair, still mounted within the circle of troops, civilian personnel, and Apache Scouts.

Mickey Free came close to Alec as he dismounted. "You're in big trouble, Major," he said in a low voice.

Alec placed an arm around the half-breed's shoulders and gripped him hard. "Damned glad you got back all right, Mick. What's this about trouble?"

"I brought the platoon back here as ordered, at least those I could round up. This Colonel Trapnell had come here and taken charge. He wanted to know why you had overstayed your patrol, and where you were. I couldn't get him to accept the idea you had gone off on your own with The Limper. Well, you can see the results." He pointed to the dark areas on the sleeves of his faded military blouse. "He busted me right then and there."

Alec stared at him. "By Jesus, Mick. I'll get them back for you!"

Mickey shrugged. "Mebbe. Mebbe not. This Trapnell is a two-bit sonofabitch if I ever seen one."

Alec gave Anne a hand down from her mare. "Your fiancé is here all right," he said in a low voice. "In all his tinsel glory. Here he comes now."

The men parted to let Trapnell through. He pulled up short when he saw Anne with her dusty deerskin dress and beaded moccasins, and beyond her the mare with its ornate Mexican saddle.

"Anne, is that really you?" Trapnell managed to get out.

She smiled. "It is, Burton, and you've got Major Kershaw to thank for it."

It was not in Burton Trapnell's nature to take Anne in his arms. Appearance, regulations, and duty came first, last, and always with him. He looked sideways at Alec. "I sincerely hope, Major Kershaw, you've some satisfactory explanation for this delay in returning from your patrol."

Alec leaned casually against his dun. "I'm hoping I have too, Colonel, but I doubt it you'll believe it. Sometimes I find it difficult to believe what happened myself."

"Aren't you going to thank him, Burton?" Anne asked.

Trapnell looked away. He waved a hand sideways in the general direction of Alec in lieu of thanking him. "Lieutenant Wicks," he said to a young second lieutenant, "please escort Mrs. Sinclair to the quarters of Captain Sawyer and his wife. I arranged with them before they left on leave to have her stay there. Anne, will you have need of medical attention?"

She shook her head. She smiled a little at Alec as Wicks escorted her to the quarters. He watched her walking across the parade ground. Suddenly, he realized he might never be able to talk with any intimacy to her again.

Burton Trapnell was damned annoyed when he saw Alec watching Anne, but he could not, of course, display any temperament within plain view of practically the whole garrison. "Major Kershaw," he said briskly. "Please report immediately to me at headquarters." He turned on his heel and stalked away.

Dennis Sullivan came up to Alec from where he had been standing out of sight of Trapnell. "You're in the soup now, me bhoyo," he said. They gripped hands together hard. There was a suspicious glint in the Irishman's blue eyes.

"I heard you were in the broth yourself, Denny," Alec said.

Sullivan shrugged. "Ah, 'twas only that I was celebratin' me promotion to post commander. Temporary, laddie, but the first time in fifteen years of service I made it. Unfortunately, it was the very day that brass-bound sonofabitch showed up."

Alec grinned. "The luck av the Irish, me bhoyo!"

Lieutenant Anthony Beaudine, post quartermaster, came up behind them. "You picked a great time to return from the dead, Alec." He shook his head.

Alec shrugged. "I didn't have much choice, Tony Soldier," he said ruefully.

"And with such a lovely lady too! We heard about the Chiricahuas raid on the wagon train. There was only one survivor that we found. He was sure Mrs. Sinclair had been killed."

Alec shook his head. "They weren't Chiricahuas, Tony."

"Are you sure?"

"They were *gambrusinos*. They dressed like Apaches."

"*Gambrusinos? This* far north?"

Alec nodded. "I am quite sure it was the same party I trailed from Muerte Springs. I lost them east of the Chiricahuas. Anne was damned lucky she was rescued from the ambush by the driver of the Rucker. I just happened to be in the area."

"Just *happened* to be there!" Tony said in astonishment. "Rescuing Trapnell's fiancée when she was on her way to meet him? Burton Trapnell, your rival at the Point and with the regiment when it was at Valverde and later at Gettysburg? Now you have the damned effrontery to show up here about a week late from patrol, without your command, dressed like a half-breed scout, and escorting Trapnell's future wife after saving her life?"

Alec inspected his dirty broken fingernails. "Oh, it was easy," he murmured.

Sergeant-Major Loomis came to them at the double-quick. He saluted Alec. "Sir, the colonel is waiting, and if I may say so, sir, damned impatiently."

They walked toward headquarters. "Do you know why he was assigned here, Alec?" Tony asked.

"Probably to further his meteoric rise in the service."

"Without necessarily having any ability," Tony said.

Alec looked sideways at him. "You said it, not me, Tony Soldier."

They paused before the headquarters porch. "What's she really like?" Tony asked.

Alec pointed toward the open window of Trapnell's office. They could see him seated at his desk writing steadily. Alec placed a finger to his lips, winked, and then entered the building.

"Well, I'll be goddamned," murmured Tony. "Old Alexander! I thought he'd sworn off ladies for life. Not women, mind you, like Belle Valois. Quite the contrary. But *ladies*? Hell, yes!"

CHAPTER 10

ALEC KNOCKED AT TRAPNELL'S DOOR.

"Come in!" the colonel snapped.

He did not look up as Alec entered. Alec stopped in front of Trapnell's desk. The colonel was still absorbed in his work. Playing his usual game, the officious sonofabitch, Alec thought. He walked over to the large ordnance map hanging on the wall and traced the location of Soledad Canyon far to the south and just west of the *camino* leading down from Tucson, crossing the border and stretching to Magdalena, Sonora, and far beyond. The notations about the Soledad country were Unmapped, Maps Not Accurate, and Unknown. He knew Trapnell would look up in annoyance.

The colonel cleared his throat. "Well, Kershaw?" he said.

Alec sauntered back to the desk. "Your pleasure, Colonel."

Trapnell leaned back and studied him. Alec had lost his disreputable campaign hat in Muerte Canyon. His issue wool shirt was threadbare and had large dried salt crescents under the arms. His breeches were powdery with dust and spotted with unidentifiable stains. Burton Trapnell wrinkled his patrician nose just a little.

Alec grinned crookedly. "It is a stink with a history, Colonel," he said dryly.

Trapnell waved a hand. "I want your verbal report now, Major."

Tattoo blew softly and sweetly across the post and bounced off the heights to die lingering in the canyons.

"That must be Counihan on the C trumpet," Alec mused. He looked down at Trapnell. "Did you know he was trumpeter with Jeb Stuart and was wounded and captured at Yellow Tavern?"

"Your report, Major," Trapnell repeated.

"Tattoo has just blown, sir. We've had a hard and dangerous ride through the canyons to get here. I'm badly in need of a bath, shave, and clean uniform. I'm sure my report can wait until tomorrow."

Trapnell shook his head. "I'll waive an extensive report, but I insist on a brief explanation."

Alec stared at him. "Explanation? What do you mean by explanation?"

"Simply this: You've overstayed your patrol. You invaded Mexican territory despite strict orders to the contrary. You took a Mexican officer as hostage and stole his horse. I think even you, Kershaw, would admit that requires *some* explanation."

"The hell I stole his damned horse!" Alec snapped. "I borrowed it for a little while. I sent the damned nag back to him when I was through with it."

"You looted his saddlebags," Trapnell continued relentlessly. "Then you turned your command over to a worthless half-breed sergeant and took off on your solitary way to God knows where."

Alec leaned forward. "Did your informant tell you that same Mexican officer also killed four of my Scouts and scalped them to collect the eight hundred pesos he could get as blood money from the governor of Sonora for the scalps of 'hostile' Apaches?"

"The point is, Major," Trapnell said icily, "that your Scouts were on Mexican territory and under your command at the time."

Trapnell had him there, Alec thought.

"Why did you leave your patrol and go off on your own?" Trapnell asked.

"We had struck the trail of hostile Chiricahuas on our side of the border. We followed them across the border."

"Against orders," Trapnell interrupted.

"Standing orders, Colonel," Alec agreed. "But General Crook has reiterated again and again—when you're on a trail, stay with it. Hang on like a saddleburr. Never abandon it."

Trapnell placed his hand on a bound set of the department orders. "*These* are the orders, Major. There's nothing in them such as you just mentioned. Come, Kershaw! Admit your guilt! You greatly overstepped your authority! Now, continue your explanation."

"Thanks, Colonel," Alec said dryly. "When we reached Muerte Springs, we found the stripped and scalped corpses of seven Mexicans. They were probably smugglers, from the newly minted adobe dollars we found with them. That's their usual means of exchange."

"Apache work!" Trapnell trumpeted.

Alec shook his head. "Not so; *gambrusinos,* who were likely scalp hunters as well."

"*Gambrusinos?* I'm not familiar with the term."

"The literal translation is 'adventurers,' or 'fortune hunters.' Rapacious bandits and killers who do anything for loot. They always kill their victims for fear of being identified. Their watchword is *Los muertos no hablan.* The dead do not speak." Alec pointed to the wall map. My Scouts were out of food and short on water. Their horses were worn out. I decided to send them back here under the command of Sergeant Free while I continued with one Scout on the trail of the *gambrusinos* which led northeast through the San Bernardino Valley and then north past the east side of the Chiricahuas to the San Simon Valley."

"Major, it was not your patrol objective to trail those so-called *gambrusinos*. It was your duty to bring your command back here to Fort Bowie. *That*, and *nothing* else!" Trapnell stood up to emphasize his point.

"Colonel, perhaps it was a dereliction of duty, but to me tracking down those bloodthirsty bastards was a helluva lot more important. Further, sir, if I had not abandoned my patrol, as you've intimated, and trailed those killers, I would not have been fortunate enough to save the life of Mrs. Sinclair. Have you ever thought of that?''

Trapnell shifted his tactics. ''But that was some days ago! You were only thirty miles or so from here. Where have you been all this time? Dallying in the mountains, I warrant! I know your type, Kershaw. No woman is safe. . . .'' His voice died away as he saw the look on Alec's face and his icy eyes.

Alec leaned forward and placed his hands flat on the desk, fixing Trapnell with his eyes. ''Burton,'' he said quietly. ''One doesn't rescue a lady in extreme distress without taking the further responsibility of making sure she has safe conduct back to her people. We were in the foothills of the Chiricahuas, short on water and food, with those bloody outlaws somewhere behind us, and on the very edge of the stronghold of the Chiricahua Apaches on the Big Mountain. Fort Bowie was thirty miles away. The country between Muerte Canyon and here is infested with Apaches. Are you beginning to understand?''

''Go on,'' Trapnell said grimly.

''I headed for the old mines at Muerte Canyon. There is usually water there. Unfortunately, it is one of the entrance ways to the Big Mountain. We made it there and found water. Just about the time we were ready to leave to come here, a raiding party of Chiricahuas passed through the canyon on their way home, laden with loot and with women and children prisoners. There was nothing we could do but sit tight and hope to Almighty God we would not be discovered. Fortunately, we were not. Then we came here.''

Trapnell nodded. ''With Anne riding another horse, and wearing Apache clothing and moccasins? Where, pray, did she get those?''

Alec shrugged. ''The dress and moccasins I had traded for from a friendly squaw as gifts for a woman I know. I planned to bring them here from patrol. I am due for a short leave. I was going to spend it in Tucson, and to present the gifts to the lady in question,'' he said with a steady gaze and complete aplomb.

After moment's hesitation Trapnell spoke slowly. ''And

the lovely little horse and silver-mounted Mexican saddle? Where did *they* come from, Major?''

"Mrs. Sinclair rode my dun until we reached the Fort Bowie road. I bought the horse and saddle from a Mexican trader whom I've known for quite some time."

"How utterly neat," Trapnell commented dryly.

Alec shrugged. "You can verify it by Mrs. Sinclair."

"I intend to and will also query her on your conduct while she was alone with you."

"In what respect?" Alec asked in a low voice.

Burton Trapnell had never been one to consider the sensibilities of other persons. He had also never learned to let well enough alone. "You must know, Major, of your, shall we say, slightly unsavory reputation with women. In addition, there are records in your dossier of heavy drinking at times, and during those times seeking the companionship of certain disreputable citizens of Tucson, including, I might add, women of shady reputation." He leaned forward and thrust an admonishing finger in Alec's face. "If you did annoy Mrs. Sinclair and perhaps take indecent liberties with her while she was defenseless and in your power, I assure you, sir, I will have charges brought against you, so help me God!"

The reaction from Alec was so instantaneous and swift, Burton nearly wet himself, both legs. A big hand shot out, grasped the front of his blouse, twisted it, then jerked him halfway across the desk so that his face was inches from Alec's.

"You pompous, insufferable jackass," Alec said quietly. "If you ever speak to me or about me in that manner again, I'll break your goddamned face!" He shoved Trapnell back so hard, the colonel knocked over his chair and staggered back against the wall, dislodging a steel engraving of General Sherman from the wall. It struck the floor with a splintering of glass.

Trapnell's first impulse was to draw his Colt and fire, but when he saw the look in Alec's eyes, he instantly decided against it. "Sergeant-Major Loomis!" he called out, trying to control the tremor in his voice. "Come in here at once!"

The worthy sergeant-major had been listening intently just outside the door. He opened it quickly. "Sir?" he said. Loomis was a very observant man. He noted the colonel adjusting the front of his blouse, his flushed face, rapid breathing, and above all the wavering fear in his eyes.

Trapnell picked up his chair and sat down. "Send the Charge of Quarters to the Officer of the Day and tell him to report here immediately. Get your pencil and pad. I want you to take some notes."

Loomis left the office. The two officers heard him order the Charge of Quarters to tell Lieutenant Wicks to report at once to headquarters. They heard the messenger's boots pound on the wooden flooring of the porch and then on the hard surface of the parade ground.

"Well, Kershaw, you've finally done it this time," Trapnell said quietly. "I'm preferring charges against you. Your patron, General Crook, will not be able to cover up for you and save you from disgrace."

"You've finally got your big chance at me, Trapnell," Alec conceded. "It's just as well. I don't want to continue my service with you hanging around my neck like the dead albatross of the Ancient Mariner."

Boot soles thudded across the parade ground and thumped on the porch. Someone knocked at the office door. A moment later Gerald Wicks appeared, slightly out of breath. He had learned to move fast at the bidding of Colonel Trapnell in the short time the colonel had been in command of Fort Bowie. Sergeant-Major Loomis came in behind Wicks, pad and pencil in hand.

Trapnell nodded. "Lieutenant Wicks and Sergeant-Major Loomis, I want you to bear witness to the charges I am preferring against Major Kershaw. Loomis, you will note these down."

Wicks looked sideways at Alec. He raised his eyebrows a little. Alec shrugged in resignation.

Trapnell stood up and passed back and forth behind his desk, crunching through the shards of glass on the floor. "The following are the charges: Firstly, Major Alexander Kershaw did overstay his allotted patrol time. Loomis, you can fill in the time element when the formal charges are prepared. Secondly, he did lead his patrol across the border into Mexican territory in direct disobedience to Department orders.

You can fill in the order number and content later, Sergeant-Major. Thirdly, while in Mexican territory Major Kershaw did take as hostage a Mexican officer in performance of his duty. He did steal that officer's horse and rifle his saddle-bags, taking certain personal items therefrom. Fourthly, Major Kershaw left his command in the charge of an inefficient noncommissioned officer and ordered that noncommissioned officer to bring the patrol back to Fort Bowie. Fifthly, Major Kershaw left his patrol command and took off for some purpose of his own.'' Trapnell's rather high-pitched voice died away. He returned to his seat.

"Is that all, sir?" asked Loomis.

Trapnell shook his head. "The final charge is: Assaulting a superior officer in the performance of his duty.''

Loomis couldn't help but whistle as he wrote down the last charge, despite an icy glare from the colonel.

"Have you anything to say for yourself, Major Kershaw?" Trapnell asked.

"Only this: I've been thinking of resigning for quite some time. I didn't expect to do so this early, but, I suppose, under the circumstances the time is as good as any," Alec replied.

Trapnell's face changed almost as though a mask had been withdrawn to reveal the real features beneath it. "You can't do that! You will face these charges in a general court-martial, sir! Do not try to evade them by resigning! I'll see to it that you're conducted under guard to Fort Lowell to stand trial! By God, I'll teach you something about military discipline and procedure if it's the last thing I ever do!''

Alec shook his head. "You're wrong. In the first place, an accused officer can request a court of inquiry when faced with charges, before he can be called before a general court. In such instance, the department commander must attend that court, and the accused officer need not be present.''

Trapnell looked at Loomis. "He's right, sir," Loomis said.

"In the second place," Alec continued relentlessly, "I've been operating under the direct orders of General Crook. Some months ago I proffered my resignation to him in order to take up private business. As a personal favor, the general requested that I remain on duty for an unspecified period of time as commander of Apache Scouts until he could find a qualified officer to replace me. He agreed to keep my resignation on file with the promise he would have it forwarded when and if I called for it. Now, Colonel, it seems as though the time has come to have that resignation honored. Good night, Colonel Trapnell.'' Alec turned on his heel and walked toward the door.

"Just a moment, Major," Trapnell said. His sentence was punctuated with the crisp double-clicking of a pistol being cocked.

Alec turned. Trapnell held his service pistol, the bottom of his hand resting on the desk and the muzzle pointing directly at Alec's belly. "Disarm him, Wicks," he ordered coldly.

Wicks looked from Trapnell to Alec, then back again.

"Damn you, Wicks!" Trapnell shouted. "Do as you are told!"

Gerald Wicks was a brave man, and also a cautious one. He couldn't resist looking at the colonel and saying, "Tell me, sir, would *you* try to disarm Alec Kershaw?"

Alec grinned a little. "Here you are, Wicks." He unbuckled his belt, heavy with the holstered Remington, cartridges, and sheath knife. He wasn't quite ready to turn over his double-barreled derringer hideout pistol.

"Confine him to quarters, Wicks," Trapnell ordered.

Alec walked side by side with Wicks to Officer's Row.

"I'm sorry about all this, Alec," Wicks apologized.

Alec shook his head. "No need."

Wicks looked sideways at Alec. "Do you really intend to resign just on account of that brass-bound sonofabitch back there?"

"Not really. It's been in my mind for some time, as I already mentioned. Perhaps it's just as well this is forcing me to go ahead."

Wicks left Alec at the door of his quarters. "I'll have to post a sentry here," he said apologetically.

"It's your duty, Gerry. Don't jeopardize your record on account of me."

Alec closed the door and lighted the lamp. His saddlebags

and other gear, including his Winchester, were all there. He
opened a closet door and removed one of his dress boots. He
fished out a small flask of Baconora from inside it. He held
it up to the light. Callahan, his dog robber, had been considerate enough to leave about two thirds of it. Alec took out the
other boot and removed another flask from it. It was suspiciously light. In fact, it was empty. "Callahan, you Irish sonofabitch," Alec said. He grinned. He took a drink and then
dropped onto his bed. He stared up at the dingy cloth that
served as a catchall for scorpions and centipedes dropping
from the ceiling. He didn't know when at last he fell asleep
with the emptied flask in his hand, resting on the floor at the
side of the bed.

CHAPTER 11

TAPS SOUNDED PLAINTIVELY ACROSS FORT BOWIE,
bouncing faintly from the nearby hills. The echoes died away,
leaving behind that lingering feeling of melancholy that always overcame Alec upon hearing the last trumpet call of the
day. Memories haunted him of the aftermaths of the battles
at Valverde and Glorieta Pass in the New Mexico Territory,
and later battles while he served with the Army of the Potomac: Fredericksburg, the Chancellorsville Campaign and
Brandy Station, Gettysburg and Cedar Creek, and finally at
Five Forks just before the surrender of the Army of Northern
Virginia at Appomattox.

He had spent the day after Trapnell's accusations and
charges had been leveled at him in his quarters with an armed
sentry standing outside the door. Private Callahan, his or-
derly, more commonly referred to as "dog robber," had
brought Alec's meals to him. Patrick Callahan had served
Alec while he was with the Army of the Potomac. This day
Callahan had brought him more than food—a Colt six-shooter
with extra cartridges and a replacement for the Baconora

brandy the dog robber had "borrowed" from Alec's reserves.

"If ye've a mind, sorr," Callahan had said casually, "me and some of the lads can arrange to get ye a horse whenever ye have a mind for the use of same."

"You mean for me to take French leave?" Alec had exclaimed.

Callahan looked back over his shoulder as though someone might have been listening, then came closer to Alec and spoke in a whisper. "As I said, whenever ye have a mind for it. And don't worry about the sentry, sorr. I'll see to it that he's occupied whilst ye take off through the back way."

Alec had shaken his head. "I appreciate the offer. No, Callahan, I'll probably be leaving soon for Fort Lowell."

"Ye'll take me with ye, sorr?"

"No. In all likelihood I'll be leaving the service."

"And then what, Major?"

"Private enterprise, Callahan."

That had been the end of that. An hour later, when dusk had settled over the post, Mickey Free showed up surreptitiously at the rear door with essentially the same offer as the one made by Callahan, and received the same refusal.

Alec had finished his arrangements for leaving Fort Bowie by the time Call to Quarters was blown. Everything but the few essentials needed to keep up his appearance while at Bowie had been packed. The odds and ends he had accumulated while at the post he had decided to bequeath to Tony Beaudine. He looked around, opened Callahan's replacement flask, and sat down to think.

A few minutes after taps, Tony showed up at the rear door and eased himself into the cramped quarters. He surveyed Alec's packing as he placed a bottle on the table. "Compliments of the estimable Myron J. Martin, post sutler," he said. "His very best brandy."

"Panther piss," scoffed Alec.

Tony shook his head. "This is not the coffin varnish he usually sells. It's his own private stock."

"Pop 'er open then, Tony Soldier. I hope you won't damage your position here at Bowie by drinking with an officer under arrest pending half a dozen lovely charges.''

"Not as far as I'm concerned. But all of us are walking a tightrope now with Trapnell taking command. He wants to make a record for himself here before he rises to greater stature elsewhere. Anyone, or anything that gets in his way is in for a chunk of hell itself.'' He slid his eyes sideways. "Like you, Never Still.''

"I have a way of doing such,'' Alec said dryly.

"Just what the hell has gotten into you this past year? Is it a hangover from the Navajo problem? I've been expecting something like this mess you're into now. God knows we're on a tight check rein here in Arizona, with the civilians howling about Apache atrocities and not being averse to committing the same thing themselves, such as the Camp Grant massacre last April of the Arivaipa and Pinal Apaches, who had been allowed to settle near the military post under protection of the army.''

Alec nodded. "Over one hundred peaceful men, women, and children, scalped, raped, and mutilated.''

Tony refilled their glasses. "Many of us deplore that horror, Alec. Sometimes you seem to take the burden of it on your shoulders alone. It was the same at Bosque Redondo with the Navajo situation. We're part of a system. We Americans are the conquerors. We've taken over this territory from the Mexicans, who in turn took it over from the Apaches. The Apaches hate the Mexicans and us. The Mexicans hate the Apaches and us. We hate them with equal venom. But Alec, when you remained in the service after the war, you took an oath to fight the enemies of the United States. You cannot remain on the fence. You must be either fish or fowl, black or white. In this system there is no gray.''

Alec emptied half of his glass. "Did it ever occur to you, Tony Soldier, that the Navajos were fighting for their own land? That the Apaches look upon this country as *theirs*? To them there is no such thing as the boundary between Arizona and Sonora. They have passed back and forth between the two places for hundreds of years. The Spaniards tried to enslave them. Their priests tried to convert them. They failed.

The Mexicans tried the same tactics, and they too have failed. They have given us hell, but nothing more than the hell they have fought against for all this time. To them there is no such thing as Spaniard, Mexican, or American. To them we are simply *indah*, the enemy.''

Tony nodded. "Sometimes, in the dark of the night, I wake up and consider the problem in that same light. But as I said before, we took an oath to fight the enemies of our country. We're in no position to rectify a centuries-old problem. We are professionals, and further, a tiny minority hanging on by our fingernails. Alec, if the Indians had the ability to ally themselves with each other and work in conjunction, they'd wipe us and our silly little outposts off the face of the West.

"Now, I don't know how you plan to handle this Trapnell business, but you must learn to follow the rules and regulations. If you want to save your commission and the possible continuation of what promises to be a brilliant career, you've got to obey orders. It's either that, or resign and go off shouting in the shadows.''

Alec emptied his glass. "Exactly,'' he agreed. That and no more.

Tony knew his man. "I think I'll wait until you're in a better mood. I know you can hold your liquor better that most men I've known, including myself, but in the past six months I've noticed you drinking more and more.'' He stood up. "Colonel Trapnell has given me orders to escort you to Fort Lowell the day after tomorrow. General Crook is there now. I am to turn you over to him along with the charges against you.'' Tony closed the door behind himself.

Alec walked to the window and looked out across the moonlit parade ground. There was no one in sight. It was almost as though he were alone on an abandoned post. To him there was always a sense of uneasiness and foreboding about these frontier posts in the midst of a hostile people and a savage environment. He pulled off his moccasins, blew out the light, stripped to the buff, and dropped on his cot with the bottle in his right hand.

* * *

Anne Sinclair and Burton Trapnell dined that evening in Surgeon Sawyer's quarters. Anne had borrowed a gown from Mrs. Sawyer's closet. It was a little large. She had not found shoes that could fit, nor any underclothing, so she wore her moccasins and had on nothing beneath the gown. She had been able to buy some dress material from the post trader, and there was a sewing machine in the quarters, but she hadn't yet gotten around to making underthings or a dress for herself.

She hardly touched her food. Burton refilled her glass with wine, eyeing her curiously over the decanter. The wine had been getting to her. While sponge-bathing she had found some of Surgeon Sawyer's medical alcohol in a half-gallon jar. She'd needed some sort of a pick-me-up before she could face Burton with any show of equanimity. The medical alcohol mixed with thick syrup from a can of peaches had been the best she could do for powerful cordial. It had a helluva wallop concealed in its golden depths, which fact she was getting uncomfortably aware of the longer she faced Burton across the dinner table. The port wine was from his private stock. Not for him were the wines carried by the post trader. The port added to the medical alcohol set up a warming glow within Anne, and the uneasy thought came to her that she had found herself acquiring a taste for Alec Kershaw's favorite drinking liquor, the potent Baconora brandy. What was it he had said? "Baconora, the drink of heroes. It isn't for everybody."

"You didn't answer my question, Anne," Burton said.

She looked up from her plate with a start. "I'm sorry, Burton. I was woolgathering."

"Do you think I was in the wrong treating Major Kershaw as I did?" he repeated.

"In part I do not think you were wrong. That is, as much as I understand military procedure. However, in view of the fact that he fought overwhelming odds to rescue me from those *gambrusinos* and got us both out of Muerte Canyon alive, I should think you'd drop those charges against him. Burton! You should have seen him! He's almost like an Apache in his methods! If it hadn't been for the way he handled them, we'd have died right there! He was magnificent!"

Burton studied her, noting her flushed face and the excitement when she spoke about Alec Kershaw. ''There's been some talk at headquarters about that very subject. He seems to have undue sympathy for Indians and an unhealthy interest in their life-ways. I recall the Navajo problem at Bosque Redondo. He was at loggerheads with headquarters about what he termed 'the cruel and callous treatment of the Navajos.' He cried about the degeneration of those damned savages, the hopelessness of their situation, and their possible extermination by starvation and disease. I recall . . .'' His voice died away as he saw the look on her face.

''I know about the situation there,'' she said quietly. ''Wasn't there a great deal of truth in what he said?''

He looked away from her. ''It was a military matter. We had orders. We were treating with an enemy, Anne. Not to change the subject, but you mentioned him handling the Apaches at Muerte Canyon? Don't you mean those Apaches who attacked the wagon train?''

She shook her head. ''They were *not* Apaches at the San Simon. They were *gambrusinos* dressed as Apaches.''

''That's not what the report indicates.''

''An investigation would prove otherwise. Alec knows who my pursuers were. You should question him about that instead of badgering him with those charges.''

Burton shrugged. ''Perhaps you're right, Anne. But those Apaches at Muerte Canyon you mentioned. They were the real thing? Perhaps they were Apache Scouts?''

She drained her wineglass. ''Absolutely not! They were Chiricahuas!''

He nodded thoughtfully.

Slowly, she began to realize the mistake she had made. She had fallen neatly into Burton's trap.

''Tell me about these Chiricahuas at Muerte Canyon,'' he suggested.

Anne shook her head. ''I should not have mentioned it.''

''Ah, but you did!''

''If I tell you about them, will you reconsider those charges?''

''I'll take it under consideration, Anne. No one is more

interested in military justice than I. I might not be able to change or delete some of the charges, but at least I can prepare a statement to the effect that Alec did rescue you and saved your life from your attackers at the San Simon and perhaps again at Muerte Canyon. But I must know the facts.''

She felt she must trust him. She was sure her story would help Alec. She told Burton of their journey through the canyons to the mines of Muerte Canyon. She told of the appearance of the Chiricahua war party returning after a raid with prisoners and loot, and of Alec's improvised operation on the wounded Apache brave.

''Then when the Chiricahuas came for Nah-delthy-ah, The Runner, which was the youth's name, Alec was ready for them. He knew of their superstitious awe of a blacksmith and his work. He worked a bar of iron when Baishan, the war chief, came for The Runner, who happened to be his younger brother. The Chiricahuas left us alone.''

Burton leaned forward. ''This Baishan? Who was he?''

Anne sipped at her wine. She felt a delightful warming glow within herself. ''That's his Chiricahua name. It means Knife.'' Her voice died away at the intent look on Burton's face.

''Go on,'' Burton urged her. ''What happened then?''

''Baishan reappeared with two horses. He said that Alec had saved The Runner's life. He let me select one of the horses to ride back here. The other he killed and gave us the neck meat for provisions.''

''You ate *horse meat*?'' Burton asked incredulously.

She nodded. ''It's not too bad. What would you have done? Starve?''

''This is unbelievable,'' he muttered. ''Go on! Go on!''

''Baishan left us,'' she said simply. ''We returned here.''

''Wearing the dress and moccasins given you by that damned bloodstained Apache Knife!''

''Would you have had me return here dressed in rags which scarcely covered me?'' she demanded. She was sorrier that ever that he had tricked her into telling the truth about Muerte Canyon.

"Was there any other communication between Kershaw and Baishan?" he asked.

She shook her head. "Nothing."

"You're certain?"

"Yes. Why do you ask?"

"Tell me," he said thoughtfully. "Did Baishan come to you unarmed?"

"He had no weapons, other than his knife."

"But Kershaw had weapons?"

She nodded. "His rifle and pistol."

"But he didn't take them with him when he met this Apache?"

"Baishan came in peace," she replied.

Burton leaned forward, fixing her with his gaze. "Do you mean to sit there and tell me Kershaw had this monstrous savage, this killer and rapist, within his power and *he did nothing about it*?"

"That is correct," she answered quietly.

He smashed his right fist into the palm of his left hand. "By God, I've got him now!"

"Burton, I spoke of those things in strictest confidence."

"This is more important than my adhering to any promise I made that you might have misunderstood. Tell me, did you promise Kershaw you wouldn't mention his saving an enemy's life when he had it in his power to kill him, then had a perfect opportunity to kill Baishan and also did not do it?"

She was puzzled, somewhat bewildered, and a little too far into drink at the moment to give a correct answer.

"Anne?" he demanded.

She reached for the wine decanter, but he was too quick for her and snatched it away. "You drink too much for a lady soon to be an officer's wife. I had begun to notice it at Santa Fe and intended to mention it here before our wedding. It's become more than just social drinking with you. I'm sure, however, that at my request you can discipline yourself to control it or forgo it altogether."

"I can handle it," she retorted. "I always have."

"If you could," he said coldly, "you would not have betrayed your new idol, Alec Kershaw."

"You can go to hell with your advice, and your damned marriage too!" she said flatly.

He shrugged. "We'll talk about that another time. I'll advise you right now that if Kershaw is brought up on further charges in reference to this business of Baishan you will be subpoenaed to appear as a witness for the prosecution."

He stood up, put on his forage cap, and took the half-full decanter with him. "I'm having a sentry posted outside your front door."

"To keep me from escaping with Alec?" she asked.

"You're drunk, Anne. You know there have been Apache intruders on this post. It's a safeguard." He walked to the rear door and bolted it, then returned to the living room. "I'll say goodnight now. Tomorrow we'll discuss your revelations when your head is clearer. By the way, Kershaw will be taken under armed guard, escorted by an officer, to Fort Lowell, where he'll be turned over to the department commander." Burton studied her for a moment. "In case you've taken an interest in Kershaw, you should know he has somewhat of a shady reputation with women. I won't say *ladies*. There's a bordello madam in Tucson by the name of Belle Valois. She's absolutely notorious. She was run out of California for operating a house of prostitution among other things. For an officer to be seen in her company is tantamount to ruining one's reputation, and in one instance an officer was forced to resign. It's said she and Kershaw are very close. I thought you should know that."

There was no answer from Anne.

He closed the door as he left.

Anne listened to his footsteps receding on the hard parade ground. "You pompous, self-important military ass! You unmitigated sonofabitch! What I ever saw in you!" she cried.

She rooted through the quarters until she found a Colt revolver and a box of cartridges. She put out the lamps and threw one of Mrs. Sawyer's dark-colored capes over her shoulders. Tiptoeing to the front door, she listened. She heard the sentry's feet shuffling on the porch. The moon was well on the wane. She returned to the back door, unbolted it and eased it open. The alleyway behind Officer's Row was already in shadows. She closed the door gently and catfooted toward the far end of the row, where Alec had his quarters.

CHAPTER 12

ANNE TRIED THE REAR DOOR OF ALEC'S QUARTERS. IT WAS unlocked. She eased it open, slipped inside, then closed the door and shot the locking bolt. The quarters were dark, the shades drawn. She placed the pistol and box of cartridges on the kitchen table. She tiptoed across the combination living room and bedroom to the front door, listening intently until she heard a faint movement from the guard outside. Then she turned toward the bed and risked lighting one of the matches she had brought with her. It popped like a toy pistol as it flared up.

Anne was charged from the bed. She dropped the match as she was driven back against the wall. The cape slipped from her shoulders and entangled her feet. A hand reached out for her throat as she twisted sideways and it caught the neckline of her gown. She tried to break free. The gown was ripped from throat to waist, leaving her breasts bared. She was hurled onto the bed. Powerful grasping hands moved along her belly and breasts, striving for her throat. It was all over in a matter of seconds.

"Jesus Christ! A woman!" Alec said incredulously.

The dropped match had set fire to the ragged fringe of the threadbare carpet. The flickering light revealed that Alec was as naked as a jaybird.

He stood up and looked down at her. "You must be a dream," he said. "I can't believe it's you."

"You'd better put out the fire," she suggested.

He looked away from her smoothly rounded white belly and breasts, picked up the water pitcher from bedside table, and doused the fire.

Alec turned to her. "What the hell are you doing here at this time of the night?" he demanded.

"Keep it low! There's a sentry outside."

"I know, dammit! Does he know you're in here?"

"No. I came in through the back. Your door was un-locked."

"What about the sentry at your quarters?"

"He was in front. I went out the back."

He suddenly was aware of his nakedness. He reached for his breeches and pulled them on over his long legs. "Do you have any idea how dangerous that could be?"

She giggled. "I have now, after coming in here."

He was silent for a moment. "I could have killed you," he said quietly. He lighted a lucifer, then snapped open the lid of his repeater watch. "Christ! It's after twelve! I hope to God no one saw you coming in here. If Trapnell finds out . . ."

She pulled the front of her gown together. "I came to warn you about him, Alec."

He lighted a small lamp and placed it on the floor with the bed between it and the window. He checked the back door and then listened at the front for any signs of activity from the guard. He took a forage cap ornament, a pair of crossed sabers with a pin back, from his dress forage cap and brought it and her pistol into the living room. She pinned the front of her dress together with the ornament.

"Why the pistol?" Alec asked.

"I thought you might need it if you planned to leave to-night."

He smiled. "I've already had several offers of help, but thanks anyway."

"Don't you think you should go? If you're taken to Fort Lowell, it will be too late to avoid being court-martialed."

"I won't run away, Anne. It would only make it worse. Would you like a drink as long as you're here?"

"I certainly need one after the reception I got," she said dryly.

She looked around the quarters while he got the liquor. They were small and cramped with a rammed-earth floor. The ceiling was no more than eight feet high and had been low-ered by a dingy linen sheet stained in various patterns from leaking rainwater that hung just below it to catch the various specimens of vermin that dropped from above. There was but one chair, a military trunk, and a long shelf lined with dusty books over which hung Alec's presentation Castellani saber. A framed Prang chromo of the Hudson River near West Point hung beside the saber. There was a small pine washstand with a cracked porcelain pitcher and dented tin basin. A mirror of bilious green hue hung above it. A small open fireplace was opposite the cot. A row of pegs on the wall held a forage cap, dress uniform, and a regulation M1860 pattern saber. Faded chintz curtains on the two small windows concealed the dust and flyspecks on the almost opaque gravel-pitted glass. An-other shelf held a row of alcohol-filled bottles, with select specimens of spiders, tarantulas, scorpions, and a small si-dewinder rattlesnake pickled in them. Anne shuddered a lit-tle.

There were various Indian artifacts throughout the clut-tered room—an Apache quiver made from the skin of a mountain lion, still filled with arrows; an Apache lance was crossed over a bow. There was a bright cheery Navajo rug in the center of the dingy, threadbare carpeting. Here and there were specimens of Pueblo pottery and Jicarilla Apache bas-kets woven of dried grasses.

One decoration drew Anne's complete attention. She rose and went to it. It was a set of armor—morion helmet, gorget, breast- and backplate, painted and varnished and fitted with tiny brass buttons.

"It belonged to a Spanish foot soldier of the sixteenth cen-tury, Anne," Alec said from behind her. "It was in West Texas, between the Pecos and Rio Grande country. The dry climate had preserved it from rusting overmuch. When I picked it up, his bones rattled in the casing. His skull was still within the helmet. We buried him where he had fallen and fired a volley over his grave."

She turned and looked at him. "Why?" she asked curi-ously.

Alec shrugged. "He was a soldier," he replied simply.

Anne sat down on the bed. Alec handed her a glass of Baconora. He shaped and lighted two cigarettes and placed one of them between her lips. He sat on the chair and studied her. The soft lamplight made her more appealing than ever, then too there was the recent memory of her belly and breasts.

"Why did you really come here, Anne?" he asked at last.

She gathered her courage. "I had dinner with Burton tonight. I had a little too much to drink. He tricked me into telling him what actually happened at Muerte Canyon." She leaned toward him. "I can't understand why I did it. Perhaps I thought he might understand and it would be of help to you."

"You don't know your fiancé very well, Anne. How much did you actually tell him?"

She bit her lip. "Everything. The operation of The Runner. About Baishan too. *Everything . . .*"

"And what was his reaction?"

"He was outraged when I told him Baishan had come in peace and unarmed and that you had met him the same way instead of killing him while you had the chance. He said I could be called on to be a witness to that effect. He feels now that he has you trapped in a corner and that you cannot escape." She searched Alec's face. "Why does he have such hatred for you? There is something beneath all this. Far more than is apparent. He said I had betrayed my new idol–Alec Kershaw."

"And how did you respond to that?"

"I told him to go to hell with his damned advice about my excessive drinking, as he termed it, and to hell with his damned marriage too!"

Alec couldn't help but grin. "That must have been interesting. In any case, I'll have to go to Camp Lowell and face General Crook. It will be up to him initially to decide what should be done about those charges."

"And if he has to send them through?"

"I doubt if I'll be able to beat those charges. Perhaps some of the earlier ones, but not this last. However, my letter of resignation has been on file with General Crook for quite some time. When I reach Fort Lowell, I plan to request him to forward the resignation.''

''And that will end your army career.''

Alec shrugged. ''Better than a court-martial and dismissal, and quite conceivably a prison sentence for collusion with the enemy.''

His powerful, alluring masculinity kept insinuating itself into her thoughts. She was already somewhat confused by the evening's events, compounded by the drinking she had done before and during dinner. Now the potent and insidious Baconora was working within her. The image of him, standing naked right before her eyes, kept reappearing in her thoughts.

Alec refilled the glasses. ''After resigning I can go about my private business. It's not a new idea with me. It has been in my mind for a long time.''

''I didn't think you would run,'' she said. She placed a cool hand on his bare shoulder. ''Take me with you,'' she pleaded.

He shook his head. ''Impossible!''

''Will you come back for me someday?''

He could not look at her. There was an unhealed wound deep within his soul from many years past, when he had lost Guadalupe, his first and possibly only love. No woman in a decade had even come close to replacing her.

''Alec?'' she asked softly.

He looked at her. Her eyes were bright with the liquor she had consumed. The fruity odor of it was on her breath. The feminine scent of her was subtle and alluring.

''Alec?'' she repeated.

''I can't promise you anything, Anne.''

They could hear the steady ticking of the wall clock on the living room wall. Then it struck one o'clock. ''It's getting late,'' he said. He really didn't want her to go.

''Then we don't know when or if we'll ever see each other again,'' she said quietly.

''No, Anne.''

''Do you remember that evening in the pass before we got here?''

''I'll probably forget it,'' he admitted.

"I asked you if you would have done it at a more convenient place."

Alec nodded.

She undid the cavalry saber pin from the front of her gown and pulled the garment back from her body, letting it drop around her waist. She placed a cool hand against his cheek. "Alec this *has* to be the time and the place," she murmured.

Alec stood up. He stripped off his breeches and then pulled her to her feet. Her gown slipped down to her ankles. She stepped out of it and kicked it to one side. He blew out the lamp, lifted her in his arms, and placed her on the bed. He stripped off her moccasins, then lay down beside her. They came together with a savage intensity that neither of them had ever experienced before. It was as though the occasion were the culmination of a dim and mysterious plan long in the making. The act burned away the aching hunger that had been within Alec ever since the loss of his first love and in Anne since she had lost her husband.

They blended together in perfect timing. Finally, he dropped limply beside her, then placed an arm under her shoulders and drew her close to him, their bodies slippery with the sweat of action. They lay together a long time, listening to the ticking of the clock, and now and then the muffled tramping of the sentry.

She cupped her hands around his face. "There's not much more time," she whispered.

There was no need to warn him. They came together again, this time with more practiced ease, as though they had been like this innumerable times instead of just once. At last they were done, at least for that passionate night.

They rested quietly. After a little while she turned to him. "Tell me about Belle Valois," she said.

He stared at her in the dimness. "Who told you about her?" he asked quickly.

"Burton," she replied.

Alec laughed softly. "That sonofabitch coppers every bet against me. What is it you want to know?"

She snuggled close. "What's she like?"

He reached for the Baconora flask and held it to her lips,

then drank himself. "One helluva woman," he said at last. "She runs a fancy house in Tucson. The best one, in fact."

"Buron said for an officer to be seen in her company was tantamount to ruining his reputation. He said you and Belle were very close."

"Rumors, just rumors," he said dryly.

"Those moccasins you gave me back when you rescued me. You said they were made by an Apache squaw. You said her name was Looking Glass. Who were the moccasins for?"

He raised himself on his elbow and studied her. "You know damned well they were for Belle. Any more questions?"

She sat up. "Is she as good in bed as I am?"

He stood up. "It's time for you to leave," he said.

She pulled the gown around her and pinned it with the saber pin. She sat back down while Alec put on her moccasins, and when he looked up at her, she placed her hands on each side of his face and kissed him, lying back on the bed to pull him on top of her. Alec got up and pulled her to her feet. He placed the cape around her shoulders and gently steered her toward the rear door. He pulled back the bolt, eased open the door, and peered up and down the darkened alleyway.

She raised up on tiptoe for one last kiss.

They clung together. The impulse came to him to carry her back to the bed, but he resisted. "Get out of here! *Vamos!*" he whispered.

She turned as she stepped into the alley. "Alec," she whispered, "*who was Guadalupe?*"

It was as though she had struck him across the face with a whip. "Go, damn you," he said hoarsely. He closed the door.

Ramon, Antonio, and Fedro were three Tucson Mexicans who had been hired by Tony Beaudine as civilian teamsters. Tonight Ramon had stolen a half gallon of tequila. After Call to Quarters they had settled down beyond the sanitary sinks to finish the bottle. At one point Fedro had gone to relieve himself. It was then he had seen the *gringa* emerge from the rear door of Captain Sawyer's quarters and walk quickly and quietly behind Officers Row to the end quarters of Major Kershaw. Curious, Fedro had loitered around the quarters. When he saw a faint light through a crack in the window curtain, he had peered through to see the officer and the *gringa* seated together on the bed. Later, the light had been extinguished. The window was partly open. Fedro had placed his ear to the opening. The sounds emanating from the darkened room were enough to raise his own manhood into a proud erection, despite the tequila he had taken on board.

Fedro had hurried back to his drinking partners and told them of what he had seen. The three of them had polished off most of the remaining tequila and then staggered in company to where he had seen the *gringa* and her lover. They knew the reputation of Major Kershaw in Tucson. He frequented the fancy house of Belle Valois, who had a group of the highest priced *mariposas* in the Arizona Territory. Therefore, they reasoned, this secretive *gringa* of the night visit must be of that particular type of whore. Now, they knew they'd never get past the front door of Belle Valois's establishment in Tucson, but this was different. This might be their chance to try one of her fancy women and not pay a copper *tlaco* for the privilege. If there was any problem, they always could leave Fort Bowie and head back to Tucson, and no one would be the wiser. After all, did not the gringos say, "The spics all look alike."

They were right on time. They heard the gringo say harshly, "Go, damn you!" Then the door was closed.

It was a simple thing for Ramon to come up behind the woman. One arm went around her slim waist; a hard dirty hand was clamped over her soft mouth. Antonio picked up her legs. Fedro went ahead to see if the way was clear. She struggled and kicked until Antonio hit her hard in the lower belly. They carried her down the slope past the sanitary sinks to an arroyo behind the wagon park. They stripped her to the skin. She was slammed down on her back.

"Who's first?" Ramon asked.

"Me," Fedro said.

"The hell you are!" Antonio said.

"Who found her?" countered Fedro.

Ramon was always the cool head, the logical one. "Let him have her, Antonio. After all, it's not as if she were a virgin. What difference does it make who mounts her first? Remember, that stud Major Kershaw probably gave her hell tonight already."

Ramon held her shoulders down and clamped a hand over her mouth while he threw a leg over one of her arms. Antonio gripped her by the ankles and spread her legs as far apart as he could. Fedro dropped his trousers and gripped his erection. At that moment Anne sank her teeth into Ramon's hand, drawing blood and a frenzied bellow from the Mexican. He pulled his hand away and released her. Anne screamed like a locomotive whistle. Antonio released one of her legs and got a hard heel right in the privates, which doubled him over and yanked a bloodcurdling roar out of his chest. Fedro was no fool. He turned to run, forgetting his trousers were below half mast. He fell, striking his face heavily on the hard gravelly ground.

Mickey Free had been unable to sleep in the Scout shacks near the corrals. He had wandered out after Taps to sleep in a wagon. The sound of muttering voices had awakened him. Then the bellowing of someone, followed by what was unmistakably the scream of a woman, galvanized him into action. He vaulted over the tailgate of the wagon and hit the ground running.

Alec had thought better of his ugly farewell to Anne. He pulled on his shirt and moccasins, picked up the Colt pistol she had left, and checked the cylinder to see if it was fully loaded. He opened the rear door. At that moment he heard a bellowing cry from somewhere beyond the sanitary sinks, seemingly echoed by the piercing scream of a woman. He ran down the alleyway toward the sound. The screaming woman must be Anne. There were no other women of the officer caste on the post, and the laundresses down on Soapsuds Row knew better than to prowl around the post after dark.

The Mexicans scattered. Ramon headed for the wagon park and ran full tilt into a short fast-moving figure coming from that direction. Mickey's knife was rammed into Ramon's belly, dragged hard one way, and then reversed, disemboweling the Mexican. As Ramon fell screaming to the ground, the dripping knife cut his throat from ear to ear. Mickey sped on.

Antonio hobbled along, his hands grasping his privates. In his confusion he had turned toward the sanitary sinks. Anne screamed again. She was crying out Alec's name over and over again. At that moment Antonio saw a tall shadowy figure standing upslope with pistol in hand.

"That's him!" Anne cried.

Antonio whirled and ran, forgetting his pain. He plunged down into an arroyo and scrambled up the other side, gravel scattering under his desperate pounding footsteps. He reached the top and turned. He knew he was safe, at least from any man hitting him with a pistol bullet in that light and from that distance.

He had regained his tequila courage. He cupped his hands around his mouth and shouted, "*Cobarde!*" Then he turned and ran. The pistol shot seemed to echo his cry. The bullet hit him in the back of the head and dropped him as though poleaxed.

The shouts, screams, and pistol shot had alerted the garrison. Lights flickered on. Men called back and forth to each other. Lanterns bobbed up and down as troopers closed in on the scene.

Alec thrust the pistol under his belt. Anne lay on the ground, naked and bleeding from scratches. She had fainted dead away. Alec picked her up and carried her toward Officer's Row.

Tony Beaudine came running, Colt in hand. "For Christ's sake, Alec!" he shouted. "What happened?"

Mickey Free came toward the troopers. His gargoyle face grinned in the lantern wash. "Greasers were after the woman," he said. He held up his bloody knife. "I got one of them. The Major got the other."

"Go find her dress," Alec said to Tony.

Burton Trapnell ran through the darkness toward the lanterns. He stopped short as he saw Alec carrying Anne. "What the hell is going on here?" he demanded.

"Mexicans. Evidently either raped or tried to rape Mrs.

Sinclair. Mickey Free heard her scream, and I did too. We each got one of them.'' He walked past the wide-eyed Trapnell toward Captain Sawyer's quarters.

"I'll take her!" Trapnell shouted.

Alec ignored him. He carried Anne to the rear of the quarters and opened the door. He took her into the bedroom and placed her on the bed. Lighting the Rochester hand lamp he turned to examine her.

"What are you doing?" Trapnell asked coldly from behind Alec.

"Examining her, Colonel. She'll be all right. Just fainted."

"Shouldn't she be examined by a surgeon?"

Alec straightened up and pulled the spread over Anne. "I'm it right now," he replied. "Sawyer isn't here. You know I've had medical training."

Trapnell eyed him up and down. "The universal man." He sneered. "I'll take that pistol, by the way." He held out his hand. Alec placed it there. Trapnell looked at it. The initials O.B.S. were inlaid in silver in the ivory buttplates . . . Orlando B. Sawyer. How had Kershaw, who had been disarmed when he was placed under arrest, gotten hold of Sawyer's pistol? There was only one answer—Kershaw had been in Sawyer's quarters with Anne!

"I'll go to my quarters now," Alec said.

Trapnell shook his head. "Wait! This is Captain Sawyer's pistol. See the initials here? How came you by it?"

"I had it," Anne said quietly. She sat up in bed, shielding herself with the spread. "I had too much to drink at dinner with you, Burton. When I awoke I needed to get some fresh air. Knowing the dangerous situation here, I took the pistol with me. When I was attacked, I dropped it in the struggle. Evidently, Major Kershaw heard my screams and came to my rescue, finding the pistol on the way."

Before God, she lies beautifully, thought Alec.

Trapnell turned to Alec. "Is that true?"

Alec nodded. "Would you doubt the word of a lady, sir?"

It was part of the code of an officer and gentleman. The colonel had nothing to say.

Alec left the bedroom and walked out the back door.

"You could at least have thanked him," Anne said coldly.

Tony Beaudine tapped at the back door, then entered the bedroom with the cape and dress draped over his arm.

"I'll take those, Beaudine," Trapnell said. "How many Mexicans were involved in his mess?"

"We found two bodies. Sergeant Free knifed one to death. Major Kershaw killed the other one with a beautiful pistol shot."

"There were three of them," Anne said.

"You're sure of that?" asked Trapnell.

She shrugged. "Positive. One held me down and closed my mouth. One pulled my legs apart. The third got ready to rape me."

Trapnell turned to Beaudine. "What are you standing there waiting for? Orders from Washington? Get out there and scour the whole damned post! I want that man!"

When Beaudine had left, Trapnell placed the cape and dress on the bed. "I'll wait in the living room," he said.

She dressed quickly. The forage cap ornament was gone. She fastened the gown together as best she could, then went into the living room.

Trapnell studied her. "Your gown is ruined," he said.

She nodded. "They were savages, Burton."

"There's something here that puzzles me," he said.

She walked to the sideboard to pour a drink of her improvised cordial, the peach syrup and 100-proof medical alcohol.

"Haven't you had enough of that?" he asked.

She turned, glass in hand. "Not quite. After that experience I need it."

He looked down at the pistol. "This is all a little too pat for me, Anne."

"What are you trying to make out of it? What is it you're trying to tell me?"

He studied her. "You said you had too much to drink and went outside for fresh air. Despite the drinking, you were alert enought to realize the danger outside during the night. You took Sawyer's pistol with you for protection. I should have thought with Kershaw's teachings of the Apache problem you would have realized that those savages can literally walk around this post at will and *are never seen by anyone*. They kill and vanish as noiselessly as they come. To my way of thinking, that would have kept you here behind locked doors no matter what your needs."

She drained her glass and refilled it. "Go on," she said dryly.

"Then suddenly you are attacked and dragged from here, dropping that fine pistol on the way. No Mexican or Apache would have left this pistol behind no matter what his purpose. Kershaw is awakened by your screaming. He rushes outside unarmed into the darkened alleyway, guiding himself to you by the sound of your screaming. Then, by sheer good fortune, in the *dark,* mind you, he comes across this pistol, snatches it up, and manages it kill one of your attackers. Now, Anne, isn't that just a little too much to be believed?"

She sipped at her drink. "Am I on trial here?" she asked bluntly.

"Of course not!"

"Then get the hell out of here with your absurd theories! I've had enough of men for this night, thank you!"

Trapnell shrugged. He walked to the rear door. "Lock this behind me," he said over his shoulder. He closed the door.

Anne shot the bolt, then turned quickly and placed her back against the door. She closed her eyes and for a moment felt unable to move. At last she returned to the living room and drained her glass. She turned the lamp down low and went into the bedroom. In bed, she lay staring up at the dim ceiling. What had she done? She herself would be safe enough. An officer's wife was supposed to be like a Roman matron, above reproach, but what about Alec? It only created more trouble for him. Burton would not let go of his suspicions.

Fedro had hidden in the wagon park until the furor died down. He clambered down from the back of a Wilson wagon. His trousers sagged about his hips. In his haste to get into the white-skinned *gringa* he had ripped the buttons off his fly. He held the front of his trousers together with one hand as he headed for one of the corrals to try to steal a horse. He knew there would be no question about who the third rapist had been once Ramon and Antonio had been identified. He heard *gringo* voices at the far side of the wagon park. *Madre de Dios!* If he was caught, he knew what would happen to him. They would not bring him in as a prisoner. They hated Mexicans as much as Mexicans hated them in turn. It would be *Ley del Fuego*—the Law of Fire. Give a prisoner a head start, then start shooting, claiming he had tried to escape.

Fedro veered away from the corrals. He had to bide his time. Perhaps he could hide out the next day and return for a horse after dark. Yes, that was it!

He stumbled over something in the dark. It was a body. He felt it warily. The corpse had been disemboweled and the throat cut. He stared closely into the contorted face. Before God! It was Ramon! Fedro stood up. Icy fear coursed through him. The body had been stripped! The soldiers would not have done it. What need would they have for the dirty and stained clothing of a greaser? There was only one answer—*Apaches*! But perhaps it had been the Apache Scouts. They weren't as particular as the soldiers, but they were deadlier, if possible, than the white men, on a par with the wild Apaches.

Fedro fled through the darkness. Perhaps Antonio had survived. He plunged down into the inky shadows of the arroyo and up the other side. There was the figure of a man standing there. Fedro was almost upon him before he recognized the bushy mane of hair and the lack of a hat. An old frontier axiom came to him in reference to fighting Apaches: "Shoot 'em if they don't wear a hat."

Fedro let go of his trousers in sheer panic. They promptly fell to his ankles as he started to run. His feet became entangled once again. He fell headlong over the stripped and mutilated corpse of Antonio. The next instant a knife was buried in his back just beside the left shoulder blade, penetrating accurately into the heart.

Baishan straightened up as he withdrew the knife. "*Yah-*

tats-an," he said. It was the term used when killing an animal rather than a human. To them a Mexican *was* an animal.

Baishan stripped Fedro, bundled his clothing with that of Ramon and Antonio, then vanished into the darkness. When he was half a mile away, he looked down on the post. Lights glittered in the clear night air. He could hear the faint sound of voices. Baishan had followed Never Still and his woman until they were safely at the fort. It was an obligation. Once they were secure there, or so he thought, he had turned his thoughts to stealing a few horses and perhaps snapping up a carbine or two. There was no use staying now. He raised his hand as though in salute to Never Still. "*Yadalanh,*" he said quietly. "Farewell . . ."

Burton Trapnell returned to his office to start making a rough draft of the report he would have to submit to the department. There was a tap at the door. It was Sergeant Fowler.

"Well, what is it, Sergeant?" asked Trapnell.

The noncom held out his hand. There was a ragged piece of cloth in it. Something on it gleamed in the lamplight. "We found this about where the lady was attacked, sir," Fowler reported. "It seems to be part of her dress. There's this saber insignia on it. Gold-plated, I think it is. I figured it must be yours. Beautiful piece of work." He placed it on the desk in front of Trapnell.

The colonel nodded. "It is, Sergeant. Thank you and good night."

The door closed behind Fowler. Trapnell unpinned the pair of crossed sabers from the material. The piece of cloth was certainly part of the gown Anne had been wearing. He studied the crossed sabers. He thought he had seen something like them before. Turning them over, he saw fine and delicate script engraving on the back. He viewed it through the magnifying glass. "Presented to Major Kershaw by the men of Company A First Cavalry, First Cavalry Division, Army of the Potomac. 1865," he read slowly. He dropped the magnifying glass. He stood up and paced back and forth for a time. Then suddenly he turned to the wall, placed his right forearm against it, rested his forehead on it, and began to beat on the wall with his clenched left fist while uncontrollable sobbing shook his frame.

CHAPTER 13

TONY BEAUDINE "DELIVERED" ALEC TO THE ADJU-tant's office of Camp Lowell and then went about his business with the quartermaster department. "Let me know how the Gray Fox deals with you, Never Still," he said cheerily as he left.

Camp Lowell had been established as a military camp in the southeast section of Tucson in 1862 by an advance detachment of California Volunteers marching toward New Mexico Territory. After the war it became the supply depot for military posts in southern Arizona and was the scene of much of Tucson's social life. Eventually, the camp was moved to the old Military Plaza east and slightly north of the Territorial capital. It was still much of a canvas city, garrisoned by officers and men of the Twenty-Third Infantry and a detachment of the First Cavalry. The camp was in the process of being established as a permanent post, with a hospital, barracks, and other buildings now under construction.

Alec waited in the outer headquarters office. He could hear General Crook speaking to the adjutant in the inner office. Alec had known George Crook during the war. Crook had served as commander of the Second Cavalry Division under General Phil Sheridan during the Shenandoah Valley Campaign of 1864, when Alec was assigned to Crook's staff. They had served together until the end of the war. A strong friendship and a bond of mutual respect had been formed between them.

After the war, a major-general by brevet, Crook had reverted to his actual rank of lieutenant-colonel and assumed command of the postwar-formed Twenty-Third Infantry. In

June 1871 he had taken command of the newly organized Department of Arizona.

To the professional army, George Crook was a soldier's soldier. He was forty-three years old, tall, broad-shouldered, sinewy of limb, and powerful of muscle. He had close-cropped gray hair and beard. He was quiet to the point of introspection, modest, unselfish, considerate, and conscientious, yet on occasion he could pronounce savage judgment on erring subordinates. He could be stubborn and independent beyond the limits usually tolerated by the military system. He usually didn't burden officers with memoranda, instructions, and orders, choosing instead merely to give them an insight into what was expected of them. The army stood in awe of his outdoorsmanship, legendary stamina, and endurance. He could meet the wilderness on its own terms.

Crook knew the Indian. He studied him as intensely as he studied birds and animals. In war against Indians Crook could be ruthless. In peace he was paternalistic, humane, and solicitous. He never made a promise to them he could not honor; in time this amounted almost to an obsession. He believed in using Indians to fight Indians. This armed his command with the natives' skill in guerrilla warfare and the psychological impact upon the enemy of finding their own people arrayed against them.

Perhaps the Apaches knew him as well in return, for with keen perception they had dubbed him *Nantan Lupan*—Chief Gray Fox.

As Alec entered Crook's office the general extended his hand. "You're looking fit, Alec," he observed. "Evidently, this life on the wildest of frontiers seems to agree with you."

Alec shrugged. "It has its up and downs, General," he dryly responded.

Crook studied him. "I see you intend to get right to the point. Now, sit down and tell me your version of this nasty Fort Bowie affair."

"May I ask how much the general already knows?"

Crook nodded. "I've read the charges brought here by Lieutenant Beaudine." He smiled faintly. "There are quite a few of them." He eyed Alec. "None of them good. The one that intrigues me most is this tale of your amputating the arm of a hostile Apache, thus saving his life, then having collusion with none other than Baishan, or Cuchillo Roja, of the Chiricahuas. What is your version of all this?"

"Is this an official explanation, sir?" Alec asked.

"Why do you ask?"

"Simply because I intend to request a court of inquiry if these charges are to be pressed. As the general knows, I do not have to be present at such an inquiry."

Crook smiled. "But *I* do, as department commander. Is that it?"

"You're very perceptive, General."

Crook nodded. "A point well taken. No, Alec, this is not an official explanation. Anything that passes between us is to be held in strictest confidence. Is that satisfactory?"

"Your word is sufficient, sir."

Alec told his version of the events leading up to the charges against him. "I give you my word, General, that's exactly what happened."

"I believe you, Alec. I think the First Charge and Specifications could be made to stick—overstaying time of patrol, crossing the border, taking the Mexican officer as hostage, looting his saddlebags and stealing his horse, deserting your command, and so forth—but a good defense counsel coupled with your excellent record might get you off with little more than a reprimand at most. The Second Charge, that of assaulting a superior officer in the performance of duty, is very serious. I can't, for the life of me, imagine what got into you. If Colonel Trapnell refuses to withdraw that particular charge, it will lead to serious consequences, perhaps dismissal from the service altogether. The Third Charge too is quite serious. I can sense, perhaps, your purpose in saving the life of the young Apache. Perhaps it was your humanitarianism. Possibly you had an ulterior motive. Probably a combination of both. It would take a Solomon to pass judgment on that one. The Second Specification of the Third Charge, that is, collusion with the enemy, is quite serious.

You will have a terrible time trying to defend yourself on that one."

It was very quiet in the office except for the ticking of the wall clock. Crook finally spoke again. "This Fourth Charge—When under close arrest and confined to quarters did leave those quarters without permission and arm himself—has me puzzled. Have you told me all the attending circumstances?"

Alec knew better than to lie to George Crook. "No sir," he said quietly.

"Why not?"

"I can't say, nor would I speak about it in any court before which I might be brought."

Crook nodded. "The witness referred to in the Third Charge would have to be Mrs. Sinclair. You should have been commended for heroism in saving her life, but if the charges are proved it would effectively cancel out such a commendation. I might have been able to recommend you for a Medal of Honor, if the circumstances had been otherwise. Alec, there is something untold here. Are you, by any chance, protecting the lady?"

"I'll have to decline to answer that, General."

"It might help your case. If Trapnell has her brought in as a witness for the prosecution, you could very well do the same as a witness for the defense."

Alec shook his head. "No!" he said bluntly.

"Then you'll have no recourse other than to request your court of inquiry, but I do not believe it will clear you of all charges."

"I do have another recourse, sir," Alec said quietly. "You have my resignation in your files. Will you accept it now and forward it through the proper channels?"

"Of course, I can't refuse to do so. However, there is one other thing I can do. I don't want to lose a fine professional soldier with a splendid record. I can stall the court-martial proceedings. The mills of the army grind exceeding slow, as you well know. As a personal favor to me, would you consider leaving the resignation in my care, and taking a leave of absence, say, for private business? During that time you might reconsider the matter. Perhaps Trapnell might also re-consider the severity of his charges.''

Alec shook his head. ''I don't think so, sir.''

''There has never been any love between the colonel and yourself, as I recall. I've often wondered why.''

Alec and Burton Trapnell had been in the same class at the Military Academy and there had been rivalry between them then, although mostly from the viewpoint of Trapnell. They had joined the First Cavalry together and served at the Battle of Valverde in New Mexico. The plain truth, and common knowledge among many officers and enlisted men, was that Trapnell had skulked at Valverde. Trapnell knew Alec had been witness to this. After the New Mexican Campaign, the regiment had been ordered east to join the Army of the Po-tomac and had fought at Gettysburg. Trapnell, feigning sick-ness, had left the field. After Gettysburg he no longer served with the cavalry and in the field. He had finished the war on a staff assignment in Washington and as a brevet colonel.

Alec remained silent.

Crook wisely changed the subject. ''Perhaps I am partly responsible for your disobedience of orders while you were on patrol. I've always been insistent that officers on a hot trail must stick to it no matter what happens. However, it was not a written order and certainly not official. It would not be a defense in any court-martial.''

''Does not the end justify the means?''

''Perhaps, but your dedication did not have concrete re-sults other than rescuing Mrs. Sinclair from those Apaches.''

''They were not Apaches, General.'' Alec quickly ex-plained about the *gambrusinos*. ''God knows the Apaches are raising enough hell on their own. But those men who raided that wagon train are every bit as dangerous. You know they stole many government weapons and thousands of dollars in paymaster's funds.''

''Then you knew when you followed their trail to the San Simon that they were not Apaches?'' queried Crook.

Alec nodded. ''I did.''

''That might pose a problem in your defense—a splitting

of hairs, so to speak. My verbal orders referred only to Apaches."

"The general knows very well where those stolen weapons will end up. The Apaches will pay for them in pure gold and at an exorbitant price. Money means nothing to them; modern firearms mean everything."

"We have no control over those *gambrusinos*. That is purely a civilian matter."

"Over which the civilian authorities have little or no control. You know as well as I do many of these outlaws are allied with territorial officials and with so-called law-abiding citizens," Alec said.

"The Tucson Ring. Many of them are civilian contractors doing a lucrative business with the Army and Apache reservations. They mean to keep the Apaches stirred up so as to keep the army here. A market for their supplies, livestock, and forage." Crook leaned forward. "Now, let's get back to you. If you insist on my keeping this resignation, I'll do so only on the condition that you take a leave of absence. When and if you decide to still request a court of inquiry, or have me forward your resignation through channels, I'll give you my word that I will do as you wish."

"That's fair enough, General."

Crook smiled in obvious relief. "Now, tell me what you intend to do on this forthcoming leave."

Alec pulled down the large topographical roller map of the southern area of Arizona Territory along the Mexican border. "You know of the Atascosa Mountains close to the border and west of the *camino* from Tucson to Sonora?"

"Very little, other than it's extremely hostile country and almost impossible to settle."

"The Altar Valley is west of the Atascosas, trending north and south. West of the valley are the Baboquivari Mountains, and beyond them the Papago Indian country. Spanish missionaries founded a *placita* they called Arivaca at the base of the San Luis Mountains. It was abandoned long ago because of Apache depredations. There is a Soledad Canyon in the Atascosas. During the eighteenth century a small visitation mission had been built there, later abandoned in favor of Ari-

vaca. In a time of comparative peace a certain Don Pedro
Aguilar came to the Atascosas and settled around the abandoned mission in Soledad Canyon. He held his ground during the Civil War, but after the war came under almost
constant attack by Apaches, Yaquis, and *gambrusinos*. Many
of his family were killed. When I was first stationed here in
Arizona Territory before you took command, I was sent down
there on a reconnoitering mission. The area intrigued me.
Don Pedro was willing to sell his holding. I paid him a down
payment. I felt it might be a good place to live after the
Apaches were finally subdued and I retired from the service.'' Alec smiled faintly. ''It seems as though one of those
conditions might be fulfilled now.''

''You may be inheriting a Pandora's box, Alec.''

Alec shrugged. ''It's a challenge.''

Crook studied him. ''Must you always seek the unknown,
perhaps the utterly impossible, in your life? What drives you?
Wherefore this restlessness?''

''Perhaps it is difficult for me to live without a challenge.''

''That well may be. What are your plans now?''

''You know of Pete Kitchen's success in holding on to his
El Potrero Rancho down along the *camino* despite constant
Apache harassment. The secret of his success is in making El
Potrero a veritable stronghold with a well-trained garrison of
employees—tough, fighting Mexicans and Opata Indians
who work the fields and his gold mine and double as fighting
men. I hope to build the same system at Soledad.''

''When are you leaving?'' Crook asked.

''As soon as possible.''

''Are you going alone?''

''As far as El Potrero. I hope to hire some help there and
later see if I can convince some of Don Pedro's people to stay
on with me.''

''You might find your grave down there.''

''I can just as easily find it up here during these times. It's
possibly just a matter of choice, General.''

Later Crook stood at his window watching Alec stride
across the parade ground. God help us, he thought, when we
lose a man like Alec Kershaw and retain one such as Burton

Trapnell. He turned from the window and sent for Sergeant Cooley. The noncom reported in a few minutes.

"Is Ben Truitt still in Tucson, Sergeant?" Crook asked.

"He is as far as I know, sir."

"Do you think you can find him?"

"I can check every saloon, cantina, and whorehouse for him, sir!"

"Go fetch him then, Sergeant."

Cooley hesitated. "I might have a hard time convincing him he should come back with me, sir. He's a helluva fightin' man."

"I'll hope you'll be able to lure him here without having to fight him. He's our best civilian scout. Tell him I need him to scout in hostile country. I imagine, next to liquor and women, that might appeal to him."

Cooley tilted his forage cap rakishly to one side and headed for the flesh pots of Tucson at the double.

CHAPTER 14

TUCSON, "THE OLD PUEBLO," LAY ALONG THE BANKS OF the Santa Cruz River. It was an ancient place whose origin was lost in the hazy past. It was ringed with rolling foothills and jagged peaks in the distance. The settlement had been built on a low ridge sloping down to the valley floor of the snaking river that flowed northward to die in the desert sands. The pueblo was surrounded by rich green flatlands, fields of grain, and fruit orchards. Beyond was flat gray desert covered with green cacti, greasewood, and paloverde. The gently rolling hills were covered with desert growths and wild grasses. The far-off Santa Catalina Mountains had ever changing hues of deep blues and reds.

The name of the pueblo Tucson had been corrupted over many years from the Pima Indian name of Stujukshon which had been variously translated as "dark mountain" or "dark spring,'' the latter because of the appearance of water standing on blackened cottonwood leaves.

Alec had emptied his quarters at Fort Bowie. He didn't anticipate returning there. He brought his uniforms and civilian clothing with him to Tucson. Tony Beaudine had brought Alec's rifle and revolver with him, turning them over to his friend when he left Fort Lowell. As a rule, no man went completely unarmed in Arizona Territory, and Tucson was known as a "paradise of devils." Alec had retained his .41-caliber double-barreled Remington derringer as well. Derringers were as much a part of a man's costume in those days as his watch, wallet, and penknife. This *stingy* gun was carried in various ways—in a pocket, tucked into the top of a boot, or thrust under a belt. Ace Carson, a professional gambler who held sway at the Congress Hall saloon, had shown Alec his method of carrying the "Little Gun with the Big Bite." Carson wore a leather-covered spring clip on a band around his left wrist. The derringer was placed under the clip, barrels pointing up the arm, and concealed by the shirt and coat cuff. It was a matter of seconds to free it from the clip, cock it, and fire it all in one swift motion. Despite the derringer's chilling appearance, it was notoriously inaccurate beyond the length of a card table. Its best target was the belly. At very short range the effect was devastating.

Alec stabled the dun at the Munoz Livery Stable and left his rifle, saddlebags, cantle, and pommel rolls in the care of the liveryman. His plan was to leave Tucson late that night after paying a visit to Belle Valois, and ride south along the Camino Del Rey to Pete Kitchen's Portrero Rancho. He could stay with Pete as long as he liked, making his preparations to go to the Soledad Rancho of Don Pedro Aguilar and spend time there getting the feel of the place. There was little doubt in his mind but what he would eventually make the Soledad his home.

Alec dined leisurely at the Shoo Fly Restaurant, then shopped around for various items he would need at Soledad, planning to have them shipped down to Pete Kitchen's place, where he could come in from the Soledad and pick them up.

It was a long and detailed list, and by the time he was done the moon was coming up.

Tucson was a beehive of activity night and day. The streets were thinly covered with floury dust through which there was a constant traffic of hulking freight wagons drawn by four or five teams of mules.

On each side of the streets sat thick-walled adobe buildings that were primitive, squat, ground-hugging, and set at irregular intervals. There were no sidewalks. In wet weather the streets were a foot deep in mud. During all seasons they were filthy, strewn with rubbish and garbage dumped there until the rains washed them away. There was a noisome manure pile at every corner. Dead animals were left where they fell. Pigs and chickens rooted through the garbage. Children, of whom the youngest were naked in hot weather, played constantly in the street at all hours. Dogs, lean and scrofulous, were more numerous than the children. They roamed through the streets in packs, hunting for food and water while yipping at the heels of passing burros, mules, and horses. Clucking, squawking chickens were everywhere underfoot.

Tucson was a place of innumerable cantinas and small *tendajons,* or stores, on the side streets. Mexican men with seemingly little to do leaned against the walls smoking cornshuck cigarettes incessantly, with smoke leaking in steady streams from their nostrils. Women in long dresses with the eternal black rebozos over their heads moved silently to the church or to the small *tendajons*. Mingling with the Mexicans were soldiers in rumpled and dusty blue uniforms, businessmen in black suits, and always there were the teamsters and the rancheros, booted and spurred.

There was a perpetual miasma of odors—rancid frying grease, spicy food, strong coffee thick enough to float a horseshoe, chili-spiced frijoles, mesquite smoke, smoky coal oil lamps, hot candle wax, and dust. And the town was always noisy with the hum of voices, thudding of hooves, squealing and grinding of ungreased wheels, the shrill cries of children, and soft guitar music. The violent oaths of mule skinners were accompanied by the pistol cracking of their whips. Drum and bugle calls sounded regularly from Camp

Lowell, and always to be heard were the somber bells of San Augustin Church.

When Alec was through with his business, he headed for the Congress Hall Saloon. As he threaded the narrow streets, the words of Tony Beaudine came back to him: *Tucson, the commercial entrepot of Arizona and the remoter Southwest. The mecca of the soldier. The Naples of the desert.* The thought was punctuated by a distant pistol shot.

The Congress Hall was the most ornate of Tucson's many saloons. It even boasted a pair of billiard tables and any game of chance a man had a mind to play. Some of the most skilled Knights of the Green Cloth in the Southwest inhabited the Congress Hall. A note of refinement at times was a lady harpist.

Tony Beaudine was at the far end of the bar. "General Crook said you had taken a leave of absence. I was afraid of that, Alec." He signaled Baldy, the bartender, for a bottle. "On the other hand," he added, "perhaps it's just as well. I don't see how you could have beaten all of those charges."

Alec shook his head. "Trapnell has all the heavy artillery on his side."

"Do you think you'll come back to the Service in time?"

Alec shrugged. "Who knows? In any case, it won't be as long as Trapnell has his sights set on me."

"You'll be going south to Soledad, then?"

Alec nodded. "For a time at least."

Tony poured the drinks. "That damned place could be your graveyard."

"It's not much different from most of this territory." Alec looked into the back mirror as a flash of something bright caught his eye. A dealer was raking in a pile of bright silver coins. The low-hung green-shaded lamp cast a pool of light on the green baize table covered with cards, chips, and piles of silver dollars. A uniformed man sat at the table. His face was half in light and half in the shadow of the lampshade. The pile of coins had been in front of him. His hands clawed a little against the tabletop.

Alec looked toward the table. "Who's the officer losing at Ace Carson's table?" he asked.

Tony glanced toward the table. "I don't know. I've never seen him before. I do know this—he's been losing steadily ever since I've been in here."

"Are those silver dollars he's betting with?"

Tony shook his head. "They're Mexican 'dobe dollars, fresh minted from the looks of them."

Baldy leaned over the bar. "It's been that way these past two nights. When he first come in here, he played with fresh greenbacks, crisp as new lettuce. He lost 'em all—a *lot* of them. Tonight he's been playing with them Mex silver dollars. He's dropped a lot of them too. Sonofabitch can't win for losing."

"Who is he?" Tony asked.

"The name is Chaffin. *Captain* Milo Chaffin. I guess that's his name, or *one* of 'em anyways. I've heard him called Pete and one time a drunken greaser called him Pedro. Chaffin cursed the hell out of him. When the greaser left, Chaffin followed right after him. Come to think of it, I never saw that greaser again."

"Maybe he's a greaser himself," Tony suggested.

"Who knows?" Baldy asked. "He speaks damned good English, but I've heard him speak spic too, and he seems to know his way around in that language. I guess he's been well educated somewhere."

Alec watched as Chaffin placed more of the silver dollars on the table. "You said he had been playing with greenbacks and then switched to the 'dobe dollars, Baldy?" he asked.

Baldy nodded. "A helluva lot of them."

"Where does he live?"

The bartender shrugged. "It ain't in Tucson as far as I know. I heard he spends a lot of time in Mexico, around Magdalena. Maybe he's in business."

"And wearing that uniform, Baldy?" Tony said. "Not likely. Do you know how he rates the uniform?"

Baldy refilled their glasses. "Maybe he just likes to dress like a soldier. There's been a lot of you here in the Old Pueblo since the war. Some even wore Rebel gray, and dared any Yankees to stop them. Come to think of it, about a year or so ago a man came in here wearin' a uniform something like

Chaffin's. Looked French to me. You know, like them officers in the Volunteer Zouave Regiments wore during the war. He had a lot more gold braid on the blouse though, and some on the cap. Chicken guts, we used to call it. He claimed he had served in Mexico with Maximilian until Maximilian was executed. He used to play at that same table where Chaffin is now. He always seemed to have a lot of money. Some of it was in gold. Kinda dangerous to flash money like that in Tucson. Chaffin and he walked out of here together one night. I never saw the Zouave fellow again. Sometime later Chaffin showed up wearing that uniform you see on him now, but without all the fancy gold braid. Chaffin claimed he bought the uniform off the hombre. You know how it is here in Tucson. You don't ask too many questions.''

Alec walked out the rear door that led to the privies. He lighted a long nine, waited a few moments, then returned inside. He paused just beyond the table. Chaffin's cap hung on a wall peg. Baldy had been right. It was a French kepi type in the French Army officer ''chasseur'' or ''zouave'' pattern. It differed from his own in that it had a lower, straighter, and stiffer visor and the crown was countersunk. There were faint dark lines on the top of the cap, as though braid had been removed. The blouse was of fine material and well made. Darker markings also showed against the material.

Ace Carson looked up at Alec. ''Want to sit in, Major Kershaw?'' he asked.

''Later perhaps, Ace,'' Alec replied.

Chaffin looked up as well, his face partly in shadow from the rim of the lamp. He was handsome in a sardonic sort of way. His complexion was dark, somewhat like a Mexican's with strong Indian blood. His hair was jet black, lank, and long, and a heavy growth of beard was on his chin, as well as a thin line of mustache on his upper lip. His blue eyes were almost startling in contrast to his dark hair and complexion. It was as though one were looking down through thin clear ice on a winter pond into intense coldness and unknown depths.

Chaffin threw his cards on the table. ''I'm out,'' he said. He looked at Alec. ''You can have my seat, Major, for what it's worth." His voice was pleasant and well modulated. He studied Alec closely.

"Thank you, but no, Captain," Alec replied. He walked back to the bar, knowing all the time Chaffin's icy eyes were on his back.

Alec leaned on the bar and reached for the bottle.

"Well?" asked Tony out of the side of his mouth.

Alec waited until Chaffin had passed directly behind them and walked down to the end of the bar nearest the door. He paused there, and spoke to Baldy.

"He's suspicious," Alec said. "Don't look at him. Baldy is right about the uniform."

Chaffin pushed his way through the batwings. Baldy sauntered down toward Alec and Tony. "He was damned curious about you two officers," the bartender said softly. "He's seen Mr. Beaudine in here before, but not you, Major, but he seemed to know who you were. He asked me if you were the same Major Kershaw who was with the Apache Scouts at Bowie and I said you were. Then he asked if you was the one who rescued a Mrs. Sinclair after the San Simon Crossing raid on the wagon train. I hadn't heard about that, so I told him I didn't know. Was that you?"

Alec nodded. Something was in his memory about that affair, something perhaps relative to Chaffin, but he couldn't bring it to mind at the moment.

"And he wanted to know what you was doing here in Tucson out of uniform. I said I figured you might be on leave and going somewhere, because you got your trail clothing on. Then he wanted to know if I knew where you were going, and I said I didn't. I wouldn't have told him if I did know."

"Curious," Tony mused. "How could he have known so soon about your rescue of Mrs. Sinclair?"

Alec shrugged. "There's always communication between Tucson and Fort Bowie—stagecoaches, mail couriers, teamsters, and so forth."

"How long has he been in Tucson, Baldy?" Tony asked.

"Couldn't say," the bartender replied. "But I hadn't seen him for a helluva long time until he came in two nights ago loaded down with greenbacks and them 'dobe dollars. I heard rumors he was mixed up with the Tucson Ring." Baldy looked up and down the bar, then leaned closer and spoke in a low voice. "They got a finger in everything crooked in this area. Smuggling is a moneymaker, as you well know. And I already told you Chaffin spends a lot of time in Mexico around Magdalena. That's sort of distributing area for Mex smugglers."

Alec was still puzzled about the man. "There's something about him that stirs my memory; but I can't put a finger on it at the moment."

Tony raised his glass. "Well, here's to you and your future, dubious as it is, in Soledad Canyon. I'm almost tempted to take a leave myself and go along to keep you out of more trouble."

Alec shook his head. "Your future is army, Tony Soldier. Unless an Apache puts a lance through your guts or a bullet in your back. You're bound to go far, perhaps as high as a star."

Tony shrugged. "There's Trapnell between me and that star. And until recently, you were there too."

Alec grinned. "Well, now all you have to do is beat out dear old Burton."

"You'll be back, Never Still. You're army to the core. I'll swear to God, if you got stuck with a knife, you'd bleed blue and gold."

Alec shook his head. "No, I think perhaps the army has seen the last of me. Maybe it's just as well."

Tony studied him. "The same old restlessness. Nothing can satisfy that—promotion, women, land, or wealth."

Alec said nothing. Tony had put his finger right on the innermost of his thoughts: the growing restlessness that nothing seemed to be able to quell.

When Tony left, as he said, "to allay the loneliness of a wealthy widow woman visiting friends in Tucson," Alec remained at the bar. He probed again into his usually good memory, seeking the man who called himself Milo Chaffin. Maybe the powerful brandy was dulling his senses. The words of Mickey Free at Muerte Springs came slowly back to him: "Smugglers, Major. Came up from Sonora heading north. Someone Indianed up on 'em. Shot them in the back. Killed the lot. Stripped and scalped them to make it look like Apache work. Took their smuggling money, horses, clothes, and guns and left during the night.''

"North to the San Simon Crossing," Alec said aloud.

He left the Congress Hall and headed for Belle Valois's establishment.

CHAPTER 15

BELLE VALOIS HAD STARTED HER BORDELLO IN A RENTED house just off the Calle Real. In time she bought the house and the one next door to it, then acquired the house on the next street, which backed up against the first two establishments. That was her private abode. There wasn't a finer palace of Elysian delights anywhere else in the Territory.

Alec knocked on the front door. A panel slid back. Hard eyes surveyed Alec. "It's Major Kershaw, Bartolome," Alec said. "Open the goddamned door and let me in. It's not too healthy in these streets tonight."

Bartolome grinned. "Or any other night, Major."

The bouncer barred the door and refastened the chain locks once Alec was inside. A double-barreled shotgun hung in brackets beside the door.

"Is Madame Valois here tonight?" Alec asked.

Bartolome nodded. "She heard you were in town. She's been expecting you."

When Belle had first started in business, she'd had the names of her original coterie of girls carved into the door lintels—Luz, Theresa, Estella, Dolores, Sophie, Betty, and so on. The turnover being what it was in Belle's profession, and the fact that she put a premium on youth and freshness, the owners of those names had long ago departed to seek other fields, in time being degraded, perhaps, to the two-bit to six-bit cribs. Thus it became the custom of the house for whoever was assigned to a room to assume the name of the original occupant.

Alec shaped a cigarette and placed it between his lips. He thumb-snapped a lucifer into flame just as he reached the door of the present Luz. At that instant a woman screamed like a wounded mare behind the door. A man bellowed hoarsely in Spanish. "You damned bitch! I pay good money for what I want. Now, you whore, do as I say!"

Luz screamed again. "Before God, señor! No! No! No! Not again! Let me alone! See? I give you your money back! Only leave me alone!"

Feet scuffled behind the door. There was hard breathing, a short scream, the shattering of glass, followed by a savage grunt. The door was opened and flung hard against the inner wall. The naked whore, wide-eyed and hysterical, hardly more than fifteen or sixteen, ran out of the room with her waist-long black hair streaming down her sweating back. She held a broken bottle in her hand. The lamplight glistened on the blood-stained, jagged points. A naked man appeared, cursing thickly, blood running through the coarse hair on his thick broad chest. He slobbered, and his eyes were hollows of madness; the animal in man was dominant in this creature, seemingly straight out of the smoky doors of hell itself. He raised his right arm. A short, curved knife blade streaked with blood protruded from the bottom of his clenched fist.

Alec threw the girl to one side, stepped in close, and slammed a right cross to the man's jaw, driving him back into the room. A blow such as that would have floored the average man, or half-stunned him. He staggered back into the room, dropping the knife and upsetting a small table. The bottles and glasses on it crashed to the floor. Silver dollars rolled across the carpeted floor in all directions.

"She's mine, you sonofabitch!" the man yelled. He snatched up a heavy chair and raised it high overhead.

Alec drew his derringer from the wrist clasp and aimed it full at the man's sweating face. "You ugly bastard," he said thinly. "Go ahead! I'll blow your face out the back of your head!"

The chair was slowly lowered. The cold green eyes held

Alec's. The man was short and thickset, inordinately deep of chest and sloping of shoulders, powerfully muscled with long arms. His legs were strong and slightly bowed. His torso was thickly covered with hair both front and back. Blood leaked from the side of his mouth and ran down from his chest lacerations into his crotch, staining his privates. Jesus, but he was really hung like a stud stallion, Alec thought.

The man slowly touched the side of his mouth, then looked at his bloodstained fingers. "You did that," he said in a low voice. "I paid good money for that damned little whore. Three times as much as that high-falutin' bitch Belle Valois usually gets for a virgin."

Alec shook his head. "No amount of money can pay for what you want, even if she is a whore."

"Put away that hideout gun and get outta here," the man warned.

"Get dressed, pick up your money, and leave," Alec countered.

The man shrugged. He knew the odds of beating out a slug at that range from the Little Gun with the Big Bite. He pulled on his clothes and boots, gathered up the scattered money, and reached quickly for his knife.

"Let it be," warned Alec.

The man smiled, but there was no mirth in his hard eyes. "Don't I know you from someplace?" he asked.

Alec motioned toward the door with his derringer. "Hopefully not."

The man walked toward the door. Alec took his eyes off him for a fraction of a second. It was enough. The reaction was instantaneous. The lamp was snatched from a stand beside the door and hurled overhand directly at Alec's face. He managed to fend it off with his left forearm. It struck the wall and smashed, dribbling burning oil down the wall to the carpet. The light temporarily blinded Alec. He dropped the derringer. An instant later a hard head hit him in the belly, driving the breath from him and hurling him back against the wall while powerful clawlike hands closed on his throat. Alec went down struggling to the floor with his growling opponent on top of him.

The flames flickered up from the oil-soaked carpeting and danced against the wall. Alec began to black out. He managed to raise a knee again and again into the man's meaty privates. He felt the grip on his throat relax. He raised his right arm and clamped a facelock on his opponent. They strained against each other, bulging muscle against lean wiry strength. Finally the man rolled sideways from Alec, releasing his throttlehold and breaking the facelock. He got to his feet and kicked Alec in the side. Alec rolled sideways and up onto his feet just in time to get a powerful backhand slash across his eyes, blinding them with tears. He charged wildly and crashed into his opponent. They struggled in the middle of the room, at times almost rigidly still, tensed against each other like a bronze statue of Grecian wrestlers. The image of their violent activity was thrown on the wall behind them like a shadow tableau.

Smoke began to fill the room. Alec went down hard from a crashing sidehand blow to the head. His hand closed on the short, curved knife, the deadly Mexican *saca tripas,* the "goes-for-the-guts." He got the boot twice before getting back up to his feet and swinging out the knife full arm. It raked across the forehead of his opponent. Blood spurted from the bone-deep, four-inch slash. It flooded down into the man's eyes. He staggered back, grunting in agony. Alec plunged toward him, grabbed him around the middle, swung him, and body-slammed him on top of the burning carpet, partially smothering the flames. Then Alec got groggily to his feet, drew and cocked his Remington, aiming to kill as his opponent rolled howling away from the fire.

Belle Valois appeared in the doorway. She moved fast. She slapped the Remington to one side, then snatched up a big flowered porcelain pitcher from a washstand used for a "whore's bath" and doused most of the flames, stamping out the last flickering vestiges. She picked up the long iron poker from the fireplace and brought it down full force alongside the prostrate man's skull, putting him into the deep sleep.

Alec coughed in the thickening smoke. He pushed Belle to one side and grabbed the unconscious man's ankles to drag him from the room. Then he leaned against the wall, coughing violently and feeling his bruised throat.

Belle came out to join him. "Alec, my love," she said dryly, "you always were one to make a dramatic entrance into my poor place of business."

Alec grinned feebly. "Nothing to it, Belle, me darlin'," he said hoarsely.

She knelt beside the man. "Bartolome!" she shouted. "Go and ask Maria for my sewing kit. *Pronto! Vamos!*" She looked at the half-naked whores and their johns crowding the long hallway. "Get the hell back to work!" she yelled. "You johns, if you're payin' by the hour, you're losing time! *Git!*"

Alec watched Belle douse the slash on his opponent's head with brandy, then sew industriously away at it. He picked up the bottle and sucked at it. The powerful liquor seemed to have little or no effect. Christ, but that had been a close one. He studied the bloody, disfigured face and the thought came to him that he had seen such a physique in another time and place, but experienced the same difficulty he had with the name Milo Chaffin, which he was positive should have meant something to him, but what had not as yet become apparent.

Belle bit off the thread close to the cut and then stood up, wiping the blood from her full lips. "That should hold him together until he can get to a doctor." She turned to Bartolome and her other houseboy, Juan. "Get him out of here, you two! I'd still like to know how the hell he ever got in here again! We had enough of him six months ago. Put two of my girls in sick bed for a week apiece! Cost me a pretty penny. Take him to the Calle Real by the back way and dump him over a fence." She knelt beside him and went swiftly through his pockets, removing the adobe dollars. She looked thoughtful. "Time lost for the girl. Ruined carpeting. Broken lamp. Busted whiskey bottle and glasses." She quickly counted out some of the dollars and deposited them in the silver-mounted leather purse she always wore belted about her wasp-waist, except, of course, when she was entertaining some of her more select clientele.

"You forgot the antiseptic brandy, and the thread used to sew him up," Alec said dryly.

Belle nodded. "That I did." She plucked another dollar from his pocket. She stood up. "You figure that should cover it?" she asked, all business.

Alec nodded. "About."

They grinned at each other.

He took her arm and the two of them walked through the hallway into the back-to-back house on the next street which was Belle's private abode. She turned before they closed the door behind them. "Bartolome!" she shouted. "I want to see you when you get back! You hear!"

Alec drew her close as they entered the sitting room next to her bedroom. She slid her smooth white arms around his neck, drawing him down to meet her lips. She thrust her body against his with a bit of a wriggle.

Alec released her and sat down on one of her plump chairs. He eyed her. Belle was always beautifully dressed and coiffured. Her hair was a natural blond. Her eyes were an incredible blue and almost too large for her oval face. Her nose was slightly aquiline, her mouth large and full. Her teeth looked like those of a china doll, small and perfect. Her skin appeared porcelain, with a roseate hue.

She came close to him and placed her fine hands on his shoulders. "Christ, but it's good to see you, Alec," she said quietly.

He placed his hands on each side of her slim waist. "Even under these circumstances?"

She nodded. "Under any circumstances."

"I suppose you've heard about what happened at Fort Bowie?"

"Who hasn't? Bad news travels fast."

He pulled her down onto his lap. She slid her arm about his neck. "How long will you be here?" she asked.

Alec shrugged. "Who knows?"

"Where will you go?"

"South."

"To that damned Soledad Canyon?" She withdrew her arm and sat up straight. "You'll only find your death down there!"

Alec grinned a little. "So everyone tells me."

"You damned fool! Can't you listen?"

Someone tapped on the door.

"*Quien es?*" Belle cried.

"Bartolome," came the reply.

She stood up and unlocked the door. "Come in," she said quietly, *very* quietly.

Bartolome was nervous. He clasped his hands in front of himself, working them against each other.

"Did you get rid of him?" Belle asked.

Bartolome nodded.

"Did anyone see you?"

Bartolome shook his head.

Belle paused. "Now, Bartolome, tell me, how did that animal get in here in the first place? How did he happen to be in Luz's room? Who was that girl in there with him?"

Bartolome smiled mechanically by raising his face muscles and showing a mouthful of teeth, but his eyes were fixed. "I'm not really sure, señora!"

"Talk!" she snapped.

Bartolome looked at Alec. Alec nodded. Bartolome looked away.

"Shall *I* tell you?" Belle demanded. "Empty your pockets on the table."

Bartolome hesitated.

"*Now!* Goddamn you!" Belle roared.

Bartolome slowly emptied his pockets—a soiled bandanna, a clasp knife, tobacco canteen and corn-shuck wrappers, a block of matches, some loose change, and a few crumpled greenbacks.

"Is that all?" Belle asked.

Bartolome held out his hands, palms upward. "Of course, señora!"

Alec looked at Bartolome's trousers. They were tucked into his boottops. The knees seemed rather full. "Jump up and down, my friend," Alec suggested.

"Are you loco?" Bartolome demanded.

Alec drew his Remington and cocked it. "Damn you! *Jump!*"

Bartolome jumped.

"Faster! Faster! Faster!" Alec chanted.

The subdued but merry jingling of metal mingled with the thudding of Bartolome's boots on the thick carpeting.

"Enough," Alec ordered. "Now, hombre, pull your pants out of your boots."

Bartolome nervously did as he was bid. Plump and shiny 'dobe dollars dropped to the carpet in a glittering pool around his boots.

"You conniving sonofabitch!" Belle spat out. "How much did that animal pay you to let him into that room?"

Bartolome pointed silently to the coins.

"Who was the girl?" Belle demanded.

Bartolome opened his mouth and closed it.

"Talk!" Alec ordered.

Bartolome smiled ingratiatingly. "Only my stepsister, señora. I couldn't find another virgin for him at such short notice. You know how it is in Tucson. She was a bastard anyway and was thinking of becoming a *mariposa*." He was flat on his back on the floor bleeding from the mouth before he realized what had hit him. "Before God!" he cried. "He's not a man to be trifled with. What he wants he gets. Once he made a capon out of a friend of mine who displeased him."

Alec blew on the skinned knuckles of his right hand. "Who is he?" he asked coldly.

"He goes by different names. Sometimes American; sometimes Mexican. At times he calls himself Bohannon, or Lasco. I've heard him called Gallier and sometimes Perez or Sanchez. In Mexico he mostly goes by the name of Diaz."

Alec stared at him. "*Diaz?* Jesus Christ! You don't mean *Chico Diaz?*"

Ramon nodded. "That's him," he said.

Alec grabbed him by the collar and hustled him from the room. "Show me where you left him!" he shouted.

Belle looked down at the pile of silver. "Well, I'll be goddamned," she murmured. She gathered up the coins, raised the seat of her plush-covered commode, lifted the chinaware chamber pot, opened a small trapdoor in the bottom of the stand, then poured them in. She added the coins from her purse, closed the trapdoor, replaced the chamber pot and plush seat, then plumped herself down and fully relieved herself.

Alec returned in an hour. He locked the door behind him then walked unsteadily to the liquor cabinet and poured a double brandy. "I hunted all over town and couldn't find the sonofabitch, Belle," he said over his shoulder. "Someone said they thought they had seen him and some other men riding north."

"Maybe you've had enough liquor this evening, love," she suggested.

He shook his head. "Not yet."

"It'll be dangerous for you to leave here tonight in that condition."

He turned and looked at her. "Who's leaving here tonight? Or maybe you want me to leave?"

She laughed softly. "Now that I've got you back in my web after all these lonely months? Besides, you know how some men perform in bed when they drink too much."

He stopped the decanter and downed the drink. "A point well taken." He sat down on the couch and rested his head against its back. He had suddenly become very tired. His left forearm ached where he had parried the lamp flung at him. His belly had been butted. His throat hurt from Chico's attempted throttling. His side was sore from being kicked. The liquor which at first had lifted his spirits had now begun to let him down.

She placed a cool hand on his forehead. "Rest," she said soothingly. "You're with your Belle now." She pulled off his boots and placed his feet on a footstool.

He opened his eyes. "You'd make a fine wife, Belle."

She grimaced. "I tried it—twice." She patted his cheek. "I could be convinced to try again with you, but you and I both know no career officer could ever marry a whore or madam and continue his career. Besides, you have no intention of marrying me anyway." She sat down close beside him and rested her head on his shoulder. "Tell me more about Chico Diaz," she added.

Alec told her everything he knew about the *gambrusino*. Suddenly, he sat straight up. "He asked me if he didn't know me from someplace! That voice! Dammit, Belle! I've heard it before!''

She stood up. ''For God's sake, let's forget that animal! Didn't you come here to see me?''

Alec nodded. ''Why else, my love?''

She swayed toward her bedroom door. She looked back over her bare shoulder with those great eyes of hers. ''I won't be long.'' she promised.

Tempting as she was, Alec's mind was filled with other pressing thoughts. Events since he had come to Tucson had moved with incredible rapidity. He had left the Service, had fought a murderous hand-to-hand fight with Chico Diaz and had marked him for life. Diaz would not forget him, ever. . . . The next time they met it would be to the death. There could be no alternative. That voice of his haunted Alec.

Belle came to the door of her bedroom and posed there, seductive and tempting in a filmy peach-hued negligee through which he could see the dark nipples of her full breasts, the silken patch at her crotch, and those lovely long legs of hers.

He went quickly to her. She led him by the hand to her wide bed. He sat down on it while she busied herself with his clothing. He was stripped in a matter of minutes. Her breathing was fast and erratic. He peeled off her negligee, pulled back the coverlet, and deposited her on the bed like a luscious pea in a pink and white pod. He placed his pistol on the bedside stand beside a brandy decanter. He lowered the Argand lamp and got into bed with her.

They came together like two virgin teenagers having their first experience at fornication. It was always that way with them. Each time they were together was like new. When they were done, they lay silently, sweat-dewed, breathing deeply, and completely content.

Belle looked sleepily at him. ''God, Alec,'' she murmured. ''You're the very best.''

''Flattery,'' he said as ne reached for the brandy.

''I should know,'' she said simply.

''I'll bet you tell that to all the boys.'' he said dryly.

Belle dozed off. Alec studied her. She was different. Most

women he had known were much alike, but Belle, and Anne too, now that he recalled her, *were* different. Belle was a master of the art, and besides that, he felt that she truly loved him. That is, if she were truly capable of loving any man. Her professional lovemaking was as assumed as her name. She was really Maggie Flanagan of New Orleans, daughter of an Irish stevedore and a creole prostitute. Her father had served in the war with the famed and notorious Louisiana Tigers, and had been killed at Kernstown. Her mother had raised her daughter in a plush bordello until she died of yellow fever. Maggie was fourteen. She had no place to go. She auctioned herself off as a virgin and had been in the profession ever since. Her first husband had been a gambler who had been killed cheating at cards. Her second had been the profligate son of a wealthy New Orleans family. He had struck it rich in California. The first thing he had done was to abandon Belle, but he had left her enough money to start her own business. She had the intelligence, drive, talent, and ambition to be a success. True, she was fading somewhat, but she still had much to be desired of by men.

Alec plumped his pillow and sat up, resting his back against it. He lighted a cigar and sat there thinking. Tired as he was, he did not seem able to sleep. The voice of Chico Diaz still haunted him.

Belle surveyed Alec with half-closed eyes. His profile was somewhat angular in the faint light of the lowered lamp. She did not need better light to see his every feature. It had been imprinted on her memory the first time she had met him. She knew much about him and yet very little in some respects. She knew there had been an unrequited love affair in his younger days. Alec hadn't told her about it. He always kept his innermost thoughts from her and probably from everyone else as well. It had been Tony Beaudine who had told Belle. She deduced that the affair had put Alec off from any kind of permanent liaison. Yet she knew he had always felt a closeness to her, perhaps more than to any other woman, at least those about whom she knew something. Still, this night, even during their lovemaking, she had sensed something different about him. There was nothing she could put her finger on, but she knew with feminine intuition that it must be another woman. Perhaps in the long months since she had seen him last he *had* found someone to replace, or at least rival that first love. Belle had never worried much about losing him. Now suddenly, she wasn't at all sure, and that fact made her sick deep inside.

Alec looked down at her. "Seen enough?" he asked dryly.

She shook her head. It was very quiet. They could hear the measured ticking of the ornate mantel clock in the sitting room. Belle laughed suddenly.

"What is it?" he asked curiously.

"We're just like man and wife," she replied. "Only a wife usually knows where her husband is most of the time. I never do. Where are you bound to this time? Back to Fort Bowie?"

Alec shook his head. "I've taken an enforced leave," he said quietly. "I wanted to resign, but George Crook talked me out of it. Still, I doubt if I'll go back to duty."

She stared at him. "You're not really going down to that damned Soledad Canyon, are you?"

"That's what I told you earlier."

She shook her head. "To a hole in the ground and a pat in the face with a spade. That is, if you're lucky enough to *be* buried. Otherwise your only mourners will be the wolves and the coyotes."

He grinned. "Don't forget the *zopilotes*—the cleanup crew."

Tears filled her eyes. "I'm sorry, Alec!" she cried.

He kissed her. "Forget it. I'll make it back someday. I'm a hard man to kill, Belle."

"*Bullshit!* Damn you! Why do you always come here and lean on me with your woes, then take off as soon as you're satisfied?"

"Is that what you really believe? Have I ever leaned on you with my woes, as you put it?"

"Not verbally, but they're there all right."

He patted her bare shoulder. "Well, darlin', I think you like it that way."

She pouted a little. "Well, anyway, you promised me a

pair of Apache moccasins when you were here months ago. Did you bring them?''

Anne had worn them thin and kept them. How could he have told her he had promised them to a whore?

"Well, Alec, where are they?" Belle demanded.

He shrugged. "I left them at Fort Bowie," he said casually.

"You're lying, as usual."

By this time the room was getting a little indistinct. The bed seemed to move up and down and sway sideways now and again. Alec placed the cigar in the ashtray, fortified himself with another drink, blew out the lamp, and half-rolled on top of Belle.

"Jesus," she whispered. "Don't you *ever* get enough?"

He closed her mouth with a kiss.

She clasped her arms around his neck and drew him down to her.

Hours later Alec awoke suddenly from a vivid dream. A hoarse shouting voice had penetrated his sleep. The dream scene was the day he had rescued Anne from the men disguised as Apaches who had been pursuing her from the San Simon Crossing. The voice was that of their leader. It was almost exactly the same as that of Chico Diaz. . . . Suddenly, and unaccountably, the dark-complected face of Milo Chaffin, with its strange and incongruous light blue eyes, seemed to stare at him from a dark corner of the room. He instinctively reached for his revolver. There was no one there. Why had Chaffin suddenly appeared? Then something Anne had said at Muerte Canyon came back to him: *You spoke of white boys being captured as Apaches and raised and trained to be warriors. I saw one such at the San Simon Crossing. He was tall for an Indian. His face was hideously painted in black and vermilion stripes. I thought he had seen me. He looked directly at me. It was eerie and frightening. His eyes were a light and icy blue, in absolute contrast to his face paint and his jet black hair. I'll never forget those eyes. Never!*

"Milo Chaffin," Alec said aloud.

Belle stirred a little in her sleep, then rolled over on her side, facing away from him.

The loose ends all began to tie in. The slaughtered smugglers at Muerte Springs and the few adobe dollars found there. The paymaster's money chest rifled from the overturned stagecoach. The *gambrusinos* aping Apaches to put the blame for their depredations on them. The distinctive voice of Chico Diaz and the distinctive eyes of Milo Chaffin. The greenbacks and silver adobe dollars Milo Chaffin had been gambling away for two nights in the Congress Hall. The silver coins Chico Diaz had paid Bartolome for a prime virgin.

Belle awoke an hour before dawn. She reached out for Alec. The bed was empty beside her. She called out, "Alec? Where are you?" There was no answer. His clothing and pistol were gone. She jumped from the bed and ran into the sitting room. His boots and hat were also gone. There was no one there.

Belle shrugged. She went back to bed. It wasn't unusual for Alec to come and go unannounced. "Oh, well," she consoled herself, "he'll come back to his Belle. He always does, sooner or later." She closed her eyes. A moment later she sat bolt upright. "Soledad Canyon! *Oh, my God!*"

CHAPTER 16

THE SUN HAD SET BEHIND BABOQUIVARI PEAK, towering forty miles to the west of the Apache-haunted Camino de los Muertos, the Highway of the Dead that stretched perilously from Tucson, past the ghost *placita* of Tubac and the gaunt, abandoned ruins of Mission San Cayetano del Tumacacori. It was another twenty miles south to the border, beyond which the *camino* reached to Magdalena, deep in Sonora. The western sky was an exquisite creation of rose, salmon, pink, and gold, done by the hand of that Master of all painters. The hot winds of the day had already reversed themselves to flow down from the higher elevations toward the valley floor of the Santa Cruz River.

Alec walked softly through the darkened echoing nave of

Mission Tumacacori into the baptistry. He climbed the narrow stone stairway to the bell tower. Staying within the shadows, he peered out of each of the four arched openings of the belfrey to the cardinal points of the compass. He did not expect to see or hear signs of human life out there in gathering darkness, but he relied on his indefinable sixth sense. It was scientifically unproven, but it was there nonetheless. He never doubted it, always relied on it.

Alec scanned the crumbling outbuildings, the long-untended fields, and the dead peach orchard. They were deserted. There would be a moon that night, but before moonrise he could continue his ride south, take cover until moonset, then go on to Pete Kitchen's El Potrero Ranch stronghold. It was the only place of safety between Tucson and Magdalena. At times the *camino* was called Pete Kitchen's Road. Pete himself had dubbed it "Tucson, Tubac, Tumacacori, Tohell."

When darkness came, he descended to the sacristy, where he had dozed during daylight. The mission was comparatively safe from the Apaches. To them, always fearful of the vengeful spirits of the dead, Tumacacori was a place to avoid. It was almost like an island of extremely fragile safety on a sea of positive peril. Superstition didn't bother the American and Mexican outlaws who preyed on travelers on the old *camino*, however.

Alec's trip south from Tucson had been delayed twelve days after he had left Belle's place. Queries about Diaz and Chaffin had led him on a will-o'-the-wisp chase, first northeast to the San Pedro, south again to the Butterfield Trail, and finally back to Tucson. He had returned there late at night, avoided Camp Lowell, his usual haunts, and Belle Valois. He had left before dawn the next day. There were vague rumors his quarry had gone south, but no one was sure, and many of them would not inform on that deadly duo in any case.

Alec slung his saddlebags over his shoulder, picked up saddle and saddle blanket, and stepped out of the sacristy into the old weed-grown cemetery, the Campo Santo. His dun was picketed at the far end of the graveyard. The dim bulk of the

roofless mortuary loomed against the night sky. He took three
steps and then froze in position. *Someone,* or *something* living other than the dun was out there. He slowly lowered his
gear to the ground and drew his revolver.

Minutes ticked past. Nothing moved.

A pebble clicked on the stony ground thirty feet from him.

He reached the mortuary, flattened his back against the
wall, and peered around the side of it toward where he had
heard the sound. A shadow moved almost imperceptibly
against the cemetery wall—one man. Alec moved almost like
a disembodied shadow himself. When there was one, there
might be more. Apaches and outlaws usually hunted in packs
like wolves and coyotes.

He passed through the sacristy, snatching up his Winchester on the way. He catfooted through the nave, ascended to
the belfry once more, cached his rifle there, then lowered
himself to the roof. He crab-crawled to the roof of the sacristy, went belly-flat, and moved to the rear edge, overlooking the Campo Santo.

The motionless shadow was still where he had last seen it.
Alec could just detect the faint miasma of stale sweat and
horse shit. He sighted the pistol on the shadow.

Something snapped. A tiny spurt of flame appeared. It rose
up to touch the tip of a cigarette and softly light the angular
planes of a lean face decorated with a thick dragoon mustache. The flickering lucifer was dropped to be stamped underfoot accompanied by the jingling of a spur. The cigarette
was puffed on, faintly lighting the face as it glowed, then letting the features darken into shadow under the wide hatbrim
as it subsided. It was obvious this stranger wanted to be seen.

Alec full-cocked the Remington. The clicking of the sear
sounded inordinately loud in the stillness.

The cigarette glowed. The stranger looked up toward him.
"What they say about you is true, Major Kershaw. You can
out-Apache the Apache." The tone was softspoken Texan.

Alec stood up. "Don't move! Raise your hands!" he ordered.

The Texan placed his hands atop his hat. "I'm alone, Major."

"Who are you?"

"The name is Truitt. Ben Truitt."

"Which means nothing to me. Where did you hear about me?"

"First time I saw you was at the Battle of Valverde in New Mexico Territory, February 1862. You called yourself Lieutenant Alexander Calhoun then. You was with MacRae's Yankee Battery. I was fifty feet from you when you got hit by a bullet."

Alec was puzzled. "What unit were you with?"

"The San Andres Light Horse—Brazos River country, Milam and San Andres actually. We were in the Fourth Texas Mounted Rifles of Sibley's Brigade. I was first sergeant of D Company." He spoke with deep pride. "Can I take my hands down now, Major?"

"Drop your gunbelt," Alec ordered.

The belt was dropped. "Hate to drop a fine Colt like that," Truitt said ruefully.

"Hazards of war, Texas." Alec dropped to the ground from the low edge of the roof. "Get in there," he added, jerking his head toward the sacristy door. "Light the candle on the table."

The soft yellowish candlelight flickered and flared in the slight breeze coming through the open door. Truitt looked at the scabrous plaster peeling from the adobe brick walls. The barrel vault overhead was stained black from many campfires. "Cozy," he murmured.

"Sit down! Hands flat on the table! Now, mister, talk and make it good!" Alec ordered.

Truitt was several inches short of Alec's six feet plus. He was broad of shoulder, with a horseman's narrow waist. His lean mahogany-hued face was bisected by a bold nose. The mouth was overhung by a thick black dragoon mustache sprinkled with gray. His long hair was black, with gray at the sides. His sun-squinted eyes were a curious-looking bottle green and as hard as jade. He wore a gray flannel shirt, a buckskin jacket, and a sweat-stained, badly faded broad-brimmed hat of Rebel gray.

"Talk is dryin' work, Major. You got any liquor?" Truitt asked.

Alec fished out a flask from one of his saddlebags and tossed it to him. Truitt drank deeply, then passed the flask back. "*Salud y pesetas,*" he murmured.

"Good health and wishes," Alec responded in English.

Truitt reached slowly inside his jacket and brought out a packet of cigars. He tossed one of them to Alec. They lighted up together from the candle, eyeing each other closely—hard gray and hard green.

"You were likely figgerin' on heading partway to El Potrero until the moon rose," suggested the Texan.

Alec nodded. "You're well informed," he said dryly.

"There ain't no 'Paches between here and there, leastways it was that way until dusk. You'll be about as safe as you'll ever get on this *camino*. In fact, I'll accompany you to Pete Kitchen's. That is, if you have a mind to allow me."

"Now, why would you want to do that, Mr. Truitt?" Alec asked thoughtfully.

Truitt grinned. "I'm just a good-hearted fella, sortta like the Good Samaritan. My friends call me Brazos. You want to know why?"

"Simple, you come from that country."

"You've got a quick mind, Yank."

Alec shrugged. "One of my better characteristics, Rebel," he said modestly.

They grinned at each other like two men who wanted to know and like each other, but neither was yet sure of the other.

"You didn't answer my question about why you wanted to ride with me to El Potrero. You see, Brazos, I don't quite buy that Good Samaritan bullshit," Alec said.

"I happened to hear in Tucson you were riding this way. I followed you as far as Tubac, then lost you. Figgered you had moved faster than I thought. I rode on past here to El Potrero and found out you hadn't gotten there yet, then backtrailed to here to make sure the 'Paches hadn't gotten you and sure enough, here you was. Simple, ain't it, Major?"

Alec shook his head. "No, Sergeant. Now tell me the truth."

"You'll need someone to back you after you leave El Potrero. I'm a fightin' man by profession. I speak good Mex and some 'Pache."

Alec studied the Texan. The rising wind whined disconsolately through the nave. "And where am I going after I leave El Potrero?" He asked quietly. "Perhaps you read it in the *Arizona Citizen*?"

Brazos shook his head. "I heard it in the Congress Hall. It was something about a rancho in which you were interested down in Atascosas Mountain country. Specifically, Soledad Canyon."

"You didn't learn that in the Congress Hall," said Alec. "One of three people in Tucson might have let it slip, but I doubt it. Lieutenant Tony Beaudine, General Crook, or Belle Valois. Neither Tony nor Belle would talk. That leaves General Crook, and why he would take you into his confidence I really don't know."

Brazos nodded. "It *was* General Crook," he admitted.

"How is it that an obviously unreconstructed Rebel like yourself gained the confidence of General Crook to learn something I had requested him to keep in absolute silence?"

Brazos reached for the flask. "The Gray Fox doesn't want anything to happen to you, Kershaw."

"Why so?"

"Because he doesn't want the army to lose you, and also because, you damned fool, he happens to think a helluva lot of you."

"Perhaps you're a government agent?" Alec asked softly.

"I'm a contract scout. Took me about seven years after Appomattox to take the oath of allegiance. I did some soldierin' down in Mexico. Scouted for the army in New Mexico. Got restless. Did some prospectin' down in Sonora. Best way to look at that country is through the bottom of a glass. I went broke. My horse died. My burro strayed with all my gear. I started back to the States on foot. Nearly got killed by scalp hunters west of Magdalena. See here?" He pushed back his straight black hair to reveal a ragged four-inch cicatrice along the scalp line. "I calls that my two-hundred-peso scar. It was bad enough when the Apaches and Yaquis tried to kill me, but when the *gambusinos* wanted to cash in my scalp because it looks like Apache hair, then it was time to split-ass out of Mexico. I returned to Camp Lowell and hired on as scout again. Couple of weeks or so ago, when you took that leave of yours to come down here, Crook sent for me and told me to keep an eye on you. Sortta like an insurance policy." He grinned.

Alec grinned back. "Well, I'll be damned! So the Gray Fox has sent me a bodyguard and an informant to boot. I'm overwhelmed with gratitude! Now, get the hell out of here! Go back to George Crook and tell him I'll return to the service when and if I'm good and ready! Tell him too that I don't need a bodyguard!"

"I got my orders, Major," Brazos said stubbornly.

"These are my orders, Texas! All *six* of them!" The hammer of the Remington clicked back into full cock.

Brazos found himself looking over the pistol barrel into a pair of chilling gray eyes. He was generally a cool one, though despite a churning gut. "Shoot and be damned to you! I got my orders I tell you!"

Alec studied him for a moment, then let down the hammer to half-cock. "You don't scare worth a shit, Truitt," he said.

Brazos grinned weakly. "It's only a front. You almost made me wet both legs right here in this holy place." He fished out a soiled fold of paper and handed it to Alec. "Take a looksee at this, if it helps any."

Alec scanned the paper.

Major Kershaw: This will introduce Ben Truitt, government scout and one of the best in the business. He could be on a par with yourself. I couldn't find a better man to send after you to make sure you don't get yourself killed on your harebrained excursion to Soledad Canyon. Ben Truitt shares some of your capacity for getting into trouble, and in and out of dangerous situations. If you must pursue a chimera, I can't think of a better companion to have with you than Ben Truitt.

Remember this too, Alec; your country and I, as your commanding officer, need you in your true capacity, that as an officer of Apache Scouts. I hope and pray you may return here before you get yourself killed in some violent and messy manner.

Sincerely,
George Crook

It was genuine. The handwriting was that of Crook and the text was pure Crookese.

"Well?" Brazos asked.

Alec nodded. "Get your horse, Texas."

Later, as Brazos rode a horse the color of distant rain beside Alec, he looked sideways at his traveling companion. "Couldn't figger out why you wanted to leave the army," he commented. "I knew your father, Colonel Calhoun, who was on Sibley's staff when we Confedrits invaded New Mexico. You were known as Lieutenant Alexander Calhoun then." Brazos knew he might be treading on dangerous ground, but, like Alec, he had the manhunter type of personality; he had to know everything in detail about his quarry. He did not really think of Alec as his quarry, of course, but rather as his responsibility.

"I heard you had changed your name from Calhoun to Kershaw after the war," he continued. "Great name, that, in New Mexico Territory. I heard about Quint Kershaw during the war. Saw him in action at Battle of Valverde. Helluva fightin' man. Is he some relation to you?"

"In a way," Alec replied.

Brazos was in rare form. "Maybe you changed your name out of admiration for Quint Kershaw after your father come over to the Confederacy?"

"Maybe," Alec admitted. It was time to change the subject. "What happened to you after the New Mexico Campaign?"

"Retreated with the Sibley Brigade back to Texas. Spent the rest of the war fightin' in Louisiana. Had a nice battery of brass howitzers captured from McRae's Battery at Valverde. *Your* old battery, Major."

Alec grunted. "Cheap profit for you Rebels. It was the only gain you got out of the whole goddamned campaign."

Brazos nodded. "Keno. Come to think of it, there wasn't much profit for either side during the war, speakin' of the good men both sides lost in it."

"You're a man of rare insight, Brazos," Alec said quietly.

The moon cast a pale glow against the eastern sky. The only sounds to be heard were the night wind rustling the brush, the soft thud of booted hooves, the whisper of girths and soft creaking of saddle leather, and now again the snorting of one of the horses.

Alec looked back along the road. It *seemed* deserted.

"You always have the feelin' of being watched in this country," Brazos said.

Alec nodded. "I had that feeling when I left Tucson and went up north about two weeks ago. Now, *Mister* Truitt, I wonder *who* could have been following *me?*"

Brazos shrugged. "Like I said, you always have that feelin'."

They rode on through the growing moonlight, a pair of hardcase fighting men, and, in a sense, drifters to boot.

CHAPTER 17

PALE MOONLIGHT SHONE ON THE DISTANT WALLS OF EL Potrero and glistened from the small creek that flowed south of the ranch buildings. Alec focused his field glasses on the environs of the ranch, sweeping the heights beyond the valley, then the fields and orchards.

"They're around somewhere," Brazos said. "I can *feel* 'Paches even when I don't see 'em. You see anybody yet? Maybe they've been here, massacred and looted, then left."

Alec shook his head. "They would have torched the buildings." Then he saw the head and shoulders of a sentry pacing on the ramparted flat-topped roof of the ranch house. The dying moonlight shone softly on a rifle barrel as he moved around the roof on his ceaseless vigil. A dog barked, then another, and soon there was a whole baying chorus arousing the echoes. The sentry ceased pacing. Moonlight reflected from his field glasses as he studied the two strangers.

They rode toward the ranch. The only real safety at night at El Potrero was to be behind thick loopholed walls. During the day fieldworkers slung rifles from their plow handles or kept them close at hand while they worked. There was a twenty-four-hour guard on the ranch house roof, and other lookouts. To go unarmed, even within sight of the house, was to invite attack.

"*Alto!*" the sentry commanded. He rested his rifle on the rampart while covering the two horsemen.

They raised their hands high. "It's Alec Kershaw and Ben Truitt!" Alec shouted. "I hope they really know who you are, Brazos," Alec said out of the side of his mouth.

"They know me all right," Brazos said.

Pete Kitchen met them at the door. The room behind him was unlighted. The old Indian fighter knew better than to silhouette himself against light. "Vicente!" he shouted. "Take the *caballos* to the stable!"

Alec thrust out his hand to grip Pete's. "Eternal vigilance is the price of safety, eh, Pete," he commented.

Pete nodded. "You always did have a way with words, Alec."

Manuel Ronquillo, the fierce-mustached Mexican who was *segundo* to Pete, lighted a lamp after the door was closed. Francis Verdugo, who was in charge of the thirty Opata Indians who had been brought up from Sonora as both farmhands and garrison, went to get food and drink. The two Mexicans were the best of frontiersmen—magnificent horsemen, expert marksmen, and topnotch vaqueros. Their intelligence was unquestionable. Their courage was legendary.

"You see any 'Pache sign?" Pete asked as Alec and Brazos sat down to eat.

"*Nada,*" Brazos replied around the warm napkin of a thick tortilla wrapping the meat, beans, and cheese fired up with hot sauces. He looked up. "But you know they're around all the same."

Pete stoked his pipe. "They hit us twice one day a month ago."

"It's that bad?" asked Alec.

Manuel nodded. "Once they attacked three times in twenty-four hours. That was during the war when there wasn't a soldier left in the whole damned Territory."

Pete poured the tequila and placed a bóx of long nines on the table. "Drink and light up," he said. "They're due about any day now. They're hanging around in the hills watching us all the time. They damned near come on schedule."

Pete was Kentucky-bred. During the Mexican War he had been wagonmaster for the old Mounted Rifles, now the Third Cavalry, along the Rio Grande. After the war he had gone to Oregon with the Rifles and taken his discharge there. He'd worked the gold fields of California for a time, then arrived in Tucson in 1853. He had settled at El Potrero, The Pastureland, north of the later established international boundary line between Mexico and the United States. He chose a hillock surrounded by 160 acres of green fields and pasturelands watered by two creeks that came together at a waterfall just west of the hillock. There he had built his sixty-foot-square stronghold. The foundation was of rock. The walls were of adobe and were two feet thick. There was an outside stairway to the roof. The roof parapet was four feet high and loopholed.

"So you're still determined to take over the Soledad Rancho?" Pete asked Alec.

Alec nodded. "This trip, of course, is only for scouting purposes."

Manuel shook his head. "This is not the time to take over that place, Alec. Look how long we've struggled to hold this place and the end is not yet in sight."

"You're still here, Manuel," Alec reminded him.

"You'll have nothing like this at Soledad. Don Aguilar has been hanging on there with his front teeth for years. They don't have a stronghold such as El Potrero. Their houses are fortified, of course, and there is the old mission church there which can be used as a refuge, but they can hardly work the fields and tend their stock with the Apaches always a threat. Then too, the *gambrusinos* are a danger.''

''Perhaps you know of the legend of lost treasures there said to have been left by the Jesuits after they were expelled from Mexico,'' Francis Verdugo put in. ''Some say Don Pedro has found it and hidden it away again somewhere in Soledad Canyon.''

Pete smiled. ''A fairy tale. My God, how many tales are there of lost treasures in these old missions? Many! How many treasures have ever been found? None!''

''Given time, I can hold that place against El Diablo himself,'' Alec said stubbornly.

Pete studied him. ''You have a lot of Quint Kershaw in you. I know the story of how he settled on the Plains of San Augustine before the war and held it against all comers, even during the war itself for that matter. Alec, my good friend, haven't you had enough of war by now?''

''Have *you*, Pete, my good friend?'' Alec challenged. ''Not by a damned sight! Why do *you* stay here under constant threat?''

Pete shrugged. ''*Yo tengo raices aqui*— I have roots here,'' he quietly replied. ''But you, you are different. You're a soldier, born and bred. You talk of leaving the army and settling in that damned and doomed Soledad Canyon, but I don't believe you, not for a moment. Your destiny is the army. One way or another, you'll return.''

Brazos nodded. ''Keno. That's why I'm here with him, Pete, risking my life and hair, to keep him from losing the same. I agree. He belongs to the army.''

Alec refilled his glass. ''Bullshit!'' he said emphatically.

''So be it,'' Pete said. ''There's no use arguing the point with you, Alec, at least now when you've got that stubborn mind of yours set on Soledad Canyon. In that case, I'll give you all the help I can. It won't be much, I'm afraid. Once you leave El Potrero, there's nothing we can do for you. The range of our rifles and our marksmanship are the best and only insurance we have of surviving. What aid will you need for your madness?''

"A pair of good pack mules. Some tools. Food supplies. A large scale map of the area."

"I can let you have everything but the map. There's no such map in existence, but you've been to Soledad before, so you should know the way."

"You'll need at least half a dozen good men with you, Alec," Manuel said. "Can we spare them, Pete?"

"Possibly, for a time anyway," Pete said with some reluctance.

Alec shook his head. "Two men, traveling by night and hiding by day, have a far better chance of getting there. Perhaps I can persuade Don Pedro to leave some of his men with me, at least after I have decided to take over the place. In time I might be able to recruit more and convince them to bring their families with them."

Later, as Alec lay in bed, Brazos pulled off his boots, shirt, and trousers. He seemed out of character at the moment. "What's bothering you, Rebel?" Alec asked.

"You think something is bothering me?" Brazos demanded testily.

Alec nodded. "It's obvious."

Brazos pushed back his hair to reveal the scar along his scalp line. "I told you about this back at Tumacacori, but I didn't say exactly where I got it, did I?"

Alec shook his head. "You didn't."

"It was in the Atascosas just this side of the border."

"So?"

Brazos paused, then spoke quietly. "I said I had been prospecting. I was actually lookin' for that treasure Manuel spoke about. That's when I was attacked. How many men have you ever seen who survived a scalping?"

"You're the first."

"So maybe I'm living on borrowed time by going back there."

"Maybe you are. You can always go back to Tucson. I'm not holding you."

It was quiet for a time. "I got my orders from General Crook," Brazos said at last.

They could hear the faint footfalls of the sentry pacing on

the roof over their heads. Somewhere in the hills east of the rancho a wolf howled twice. A moment later another wolf howled, this time from the north. Minutes passed, then a solitary howl came from the south. It was quiet again. The sentry had stopped pacing.

"Best imitation I've ever heard," Brazos said. "But they forgot the west."

A moment later a wolf howled from the west.

Alec raised himself on an elbow. "Chiricahuas—two-legged lobos calling to their brothers. The people of the desert, canyons, mountains, and moonlight. They own everything out there, and yet they own nothing."

As Pete had said: *The range of out rifles and our marksmanship are the best and only insurance we have of surviving.*

Alec blew out the lamp.

The Chiricahuas were still in the hills the next day and for a week after that. There could be no leaving the ranch until they were gone. One day smoke plumed up to the south and raveled out against the clear sky like lank black hair stretched across faded blue linen. The next day a traveler told of an ambushed wagon train. There had been no survivors.

At El Potrero the even tenor of life went on despite the constant Apache threat. There were rolling grasslands and hills to the west and east. During the day the Apaches could not be seen but they were always there, hidden in the grass. At dusk they moved in closer. They had spidery patience, waiting, waiting for the one chance to strike.

Pete Kitchen had planned well, a testimony to that being his lone survival in an otherwise abandoned area. There was plenty of water in an ever-flowing stream that ran a hundred feet south of the house. In addition, there was a hand-dug well about sixty feet deep at the rear of the house and twenty feet from the smokehouse, where Pete smoked his hams and bacon for sale in Tucson and to the various army posts. They were famous throughout the southern part of the Territory. There was a big hay shed, with one-room adobe quarters for the Indians and Mexicans who worked on the ranch backed up against its east wall. The hay shed was fifty yards behind the house and faced it. A dugout afforded shelter for the women and children in case of attack.

The ranch had its own graveyard, with a six-by-eight-foot mortuary close by it. There Pete buried travelers who had been killed on the *camino*. There were quite a few of them. Two of Manuel Ronquillo's sons killed by Apaches lay there. A man named Wright and two boys who had been ambushed at dawn one morning at the corner of a field just south of the house were buried in the graveyard. One day a man named Tiburcio had gone to the waterfall at the spring without his rifle. Pete had found him dead, floating in the pool, the next day. He was buried beside the others.

El Potrero was a busy place from dawn to dusk despite the constant threat of attack. The clanging of the blacksmith's hammer echoed from the hills, mingled with the braying of mules, the shouting of men, and the cries of the children at play or work. The forge glowed most of the day as shoes were beaten out for horses, mules, and oxen. Wagons were mended. Tools were made. A constant *tap, tap, tapping* came from the saddle shop where saddles, harness, and other leather goods were made. Smoke rose from the chimneys of the house, quarters, and the smokehouse. Chickens scratched and squawked underfoot. Laundry was beaten clean by the *lavenderas*, the laundresses, on the flat rocks along the creek fifty yards south of the compound. Pete's far-famed hogs wallowed in the mud pits below where the laundry was washed. The hogs were always a favorite target of the raiders, who sometimes shot them full of arrows until they looked like gigantic porcupines.

Pete had invited Alec and Brazos to ride with him on one of his customary inspection trips, a part of which was to check on La Loma de Oro, his gold mine a mile and a half east of the stronghold. It was another reason for him to hang on at El Potrero.

Santiaguito, Pete's twelve-year-old son, came dashing up on his pony as the three men mounted. "Can't I ride with you, Father?" the boy shouted.

Pete shook his head. "Too dangerous, son."

"But the Apaches have left!" the boy cried.

"We're not sure of that, Santiaguito. No, you must stay here. Don't stray too far. We'll be gone only an hour or so," Pete explained. He touched his riding mule with his heels and rode toward the rutted trail that led to the mine, leaving behind a badly disappointed boy, who had taken greatly to Alec and Brazos.

"He's a good boy, but badly spoiled by everyone here, including myself, I'm afraid," Pete said. "He must have his way. I want to try and break him of that habit. Otherwise, when he grows up and has to make his own way in the world, he'll have one helluva time. All this will be his someday. He'll have to learn to control himself before he can control other people."

Brazos smiled. "He's a fine boy, Pete. If I was to have a son, I'd want one just like him."

"Hear, hear," Alec said.

La Loma de Oro was a busy place. Twice a month the *arrieros* would bring their *conducta* of burros up the straggling trail to pack the ore in cowhide sacks to be taken out, melted, and turned into gold ingots. At least a third of Pete Kitchen's men stood guard in the mine compound, for every gringo outlaw and Mexican *ladrone* in the Southern Arizona Territory and Northern Sonora knew of Pete Kitchen's mine.

The staccato clanging of the alarm at El Potrero carried to the distant hills and echoed back and forth. Pete, Alec, and Brazos had already left the mine and were riding to the east, out of sight of the stronghold. Without a word Pete turned his mule, kicked it hard in the sides, and set off at breakneck speed down the slope heading home. Alec and Brazos followed him, yanking their rifles from their sheaths and levering rounds into the chambers. A sound like the cracking of a huge shingle came from near the stronghold, followed by a rippling, irregular crackling of gunfire.

When the three hard-riding horsemen came in sight of El Potrero, they could see the field hands running toward the stronghold followed by a few mounted men who turned in their saddles and fired back at unseen targets. Puffs of gunsmoke rose and were carried off by the fresh wind. Manuel

Ronquillo was one of the horsemen. He reined in his horse, turned in the saddle, sighted carefully, and then fired. A staggering, hatless figure came out of the concealment of a *bosquecito*, spun around once, and then fell heavily. Plumes of smoke followed by thudding discharges came from here and there among the trees and brush. One of the retreating field workers was hit and fell. Manuel drew his horse to a halt, slid off, threw the field worker over the saddle, then set off at a dead run, leading the horse to the stronghold. The loopholes in the buildings and on the house roof spouted thick white smoke. A haystack upwind suddenly burst into flames. The smoke began to drift toward the buildings. In a little while swiftly darting figures used the cover of the smoke to get near the stronghold.

Pete galloped past a brushy ditch. An Apache with bent bow popped up like a jack-in-the-box, aiming for his back. Alec and Brazos fired at the same instant. The slugs drove the warrior back into the ditch. The arrow flighted harmlessly upward.

They galloped into the ranch compound, dismounted, and flung the reins to some of the nearby ranch hands. The horses were led at a run into the big barn, the door slammed shut behind them. The kitchen door of the house was opened just long enough for Pete, Alec, and Brazos to enter, then was shut as well and barred behind them.

Pete looked about. "Where's Santiaguito, Rosa?" he shouted to his wife.

Her face paled. "Was he not with you?" she cried.

"Christ no!" Pete yelled. "The rest of you! Look for him!"

Men and women scattered at his order. Some of them went through the rooms, others ran through the gunfire to the dugout, hay shed, barn, and other outbuildings. In a few minutes they all reported. The boy could not be found. No one had seen him.

Alec went up the ladder two steps at a time to reach the roof. He crouched low and ran to the parapet. Francis Verdugo silently pointed to a haystack two hundred yards south of the house. He handed his field glasses to Alec. Alec stood up straight, heedless of the Apache bullets, and focused the glasses on the haystack. A pony stood close to it. Even as he watched, the pony stampeded toward the stronghold. Then he made out a small form at the foot of the stack. At first Alec thought he was dead or wounded, then he realized with horror that incredibly, despite the noise of the guns, the boy was sound asleep. A hundred yards beyond the haystack a group of warriors came from hiding and trotted toward the boy.

Alec, followed by Francis and five of the Opatas, plunged down the outside staircase. Just as they did so, Brazos came from within the house and followed them. They sprinted toward the haystack.

A bullet plucked Francis's hat from his head. One of the Opatas went down with a leg wound. Arrows flew toward them, the sun flashing from the polished shafts.

No spurred and booted white man could outrun a moccasin-footed Apache, or even give him a good race, Alec knew. The average Apache could even outrun a horse on the side of a mountain. The warriors reached the haystack first and loosed their cane-shafted arrows tipped with obsidian or razor-sharp tire iron into the boy who had just sat up. The Apaches then turned and loosed a cloud of shafts toward the approaching men. One of the Indians drew a knife, bent, and gripped the boy by his long dark hair, then swiftly circumscribed the small head and yanked the scalp free. He waved it in the air, scattering bright droplets of blood while he yelled in triumph. He probably knew who the boy was. It was a great victory over Don Pedro. The Apaches ran back to shelter without losing a man. They had a great prize, a medicine scalp, that of the beloved son of that White-Eye devil who had so long defied them with his cursed stronghold in the very heart of their country—the country of the Chiricahuas, and none other—Spaniard, Mexican, or American.

Francis reached the haystack first. A trio of flaming arrows plunged into the dry hay, and it flared up at once. The Mexican stared at the small body, stuck with arrows like some strange growths. He snatched up Santiaguito, threw him over his shoulder, and ran heavily back toward the stronghold. Alec, Brazos, and the Opatas gave him covering fire.

Brazos turned toward Alec. His eyes were wild. "Let's charge the filthy, murderin' sonsofbitches!" he yelled hoarsely. "Come awn, damn you! We can get a few of them at least!"

"Get back to the house, you damned fool!" Alec shouted.

A bullet plucked at the slack in Brazos's jacket. Another ripped through the crown of his hat. He dropped his smoking empty Spencer. He drew his Colt with one hand and his bowie knife with the other and turned to charge like a berserker. The eerie Rebel yell began to rise in his throat. It was promptly cut off when Alec slammed the eight-inch barrel of his Remington pistol alongside Brazos's skull and dropped him neatly. Before he hit the ground Alec caught him and lifted him over his shoulders, then dog-trotted toward the house.

The attack subsided as suddenly as it had come. Thick smoke from burning haystacks and several wooden outbuildings soared upward, mingling with the gunsmoke. Under that cover the Apaches swiftly withdrew, carrying their dead and wounded, except for three who lay out in the open within excellent gun range from the roof of the house. It became very quiet except for the crackling of flame and the occasional crying out of one of the wounded at the stronghold.

The hatless men and the women with their black rebozos over their heads stood in the bright afternoon sunlight beside six open graves. Five were for grown men; the sixth was for a twelve-year-old boy—Santiaguito. Two of the larger graves were for an Opata and a Mexican. Three held the bodies of the Chiricahuas who had been left behind by their war party. It had been the wish of Doña Rosa that it be so. She and the women of the house had recited Ave Marias and burned candles for the souls of the newly dead. Brazos had asked Doña Rosa if she had included the Apaches in her prayers. "Oh, yes, Señor Brazos. They are all God's children, are they not?" She had replied simply. Brazos had had nothing to say.

Alec, always the observer, looked at the faces of the mourners as the dirt was shoveled in on top of the crude wooden caskets. He gazed in turn at the tear-stained faces of the women, the awe and curiosity of the younger children, the expressionless faces of the Mexican men, and the stolid bronze faces of the Opatas.

"Though I walk in the Valley of the shadow of Death," Pete began. His face was as expressionless as that of an Opata. For the first time in his fifty years he had, overnight, begun to look his age. He had dearly loved the sunny-dispositioned Santiaguito. Deep within himself he felt he was responsible for the boy's death. He blamed no one but himself, although it had clearly been the duty of the field workers to bring the boy in from the fields with them at the sound of the tocsin. He completed the prayer and raised his head. Without another word he put on his hat and stalked to his riding mule. He mounted, touched the mule with his heels, and rode toward the trail to the mine and then beyond.

At dusk Manuel Ronquillo walked with Alec and Brazos to their horses and a pair of small but sturdy Sonoran pack mules. "Don Pedro asked me to say farewell to you," he said. "His heart is full, my friends."

Alec nodded as he tightened his saddle girth. "We understand."

Manuel placed a hand on Alec's shoulder. "He also said to ask you not to go into the Atascosas, at least for some time. Until it is quieter, at least."

Brazos spat to one side. "And when will that be, amigo?"

Manuel shrugged. "Who knows the minds of Los Indios Diablos? Even God himself would have trouble guessing. Your great peril will be between here and Don Alvarado's rancho. Once there, the old mission is a safeguard against attack. The Apaches' superstition is a better weapon against them than bullets. However, as you know, this does not apply to the rest of the rancho. Once the Apaches attack, Don Alvarado and his people run to the mission for safety."

Alec turned. "I don't intend to spend my time in Soledad Canyon sitting on my ass in a mission church, scared to death of a bunch of Apaches."

Manuel handed each them a flask of Baconora and a thick packet of black Sonoran twist cigars. "My prayers and hopes go with you, my friends, along with these simple gifts."

They mounted, and each of them took the lead rope of a pack mule. They rode down the slope toward the *camino*.

"Vaya con Dios!" Manuel called out. He watched their shadowy figures until they vanished into the darkness. *"Vaya con Dios,"* he repeated to himself. He paused. *"Acaso,"* he added quietly. "Go with God—*maybe.* . . ."

CHAPTER 18

ALEC AND BRAZOS REACHED THE VICINITY OF SOLEDAD Canyon in the lonely, completely isolated Atascosas range. It was several hours before dawn. They had traveled slowly and laboriously from El Potrero through some of the roughest terrain imaginable. It brought back to Alec the memory of Anne's and his journey through the foothills of the Chiricahuas to Muerte Canyon. It was the first time he had thought of her in two weeks.

They had halted on the heights overlooking the dark depths of Soledad Canyon. It was cold, but there could be no lighting of a fire for coffee. A pinpoint of light in that high clear atmosphere could be seen for miles. They sat there huddled out of the wind in the cold shelter of a rock gully, gnawing on tough jerked beef and hard biscuits.

Alec finished eating and passed his flask to Brazos. "Cheer up, Rebel. There will be good tortillas and frijoles, and coffee laced with brandy at the rancho."

"Piss!" Brazos retorted sourly. His head still ached at times from the buffaloing Alec had give him at El Potrero. Still, he was grudgingly grateful it had been done by an expert—an amateur could have fractured his skull.

Brazos finished eating, picked out a bit of stringy beef from between his teeth with a dirty fingernail, drank deeply, wiped his mouth, and looked sideways at Alec. "If they're still there," he said quietly.

Alec glanced up at the eastern sky. The stars had begun winking out. The first faint trace of pewter light tinged the darkness. "We'll know soon enough."

"You couldda mebbe talked me out of chargin' them 'Paches," Brazos growled.

Alec leaned back against a boulder and pulled his heavy serape up around his neck. "*Bullshit*, Mr. Truitt! You're like all them damned Texicans, always ready to charge hell with a bucket of water. I've seen you Rebs in action too many times."

Brazos shrugged. "You might be right at that, but I still think you should have *tried* to talk me out of it at least."

"Jesus! With bullets fanning my ass all the way back to the stronghold while carrying you on my back?"

They grinned at each other in the dimness.

The sky brightened, became translucent with mother-of-pearl light, then with a vast silent explosion the full glory of a southwestern sunrise burst across the landscape. Soon they could feel the first faint heat of the coming day.

They surveyed the terrain through their field glasses. The elevation was about four thousand feet. The Sonoran border was ten miles south. To the northwest were the Las Guijas Mountains. To the north were the Cerro Colorados, and beyond them the Sierraitas. Beyond these two ranges and between them and the Baboquivaris was the Altair Valley. Baboquivari Peak was just catching the first warming glow of the rising sun.

A thin tendril of smoke rose high in the quiet dawn air from about the position of Soledad Rancho.

Brazos looked sideways at Alec. "Breakfast fires?"

The sun had not yet lighted the deep canyon. There wasn't much of man to be seen unless one knew where to look. The pale walls of the old mission church and its belfry were just about visible. The smoke did not rise from there.

"Well?" Brazos queried.

Alec cased his glasses. "Can't tell anything yet."

They led the horses and pack mules down the precipitous slopes strewn with great jagged chunks of rocks protected by a bristling chevaux-de-frise of cacti and thorned wait-a-minute brush. They kept as close under cover as possible. At times one or the other of them would scout ahead seeking the best route. It was near to noon when they reached level ground at the foot of a vast talus slope. The smoke was still hanging against the sky, but the morning wind blowing up the heights had thinned and raveled it out. The rancho buildings were as yet unseen behind a dense screen of trees and shrubbery. Only the tiled roof of the mission topped by its bell tower was visible, the arched belfry looking for all the world like a huge gaunt skull with staring empty eye sockets.

It was inordinately quiet. The wind was blowing toward the heights down from which Brazos and Alec had descended.

Brazos scratched inside his shirt. "Should be hearin' something by now—a braying mule, sounds of work, maybe people calling out. . . ."

They looked at each other. "Stay here," Alec said at last.

"I'll go," offered Brazos.

Alec shook his head. "Keep yourself and the animals under cover."

Alec removed his spurs and took his Winchester. He worked his way toward the rancho, taking advantage of every scrap of cover. He crossed a fallow field into the edge of the thick grown bosque of trees that had sprung up, watered by the ever-flowing springs of the canyon, and which served to conceal the rancho from view.

The pungent smell of woodsmoke came through the trees. Alec stopped short. The odor was mingled with something else. It instantly brought back a horrifying memory to him— the night after the Battle of Chancellorsville, when the dry woods had caught fire from the gun flashes, trapping the screaming wounded along with the silent dead in the thick blazing tangle. Both Union and Confederate troops had worked side by side in some cases to get the wounded out of the roaring inferno. They had saved some. Most had been burned to death. He passed a dirty hand across his face as though to erase that memory. It did not remove the stench of burned flesh.

He moved on, then stopped short again. A flask made from a dried animal stomach lay at his feet. He picked it up. The stopper was missing. It was empty, but the pungent smell of tequila was still present within it.

He stalked closer toward the rancho. The smell of burned flesh became much stronger. He reached a clearing bright in the sunlight. A faint trace of shadow moved across it and then was gone. He looked up. High in the sky over the canyon and almost in the eye of the midday sun a *zopilote* hung on the wind with motionless white-patched, black wings. It was likely the scout. There would be others before long.

It was unnaturally quiet. There were no sounds of life from the fields and rancho, no chirp of bird, no bray of mule or whinny of horse, voice of man, woman, or child at play. There was no sound except the faint dry rustle of wind-stirred leaves.

Alec saw the first of the rancho buildings through the screen of trees. Now, added to the leaf rustle could be heard the faint chuckling of the water running through the stone-lined *acequias,* or irrigation ditches, through which the springs had been channeled to water the garden, orchard, and the fields beyond. The smell of burned flesh had become a noisome stench.

There would be no one alive there. He leaped across the *acequia,* took three full strides, and saw the first of the bodies sprawled on the beaten earth of a path. It was a woman. Her wide skirts and many petticoats had been pulled up around her head. She was naked from the breasts down to her sturdy legs clad in white cotton stockings. The light-colored earth around her concealed head was stained black with drying blood. Alec flipped down the skirts and petticoats from her head, disturbing a swarm of buzzing flies. The woman's throat had been cut. She had been scalped, ears and all. The face flesh, released from the taut pull of the scalp, had sagged into a grotesque caricature of what probably had been a pretty young female Mexican. Alec had long been used to the sight of violent and bloody death, but this was almost too much for him. He flipped the clothing back up over her head and pulled down one of the petticoats to cover her nakedness. There was no doubt in his mind but what she had been brutally raped.

He walked around the compound. The large ranch house

had been gutted by flames. The fire had eaten through the roof beams and allowed the flat earthen roof to collapse into the interior, a still smoking mass of beams, earth, furnishings, and likely some of the dead who had been trapped within. There were other bodies scattered like windblown chaff in every direction. All had been scalped—man, woman, child. All the women, regardless of age, showed bitter and bitten signs of rape. One woman floated face downward in the pool at the springs, with her skirts floating over her. The water was still tinted pink from the blood. There was no need to go into the fields to seek other dead. They would be there. Already the *zopilotes* were winging in that direction.

Alec walked to the old mission church, hopeful that perhaps someone had survived, although he knew better. The wide double door gaped open. Dark spots of blood stained the well-worn stone steps and entry pavement. He padded through the shadowed, echoing nave toward the sanctuary. The primitive, age-darkened oil paintings of the Virgin and Child and various saints had been slashed through, with their throats cut. A carved crucified Christ was broken in two at the neck, the head, hanging awkwardly to one side, was held in position by a few wood fibers.

Alec stooped short at the sight of a male body sprawled in of the altar, lying on its back along a low stone step. He had been scalped, and the side of his skull was crushed in. The jaws had been broken and the mouth hung open, thick with drying blood. He was Don Alvarado, a man who had always been inordinately proud of his thick thatch of gray hair and mouthful of gold teeth. Both his vanities had been brutally torn from him. Alec hoped to God he had not been alive during that obscene violence. He had evidently sought sanctuary in the church.

"Sanctuary?" Alec bitterly asked aloud, thinking of Manuel's words. "What sanctuary?"

He covered the old man with a hanging torn from the wall. "Heaven receive your soul, Don Alvarado," he said softly. "You earned peace and rest long, long ago."

Alec returned through the tomb-quiet of the compound. It must have been Apache work. The skulls of every one of the dead had been crushed to let out the vengeful souls. Yet Manuel had said they would never directly attack the old mission church, being held back by superstition. The Mexican knew that country and its lore and legends better than anyone. Still, they had done so. It was a puzzler.

Alec and Brazos tethered the horses and mules upwind at the edge of the woods to avoid as much as possible the stench of blood and death. Even so, the animals shied and whinnied, plunging about at the ends of their tethers and trembling violently.

Brazos gripped his Spencer so hard his knuckles turned white. His eyes were wide in his head as he walked around the rancho amid its horrors. He looked like he had been at El Potrero when he had seen the body of poor little Santiaguito.

"Take it easy," Alec counseled. "There's nothing we can do about it now."

"Did they get *all* of them?" Brazos demanded.

"I found no live ones," Alec replied quietly.

Brazos looked toward the rutted road that led south through a narrow pass to the border. "How long ago you figure they was here?" he asked.

Alec shrugged. "They probably hit this place just before dusk, about the time people were eating their evening meal."

"Murder, rape, and loot! It's their only way of life." Brazos spun on a heel and ran back toward the animals.

"Where the hell do you think you're going?" Alec demanded.

"To cut for sign! Maybe they haven't gotten too far yet!" Brazos flung back over his shoulder.

"They're long gone, you damned fool!" Alec shouted. "You know they don't stay any longer than they have to after such a raid!"

Alec waited until Brazos reappeared, fighting his shying gray. He held up a hand to halt him. "Listen, Brazos," he said quietly, "they're long gone. You know how fast they can move. Don't leave here." He reached for the reins.

Brazos's face was a set mask, wide-eyed, with teeth showing behind his tightly drawn lips. "Get out of the way, damn you!'' he grated. ''You won't stop me with a buffaloing this time, Kershaw!''

Alec knew better than to try. There was a madness in the Texan; the *killing* madness.

The gray was off in a shower of gravel.

Alec found a plow. He hitched the mules to it and plowed deep in a soft patch of earth shadowed by the trees behind the church, and beside the simple Campo Santo of the rancho. He deepened the furrow with a spade.

Brazos returned late that afternoon on his worn-out horse. He found another spade and without a word he attacked the earth and made it fly until the mass grave was deep enough for all the bodies.

When they were done, Alec handed Brazos the brandy flask. ''Well?'' he asked.

''Left a trail as wide as a caravan on the Santa Fe Trail. Headed straight for the border. I found their last night's camp on the Sonoran side.'' His voice died away.

''Go on,'' Alec urged. ''Get it out of your system, man!''

The set mask had returned; the eyes looking through it seemed haunted and far away. ''They had taken three younger women with them. Had a helluva drunken celebration, looks like. Empty liquor keg. Broken bottles. Empty flasks. Blood splattered all over the ground where I found the stripped bodies of the women.'' He paused, got control of himself, then continued in a dull monotone. ''Mass raped. Throats cut. Pumped full of bullets. Scalped, ears and all.'' Brazos turned on a heel and stalked away.

Alec waited, smoking a cigar to get the smell of death and decay out of his nostrils.

Brazos came back slowly. He picked up the flask of Baconara and emptied it.

''How many do you figure there were?'' Alec asked.

''Twenty-five or thirty. It's not like Apaches to waste cartridges like that. Cutting a throat is *dead* dead.''

They loaded the bodies on to the balky, trembling mules and brought them to the grave. The bodies were bloating and emitting pent-up gases. Alec and Brazos wrapped them in whatever they could find—blankets, saddle blankets, extra clothing, serapes, and canvas, some of the items partially charred from the flames, and many of them bloodstained.

Alec removed his hat after the bodies were laid in the grave. "The Lord is my Shepherd, I shall not want . . ." he began. When he was done, they quickly filled in the grave, then hauled rocks from a nearby hillside to cover the earth. As a final deterrent to wolves and coyotes, they sprinkled gunpowder from a keg they had found in an unburned shed and touched it off. They stood there in silence as it hissed and flared, then the smoke drifted off in a pungent white cloud.

"Amen," Brazos said as they turned away.

The sun was slanting far to the west over the Baboquivaris. An eerie quiet fell over Soledad Canyon. Even the birds were silent.

Brazos hammered together a cross out of rough timber while Alec cooked a meal over an open fire well upwind from the grave. The Texan drove the cross down into the soft earth. He tamped the soil tightly around the shaft.

They lighted cigars over their brandy-laced coffee. "What's next?" Brazos asked.

"This is my place now," Alec replied.

"You can't work it alone, and you sure as hell won't get any Indians or Mexicans to come here to work. They never did like this place anyway. They'll shun it like the plague now."

"That's the bitter truth," Alec agreed.

"Anyway, the 'Paches won't be back, at least for a helluva long time." Brazos studied Alec. "I can't figure you out, Kershaw. Doesn't all this bother the hell outta you? Don't you want to track them down and wipe them out like piss ants?" His voice died away as he saw the look on Alec's face.

"You're certainly not dumb enough to really think this doesn't bother me. I'm not like you, running around half-mad, shouting for vengeance. I keep these things within myself."

Brazos nodded. "It was stupid of me to say what I did."

"Forget it, Rebel." Alec relighted his cigar and puffed it into life. "If I'm one way, Brazos, that is, to keep things inside, why are you just the opposite? You strike me as a first-rate fighting man, a professional to the core. But no professional would go off half-cocked like you did at El Potrero and again this afternoon. Why?''

After a moment or two Brazos spoke quietly. ''It's usually not my way to talk about it.''

''You don't have to. Forget it, Brazos.''

The Texan shook his head. ''I can tell you, Alec. You see, I went back to Texas after the war, back to the Brazos, intending to join my family again and the girl I had planned to marry. I found out they had wanted no part of Yankeedom in Texas after the surrender. They'd pulled out and gone up to the Double Mountain Fork of the Brazos south of the Panhandle, as far away as possible from the Yankees. I started out to find them. I was stopped by a cousin of the girl. Her family and mine were kin and had gone together to the Double Mountain Fork. Wasn't no use in going, my fiancée's cousin said.'' His voice died away. Then he spoke again in the same dull monotone. ''The Comanches had got them all. I went away to Mexico with Jo Shelby then. When I came back, I rode up to the Double Mountain Fork of the Brazos. It's a vast tawny land of wide open plains, where you can see the sky from under a horse's belly. Nothing there but grass, sun, wind, and solitude, and a mass grave that the wolves and coyotes had dug up right after the burial. Mebbe I went a little loco then. I don't remember much for days. Now, when things happen like the killing of little Santiaguito and these people here, the madness comes back and I ain't fit to be around anybody.'' He looked sideways at Alec. ''You know,'' he added, ''I can't see anything in front of me then but the murdered through a red mist like blood.''

''You had better learn to control it, Brazos,'' Alec advised. ''If you don't, it might very well lead to your death.''

There was a hauntedness to Brazos's eyes. ''Maybe it will. *Maybe it will . . .*'' It was as though it didn't really matter. Part of him might very well have been buried with his family and the girl he had loved back on the Double Mountain Fork of the Brazo.

The rancho and its environs were deathly still. Alec left

Brazos with his morbid thoughts and scouted around through the bosque and orchard, checked the animals, then headed back. Something rolled underfoot. He picked up an empty Spencer .56/50 rimfire cartridge case. In a few minutes he had found a dozen more. He walked slowly around the compound and found another score of the same empty hulls. He returned to Brazos.

The Texan nodded as Alec showed him the shell cases. "I can do better than that," he said. "Look here." He went to his saddle and returned with a Spencer carbine. "It's exactly like mine, Alec. I found it lying behind a rock, where those raiders had camped." He handed it over.

Alec knelt close beside the fire and examined the carbine. It was marked "Spencer Repeating Rifle Pat. March 6, 1860. Manufactured at Providence, R.I., by Burnside Rifle Co., Model 1865." It was also stamped "U.S." The weapon showed no traces of hard usage so customary in the Territory, and no indication of the rough and careless use typical of Indian handling. He knew this particular model, although manufactured during the latter part of the Civil War, had not been delivered until after Appomattox. Some of them had been issued to troops in the West, but the majority had been stored in arsenals.

"Well?" Brazos asked.

Alec looked up. "This has hardly been in use long. Have you seen many of these in the hands of the troops?"

"Only a few. Most of them have the Sharps single-shot cartridge carbine."

"Where did you get yours?"

"It was issued to me at Fort Lowell, part of a shipment that had come in from New Mexico earlier this year. About March, I think it was. What's on your mind, Alec?"

"You know about the recent so-called Apache raid on the wagon train at the San Simon, of course."

Brazos nodded. "That was when you rescued Mrs. Sinclair."

"There were cases of Spencers, Sharps, and Colts in that wagon train, as well as thousands of dollars of paymaster's funds in greenbacks. The raiders got away with the lot, and they weren't Apaches, Brazos. They were *gambrusinos*. I'm quite sure they were the same bunch who hit a group of Mexican smugglers at Muerte Springs, killed and scalped them, made off with their horses and mules and thousands of Mexican silver 'dobe dollars. In both instances the raiders tried to make it look like it was Apache work, the same as the murderers who hit this place.''

Brazos stared at Alec. "How can you be sure of that?"

"There are many signs that they were not Apaches if you tie them all in together."

"Such as?"

"Apaches don't scalp much as a rule. They might take a few for a victory celebration or ritual purposes, then they are discarded. They don't keep them as trophies like the Plains tribes. Apache war parties also do not rape while on the warpath. Their warfare is based on their religion. They think rape weakens their medicine. And I've never seen this particular model of a Spencer in their hands, and even if they had them, they'd never waste cartridges like we've seen here. I've seen them fill bodies with arrows until they looked like porcupines, but *never* have I seen them waste cartridges on the wounded or dead. Also, if they *were* Apaches who raided here, why would they suddenly violate one of their taboos by pursuing Don Alvarado into the mission church, a place of which it is well known they have a superstitious dread? In addition, you saw the body of Don Alvarado, with his jaws broken open so that the gold in his teeth could be pried out. Apaches have no use for gold. It means nothing to them other than what they could trade it for—weapons or liquor mostly. Further, no Apache would ever be careless enough, or drunken enough, perhaps, to leave behind a fine repeating carbine like the Spencer you found. I think the killers of the smugglers at Muerte Springs, the raiders of the wagon train at the San Simon, and the bunch who raided here are quite possibly one and the same.''

They sat silently in the dimness illuminated only by the dying flames of the fire. At last Brazos spoke. "How much longer do you figure on staying here in this stinking charnel place?"

Alec stood up. "I can't work this place alone. As you pointed out, no one would come here to help me now after this massacre. There is nothing of value to be stolen. No one else to be murdered and left for the wolves and coyotes."

Brazos stood up. "And those raiders left a trail a blind man could follow."

They doused the fire, cached that which they would not need on the manhunt trail, turned the pack mules loose, and rode from that silent place at moonrise. Somewhere on the heights wolves howled. This time they would not be Apaches. The mass grave would no doubt be excavated by digging paws as soon as the man creatures were well gone.

Alec and Brazos cleared the pass and rode southeast into Sonora. By the time the moon had fully risen, illuminating the vast leanness of the desert, the trail of the raiders could be followed even without the two manhunters dismounting to cast around for sign.

CHAPTER 19

ALEC AND BRAZOS PASSED NORTH OF MAGDALENA, FOL-lowing the trail of the raiders. They wanted no part of Mexican officialdom. Both of them figured there might be a price of their heads—Brazos because he had served in the past with Maximilian and for a few later indiscretions, Alec due to his recent confrontation with Captain Ramon Gonzalez, Tenth Cavalry. If either or both of them were caught in Sonora, there would be no trial, but hangrope justice, or perhaps the notorious Mexican Ley del Fuego, the "Law of Fire," during which the prisoner was given a head start of say fifty yards more or less before the shooting would begin. If a mistake were made, the executioners would piously cross themselves and say, *sotto voce*, "God will sort the souls."

It was an aging *arriero*, a muleteer, who had once lived in the remote and almost forgotten *placita* of Los Padres, who gave them the destination of the raiders. "There can be no doubt but that the men you seek are heading for Los Padres on the Rio San Tomas.''

"Why are you so sure?" Alec asked.

The old man quickly crossed himself. "Because that is the place of such *gambrusinos* and scalp hunters. It is worth one's life and scalp to go there. The few people who live there are virtually the slaves of the damned *ladrones*. The only reason they are left alive is to maintain the place, grow food, and supply their daughters and young wives for the pleasure of those hellions. Even the soldiers will not go there."

"Who leads these outlaws?" Alec asked.

The muleteer looked quickly back over both his shoulders as though he might be overheard. "A demon straight out of hell itself—Chico Diaz," he said in a rusty whisper.

The little *placita* of Los Padres was twenty miles south of the border and northeast of Magdalena, situated on the headwaters of the Rio San Tomas. Headwaters was an exaggeration. The riverbed was almost perpetually dry except during the rainy season, but there had always been good wells in the area, tapping a large reservoir of groundwater trapped above a vast shelf of hardpan. The first sight Alec and Brazos caught of Los Padres upon the dun-colored monotony of the desert was a line of cottonwoods along the course of the dry riverbed with an eroded church belfry rising gaunt above them like a great rotten tooth. There two hills met on the valley floor. That was the way of towns on the Sonoran Desert—sandy streams converged, spring runoffs and summer rainstorms collected and flowed until they sank into the arid ground. Cottonwood trees took root and grew where water was and so too it was the way with towns.

Alec and Brazos lay hidden on one of the two hills that met at Los Padres, waiting while the sun sank and long shadows pooled themselves, inking in the hollow places first. They could plainly see the small plaza bordered with scrofulous and sickly paloverde trees gray with dust. People moved listlessly about it and the few straggling streets, but they were too far away to be identified as *gambrusinos*. There was no doubt but what the outlaws were in the town. Their trail had been obvious for some miles. A large walled corral was filled with horses and mules, far more than would have been needed to serve the few townspeople. There seemed to be much activity around the old church and mission buildings, but the area was shielded from a good view by the tall cottonwoods along the riverbank.

Smoke began to rise from the house and some of the mission buildings as dusk came over the land. The wind died away as the desert cooled with the coming of darkness. There would be a last quarter moon that night. As the shadows lengthened, the pale yellow lights from the town seemed to twinkle in the clear atmosphere.

The faint sound of a guitar came to the two tired, dirty, and hungry men on the hill. The wind had begun to shift. It brought the faint odor of cooking food to the men.

Brazos scratched inside his shirt. "I swear to God I can smell chili frijoles," he muttered.

"Smells more like chamaca," Alec suggested.

"You like chamaca better than chili or tacos?"

"Right now I'd settle for anything."

"We got any of that brandy left?"

Alec shook his head.

There was a long silence.

Brazos drank the last of the water in his canteen. "What the hell are we doing here anyway? Sitting on our tired asses on a barren hilltop twenty miles from the border without food, water, or brandy? Two goddamned fools thinkin' of taking or maybe thirty hardcases! *What the hell for?*"

Alec grunted sourly. "You act like it was all *my* idea."

"You could have talked me out of it if you had tried."

"Bullshit!" Alec snapped.

Brazos grinned wryly. "Well, we're here, ain't we? What's next, Major, *sir*!"

Alec looked down at the town, now quite dark except for a few glimmers showing through cracks in the shutters. The only place where lights were carelessly shown was in the church and in one of the old mission buildings. "We need food and water first. It's all down there. We'll have to go in to get them. Do you have any better suggestion?"

There was no reply from Brazos.

It was close to midnight when two dark and furtive figures slipped noiselessly down the hillside to the riverbed just north of the *placita*. Guitar music, voices, raucous singing, and boisterous laughter came to them from the church. Alec stood watch while Brazos went for water. He came back with four dripping canteens. They drank thirstily. Brazos went to water the horses.

Alec moved like a disembodied shadow through the side streets. The townspeople were evidently sitting tight in their houses, fearfully awaiting results of the drunken brawl in the church. Some of their women were no doubt in there. It was the price one paid to live in comparative peace in Los Padres.

Alec broke in through the rear door of the small *tendajon* and found bread, dried beef, and fruit. He was lucky enough to come upon a half-gallon jug of tequila hidden behind some canned goods. He cached the food and tequila just north of the church. In passing a long, low warehouse between the river and the church he had scented a sweetish, sickening stench. He returned and managed to pry open a window shutter with the blade of his sheath knife. He slipped inside and was immediately enveloped by the stench. His empty stomach almost revolted. He risked lighting a lucifer, then turned away, sickened even more. There were bales of dark hair still attached to the reeking scalps stacked along one wall. He searched through the darkness and located case after case stacked to the ceiling. The lettering on them identified them as United States property, and their contents as Spencer repeating carbines and Colt revolvers. Other cases held cartridges for the weapons. There was no doubt as to their origin.

Baishan and his warriors had moved in after dark from the south close to Los Padres. They had been raiding as far south as Ures on the Rio Sonora without much success. They had lost two warriors and one novice. All they had to show for it was half a dozen horses and a pair of mules, and nine old rusty muzzle-loading muskets with the stamp of the king of Spain on them. They had also captured three sturdy boys ranging in age from nine years to twelve. Perhaps they would in time replace the Chiricahua losses on the raid.

The Chiricahuas had passed Los Padres on their way south. At that time the big corral had held only a few horses and mules, hardly worth the bother, and further, it was known to be a den of the *Nakai-Yes—gambrusinos* and scalp hunters. It was a place to be avoided. Now, however, it was quite evident that the *gambrusinos* had returned and brought with them a wealth of fine mules and horses. The corral was almost full to overflowing with them. The temptation was too much for the Chiricahuas. They had to salvage some measure of success from their raid.

The *Nakai-Yes* were deep in their drinking and carousing. So sure were they of their impregnability in Los Padres, they had not set out sentries. Too, they were sure of the safety of their horses and mules because of the high-walled adobe brick corral they had forced the people of Los Padres to build for them.

Baishan's warriors worked noiselessly, smoothly, and with utmost efficiency. Buckets of water were brought from the well nearest the corral. Two warriors scaled the wall. They dropped rawhide reatas back down to warriors waiting below. They then jumped down inside the corral. A pair of warriors scaled the reatas from the outside, bringing up with them a reata apiece attached to the bail of a full water bucket. They drew up the water buckets and straddled the wall top, slowly pouring water on the reatas held on either side as they were sawed back and forth. The tough rawhide cut into the wet adobe inch by inch. As the buckets were emptied they were lowered, instantly refilled, then hoisted up again. When the sawing reatas wore out from the constant friction, they were replaced. The townspeople had not bothered with the safeguards used by many ranchers in Sonora, who mixed sharp bones and flintlike stones into the wet adobe bricks to forestall just such a procedure as was now being practiced by the Chiricahuas, nor had they bothered to trough the wall top, fill it with earth, and plant it thickly with spiky cactus.

Alec clambered out of the window and flattened himself against the wall. Discretion told him persistently to get the hell out of there. He had his evidence, but whom could he turn to for help? Brazos and he could not turn the trick alone. He could not go to the Mexican authorities. True, they might believe him, and even take steps to investigate, but what would be the result? The weapons were United States property—they hadn't been stolen from the Mexican government and might very well make a nice addition to their own arsenal. The scalps would mean nothing to them. The State of Sonora paid money for them. They didn't question the sources. After all, hair was hair, and if it was the same color as Apache hair, who was to know whether or not it was Apache? In addition, Alec did not know for certain whether or not this was the band of Chico Diaz, and if Milo Chaffin, or whoever he was, was one of his subordinates. There was but one way to find out.

He eased into the thick shadows of the cottonwoods and worked his way toward the rear of the church. *Where the hell was Brazos?* The Texan hadn't been too keen on coming into Los Padres despite his hatred of those who had destroyed Soledad Rancho and its people. Maybe he had pulled foot and headed back to the border.

Any noise Alec might have made was fully drowned out by the raucous din emanating from the church. Lamplight flooded from the windows and cast oblong panels on the sun-baked caliche of the ground. Now and again fleeting shadows passed across them. The sound of guitar, violin, and tom-tom came from within the building.

The years had caved in the roof of the sacristy, filling the interior thigh-deep with roof beams and broken tiles. Alec entered and crawled across the room to the doorway that led into the sanctuary. The door was still there, hanging on a lower hinge, and tilted sideways, allowing a narrow triangular opening into the interior.

Alec peered through it. The scene he saw might well have been a poor imitation of a woodcut of Dante's *Inferno*. A half-naked woman was cooking over a fire set in a hole in the sanctuary floor. Here and there on the floor of the nave lay men and women dead drunk. One pair was coupling openly in the middle of the floor. Wood and tobacco smoke lay in thick, rifted layers high up beneath the vaulted ceiling. Bottles and fragments of food were littered from one end of the nave to the other.

Then Alec saw him—Chico Diaz, swaggering in from the front of the church. The angry red scar of the cut Alec had dealt him across the brow at Belle Valois's place shone vividly. He moved among his minions like Satan at a Black Mass, lacking only horns, a tail, and cloven hoofs. Chico was drunk, but not so drunk that he was out of control. His eyes darted back and forth, seeing everything, missing nothing. He turned and shouted back to someone at the front of the Church. Then Milo Chaffin appeared wearing the uniform Alec had seen him in at the Congress Hall. The two of them spoke together. Chaffin grinned and slapped Diaz on the shoulder, nodding all the while. Some new deviltry being planned, thought Alec. He had his evidence. It was time to go. He clambered back over the broken tiles and roof beams to leave the sacristy.

Adolpho Gomez, *segundo* to Chico Diaz, staggered a little as he left the church, dragging a sixteen-year-old girl along by her wrist. He unbuttoned his trousers to urinate against the back wall of the sacristy just as Alec dropped to the ground from a sacristy window with his back toward Adolpho and only five feet away. The girl screamed. Adolpho had left his pistol within the church, but he never went anywhere without his hideout knife, the short, curved, and deadly *saca tripas*, gets the guts. Alec whirled. His rifle was in his left hand. He ripped the derringer through the wrist spring clip, cocked and fired it sideways toward the belly of the Mexican at the same time Adolpho knife-struck Alec on his left hand side. The blade slid down through the skin and penetrated deeply below the lower rib. Adolpho bent over from the impact of the slug. The second bullet struck him on top of the head. He was dead when he hit the ground. The girl ran screaming off into the darkness.

Baishan had come to the plaza to withdraw his sentries. The pistol shots sounded within fifty feet of him. He jerked his head at his sentries. "*Ugashe! Ugashe! Ugashe!* Go! Go! Go!" he shouted.

An uproar broke out in the church. Men shouted. Boots

thudded against pavement. Baishan turned to run, then saw the tall man staggering toward him out of the shadows, holding one hand hard against his left side and carrying a rifle in his right hand. Baishan drew his knife for the killing thrust. Light from a window of the church fell full upon the face of the man. There was instant recognition from Baishan. How Never Still came to be there was beyond the comprehension of the Chiricahua, but it was obvious he was among enemies. All that mattered was that he was there, obviously wounded, and would likely be killed within a few moments.

"Perico!" Baishan shouted to one of his sentries. "Cover me!"

Alec fell toward Baishan. The Apache lowered a shoulder, then grasped Alec's right arm to draw him across his shoulders. Alec dropped his Winchester. Perico snatched it up, levered a round into the chamber, and opened fire on the shouting men running from the church. Baishan trotted slowly toward the corral. A rifle cracked. The slug creased Alec along the left side of the head. He seemed to fall head over heels into a deep black void, and then knew no more.

Perico held back the Mexicans from the shelter of a cottonwood, emptying the full magazine of the repeater, then he raced after Baishan. The other warriors and novices were already driving the horse and mule herd through the gap they had cut into the wall.

"Drive them north!" Baishan ordered.

They loaded Alec across a saddle, tying his wrists and ankles together under the barrel of the horse. There was no time to tend his bleeding wounds. A novice mounted his horse and galloped off into the darkness, leading Alec's alongside the running herd, with the herd between them and the Mexicans. In a few moments the Chiricahuas were beyond the river, heading north to the border and safety.

CHAPTER 20

THE APACHES DROVE THE STOLEN HERD HARD, EVEN though they knew the people of Los Padres had no means of pursuit. It was the Chiricahua way—come unseen, ambush or steal as swiftly as possible, then head back to their stronghold. If pursuit came too close, they would scatter like quail, and either rendezvous at some predesignated place, or if that was not feasible, return home alone. By the false dawn they had reached the vicinity of Muerte Springs, but the main party rode past it, giving it a wide berth. It was too dangerous for such a large herd and a score of warriors to stop at the springs, and in any case, there was a superstitious taboo about the place.

Despite the taboo, however, Baishan; Perico, or White Horse; and Klij-Litzogue, Yellow Snake, decided they must stop at the springs. Their wounded charge might not be able to live through the sun-cursed and waterless ride across the desert to the Chiricahua stronghold.

There was always a brooding silence about Muerte Springs. It was so real to the senses, it seemed to have a solidity to it. There were no birds to chirp a sleepy welcome to the coming day. Perico and Klij-Litzogue watered the horses while Baishan tended to Alec. They were in a hurry. They knew they could outrun any late pursuit from Los Padres, but they also knew they could not outdistance the vengeful spirits who haunted Muerte Springs. There was no sign of them now. They could be resting or perhaps were abroad on the desert. How long would it be before they awoke or returned to the springs? Still, Baishan's warriors knew of his debt to the white man they had called Never Still. According to the code, it was a debt that must be repaid, however difficult.

Baishan soaked free the wadded cloth, now stiff with dried blood, he had stuffed inside Alec's shirt to staunch the bleeding. It was one of Alec's shirt-sleeves. The Apache examined the ugly wound. It might be too early for signs of infection. He had some experience in treating wounds, but those had been in Chiricahua flesh. Perhaps such treatment might not work on a White-Eye.

"The sun is rising, Baishan," Perico warned.

Baishan jerked his head. "Leave now if you are afraid," he said angrily.

They would not leave him out of loyalty and pride, frightened as they were of this haunted place.

Baishan removed the headband he had bound around Alec's temples over the scalp wound. The Apache nodded. The wound was superficial. He bathed both wounds, then hacked off one of the fleshy joints of a nopal cactus and split it down the middle. He twisted the bullet from one of his rifle cartridges, sprinkled the powder over the belly wound, and ignited it. The cauterization forced a sudden groan from Alec. He opened his eyes, saw the stern face of Baishan above him, then lapsed back into unconsciousness. The Chiricahua placed the split cactus joint on the wound and bound it into place with a strip of cloth he cut from his own *himper,* the kiltlike garment he wore above his baggy white trousers. He then cleansed the scalp wound and bandaged it with Alec's remaining shirt-sleeve.

The sky was lightening with the coming of the sun.

"Hurry!" Yellow Snake pleaded.

They hoisted Alec into a saddle, then bound him in position with their reatas. They rode swiftly from Muerte Springs.

The sun rose, coloring the eastern sweep of the sky with amber mare's-tail clouds. It was as though half the sky were afire.

White Horse turned in his saddle. "Look," he said, pointing.

Faint dust was rising a few miles south of the springs. *Gambrusinos* or Mexican soldiers? The Chiricahuas quirted their horses into a dead run. They could ride them to death and shift over to the spares if necessary. Their safety was almost assured, but would Never Still survive the hell of the day and the arduous ride?

Brazos saw the dust just beyond Muerte Springs as the sun came up. He urged Alec's dun on toward the springs. His gray had gone down ten miles out of Los Padres. Brazos had gone into the town just in time to hear a woman's scream instantly punctuated by two shots, and another scream, followed shortly thereafter by more shooting. He had reached the rear of the church, skirted a mission building, then saw an Apache staggering past, bent under the weight of a man wearing a hat. Lamplight from a flung-open door fell on Alec's bloody face. Another Apache had stepped in behind them and opened fire on the *gambrusinos* streaming from the church. Brazos had darted back into the shadows and almost ran into several swift-moving, bushy-headed figures running noiselessly toward the big corral. A few moments later there came the thundering rush of a herd being driven from the corral toward the northern darkness. Brazos had seen Apaches riding like centaurs, forcing the herd onward. In a little while he'd caught sight of one of them leading a horse with a man lying belly downward across the saddle. There was no question in his mind but that the man was Alec.

Muerte Springs showed no signs of life as Brazos cautiously approached it, leading the weary dun. He put the field glasses on the almost indiscernible wisp of dust rising out on the desert to the northeast. Far beyond the dust rose the looming Chiricahua Mountains. A broad trail of hoof-marks passed the springs to the west and continued on to the northeast. There were other hoofprints around the springs themselves, mingled with moccasin tracks. He watered the dun, then prowled around, cutting for sign. An empty rifle case rolled under his foot. The rim was not marked by a firing pin, so it had not been fired. A moment later he found the bullet. A wad of bloody cloth lay beside the pool. Brazos opened it out. It was a sleeve from a heavy gray issue army shirt patched at the elbow with buckskin. It was from Alec's shirt.

Brazos led the horse to the northeast. It was a country dominated by the Chiricahua Apaches. No white man in his right mind would cross that vast expanse during daylight hours. The Texan felt he had no choice. Once, late in the afternoon,

he saw dust rising far behind him in the vicinity of Muerte
Springs. He plodded on. The Chiricahua range seemed to
grow in stature and become increasingly ominous the closer
he came to it. The feeling came over him that a man in that
vast sun-ravaged terrain could be likened to a louse crawling
over the body of a giant.

CHAPTER 21

THE BIG MOUNTAIN, CALLED THE CHIRICAHUAS MOUN-
tains by white men, was where Baishan brought Alec. It was
a virtual Eden, hardly marked by the Chiricahuas, whose
stronghold it had been for untold generations. Before their
time it was the home of the Ancient Ones, those who had
dwelt in the great caves honeycombed in the creek canyon
walls and left their crumbling rock dwellings there. The range
was forty miles long and twenty wide at its broadest point,
rising to crests almost ten thousand feet high. The mountains
stretched north and south, a giant rampart between the San
Simon Valley to the east and the Sulphur Springs Valley to
the west. The Big Mountain was a complicated maze of soaring peaks and deep canyons, with a climate, vegetation, animal life, and scenery so different from its surroundings, it
was as if it were an isolated island far out at sea.

The creek canyon was a gigantic gash driven into the very
heart of the mountains. The result was a vast kaleidoscope of
colors. Buff-colored rock, shaded into streaks and patches of
glowing salmon and bright pink, seemed as though it had been
daubed on with a mammoth painter's brush. Brightly tinted
cliffs and castled rock rose high on both sides. Tributaries of
the creek tumbled down steep, heavily forested slopes in cas-
cades and miniature waterfalls to form the crystal-clear main
stream. Pines and oaks studded the canyon walls, making soft
patches of green against the bright-colored rock.

The upper part of the range was covered with a magnificent northern evergreen forest broken only by jewellike

meadows. Groves of white-stemmed aspens sheltered feathery fern brakes and luxuriant underbrush. Each summer the Chiricahuas were a fairyland of wildflowers. Sunny slopes were spread and dappled with golden helenium. Meadows were abloom with iris, verbena, and larkspur five to seven feet high. The shaded woods were brightened by columbine, Indian paintbrush, silene, penstemon, meretensia, and many other varieties.

The Big Mountain had the exhilarating sweep of spaciousness. Great rocky ribs were outflung from the lofty serrated backbone of the heights. From the uppermost areas could be seen the vast green hollow of the main creek valley, and far out to the east, over the level amber stretches of the San Simon Valley, the blue New Mexican mountains lined the distant horizon.

It was to this remote eyrie Ben Truitt came seeking Alec Kershaw.

Vague, indistinct, and confusing memories drifted in and out of Alec's mind as he lay on a pallet of grass and deerskin in a wickiup of the rancheria of the Chiricahua Apaches somewhere on the Big Mountain. He remembered a tortuous and agonizing ride across the desert and up into the mountains. Sleep had been the only relief from the pounding headache and intense fever that at times threatened to drive him out of his mind. He knew, of course, that somehow he had been rescued by Baishan from certain death at Los Padres and brought here. He had recognized Kaw-Tenne, Looking Glass, who was a female *diyi*, or medicine person, with many powers, among them treatment of the severely or critically ill, those hovering at death's door. It was she who had made the moccasins Alec had intended for Belle Valois, but instead had given to Anne at Canyon Muerte. Although Baishan and Looking Glass came and went, there was one person who remained steadfast beside Alec's bed, sleeping on a pallet across the large wickiup. He was The Runner. In a moment or two of lucidity the young Chiricahua had told Alec he was a student of Looking Glass's in his aspirations to become a *diyi*. His reasoning, of course, was that his rescue from certain death by the removal of his gangrenous forearm was a sign from Herus, or Child of the Water, son of White Painted Lady. Therefore he must dedicate his life to healing the sick. He had much to learn, and there was no better mentor than Looking Glass, whose famed skill was known throughout Apacheria and who was in almost constant demand, like a physician on call.

It had been the high-pitched ululating cry of the women welcoming back the victorious raiding party from the great feat at Los Padres that had brought Alec back from the deep blackness that had overwhelmed him. He'd had the impression of sliding down a slippery mound of sand into the unknown depths. There were vague, indistinct, and dreamlike recollections of being guided to a camp where someone whose face was nothing but shadows had offered him fruit. Something had warned him to refuse. Upon awakening, he had told Looking Glass of his dream. A look of intense horror had crossed her face. "You have been in the underworld," she had whispered, glancing back over both of her shoulders. "Thank Yosen you refused the fruit. Had you taken it, you'd have had to remain there. I fear for you, Never Still. If it happens again . . ." Her voice had died away, and she hurried deeply distraught from the wickiup. Her warning was plain enough—the next time it would be death.

Alec was not sure how many nights the Victory Dance would continue. The horses and mules would be distributed among the whole band. Some of the mules would be butchered and eaten at the feast. Each member of the raiding party would have his chance to dress and act as he had done during the raid, while singers described his heroics in detail. The thudding of the drums, the shuffling and stamping of moccasined feet, and the continual singing had been going on for four nights, The Runner told Alec. This night would be the time for the Circle Dance, when the men and women danced in separate lines, alternately approaching each other, then dancing apart. It would last all night.

Alec lay half-awake, burning with fever, watching the shadows of the dancers passing back and forth between him and the blazing bonfire in the center of the camp. Finally, he fell into a troubled sleep. The forbidding darkness came again. He felt himself on the steep sand slope, sliding down, and down, struggling to climb back to the light, gaining one step, losing three, and descending ever lower and lower. He started awake and sat up, crying out in fear.

Looking Glass came quickly to him. She place a cool hand on his burning forehead. "Is it the dream again?" she asked.

Alec nodded. He fell back heavily on the pallet, staring up at the low roof.

"How does it look?" The Runner asked.

She shook her head. "Get Baishan! *Quickly!*"

The chief came to the wickiup, still wearing his battle dress and carrying the weapons with which he had performed the Victory Dance.

Looking Glass crouched beside Alec, her mouth close to his, blowing the power from her lungs into his. She looked up at Baishan. "There is fire from some evil spirit within his body. He has gone twice down into the underworld. If he slips past me and goes there again, he won't return. I have done all I can. There is only one way he can be saved now. The Curing Dance."

Baishan nodded. He left the wickiup and immediately put a stop to the Circle Dance. He rapped out his orders for the Curing Dance to begin.

Brazos heard the shouting voice and then the sudden cessation of the thudding drums and the cries of the dancers. He lay hidden atop a low cliff overlooking the Chiricahua rancheria. He had lucked out in his approach to the camp, and had crept in close under cover of darkness. So secure were the Chiricahuas in their stronghold, they had but a few sentries out, and most of them quite far from the camp itself, watching the outer trails. Brazos had avoided those guards. It had been simple enough to locate the camp. He had followed the dull throbbing of the drums for three nights, hiding out by day, guided to the rancheria by the pounding as a fog-bound mariner is guided by foghorns or channel buoy clanking bells. There had been no sentries on this cliff.

The fierce and realistic pantomiming of the dancing warriors and the ominous beating of the drums had made his skin crawl. He wondered whether he was going mad, to have been stupid enough to come to the very heart of the Chiricahua stronghold. Or perhaps it was the tequila he had been absorbing steadily ever since he had entered the Big Mountain country. He was almost positive that his likelihood of finding Alec still alive was minimal. He was utterly exhausted from his ride to the Big Mountain and his perilous ascent to the area of the rancheria. The terrible fear of the Chiricahuas had ridden his back like a harpy. He had had very little food on the journey. That and the powerful tequila had made his mind do strange things. He knew he should turn back. Still, he struggled with overpowering drowsiness and fought to keep his eyes open. If he fell asleep for too long, it would be only a matter of time before he was discovered by the Chiricahuas. In that case his end was too horrible to comtemplate.

Eerie quiet settled over the encampment, broken only by the faint Aeolian humming of the night wind through the tall pines, and the subdued crackling of the bonfire in the center of the dancing area.

Time passed. Brazos dozed on and off. He opened his eyes to see a tall man brought out to lie on a pallet near the fire. His bare torso was bandaged below the rib cage. Another bandage was bound around his temples. There was no mistaking Alec Kershaw! What were his captors up to? It could not be torture and death. They would not have brought him all the way to the Big Mountain if that had been their intention.

Wood was piled on the fire. It blazed up. Smoke and sparks soared up to and above the treetops. The people gathered silently in a ring around the dancing ground. A drummer thumped a stiffened rawhide with a hooped stick. The people began to sing. The eerie whine of a cane flute rose above the singing, almost as though it were a signal to someone, or *something*. . . . It was well after midnight. There was a feeling of taut expectancy in the air. The people were waiting, waiting for something to happen.

An eerie buzzing sound like gusts of wind-laden rain came from the dark woods. Through half-closed eyes Brazos saw a grotesque black-hooded man-figure suddenly appear as though engendered from the shadows and wreathing smoke. He was bare from the waist up and wore an elaborate arc-shaped framework on his head. His torso was painted white with black dots. His waist was girdled by spruce branches. Feathers on each side of the hood appeared like donkey's ears. He held a forked stick in his left hand and a long cord in his right. At the end of the cord was a flat rectangular piece of wood painted in primary colors. He twirled the wood around his head and from front to rear, causing the peculiar sound Brazos had heard.

In his exhausted, tequila-laden state, Brazos was only dimly aware of four more masked figures who joined the first dancer. They danced in a peculiar strutting style, like great turkeys, advancing to and retreating from Alec. Brazos removed his hat for better concealment. He bound tall-stemmed grasses and thin leafy branches around his head. He bellied closer and closer to the edge of the cliff until he lay right on top of it, twenty feet above the talus slope that extended downward another sixty feet or so to the level ground just short of a row of wickiups.

Hours passed, and still the figures came and went at intervals. The people sang and shuffled in a sober sort of dance. Once Brazos saw a rather plump and very attractive squaw approach the dancers, sprinkling them with a yellowish powder and blowing her breath on them. There was something strange-looking about the right side of her face. At first Brazos thought it was painted. He risked putting the field glasses on her as she turned toward the fire. Brazos closed his eyes in a sudden horror. The right side of her face was a mass of scar tissue, as though it had once been thoroughly raked and ravaged by the red-hot tongs of Satan himself.

The interminable dancing went on and on. The sky began to gray with the coming of the false dawn. The singing and commotion rose to a higher pitch until the din became horrendous. The scarfaced squaw dashed about sprinkling her powder. The chanting became louder. The din was ear-grating.

Brazos had fallen asleep. The cliff edge crumbled. He fell

and landed heavily on the decomposed granite of the talus slope. The breath was knocked out of him. He tumbled ass-over-teakettle down the slope, enveloped in a cloud of dust. He crashed into the fringe of brush at the bottom of the slope, passed between two wickiups, and came to a dust-and-smoke shrouded halt at the very edge of the dancing ground, not twenty feet from the nearest dancers.

The drumming, singing, and dancing stopped abruptly. There was an immediate and compelling silence broken only by the subdued crackling of the dying fire, the soughing of the fresh dawn wind through the treetops, and the hissing of the subsiding decomposed granite of the talus slope.

Brazos got slowly to his feet. His attempt to refill his lungs made an eerie husking sound. His Colt was in its holster. His Spencer lay at the top of the cliff. He knew he'd not be able to get more than one round fired out of the six–gun before he'd be overwhelmed. The Texan had always been a good poker player. It was time to bluff, or to die suddenly. He forced a careless grin onto his dry, bewhiskered countenance and slowly raised his arms. The icy sweat of fear ran down his sides. He wet himself, both legs.

The Chiricahuas are a brave people, afraid not of mortal man or savage beast, but they are dreadfully fearful of their gods and the Mountain Spirits. The hooting of Bú, the Owl, that moon-eyed bird of the night who speaks in the voice of the recent dead, could stampede the bravest war party.

The tense moment hung in the balance as the awed people stared at this mysterious being who had appeared as though dropped from the sky, wearing a headdress strangely similar to that of the masked dancers of the Mountain Spirits who had just completed the Curing Dance, looking at them with alien eyes through the wreathing dust and smoke, while raising his arms in a threatening gesture.

Alec had regained full consciousness with the coming of the dawn. The burning pain in his side wound seemed to have subsided. The throbbing in his skull had abated. He raised himself on his elbow and looked toward the strange apparition who had stopped the Curing Dance by his abrupt appearance.

Baishan broke the spell. He drew his knife.

"Beware the *Gode*, Baishan!" Alec shouted with all his power.

The cry stampeded the entire band, including Baishan. Men, women, and children flew in all directions away from the Gode, legging it at full speed, crashing through, over, or under anything in their way—each other, wickiups, underbrush, rocks, and logs, at frenzied speed. In a matter of moments there wasn't an Apache in sight. The noise from their stampede through the forest died away.

Brazos slowly lowered his arms. He hiccuped. "Well, I'll be goddamned," he drawled.

Alec sat up. "You've got a helluva spectacular way of making an entrance, Rebel," he suggested dryly.

Brazos grinned weakly. "It wasn't rehearsed. Sortta made it up on the spur of the moment."

"Just what the hell do you think you're doing here?"

Brazos shrugged. "I'm your blood brother, ain't I? Besides, I got my orders from General Crook to take care of you and bring you back to the army, where you belong. Who's this Gode anyway?"

"A vague, shadowy, and dreaded spirit being," Alec explained. "Sometimes it comes in the night to warn you. It's usually used to frighten a child. He preys on disobedient children. It was the only thing I could think of at the moment."

Brazos grunted. "Good thing you did, or I'da been wolf bait by now. What happens when they come back and find out who I really am?"

"We sit tight and find out. Have you any other suggestions?"

Long, slow moments ticked past. Baishan returned first. None of the other warriors could be seen nor heard, *but they were there,* just within the shadows, fingers on triggers, hands holding bows with nocked arrows, or razor-edged knives.

Baishan held Alec's Winchester pointed at Brazos's face. "Who are you?" he demanded in Spanish.

"A friend," Brazos replied coolly.

Baishan shook his head. "No White-Eye is our friend."

Brazos tilted his head toward Alec. "*He* is."

Baishan nodded. "The only White-Eye who is."

It was very quiet again. Brazos knew he was going to die.

Alec got painfully to his feet. He carefully and gently pushed the barrel of the rifle away from Brazos's face. "This man is my blood brother and friend," he said quietly. "Before you kill him, you must kill me first."

"You know I can't do that," Baishan said. "All right, my brother. He can stay, but only for the length of time Holos the Sun takes to cross the heavens seven times. Then he must leave. Agreed, my brother?"

Alec nodded.

That was all there was to it. The Chiricahuas, of course, knew Never Still had certain powers. He had saved the life of The Runner from the black poison death by removing an infected arm. They had never before seen anyone recover from the black poison sickness. Was he not of the Pesh-Chidin, the Spirit of Iron? Perhaps this curious-looking blood brother of his had been summoned by Yosen to appear out of the sky in response to the Curing Dance to help him recover from his wounds. Baishan did not question it.

Brazos moved into the commodious wickiup of Looking Glass, the scarfaced squaw he had seen at the Curing Dance. There didn't seem to be a sexual relationship between Alec and the squaw, but there certainly was a powerful attraction between the two of them, grounded, most probably, in their respect for each other. Brazos found it difficult not to stare or even look at the right side of her face. The first evening that he stayed in the lodge she brought food for him and Alec. She smiled at Brazos. It was almost a grotesque caricature of a smile, due to the severely damaged muscles and nerves in the right side of her face.

When she left that evening he looked curiously at Alec.

"When she was a young girl a mountain lion came into the camp one dark night," Alec explained quietly. "He seized her head in his mouth and dragged her into the woods. She had managed to snatch up a long-bladed knife made from an old Spanish bayonet. She somehow drove the knife into the mountain lion's belly and probed for the heart. In its agony the beast dropped her; while thrashing in its death throes its claws raked the right side of her face to the bone. The eye was spared. Since that time she has been considered to have great magical powers. A few years later Looking Glass was struck by lightning, but survived. That convinced the Chiricahuas she had no choice but to become a *diyi,* or medicine person. She is well respected not only by her own people, but by members of other bands. She is said to have miraculous curing powers. She feels that she must always respond to any call of distress no matter where it comes from or how far she must travel. She always goes, God bless her. If asked why she does these missions of mercy, she simply says it is the will of Yosen.''

Alec passed his tobacco pouch and corn-shuck wrappers to Brazos when they had finished eating. ''Ignore her disfigurement if you can. It's difficult, I know, but just notice the deep sincerity of her smile, the great human warmth within her. I'll admit it's not easy. It took me quite a while.''

Brazos rolled a quirly and lighted it with a splinter from the fire. ''You've known her for some time?'' he asked, glancing sideways at Alec.

''About two years.''

Brazos hesitated. ''Just what is she to you?'' he asked.

''Only a friend. There's nothing between us other than that, if that's what you mean.''

After a moment Brazos spoke. ''Perhaps not on your side.''

Alec studied the Texan. ''So?'' he queried quietly.

''I'm not so dense that I can't see she's got it in her head for you, Alec.''

Alec looked down into the fire. ''She's her own woman. Further, she has saved my life. I haven't been exactly interested in having a woman since Los Padres. I wouldn't want to lead her on, thinking the feeling was mutual between us.''

Brazos scratched inside of his shirt and then drank the last of his coffee. He hummed a few bars of ''The Yellow Rose of Texas.'' All the time he avoided looking at his friend.

Alec lay back on his pallet and blew a smoke ring. He

watched it drift upward toward the smoke hole in the center of the roof. "What's on your mind, Rebel?" he asked.

Brazos lowered his voice. "Would there be any trouble if I tried to take up with one of them? I've always had a sort of hankerin' to try one. Any chance of that?"

"Fair enough, if the woman is willing. For God's sake, keep away from the virgins and married women. Divorcees and widows are fair game, but only with their consent, mind you. I'll ask Looking Glass for a suitable candidate." Alec grinned.

Brazos nodded. "*Gracias.* Now, this Curing Dance, or whatever it is, do you believe in it?" He studied Alec closely.

Alec recalled the eerie, powerful ceremony. The incessant drumming and singing, the slap, slap, slap of moccasined feet of the mysterious, so-called Ghost Dancers on the hard-packed earth, had created a charged atmosphere in which anything might happen, as, in fact, it had. He knew from his own medical training that he might have been on the verge of death, and yet at this moment he felt renewed strength and a well-being he had not known until the ceremony had been concluded.

"Alec?" Brazos asked quietly.

"You were watching. Didn't you feel anything?"

Brazos looked away from Alec's penetrating gaze. "Well . . ." he started to say. His voice died away. "Oh, shit!" he suddenly burst out. "It was *mucho* tequila on an empty belly. That's all!"

"Look at me," Alec said.

Brazos looked into his eyes.

"I was seriously wounded. The wound was infected. I knew that. Have you ever seen a man survive an infected belly wound?"

Brazos shook his head, looking away again.

"Admit you may have seen something unknown, or *felt* it at least," Alec suggested.

Brazos looked at him again, and for an infinitesimal fraction of a second he *thought* he saw something; something that put an icy chill throughout his body and made him doubt his reason.

Alec knew when to change the subject. "What made you really come after me? You knew the odds against getting here, finding me, and, more than that, leaving here alive were at least a thousand to one."

Brazos spat into the fire. "I already told you. I got my orders from Crook. I followed them."

There was a moment of silence. "Is that *all*, Brazos?" Alec asked at last.

Brazos knew what Alec was probing for well enough. What he had not been able to account for was the powerful drive he had felt actually urging him on and on when he was almost physically exhausted. There must be some reason for it, likely something spiritual, and for another fraction of a second he thought he *knew*, and then it was gone like the passing shadow of a hawk high overhead.

"Brazos?" Alec queried quietly.

"I already told you," his friend insisted. "There was nothing else!"

"You know you're full of Texican bullshit, don't you?" Alec asked.

Brazos waved a deprecating hand. "A mite, Major, just a mite. Surely comes in handy, especially at trying times like this. By the way, you got any drinkin' liquor?"

They grinned at each other as Alec reached for the bottle.

The level in the liquor bottle was considerably lowered when Looking Glass returned. There was a snub-nosed woman with her, plump of figure, and perhaps in her middle thirties. She knew Alec, of course, and fixed an intent and almost predatory gaze on Brazos. Her name was To-Klani, or Plenty Water. She had lost her first husband in battle and had been summarily divorced by the second. After her divorce she had become fair game for the young men of the rancheria eager for their first sexual experience. She also served with great willingness as an offering for the unmarried returnees of a victorious war party. If the Chiricahuas had such a thing as a prostitute she would have been considered the next thing to one.

Looking Glass squatted beside Alec. She placed a cool

hand on his forehead. "Plenty Water is willing to take your friend into her wickiup as long as he stays here in the camp."

Alec looked quickly at her. "Why can't he sleep here?"

She shook her head. "You're not fully recovered yet. He would be in the way."

Alec looked into her fine eyes. He knew without being told that she didn't want to share him with anyone else.

"You can go with her," Looking Glass said to Brazos in Spanish. "You can stay with her. She has no man. She is a good woman. She'll cook for you."

Brazos slewed his eyes toward Alec. "What's the matter with her nose?"

Alec shrugged. "Her second husband bit off the tip of it, then divorced her."

"Why?" demanded Brazos.

"Adultery, Rebel. Sometimes they merely slit it. He wanted to mark her well."

"He sure succeeded," Brazos said dryly. "Oh, well . . ." He glanced at Looking Glass. His meaning was clear enough. If Alec could live with her and her hideous scarred face, he thought he could last a week with the divorcee and her snub nose.

After Brazos left with Plenty Water, Alec studied Looking Glass. "What made you pick her?" he asked.

The squaw was fussing about the place, tidying this and that. She glanced coyly over her shoulder. "*She'll* keep him plenty busy," she said. She rolled her eyes upward.

Alec cracked up.

CHAPTER 22

HOLOS HAD CROSSED THE HEAVENS SEVEN TIMES. THE Runner guided Alec and Brazos to within half a mile of where the trail led down into Muerte Canyon. They had already said their farewells to the people of the rancheria. Only Looking

Glass had not been there. She had fled into the woods rather than say good-bye to Alec.

The Runner removed the four-stranded *izze-kloth* or medicine cord, from around his neck and held it out toward Never Still. Alec placed it around his own neck. He could not speak. The gift was a powerful token of the love and friendship that had grown between them. The Runner could not have expressed it better. The cord was sacred, made by blind old Black Wind, chief medicine man of the Chiricahuas. It was strung with beads and shells, pieces of sacred green chalchihutl stone, a diamondback rattle, petrified wood, eagle down, the claws of a hawk, and the talons of a bear. There were small buckskin bags of *hoddentin,* the sacred pollen of the tule, a variety of the cattail rush that grew in little ponds and *cienagas* of the Southwest. The pollen resembled cornmeal and was used for protection on the warpath, to detect pony thieves, help the crops, and cure the sick. The Runner kneed his pony around, back toward the rancheria and rode slowly away until he was lost to sight in the deep shadows of the woods.

Brazos looked curiously at the medicine cord. "I thought they set a big store by them things. Sorta like a Bible, ain't it, in a manner of speaking? What'd he mean by giving it to you?"

Alec fingered the sacred cord. "It's either an indication of his great love and friendship for me in our parting, or he doesn't expect me to leave and thinks I will bring it back to him."

Brazos spat sideways. "Fat chance of that last, eh?"

Alec did not reply.

They rode on toward the canyon. As they rounded a curve in the trail, he thought he saw a movement out of the corner of his eye, a second sight of something lighter than the dark foliage, keeping a noiseless pace alongside the trail. Alec pointed in its direction.

"Painter?" Brazos asked in a low voice.

Alec shook his head. "You know they usually keep away from humans as much as possible. There are exceptions though. Looking Glass' face is a prime example."

The faint trace of the rising moon diffused the sky to the east. The canyon rim was a few hundred yards to the north.

"There!" snapped Brazos. He yanked his revolver from its sheath.

"Wait!" cried Alec. He held out an arm to stop Brazos from shooting. A figure stood in the center of the trail. It was Plenty Water, wearing only a buckskin breech clout, holding out her plump arms toward the two white men.

Brazos paled. "My God," he murmured. "I thought I had serviced her enough last night and even this morning."

Alec grinned. "All she wants is a last farewell tumble in the grass with you, Rebel. Surely you can't deprive her of that."

Brazos looked quickly back over his shoulder.

"You can't go back, Rebel," Alec said cheerfully. "You know the rules. Besides, you were the horny boy who always had a sorta *hankerin'* to try one of them, as you said."

"Jesus, Alec! This is more than a try! It's been like an ordeal all week long! It was all I could do to get it partway up this morning!" There was a haunted look in his eyes.

"You're trapped," Alec said. "You can't outrun her, or satisfy her, for that matter. Go to your doom like a brave man." He kicked his horse with his heels and rode past the woman, tipping his hat as he did so. "Howdy, Missus Truitt," he said politely. He could hear Brazos cursing him as he rode on toward the canyon. When he looked back, Brazos's horse stood alone on the trail. The long grass and shrubbery at the side of the trail was shaking in a violent manner. There were ecstatic cries from Plenty Water and nothing but desperate silence from Brazos.

The moon was just appearing, illuminating the landscape with a soft silvery glow. The canyon at Alec's feet was still deep in shadows. He opened the *hoddentin* pouch and took a pinch of pollen between his fingers. He held out his arm and flicked the golden powder toward the rising moon. "*Gun-ju-le, Klego-na-ay. Inzayu-ijangle,*" he murmured. "Be good, O Moon! Do not let me die." He finished the prayer with a short and snappy "Ek!" to draw the moon's attention to his prayer. Alec rolled and lighted a cigarette and watched the moon rise slowly in a display of cool beauty.

"I'm beginning to believe you think you're one of them," Brazos said weakly from behind Alec.

"When in Rome," Alec murmured.

"What the hell are you talkin' about?" Brazos demanded.

Alec shook his head. "Nothing, nothing."

Brazos stood beside him. Now and again he looked back over his shoulder into the dark woods. "Jesus," he said quietly. "I'm damned glad we have to get out of here anyhow."

Alec studied him. "Your face is pale and drawn, stud, but beneath it all is the demeanor of a well-satisfied man."

Brazos grinned weakly. "She's some punkins, that woman." He looked down over the rim of the almost sheer cliff below them. The faint light of the rising moon just picked out the hairline marking of the trail against the huge bald dome of weathered rock that towered hundreds of feet above the depth of the canyon. He looked back at Alec.

Alec shrugged. "We have no choice. You can see now how a few warriors armed only with rocks could hold off a regiment of soldiers on that trail."

"It's getting late," Brazos warned. "We're burning daylight. If we're going to go down *that* trail, we haven't much time. Once the moon passes overhead, the canyon will be in darkness again. We don't want to be caught on it then." He studied Alec. "You *are* coming with me, aren't you?"

Alec had suffered a definite feeling of loss when he had left the rancheria. It was growing worse by the minute. When would he ever have another chance to study these remarkable people? What would he go back to in his own world? His army career was in extreme jeopardy, possibly about to end in disgrace and dismissal. He could not return to Soledad Canyon for a long time, perhaps never. His beloved Guadalupe was lost to him forever in a Mexican convent. Anne might still marry Trapnell. Belle Valois would always be there, but there was no great future for them as a pair. He knew she would never consent to live in Soledad Canyon if he decided to return there.

"For Christ's sake, Alec!" Brazos snapped. "You can go

back to the rancheria, but I can't! Are you coming with me or not?''

Alec took a bottle of tequila from his saddlebag. It was a parting gift from Looking Glass. He handed it to Brazos. The Texan drank deeply and handed the bottle back.

Alec saw the somber face of Baishan and the always smiling face of The Runner. He drank. The image of Looking Glass swam into view, and miraculously her features were unscarred, as she had been before the mountain lion had destroyed half of her face.

''You're going back, aren't you?'' Brazos asked quietly.

Alec nodded.

''What do I tell the general?''

''You'll think of something, I'm sure.''

Brazos took the reins of his horse. ''Any messages?''

''For whom?''

''I was thinkin' of the lady you saved down in that damned canyon below us.''

Alec shook his head. He drank again and handed Brazos the bottle. ''Save this until you reach the bottom, Rebel. I wouldn't want you to fall off drunk.''

They gripped hands. Brazos led his horse to the top of the trail. He turned. ''God help you, Major,'' he said quietly. ''I hope he helps you to find yourself. No one else can.'' He led the horse onto the trail and then was lost to view. Alec could hear the hooves on the rock and the rattling of displaced gravel hissing over the edge of the trail.

After a time Alec leaned out over the rim. ''*Vaya!*'' he called out. ''*Vaya, vaya, vaya,*'' the canyon echoed until it died away.

He heard a faint farewell rising from the depths. Then it was quiet again except for the sound of the wind through the canyon and the rustling treetops.

It was long after dark when Alec returned to the rancheria. A spit of rain was in the air. There had been social dancing that night, but only a few of the dancers were left, and they were merely going through the motions. The fires were thick beds of ashes through which red ember eyes winked open and shut now and again. It was very quiet except for the soft thudding of the drum and the slap and shuffle of moccasins on the hard ground.

A lone figure sat hunched under a Mexican blanket at a small dying fire to one side. Alec walked over to him. The sleeper's left arm was but a stump. Alec took off the medicine cord and placed it about The Runner's neck.

Alec entered the wickiup. The fire in the center of the floor was a thick bed of ashes. Looking Glass's pallet was unoccupied. Perhaps she had not returned yet. He was tired. He was not yet fully recovered from his wounds. It was quietly pleasurable to be back in the comfortable lodge, with its mingled aroma of tanned hides, flavorful smoke, and the evergreen branches forming the low roof. He began to undress. It was then he noticed the faint scent of crushed mint and dried flowers. He stripped, downed a stiff drink of tequila, and dropped to his knees to crawl onto his pallet.

He reached to throw back the blankets. Almost as though the thought had energized the action, the blankets were thrown back. The odor of mint and dried flowers intensified, and he detected another faint aroma, the woman scent. Looking Glass sat up in the bed. "Never Still," she whispered softly, "I knew you would return."

He lay down beside her full-bodied nakedness. She threw the blanket over him and enveloped him with her strong arms and legs. Rain began to patter gently on the roof.

"You can't stay with these people," a voice whispered into Alec's left ear. *"This is not the place for you. You must leave."*

He awoke with a start. Looking Glass was sound asleep at his side, lying belly down, her right arm thrown protectively across his chest. It was raining harder, pattering steadily on the roof and the hard ground outside. The rain-laden wind rushed through the treetops, rustling and thrashing them around.

A faggot popped in the fire pit, sending up a shower of sparks, faintly lighting the interior. Alec half-expected to see someone within the wickiup. There was no one there. The firelight died. He crawled to the doorway and pushed aside the stiffened hide that closed it. It was dark outside. Shrugging, he returned to bed. For the life of him, he could not remember if the bodiless voice had spoken English or in the dialect of the Chiricahuas, so accustomed had he become to the Apache tongue. He was sure the speaker had not been Looking Glass.

"What is it?" She asked, drawing him close.

"Nothing," he said.

She was silent for a moment. "You heard something," she whispered at last. "But there was no one there? No footprints?"

"Yes," he admitted reluctantly.

She shivered. "There are many ghosts in our lives. Sometimes they speak a warning to us in the voice of Bú, the Owl. Sometimes it is a human-sounding voice. There are many spirits on the Big Mountain."

Alec laughed. "Nonsense! There are no such things!"

"Tell me you truly believe that."

He could not.

CHAPTER 23

IT WAS THE TIME OF THICK WITH FRUIT, LATE SUMMER and early fall. In the slow passage of weeks since the Curing Dance, with the loving care of Looking Glass, Alec had gained back his strength by following the rigid training regimen of the Chiricahua boys and novice warriors. No white man, with the possible exception of a Spartan, was ever trained as thoroughly. Training started as soon as a boy learned to walk. The youngsters were aroused just before dawn and told to run to the top of the mountain and back before daylight. They rode horses downhill at reckless speed without the use of a rope. They developed the fine art of hiding. It was unbelievable how they could seemingly disappear into thin air. The older boys played at dangerous games of war, shooting wooden-tipped arrows or hurling stones from their deadly accurate slings at each other. Sometimes bones were broken, and even death occurred. Above all, the boys were trained to run. They were taught that their legs were their best friends. They ran long distances with a mouthful of water and were required to spit all of it out at the end of the course. The girls too were taught to run. Some of them were more fleet than the boys.

Looking Glass had gone to Sonora. Her mother was extremely ill. She was a Mexican of San Tiburcio who had been a *captiva* of the Chiricahuas. Indah-yi-yahn, He Kills Enemies, a famous warrior, had taken her as his wife. Later he had been killed in battle with Mexican troops. She had raised Looking Glass on the Big Mountain. When Looking Glass had become full-grown, her mother had left the rancheria to return to her people in San Tiburcio, on a fork of the Rio Bavispe, eight or nine days travel to the south from the Big Mountain.

In a land where Apache and Mexicans had been sworn enemies for centuries, there was an unusual neutrality about San Tiburcio. Twenty-five years before there had been an open market there between Apache and Mexican. In the year 1848 a mixed band of outlaws—Mexicans, Americans, several Pima Indians, and a halfbreed Zambro had attacked San Tiburcio, thinking to catch unawares the townspeople and Chiricahuas supposedly trading there. The Chiricahuas, however, had been delayed in their arrival. They rode up in time to find Hell in full swing. The Chiricahuas attacked just before dawn and slaughtered the outlaws to a man. The townspeople could not resurrect their dead nor restore the virginity of their daughters, but they could show their gratitude to the Chiricahuas. For a quarter of a century they had kept a peace pact with their saviors.

Looking Glass had traveled there with a small party, other women and girls, some boys and novices, and a few warriors. The Runner had gone along. They would ride by night and hide by day, moving by a circuitous route well east of Muerte Springs. They expected to be gone at least a month. In the meantime Perico, White Horse, who was the usual war leader after Baishan, had left the Big Mountain for a horse and mule raid to the west. The Chiricahuas had become short of good horses. Alec had an idea of where they intended to find them. What could he say? He was living in tenuous balance between two warring factions.

He was lonely after Looking Glass's departure, but the gap was filled every evening by the *yoshti,* or intimate talk among friends. During these talks he learned a great deal more of The People and their life-way. Their culture and history was verbal, passed on from father to son, and from the elders to the young. That was the way it was; that was the way it would be.

The days were still pleasant, though cooling fast. The nights were often cold, a warning that Ghost Face was not far away. One night when they held the *yoshti,* all the elders and remaining warriors were there—Baishan, Colored Beads, and Black Bear, who wore a necklace of bear claws around his strong neck, indicative of the fact he had, armed only with a knife, performed the prodigious feat of killing a bear. He had the scars to prove it as well. Hair Rope had been so named because he had once roped a Mexican officer and dragged him to death behind his horse. Corn Flower had gained his name by hiding in a field of corn flowers while Mexican soldiers passed within a few yards of his hiding place. There were others, well-known warriors all.

Intchi-dijin, Black Wind, had joined the circle around the big fire and listened to the counsel, now and again asking Alec pointed questions. He was the grandfather of Baishan. Black Wind had been a great warrior in his day. He was very old. His hair was pure white. There was little flesh on his shrunken body. His ribs were ridged under the taut dry flesh. His eyes were an opaque white. He had been blind for over forty years. Black Wind could no longer see with his eyes, but Yosen, taking pity on him, had granted him the power to see with his mind. In that respect his sight was greater than that of any man. It was greater even than the telescopic vision of the high-soaring golden eagle. In addition, he had been given some "power" to see into the future. It was not revealed to him in exact detail of course, but clearly enough to have established him as a prophet long ago.

The old prophet tolerated Alec, though Alec had the gut feeling that Black Wind had not approved of a White-Eye being brought to the stronghold. To him a White-Eye was simply *Indah*, The Enemy. The two were the same.

They smoked wild tobacco wrapped in dried oak leaves. All of them, as the saying went, "had caught their coyote." It was one of the customs of The People, a requirement to take up the habit. No one knew the origin of it, long lost in the shadows of antiquity.

The talk for some nights had been about whose country this was. Alec found himself alone in his opinion. There was no animosity toward him, just an intense and probing curiosity about how the White-Eyes stood on the subject. To the Chiricahua way of thinking, one owned the entire land and yet owned nothing of it. They could not understand why the Mexicans and the Americans must allocate certain areas of land and say, "This is mine and no other's place." It was bad enough that they did this in certain parts of the land, but to claim *all* of it for their own purposes was beyond Chiricahua comprehension.

"We do not understand this border, of which you speak, Never Still," Black Bear said. "This line, which no one can see on the land, on one side of which is Mexico and the other the United States. How did this come about?"

Alec rolled another cigarette. "It was done by a treaty between the two countries," he explained. They had been over this before.

"When I was young," Black Bear said, "there was no line. The Mexicans said all of this was *their* land. Then the Americans came and said it was *their* land. How is this?"

Alec lighted his cigarette and looked over the flare of the burning splinter. "There was a war. The Americans won. The Mexicans agreed to let the Americans have all this land north of that invisible line as theirs."

Corn Flower leaned forward. "We understand war. That is our way of life. But this invisible line we don't understand. For generations, long, long before even the Mexicans came here, it was *our* land as far as one could see in every direction and beyond. We could go anywhere in that land. Then, one day, we were told the land was no longer ours, and that we must listen to the laws of the Mexicans on one side of the line and to the Americans on the other. How is this?''

It was almost impossible to make these people comprehend.

Baishan spoke quietly. ''Yosen created this land for The People. Each tribe had its place. Now we are told that is no longer true. Did Yosen have no use for The People when he created them?''

''How can he let it be that we must obey the laws of these American people who have been here only a few years?'' asked Hair Rope.

Alec thought for a moment. There must be some way to explain it reasonably well. ''The Americans are a large tribe,'' he said at last. ''Their numbers are like the leaves on the trees. They are a strong people and well armed. They think of all this vast land as theirs. There is no way you can defeat them.''

Black Bear laughed. ''I shit on them and their laws. I do not believe there are so many of them. If there are, where *are* they? Do you remember ten years ago when all the American soldiers left this country? We Chiricahuas drove them from this place.''

There was no way Alec could explain the Civil War, and he didn't intend to try. ''But they came back, did they not, Black Bear? Now there are more of them than ever before, and many more will come in time. You can't defeat them, as I said.''

They were quiet for a long time, occupied with their own thoughts.

Black Wind raised his head and looked across the fire at Alec. ''When I was young, I walked all over this country and saw no other people but the Apaches. After many summers I walked again and learned another race of people had come to take it. Why is that? Why is it that we Chiricahuas seem to want to die? That we carry our lives in our fingernails? We roam all over the hills and plains and want Heaven to fall in

pouch and held them out to Alec. The firelight shone dully on the brass. They were rimfire .56/50 Spencer hulls.

It became very quiet except for the crackling of the fire.

There was no need for orders. The warriors went for their weapons. The novices rounded up the horses.

Alec went to the wickiup and dressed for the war trail—baggy white trousers, thigh-length moccasins tied below the knee, a red and white checked white man's shirt, and a buckskin vest. He wore the kiltlike white cloth *himper* over this trousers. He tied a calico band around his forehead and long mane of hair. He painted parallel lines of white bottom clay across the bridge of his nose and cheekbones. He placed his rifle, pistol, and trail gear outside the wickiup and reentered it. He looked around the interior, where he had spent so much time in comfort and happiness. He replenished the fire, and then threw everything belonging to Looking Glass on it. It began to smolder, and then burst into flame. The last thing he did was to take a faggot from the fire and hold it against the dry evergreen branches forming the inner roof of the wickiup.

Alec strode toward his horse. He had shaved off his dragoon mustache and short beard weeks ago. Apaches disdained all facial hair. Now, with the exception of his dark ruddy hair and his gray eyes, he was to all intents and purposes a Chiricahua warrior ready for the war trail.

He could hear the flames crackling behind him. There were other fires springing up throughout the encampment as the wickiups of those who had died at Los Padres were burned.

Baishan tightened the girth of his Mexican saddle. "This is not your fight, Never Still," he said.

Alec shook his head. "I know those animals who call themselves men. It has been my fight longer than it has been yours."

By dawnlight they were at the foot of the Big Mountain, fifteen Chiricahuas and one white man.

CHAPTER 24

ALEC KERSHAW CAME INTO SAN TIBURCIO FROM UPWIND. The fearsome stench of corruption was borne on the early morning wind. The once pleasant town was a blackened ruin; the collapsed roofs had thankfully buried the dead within. Gaunt coyotes slunk away at Alec's approach. They would return as soon as he was out of sight. The heavy brooding silence he had noticed from a distance was now broken by the hissing and low grunting of the vultures and the harsh *kraak, kraak, kraak* of the white-necked ravens. There were so many of the carrion-eaters tearing at the bloated flesh of the bodies scattered through the streets and on the plaza, it would be only a matter of days before there would be nothing left but cleanly picked bones. There could be no identification made of the corpses, nor would Alec have wanted to do so. He preferred to remember Looking Glass and his other Chiricahua friends as he knew them.

The raiders had been thorough. Anything they could not take with them had been wantonly destroyed. The wells had been polluted by bodies dumped into them. San Tiburcio's destiny was to be a haunted ruin.

Los Padres was about twenty-five miles or more due west. There was a range of rugged hills lining the east side of the Rio San Tomas Valley, wherein Los Padres lay. There would be a late moon that night. Baishan wanted to attack before the moon rose. There was no doubt but what his warriors could make it. Alec was the unknown quantity. There were only five horses left after the killing ride from the Big Mountain. Two of the warriors would ride far ahead as scouts. The remaining horses would be used in the ride-and-tie system. Three warriors would ride a few miles, tie the horses, and proceed on foot. The first three warriors arriving at the horses would ride on some miles, then leave the horses for the next relay, and go on afoot. Baishan had wanted Alec to ride all the time, but he had refused.

When darkness came, the war party was strung out for some miles. Alec slogged on alone. No white man could keep up with an Apache on the move. He had known his Scouts to cover forty miles a day on foot. Their water discipline was incredible. Sheer stupid pride had caused him to refuse Baishan's offer of a horse. He could feel every ache and pain in his body. His side wound burned. He head throbbed and pounded. His mouth and throat were brassy dry. His moccasins were worn thin. Sweat streamed down his body. In a sense, he was stronger than many of the warriors, but it was a different type of strength. This was their game. They had been trained for it since they had learned to walk.

Up, up, and still up! Alec felt his way up the steep, narrowing gully that led up to the top of the ridge beyond which was the Valley of the San Tomas. The higher he climbed in the Stygian darkness, the steeper it got. The uneasy feeling came over him that perhaps the Chiricahuas had gone on without him. Perhaps he had wandered from the trail and was ascending the ridge in the wrong place. Dislodged stones clattered down the rocky trough far below him. His breathing was so harsh and labored, he could not have heard anyone near him. No one had passed him in the gully. He was *almost* sure of that.

Sheet lightning had begun to flicker eerily around the fringes of a bank of low-lying clouds that was passing slowly overhead. Alec could just about make out the gunsight notch high above him which would mean the ridge top. Now the gully was so steep, he had to help his progress by placing his hands on rock surfaces still warm from the heat of the past day. He thought always of rattlesnakes being disturbed and striking with deadly accuracy through the darkness.

His legs began to feel wooden, almost like a form of paralysis. He staggered on. To hell with these damned Chiricahuas! They didn't seem much concerned about him. He stopped and placed his sweating back against a rock ledge. He closed his burning eyes.

Lightning flashed, followed by an ear-splitting thunderclap. Alec opened his eyes once more. The terrain was lighted by an eerie greenish glow. There, not ten feet from Alec, were three grinning warriors. It gave him one helluva turn, and for a second or so he thought he was going to embarrass himself in front of them. They were Corn Flower, Black Bear, and one named Strong Swimmer. It was as though they had been shaped out of the darkness and given life by the lightning flash. Christ, he thought, *if they had been enemies . . .*

Alec almost crawled out of the gully to the ridge top. He got to his feet and walked on toward the waiting warriors, trying to act as nonchalant as possible. It was a hell of an effort. At last he could bear it no longer. He sat down on a rock, pulled down his moccasins around his ankles and began to massage his calves.

Black Bear cut a branch of nettles, rolled down his moccasins, and beat his calves with the thorny growth. The blood flowed down his legs. He handed Alec the branch. Alec followed suit, trying not to cry out in pain and to maintain a stoic expression. When he was done, he found that his legs did feel better with the flow of fresh blood.

Of the five horses, there were only three left. One had been ridden to death by one of the scouts. The other had fallen and broken its leg. The remaining three were through. They stood with hanging heads, shivering spasmodically from their manes to their hooves. Yellowish foam hung in strings from their mouths. They probably would not live through the night without water.

"Can we water them a little at least?" Alec asked Baishan.

Baishan shook his head. "They'll die anyway."

"We can get more water at Los Padres."

"Perhaps. Perhaps not. If we are driven off, we'll have only enough water to get back across the border."

"Kill them, at least," Alec said.

Baishan shrugged. "Why bother? We're moving on right now."

The soft lights of Los Padres shone through the darkness. The clouds had moved on, accompanied by the lightning. The sky to the east had cleared, waiting for the moon.

The sound of music and singing came from Los Padres. A

liquid bird call came through the darkness and was echoed by Baishan. Colored Beads came to the war party. He had been in the town. None of the townspeople were in the streets. Their doors and windows were closed and no lights showed. There were three *gambrusino* sentries, one at the corral, another in the plaza, the third outside the *bodega,* where Alec knew the guns and scalps were stored. The corral was full of many good horses and mules. The gap in the rear wall had been carelessly boarded up. The *gambrusinos* were carousing within the old church.

"How many of them, do you think?" asked Alec.

"Many. Thirty maybe. Maybe forty. I'm guessing, Never Still."

Baishan looked at Alec. Alec knew what he was thinking. The Chiricahuas were outnumbered. The *gambrusinos* were better armed with revolvers and *petiltows.* The Chiricahuas were armed with single-shot rifles and carbines and only a few pistols. Alec had the only repeating rifle. The Chiricahuas were guerrilla fighters who fought only when they had great advantage.

This was the moment of truth for Alec. They could not defeat the *gambrusinos* without those repeating carbines and revolvers stored in the bodega. If he armed the Chiricahuas, who were still enemies of all white men, they would have the firepower of a squadron of cavalry. Very few troops in Arizona Territory were equipped with repeating carbines. Those in the warehouse had been destined for that very purpose. Then he remembered the wagon train at the San Simon; the slaughter at Soledad Canyon; the bloody massacre at San Tiburcio. He had the power to destroy the *gambrusinos.* There might never be another chance. He must risk it now and face the consequences later.

Baishan pointed wordlessly to the east. The faintest trace of the rising moon could be seen.

CHAPTER 25

DARK AND FURTIVE FIGURES CROSSED THE DRY RIVERBED. Alec and Baishan crept to the bodega. The sentry never knew what killed him. Flat Nose dragged the body away and returned, putting on the sombrero to take the sentry's place at the door.

Alec entered the bodega. He had to enter alone. No Chiricahua would go into that charnel house of baled scalps. He opened one of the side windows facing the river. He passed out five cases of Spencers, three of Colt revolvers, and a case each of Spencer and Colt cartridges, along with a box of extra magazine tubes for the carbines. Then he barred the door from the inside and went out the window.

They carried the cases across the river. There were twenty Spencers and thirty-six revolvers, enough to give each warrior a carbine and a pair of Colts. The thin coat of cosmolene on each weapon was hastily wiped off, and cloth patches were run through the bores to clean out the storage grease as much as possible. Alec quickly instructed the warriors how to load the stubby carbines by means of a tin loading tube containing seven cartridges thrust up into the buttstock through the loading gate in the butt plate. Each warrior thrust two extra loaded tubes under his belt and filled his pouch with extra cartridges for the carbines and revolvers. The war party now had the equivalent firepower of a company of cavalry armed with single-shot carbines and two revolvers. The thought was uneasy in Alec's mind, but he was fully committed now.

He loaded an extra Colt for himself. He looked around at the grim faces of the Chiricahuas. "Don't kill any of the women, my brothers. Some of them may be from San Tiburcio and others from this town."

Black Bear grinned. "Why kill them, brother? We'll need them to replace our women who crossed the canyon at San Tiburcio."

That wasn't what Alec had in mind, but at least it was better than having them killed. "Another thing," he added. "There are two of those *gambrusinos* I want for myself. Chico Diaz and Milo Chaffin. I've described them to you. I know it won't be easy to capture them alive, but they are to be *mine*. You understand?"

The first warriors moved up to take their stations for the attack. Baishan looked at Alec. "It will be hard for them to hold back once the killing starts, Never Still. The *heshke,* the wild killing craze, may overcome them. Then they'll kill until no one is left alive. I am like that myself. You understand? Do you want those two men for prisoners?"

Alec nodded.

"Where will you take them? Back to Big Mountain? Or to the soldiers?" He shook his head. "They must die here. They are too dangerous to be taken as prisoners. They must die here! There is no other way!"

Baishan was right. He was the war leader and must be obeyed. Alec knew he could never bring those two killers to the white man's justice. There was a powerful possibility they might be part of the Tucson Ring. If so, they might never endure hangrope justice.

Baishan went ahead to be with his warriors.

Alec was alone. He crawled back in through the bodega window. He piled straw from the floor along the bases of the baled scalps and laid a train of it to the remaining cases of carbines, revolvers, and cartridges. There were a number of large cans of Curtis and Henry black powder resting atop the upper cases. He quickly opened one of them, poured gun powder along a long strip of cloth he found, rolled it tightly together, and placed one end in amid the straw piled against the cases. He put bits of wood on the straw to add fuel to the coming flames. If he must arm the Chiricahuas, at least he could prevent them from getting their hands on the remaining weapons and the many boxes of cartridges. They had enough with them now for the attack and victory. It was the best he could do. He dropped a burning match on the straw in the middle of the floor. The flames began to eat their way toward the improvised cloth fuse. He climbed out the window and closed the shutters.

Black Bear was waiting for him at the rear of the church. He would provide cover for Alec. Alec crawled over the jackstraw jumble of timbers and broken tiles in the ruined sacristy. Faint light shone between the edge of the loose interior hanging door and the jamb. He peered through the gap. A man and a woman lay on a bed in a small room, beyond which was the sanctuary of the church. They were both naked. The woman lay on her back snoring lustily. The man was on his side facing away from Alec. Alec shifted a little. A tile slippped beneath him and clattered against some others. The man rolled over and raised himself on his elbow to stare suspiciously at the door. He was Chico Diaz!

Alec dropped his hand to his Colt. He must wait. Any shooting now might alert the *gambrusinos* before the attack was ready. Chico droppped back on the bed. Alec retreated, lighting a fire under one of the shattered roof beams. He returned to Black Bear. Their assignment was to cover the rear of the church and the roofed arcade behind it, leading to some mission buildings on the west side of the church.

Smoke rose from the sacristy. The crackling of the fire became apparent. Sparks began to ascend. The wind had risen. Sparks were carried into the bosque of cottonwoods. Some of them drifted down atop the piles and windrows of yellowed dried leaves on the ground. The leaves began to smoke, and then burst into tiny twinkling fires.

Startled, muffled screaming came from within the church as smoke seeped into it through the half open windows. Naked and half-naked men and women ran out onto the broad raised paved area fronting the church. They were perfect targets silhouetted in the light emanating from the church and the growing moonlight. The Chiricahuas were basically not good marksmen and had no experience with the Spencer. It didn't really matter. Alec had insisted that they should not shoot the women. It was almost impossible to spare them now.

It was like shooting fish in a barrel. Those that weren't shot down ran back into the smoke-filled church and slammed shut the double doors. Slugs thudded into the thick wood. Some of those inside tried to escape through the high windows. The flat-nosed 385-grain Spencer bullets slammed them back within the church.

Gambrusinos and their women in other buildings ran outside in the firelight and moonlight. Most of them died before they got a few feet. The gray smoke from the fire and the white black-powder smoke mingled together and rose in a wind-driven pall high above the town. The church doors were opened. A dirty white cloth was waved on a stick through it, and then the people rushed outside again crying and screaming for mercy.

The *heshke*, the wild killing craze, overcame the Chiricahuas. "*Zastee! Zastee! Zastee! Kill! Kill! Kill!*" they shouted. They emptied their carbines and revolvers into the people massed in front of the burning church. Then they rushed in with carbine butts and knives. They crushed in the skulls to let out possible vengeful spirits, then hacked away in ferocious frenzy with their knives. Blood glistened in the firelight glare. Runnels of it ran across the pavement and trickled down the steps.

Alec ran to Baishan. "They surrendered! Stop the killing! There are women there! They surrendered, goddamn you!" he shouted.

Baishan turned the contorted mask face of a crazed killer toward Alec. The *heshke* had seized him as well.

To Alec it was almost as though the red-hot doors of hell had been flung open to let one view the unspeakable horrors within. He fled from the scene to find Diaz and Chaffin.

Smoke had been rising from the bodega. Suddenly, there was a heavy thudding explosion from within it, and the roof rose into the air, scattering itself and fragments of baled scalps and gun cases far and wide. They crashed down on *gambrusino* and Chiricahua alike. The explosion glared up through the smoke pall and reverberated like distant thunder along the hills lining both sides of the valley.

Alec was hurled back by the blast over the edge of the riverbank. He lost his grip on his Winchester. He stood up, dazed, to see a man wearing nothing but trousers lower himself from one of the church belfry openings to the roof of the church. He clambered toward the rear of the building, then dropped to the roof of the arcade and jumped down into the flaming bosque. It was Chico Diaz!

Alec ran through the bosque. The burning leaves seared through his moccasin soles. The smoke was thick. The crackling of the flames drowned out other noises. He came out into a small cornfield. The bosque continued on the other side of it. It too was beginning to flame from drifting sparks.

Chico Diaz peered through the drifting smoke in the cornfield. He thought he had seen some movement on the other side. He was in a helluva fix. He had managed to grab his trousers before he escaped from the church. He had snatched up a loaded Colt. His sheath knife was attached to his trouser belt. He knew none of his men would survive the massacre in Los Padres. The surprise had been complete. How could he get clothing, water, and a mount to make good his escape? At the moment his chief concern was to make sure he wasn't being followed. Then he was sure he saw another movement, and a tall Apache appeared through the drifting smoke. He fired at him.

Alec hit the dirt. The bullet smashed into a tree behind him. He bellied through burning leaves to reach the riverbank, rolled into the dry riverbed, and crawled along the bank toward the far side of the bosque from where he had been fired on.

The woods behind Chico were burning now. He ran back through the smoke, then paused and looked around. Something thudded to the ground behind him. He turned and fired twice, blindly, from the hip. He saw no one.

A gun cracked behind Chico. He whirled and fired again. There was no one there. He ran farther into the bosque and full tilt into a thick-boled cottonwood. He rebounded and fell flat on his back. His trigger finger tightened, and the gun discharged into the air.

Chico got up on his hands and knees, peering under the smoke.

"Over here, Chico," the voice said in Spanish twenty feet behind him.

Chico fell sideways and fired at the same instant. He recocked the pistol and pulled the trigger again. The hammer fell on an empty cartridge case. He got to his feet and drew his knife.

The tall Apache stood in the shadows and smoke. The moonlight filtered down through the leaves overhead. The painted face was indistinct. Chico hurled his knife overhand with blinding speed.

Alec jumped sideways. The knife passed right where his throat had been and thudded into a tree. He caromed from a tree and dropped his Colt as he went down. Chico plunged to the tree to yank his knife from it. He turned and went into a knife-fighter's crouch. The moonlight shone on the bestial grimacing face of a cold-blooded killer.

There was no time for Alec to find his Colt. He drew his knife. He had learned some of the skills of knife-fighting while a teenager on his mother's Rio Brioso rancho in the New Mexico Territory. Old Santiago Zaldivar, a past master of the art, had taught him. Santiago had said with emphasis, "A knife fight is short. There is not the honor or the tradition of the duel in it. Your opponent may die slowly from many cuts, but at once with the thrust that is right. Fight with the point, *not* the edge of the knife. Keep calm. Remember, *a knife fighter kills, or is killed. . . .*"

They circled in the small clearing in which they stood. Smoke thickened and swirled around them. The heat of the flames was more intense.

"You are not Apache," Chico said. "Mexican, perhaps?"

Alec shook his head. "No, but you know me, Chico Diaz," he said in English.

Chico struck swiftly, feinting high then low. Their blades clicked sharply with Alec's parry.

"Where do I know you from?" Chico asked as he circled again.

"One night in Belle Valois's place in Tucson. It was I who gave you that lovely scar on your forehead."

Chico's eyes narrowed. He tried to mentally erase the white paint bars across the nose and cheekbones. Then he looked into the cold gray eyes and he *knew*. . . . It was no time to question how his opponent whom he knew as a United States Army officer came to be here dressed as an Apache.

Chico tested Alec's reactions. His blade moved swiftly, reflecting the moonlight. His knife came in high for the face, then dropped low, turning sideways into the thrusting, slashing, disemboweling stroke.

Alec sucked in his lean gut. The knife tip cut through his shirt and scored a thin red line across his belly. He leaned forward from the hips and thrust for Chico's throat. The knife was blocked by an upraised forearm. Alec dragged it back, furrowing the skin.

They closed. Blade locked against blade. Their left hands each locked onto their opponent's left wrist. Their right arms rose overhead as they strained, chest to chest. Chico was the more powerful. Alec had been weakened by the arduous march to Los Padres. Chico spat full in his face, half-blinding him. Alec's instant reaction was to raise a knee squarely into Chico's privates. Chico's head went down involuntarily. Alec broke Chico's hold and backhanded him alongside the head.

They staggered apart, breathing harshly, sweat dripping from their faces and blood from their wounds. Chico closed. Alec sidestepped and slammed a hard elbow against Chico's temple, then jumped sideways, wiping the saliva from his eyes. Chico went down, rolled over through the smoking leaves, and came up onto his feet to close again.

They met and fought. Their moonlight shadow figures aped their every move in grotesque imitation. They leaped in close, retreated, swayed sideways, forward, and backward, with their blades clicking and clashing, feet stamping hard on the ground, sweat flying from their faces, fighting like great clawing cats or fang-slashing lobos. They broke apart at last.

They circled warily, their breaths coming harsh, quick, and erratic in their dry throats. They coughed now and again from the thickening smoke.

"You're going to die, renegade," grunted Chico.

"After you, scalp hunter," Alec responded politely. He

charged, driving Chico back. There was a mass of burning leaves not far behind the *gambrusino*.

Chico fell back before the desperate charge. He grinned. He knew he had Alec now. Just then his bare feet plunged into the thick mass of leaves. His face changed. He screamed harshly and looked behind him.

Alec closed in, turning his knife hand so that the big knuckles were outward, and smashed his fist with stunning force against Chico's jaw. Chico staggered sideways against a tree. Alec closed in again. His blade sank deep into the lower part of Chico's hairy paunch. He dragged the knife with brutal power across to the other side of the belly, reversed it, slanting upward, back again, then reversed it again in the disemboweling, killing Z. Chico went down flat on his back in the burning leaves and stared upward at Alec with glazing eyes. "*Yahtatsan!*" Alec savagely shouted, as though he had killed an animal rather than a man.

Milo Chaffin had seen the firelight glowing against the eastern sky as he approached Los Padres. He had been in Magdalena for five days, blowing his share of the loot from San Tiburcio. Bartolome Calderon had been with him. Now they rode to the side of a ridge overlooking the town at close range, dismounted, and walked up to the ridge top. Milo put his field glasses on the the town just at the time the bodega blew up.

"Let's get out of here!" Bartolome pleaded. He turned and ran down toward the horses.

Milo smiled. "As you wish, amigo," he said, drawing his pistol.

The bullet crashed into the back of Bartolome's skull.

Milo emptied the dead man's pockets and took his weapons. He mounted his own horse and led the other to the north and then down into the Valley of the San Tomas toward the far end of the burning bosque. He dismounted and took out his officer's uniform from a saddlebag. He had worn it in Magdalena to attract the señoritas. It was one of the best investments he had ever made.

He thought he heard voices in the bosque. He took his

Henry rifle and walked quietly into the woods. Then he saw them, Chico Diaz and a tall Apache engaged in a deadly knife fight. Milo could have killed the Apache and saved Chico the trouble, but he didn't want to alert other Apaches who might be somewhere in the smoke-filled woods. Besides, who could best Chico in a knife fight? Further, Milo reasoned, why should he bother with Chico at all? If he revealed himself after Chico won, he'd have to take the sonofabitch with him. Then it would be only a matter of time before Chico tried to kill him for the horses.

It was all over. Milo Chaffin, hardened killer that he was himself, turned his head aside at Chico's end. Milo studied the tall Apache. He narrowed his eyes. This was no Apache! Perhaps he was a Mexican. There were some of them who had been raised as warriors. He shook his head. There was something about the features and the stance he should have recognized. The Apache turned and ran from the woods in the direction of Los Padres.

Milo was a few miles from Los Padres, riding hard for the distant border, when he suddenly remembered. "Christ!" he cried. "That was Major Kershaw! It *had* to be him. And I had the sonofabitch right under my gunsights!"

CHAPTER 26

BEN TRUITT MET THE CAVALRY COLUMN FROM FORT Bowie a mile from long-abandoned Camp Farrar at the base of the Pedregosas. He watched the column moving slowly, accompanied by a tall plume of dust.

Colonel Burton Trapnell galloped alone toward Ben on a splendid bay horse. Ben stood up from where he had been squatting in the shade of his own mount. Trapnell was a very formal man, even with civilian employees like Ben.

Trapnell drew rein and dismounted. . "Well, Truitt," he said briskly, "is there plenty of water at Camp Farrar?"

Ben shook his head. "The wells have been plugged and mebbe polluted, probably by the Chiricahuas."

"How is that?" demanded Trapnell. "They couldn't have known of our coming. We moved fast and at night, until today."

Ben silently pointed toward the looming, hazy Chiricahua Mountains of which the Pedregosas were a sort of appendage trending slightly south and west. "They could see your dust for miles, Colonel. Nothing much moves in this country they don't know about."

"Where is the nearest water?" Trapnell asked impatiently.

Ben jerked his thumb over his shoulder. "Over twenty miles south of Camp Farrar."

Trapnell nodded. "Good! We'll have to continue on, then. A forced march should do it."

Ben shifted his wad of Wedding Cake from one side of his mouth to the other and spat copiously. "That's Muerte Springs, Colonel. About five miles into Mexico."

Trapnell stared at Ben. "Are you sure? There's nothing on this side of the border?"

Ben wiped his mouth with the back of his hand. "*Certain* sure, sir."

"But this is impossible! Your Apache Scouts positively assured me there would be water here."

Ben shook his head. "You call that bunch of coffee coolers Apache Scouts, Colonel? A bunch of Arivaipas, Tontos, Coyoteros, and Mimbrenos, practically all of whom were kicked out of their own bands. Some of them are half-breeds, one is half Navajo and two of them are really Mexicans playing the part of Apaches."

"Dammit, Truitt! I was assured these were some of the same men Major Kershaw had in his Company D."

Ben laughed softly. "Jesus Christ, Colonel. You got taken hook, line, and sinker. Kershaw's Scouts were *real* Apache Scouts! They left the service after Kershaw did. To top it off, you refused to return Mickey Free's stripes to him. Mebbe Mickey might have got some discipline out of these damned coffee coolers, but he was too smart to come along."

"Then, why did you agree to lead them?" Trapnell demanded suspiciously.

Ben shrugged. "I figgered you might need a hand, Colonel. God knows you needed someone with experience handling that rabble."

Trapnell mounted and rode back toward the column.

Ben drank from his canteen, swilled the water around in his mouth, and spit it back into the canteen.

The cavalry column was actually under the command of Captain Gerald Bascomb. It consisted of a two-company provisional squadron of eighty men. They were slated to join General Crook's column now forming at Fort Huachuca for a campaign along the border. In addition to the squadron, there was a twelve-man headquarters detachment destined for Fort Huachuca service, four supply wagons, and a Rucker ambulance. Mrs. Anne Sinclair, the colonel's fiancée, rode in the Rucker.

Captain Bascomb was an experienced field soldier. His original trip plan had taken into consideration every factor—availability of water, roads, and ease of travel. The plan was to travel westerly from Fort Bowie, on the Butterfield Trail, then to turn left following the San Pedro River Valley southeasterly for twenty-five miles to the Huachucas, then west twelve more miles to Fort Huachuca, a total mileage of ninety-five. There would be no lack of water or grazing. It was a well-thought-out plan, logistically correct, and allowing for a safe margin of error. There was one factor, however, that he had not taken into consideration. Colonel Burton Trapnell had requested and received command of the newly formed quasi-district from the Huachuca Mountains east to the New Mexico Line, thence south to the border, roughly two thousand square miles of vast and rugged terrain haunted by the warlike Chiricahuas.

Trapnell need not have taken the responsibility of district command. He could have safely remained at Fort Bowie. After all, it was only a temporary assignment on his certain way to the coveted star of a brigadier general. However, it seemed as though the sands in the hour glass of promotion did not run quickly enough to satisfy him. Fort Bowie was a backwater. He felt that he needed field service to accelerate his advance. He had none, ergo he had volunteered and been accepted to command the new district.

The first hitch in Bascomb's careful trip plan had been caused by a two-day delay while waiting for Trapnell, who was to travel with the column. Valuable time had been lost. George Crook was waiting for the squadron. When he set the date and time for an event, he expected it to be kept and would brook no excuses. Trapnell, in order to cover up the fact that he had caused the delay, had suggested marching directly southwest in a straight line from Fort Bowie to Fort Huachuca, which would cut thirty-five miles from the longer route. Bascomb had coldly pointed out that Trapnell's route would take them directly across the Sulphur Springs Valley to the Dragoon Mountains. There was always a good supply of water there; there was also an oversupply of Chiricahuas, for the Dragoons were the impregnable stronghold of Cochise. There had been no alternative but to alter the plan and march almost due south between the Swisshelm Mountains and the Chiricahua range to Camp Farrar at the base of the Pedregosas. Bascomb had complained that the water supply at Camp Farrar was uncertain at best. Trapnell had assured him, on authority of *his* Apache Scouts, that the supply was always adequate. Bascomb could have asserted his authority as column commander, but Trapnell had a habit of overriding anyone who stood in his way, and beyond that, Bascomb knew of Trapnell's record as a member of the Benzine Board and his most recent assignment to the Inspector-General Department. Bascomb had a fine record, but he also had intermittent bouts with a drinking problem. There was nothing he could do for his own personal safety in the service but to allow Trapnell to have his own way. He soon had cause to regret it when he heard of the lack of water at Camp Farrar.

Colonel Trapnell's assumed command of the column had been a disaster from the start. In his haste to make up lost time he had violated one of the primary rules set down in *Cooke's Cavalry Tactics*, the Bible of the cavalry arm. "*Cavalry is a delicate arm,*" Cooke stated. "*Its whole existence and efficiency depends upon the care and condition of its horses.*"

Standard operating procedure in the field was to have the men march afoot leading their mounts the large percentage of march time. Trapnell had reversed this rule. His water discipline had been criminally lax. The column was down to its last reserves of water as it reached Camp Farrar.

There was no choice for Trapnell but to continue on to Muerte Springs, violating the borderline on the way, then march west sixty miles to Fort Huachuca. What had been planned as a comparatively easy journey of ninety-five miles with adequate water and forage had developed into a grueling total of 130 miles on short water rations and approximately three to four days of delay. George Crook would be far from pleased with the performance.

Anne Sinclair rode in the Rucker ambulance. Her *ruano estrella,* the roan mare given her by Baishan, was tethered to the tailgate. Outwardly, it might appear as though she had reached a reconciliation with Burton after the Kershaw affair at Fort Bowie. Such was not the case. Before Ben Truitt had showed up at Fort Bowie, all Anne had heard about Alec was that he had vanished in the remote and hostile Soledad Canyon area. Ben Truitt had officially reported to Colonel Trapnell that Major Kershaw had left the army at Fort Lowell to take up ranching and that he had been driven from Soledad Canyon by the Chiricahuas. Privately, he had told Anne that Alec was alive and with Baishan and his warriors on the Big Mountain recuperating from his wounds suffered at Los Padres. When Burton had asked her to marry him after all, she had agreed on the condition that the ceremony be military and performed at Fort Huachuca, where he would take up his new district command. She felt no guilt. She had known she was in love with Alec ever since she had been with him at Fort Bowie. She had resolved to do anything in her power to find and rejoin him. It was as simple as that.

The column ground to a dust-shrouded halt on the weed-grown parade ground of Camp Farrar. Every man's eyes were on the two wells. They knew no water was to be had. If there had been water, the Apache Scouts would already have been at it.

Colonel Trapnell beckoned to the trumpeter. "Officer's

Call, Tucker,'' he ordered. The brassy call stuttered out and awoke the echoes in the nearby barren hills.

The column was about three quarters short of the officers required on the Tables of Organization. In fact, outside of Trapnell and Bascomb, there were only three more. They were a mixed bag. First Lieutenant George Worley was an old veteran who was waiting out the last three months required to complete his thirty years. His only interest was hanging on with his front teeth until retirement. First Lieutenant John Cleveland was a quartermaster officer reassigned to Fort Huachuca, temporarily assigned to the cavalry squadron for the trip to the fort. He had no cavalry experience. Second Lieutenant Archer Jardine was a ''shavetail,'' fresh from the Military Academy. He should have been allowed to remain at Fort Bowie long enough to learn the ropes, but due to the shortage of officers he marched with the column.

Trapnell stood gazing to the south, holding his white gauntlets in his right hand and slapping them against his left palm.

''We're here, Colonel,'' Captain Bascomb said quietly from behind him.

Trapnell turned slowly, as though coming out of deep thought. ''Gentlemen,'' he said, ''as you no doubt can see, there is no water here at Camp Farrar. I was misinformed as to that fact. This will necessitate a forced march twenty miles south to Muerte Springs. I'd like your opinions and suggestions, if you please.''

Bascomb stared at Trapnell. ''Unless we can call on Moses to strike this ground with his staff and bring forth the gushing waters, Colonel, I can't see any other alternative,'' he said wryly.

''Sarcasm is of no help, Captain,'' Trapnell retorted. ''Is it agreed then that we continue the march to Muerte Springs?''

Bascomb turned on a heel. ''For Christ's sake,'' he said, and that was all.

''I haven't dismissed you yet, Captain!'' Trapnell called after Bascomb. He did not turn back.

When the other officers had returned to their posts, Trapnell called Ben Truitt to him. ''Where are your Scouts?'' he demanded.

Ben pointed south. "I sent them on ahead. That's dangerous ground out there, Colonel."

Trapnell nodded. "Good! Good! I assume they will continue
on to the springs, then report back to me on the conditions
there?"

Ben shifted his chew. "I expect so." How could he tell
Trapnell the Scouts' customary technique when in hostile
country was to disappear, sit out any danger in a place of
comparative safety, then reappear afterward and claim they
had been lost. Any veteran could have told Trapnell an
Apache *never* got lost. Ben mounted his horse and rode on
ahead. A mile from Camp Farrar he looked back. The telltale
dust plume was rising again to be borne on the hot dry wind.

Milo Chaffin reached Muerte Springs at dusk the day after
he had fled from Los Padres. He had been forced to travel by
night and hide out by day. It was not safe even for a well-
armed man with two fine horses. The springs were deserted.
The carrion-scattered bones and skulls of the smugglers didn't
bother Milo. After all, he had been one of the killers. He
didn't intend to stay long at the springs. The Apaches who
had attacked Los Padres would certainly be on their way north
with their stolen horses and mules and the fine firearms they
had likely looted from the *gambrusino* bodega before blowing it up. Milo knew Apaches generally avoided Muerte
Springs unless it was absolutely necessary to go there. He was
sure they'd have to stop this trip to water the stolen horses
and mules. They'd never make it to the Big Mountain with
them otherwise. Then too, the renegade Major Kershaw was
with them. In a sense, Milo would rather face the Chiricahuas than face Kershaw. He figured on moving north after
dark, hiding out in the malpais during moonlight, then heading for the border and the United States after moonset.

Milo made a small, virtually smokeless fire to heat water.
He'd have to shave off his mustache and the short beard he'd
acquired after he had left the Arizona Territory the last time.
Also, in order to shift back into his chameleonlike role of an
American officer, he'd have to remove the Mexican braid

from his kepi and blouse. He began picking at the kepi braid threads with his sheath knife.

"Drop that knife! Stand up! Raise your hands! Turn around slowlike!" a hard voice ordered sharply in Spanish from behind him.

Milo did as he was ordered. A lean man wearing a broad-brimmed hat of Rebel gray stood fifty feet away, just at the edge of the faint firelight glow.

Ben Truitt eyed the uniform. "You in the Mex Army?" he asked.

Milo slipped easily into one of his many characterizations, gambling on the man's Texan accent and the gray hat. He nodded. "I'm an American though," he replied in English. "Captain Steven Crozier, Regiment Fronteras Fusilieros. I was one of the unreconstructed Rebels who left Yankeedom after the war. Fought with Juarez. Stayed in Mexico rather than return to the States." He studied Ben. "This is Mexican territory, you know." His excellent hearing caught the faint rumbling of wheels and thudding of hooves in the narrow, twisting pass through the malpais to the north of the springs. "Who are you?" he added.

"Ben Truitt. Civilian scout, U.S. Army. I'm with a column coming here for water," Ben replied. He eyed Chaffin. "You look familiar somehow. Maybe I met you in Mexico? I was with Jo Shelby."

Milo smiled. "I was with Juarez, as I said. Maybe we saw each other through gunsights." Then he remembered Truitt. He had seen him in Tucson, but at the time Milo had been in his American officer disguise. Thank God he had not had time to shave and remove the uniform braid.

Ben looked around. "Seems strange for a Mex officer to be here in this death trap all alone. You can put down your hands, Captain."

"Thanks. I'm actually on a mission to the United States. I was ordered across the border to contact the first United States troops I could find."

Ben shrugged. "You've done that without crossing the border."

Milo immediately recognized Colonel Trapnell when he

arrived. He had never seen Anne Sinclair, but he knew at once who she was from a description Chico Diaz had received from an informant at Fort Bowie.

Ben introduced Chaffin to Trapnell. "He says he's on a mission to the United States to contact the first U.S. troops he can find."

"And, thank God, I have managed to do so," Milo said fervently. He pointed south. "Apaches attacked Los Padres on the Rio San Tomas. It is assumed they massacred all the inhabitants. They are now moving north and probably will water here. My government needs help in apprehending them."

"Have you no troops of your own?" queried Trapnell.

"We have none available at this time. They were ordered to San Tiburcio because of rumors of a raid there. My commanding officer felt that inasmuch as these raiders obviously intend to return to the United States, it would be to the best interest of both governments to stop them in any possible way."

Trapnell shook his head. "We're under pressing orders to march to Fort Huachuca and are already several days late. If you like, you can ride with us and present your case to General Crook, the department commander."

That was the last thing Milo wanted to do. Once there, someone was sure to recognize him for who he was. "I understand, Colonel. However, there is an aspect of this matter which should hold your interest. I'm sure you will recall the Apache raid on the government wagon train at the San Simon Crossing some time ago. Those raiders were not Apaches, but *gambrusinos* disguised as Apaches. They managed to escape back into Mexico with a great quantity of United States repeating carbines and revolvers, with many cartridges to boot. They were led by the notorious Chico Diaz. The loot was stored in the very same town of Los Padres the Apaches just attacked. You may be sure, sir, the savages have taken those firearms with them. It should give them the firepower of a squadron of cavalry. Can you imagine the result if they manage to return unscathed to their stronghold? The border would become aflame and run red with the blood of American and Mexican soldiers and civilians alike."

Anne had been watching the glib Mexican officer. The

vague thought came to her that she had heard his voice somewhere. Suddenly, he looked directly at her as though he had
read her mind. She was startled. From the side Chaffin looked
Mexican, with his straight black hair and olive complexion.
It was his eyes that had surprised her. They were an incredible, icy-looking blue. There was something alien and predatory about this strange-looking man who had seemed to
appear out of nowhere in the vast emptiness surrounding
Muerte Springs. An uneasy foreboding crept through her.

"This might be a splendid opportunity for you, Colonel,"
continued Chaffin. "The Apaches stand to play right into
your hands. I have no doubt they'll come here for water. It's
a perfect place for an ambush."

Trapnell hesitated. He ran the thought through his mind.
He was tired and worried about his possible reception by
General Crook. There was no way he could foist the blame
for the dilemma he had caused by usurping Bascomb's right-
ful command. By God, this might just be his big chance. If
successful, it would clear the blame from his shoulders, accelerate his rise to that coveted brigadier general's star, and
with a smile and nod from Dame Fortune there might even
be a Congressional Medal of Honor to add to his laurels. It
might just be worth a gamble at that.

Captain Bascomb had overheard Chaffin. He didn't like
the looks of the man. The watering should be completed
within an hour. They could clear the springs before full
moonrise and be on the way to Fort Huachuca.

"Captain Bascomb!" Trapnell called out. "I want you and
the other officers here."

"We'll soon be ready to move out, sir," Bascomb reported. "If there are Apaches in the area, this will be a bad
place to get caught. The desert will be as bright as day once
the moon is up. If we're on the road, we'll be safe from their
attack."

Milo Chaffin pointed east. There was the faintest trace of
pewter light forecasting the rising full moon. "If the colonel
is thinking of ambushing the Apaches, you'd better start
making your dispositions. I'd suggest moving the ambulance

and wagons, horses and mules beyond the pass. There is a box canyon there which would be ideal to hide them in."

Bascomb stared incredulously at Trapnell. "Surely you're not thinking of ambushing those Apaches, Colonel?"

"I'm seriously considering it," Trapnell replied.

Bascomb shook his head. "We've got strict orders to report to Crook at Fort Huachuca. We're already late. You don't know the Apaches, sir. They're familiar with every yard of this terrain. They can travel across it like phantoms and not be seen unless they *want* to be seen. I strongly advise against ambushing them, or, to be correct, *trying* to ambush them."

"It is to be my decision, Captain," Trapnell said stiffly.

"You cannot risk this foolish action! You had better make your decision to move out, and damned fast!"

"That's enough, Bascomb!" snapped Trapnell.

"This is no time for glory-hunting, if that's what you have in mind! Come, do your duty! Forget this madness!"

Milo began to see that Bascomb might very well win his point. He'd have to play his last ace. "May I have a private word with you, Colonel?" he asked.

They walked together near one of the burned-out adobes. Ben Truitt happened to be relieving himself against a wall within easy earshot.

Milo drew Trapnell close to himself. "I didn't want to mention this in the presence of the other officers," he said. "I know you're acquainted with Major Alexander Kershaw, who once commanded Apache Scouts at Fort Bowie. Is that not true?"

Trapnell stared at him. "It is. He resigned his commission rather than face my court-martial charges. The last I heard of him was that he was missing, presumed dead, in the Soledad Canyon area."

Chaffin shook his head. "That is not true. You're probably aware of how friendly he had been with the Chiricahuas."

Trapnell eyed him. "How could you possibly know that?"

Chaffin smiled. "We have our sources of information, as you do yours, Colonel. I know you find this difficult if not impossible to believe, but Alexander Kershaw was seen with the Chiricahuas during the Los Padres raid. In fact, according to reliable witnesses, he was dressed and acted like one of them even to the extent of killing Mexican citizens in cold blood.''

Trapnell shook his head. "You must take me for a complete fool, Captain Crozier. Why should I accept this preposterous tale?''

Chaffin looked around, then leaned closer to Trapnell. "Because I saw him myself,'' he said in a low voice.

"You are certain of this?''

Chaffin nodded. "Positive!''

Trapnell began to draw his gauntlets repeatedly through the palm of his left hand. He seemed far away from Muerte Springs. "It *is* preposterous,'' he said softly, "and yet I have it by a reliable witness of my own that he has been in collusion with Baishan, chief of the Apaches, in the Chiricahua Mountains. I would not put it past him. The man is a known Apache lover. When he was with his past command of Apache Scouts, he was said to have acted more like one of them than as an officer of the United States Army.''

"There isn't much time,'' Chaffin reminded him.

Trapnell nodded. "Napoleon believed in his star,'' he mused. "Why cannot I? This is a heaven-sent opportunity!'' He smashed his right fist into his left palm. "By God! I'll do it!''

Captain Bascomb and the other officers were standing where Trapnell had left them. Now and again they glanced uneasily at the lightening eastern sky beyond the mountains.

Trapnell strode to them. "It is our duty as soldiers to strike the enemy wherever and whenever possible, gentlemen! We cannot overlook this opportunity! My decision, therefore, as district commander is to ambush the Apaches. We'll move the wagons, ambulance, horses, and mules into the box canyon for concealment. Captain Crozier will show you where it is. Captain Bascomb, assign a guard detail for them. Lieutenant Worley, take charge here and eradicate all traces of our presence. See to these matters at once, gentlemen.''

Captain Bascomb held up a hand to stay the other officers.

"Colonel Trapnell, as commander of this column under orders for Fort Huachuca, I strongly protest this action."

Trapnell stared unbelievingly at him. "By God, sir, this smacks of insubordination! Refusing to obey the orders of a superior officer in the field! Cowardice in the face of the enemy! *Mutiny!*"

Bascomb shrugged. "It is your privilege to make those charges, sir, but *only* when we reach Fort Huachuca. You are not due to take up district command until then. *I* am in command of this column, and always was until I was foolish enough and weak enough to let you overrule me. Therefore, I intend to take *my* command to Fort Huachuca as ordered."

"The moon is rising, Colonel," Milo reminded him.

Trapnell, for the life of him, would not and could not let this golden opportunity for glory and sweet revenge on Alexander Kershaw pass him by, and yet he knew Bascomb was fully within his rights to refuse the squadron to him. "Captain Bascomb," Trapnell said. "Can you not at least allow me enough men to ambush these red hellions?"

Bascomb shook his head. "These men are destined for Fort Huachuca."

Trapnell became desperate. "I can hold my headquarters section here. With them and my Apache Scouts I can succeed. That will give me a force of thirty-seven men, certainly adequate enough to defeat the hostiles."

Bascomb stared at him. "Twelve clerks and pen pushers and twenty-five coffee coolers who'll vanish before the first shot is fired, if not sooner? For God's sake, Colonel! That's suicidal!"

"I'll take the risk," Trapnell insisted firmly.

Captain Bascomb wasted no time. He formed the column with the four supply wagons at its end and the Rucker ambulance at the tail. Anne had no choice. She had to go with the column.

Ben Truitt sauntered past the Rucker. "I overheard Crozier telling Trapnell that Alec was with the Chiricahuas at Los Padres dressed like them and killing like them as well."

Anne stared at him. "Is that possible?" she asked.

Ben nodded. "Something tells me it is."

"I'll stay here, then," she said.

He shook his head. "Trapnell will never allow it. It's best that you go on to Fort Huachuca. This is no place for you. Whichever side wins this fracas, there ain't likely to be any survivors on the losing side and damned few of the winners."

"I know Burton," she said, almost as though to herself. "If he wins, Alec will not be a survivor. Will you remain here?"

He grinned. "I'll go scoutin'," he said. "That's my job, isn't it? Besides, I'm not army. I'm a civilian under contract. They can't court-martial me."

The column moved out. The sound of its passage was soon gone. The dust settled slowly. Trapnell suddenly seemed to be in his element. He had a few men take the horses to the box canyon Crozier had mentioned. The good Mexican officer would guide them there. The remaining troopers were set to work cleaning up traces of the column's presence at the springs. Their work might fool a white man; it would never fool an Apache. That trenchant thought was in Ben Truitt's mind. The soldiers kept looking back over their shoulders as though being secretly watched by the Chiricahuas.

Fifteen of the Apache Scouts were to remain with Trapnell. The remaining ten were to scout to the south in a fan shape from east to west. They trotted out afoot and were soon lost to view. The Scouts who remained watched Trapnell with enigmatical expressions. The man with the silver eagles on his shoulders was mad. *He thought he could ambush Chiricahuas.*

By the time the moon rose about the eastern mountains, Muerte Springs seemed as deserted as it was most of the time.

CHAPTER 27

PRIVATE LOGAN DROVE THE RUCKER AMBULANCE AT THE tail end of the supply wagons. He usually kept it to the windward side to avoid the dust stirred up by the marching col-

umn. This night the wind was coming from due west, directly
onto the column, driving the dust toward the wagons and ambulance. In his haste to get away from Muerte Springs, Captain Bascomb had relegated Lieutenant Worley to arrange
point riders, advance party, and flankers, but had not mentioned a rear guard. Worley, with the privilege of thirty years
of service, had in turn relegated the task to Lieutenant Jardine. Worley had not mentioned a rear guard. Young Jardine
did exactly as he was told, and rode proudly with the advance
squad. The Rucker was partially obscured by the blowing
dust. The moon was not yet high enough to light the desert.

Logan was exhausted. He had been in Fort Bowie post
hospital with a high fever and had just been released in time
to join the column. Lieutenant Worley had assigned him to
drive the ambulance because of his condition. The march to
Muerte Springs had been hell on men in good health. It had
certainly done Logan no good. He constantly nodded. The
mules patiently plodded after the last supply wagon but con-
sistently lost ground.

Anne had been watching Logan ever since they had left the
springs. When she was sure he was sound asleep, she clambered over the back of her seat and rooted through one of her
suitcases. She took out a pair of officer's breeches and a shirt
altered to fit her by one of the post laundresses who doubled
as a dressmaker. She quickly stripped off her traveling costume and underskirts and put on the breeches and shirt. She
pulled on a pair of boots and donned a lightweight leather
jacket. Placing an officer's campaign hat on her head, she
buckled a pistol belt with holstered Colt revolver, cartridges,
and a sheath knife around her slim waist. She stealthily removed Logan's Spencer carbine from under his seat. The
ambulance was now trailing far behind the last wagon and
was veiled in dust. No one saw Anne untie the mare's reins
from the tailgate. She took a full canteen with her and dropped
over the back of the Rucker, then waited until the column had
moved on a quarter of a mile before she mounted the roan and
touched her with her heels, turning to ride back toward the
malpais country.

Anne dismounted at the base of the chaotic conglomeration of cracked, fissured, and riven black rock forming the malpais mass. The moon was now illuminating the terrain, and she knew she must get under cover. The northern entry of the pass leading to Muerte Springs was to her left, but she felt that to enter the pass might invite detection, or possibly gunfire. Burton would certainly have his men in position by now, and they might have itchy trigger fingers. Also, the Apaches might have reached the area by this time, and as Alec had told her, "Apaches are seen only when they *want* to be seen."

She led the roan into a shallow canyon that might in time lead her to the pass. Up until that moment she had been so occupied in getting away from the column, she hadn't really considered her position. Slowly and inexorably the reality of it came over her. *What had she done!* She was alone now in deadly hostile country. She knew enough about the Chiricahua Apaches to realize it would hardly seem possible Burton and his motley command could surprise and ambush them. Still, it might come about, and if Alec truly was riding with the oncoming Chiricahuas, she knew Burton well enough to know that he would see to it that Alec was killed. Even if Burton didn't shoot him or have him shot, if he could capture him and take him to Fort Huachuca, it would mean life imprisonment for Alec if not execution.

The roan whinnied sharply.

Anne quickly raised the Spencer and looked around her. Ahead was what looked like an opening into a basin. She tethered the roan to some brush and moved forward. There was at least a score of horses picketed in the basin. The moonlight was bright enough for her to recognize the black McClellan saddles. Two horses were much closer to her, and they had Mexican-style gourd-horn saddles. She thought they were those belonging to the Mexican officer Captain Crozier.

The roan whinnied again.

Anne whirled. A uniformed man stood fifty feet behind her. It was Captain Crozier himself. He smiled and touched the fingertips of his right hand to the bill of his kepi. There was no one else in sight.

"What are you doing here?" Anne asked.

Chaffin shrugged. "I volunteered to show this box canyon to the soldiers who brought their horses and those of the Apache Scouts here for safekeeping." He studied her. "May I ask what *you* are doing here?"

She tried to remember where she had heard his voice and seen those strange eyes, so greatly in contrast to his complexion and dark hair.

"I am curious," Chaffin said. "Why did you return, and in such a fetching costume?" He boldly looked down at her long slim legs.

"I thought to take cover here until I found out what happened at the ambush," she replied.

He nodded. "I see. You changed into that trail clothing, armed yourself, left the safety of the column, and then rode back here just out of curiosity to see the outcome of an ambush which is probably doomed to failure." He shook his head. "It doesn't make sense."

Anne still held the carbine at hip level and pointing at his belly. "It does to me," she said quietly.

He tilted his head to one side. "Are you quite sure there isn't some other explanation?"

She stepped back a little. "Get out of my way," she ordered.

He looked with amusement at her ready Spencer and apparent determination. "You can't be that much in love with that ass Trapnell. So there must be some other compelling interest drawing you back here."

"You forget yourself, Captain Crozier," she said coldly.

Chaffin shook his head. "If it is not Colonel Trapnell, then it must be someone else. Now, let's see . . . Ben Truitt? No." He half-closed his eyes, then opened them quickly. "I think I have it! Whoever he is, he's not with the ambushers. Yes, that's it! Now, who else will soon be in this vicinity? Ah, the Apaches! Perhaps you are interested in one of them?" He shook his head again. "That's hardly possible for one in your social position."

"Get out of the way," she repeated.

Chaffin did not move. "That leaves but *one* man. . . . A

renegade army officer. An Apache-lover. Shall I *name* him, Mrs. Sinclair?''

She stared at him. ''How do you know this?'' she demanded.

He cocked his head sideways and looked thoughtfully upward. ''The Sir Galahad of the Army. Or is it Sir Launcelot? Whatever . . . We commoners know him as Major Alexander Kershaw.''

Slowly, ever so slowly, Anne began to fit pieces together in the intricate puzzle that was this strange man standing before her. She looked into those eerie eyes, and then it came back to her in a wild and fearful rush—those were the same eyes she had seen peering from a face hideously daubed with black and vermilion stalking like a demon through the dust and powder smoke veiling the San Simon Crossing.

He smiled thinly. ''You know me now,'' he said quietly. ''You've recognized me from somewhere. It's these damned eyes of mine, they give me away like the kiss of Judas.''

Anne backed away slowly. He was between her and her horse. Perhaps she could reach one of the herd horses. She caught a heel on something and staggered backward, momentarily lowering her carbine. Chaffin moved like a panther. He grasped the barrel of the carbine, pushed it to one side, and hit Anne on the point of the jaw with a jolting right cross that dropped her flat on her back. She had enought sense left to reach for her Colt. He stepped in close, placed a foot on her wrist, reached down and plucked the Colt from its holster, then stepped back, grinning like an ape. A thin trickle of blood leaked from the corner of her mouth.

Milo thrust the Colt under his belt. ''I see your blood isn't really blue like the rest of us lowbreds. You asked me what I was doing here. Simple. I was waiting until moonset to get the hell away.'' He eyed her. ''Too goddamned bad you had to figure out who I was. I might have let you live.''

Anne knew him for certain now as one of the will-o'-the-wisp *gambrusinos* who crossed back and forth over the border at will. A man with many names, faces, and roles. They had a saying among themselves, or so Alec had told her: *Los muertos no hablan. The dead do not talk.* She knew now she'd never survive to identify him.

He pulled her to her feet and led her to a shallow cave, the rear of which curved to one side. He threw her on the ground and tied her wrists and ankles together, bending her body like a bow. "Sit tight, little lady," he said. "I'll take a look-see toward the pass. You see, whoever wins at the springs would probably kill me on sight." He grinned. "That is, if anyone can find me. Meanwhile, take it easy. When I get back, we can spend a quiet evening here in the malpais, well hidden from prying eyes."

The Chiricahuas were driving the captured herd of horses and mules hard to the north. Foam dripped in yellowish strings from the mouths of the animals. The trail back to the Valley of the San Tomas was littered with dead, dying, and foundered horses and mules, food for the wolves, coyotes, and *zopilotes*. The goal for the Apaches was Muerte Springs. They had no other choice. The herd and the wounded warriors might not survive to reach the Big Mountain without water.

Scouts sent south from Los Padres had returned with a warning that a large body of Mexican cavalry was riding fast toward the *placita*. There were far too many soldiers for the Chiricahuas to ambush. Their horses were fresh and they had a caballada of extra horses for the pursuit. Baishan had been forced to leave the Valley of the San Tomas and veer hard right to deceive the Mexicans into thinking the Chiricahua goal was actually not Muerte Springs. Once the Apaches were sure the Mexicans had been deceived, they could veer left again and make a beeline for the springs.

There had been too many casualties at Los Padres. Nakai, the Mexican, and Antelope had entered the bodega in search of loot and had vanished in the explosion. Curly Haired, a novice, had been shot to death. Strong Swimmer was missing. Flat Nose had a bullet-shattered left thigh and was riding now with a splinted leg and an inward intensity of agony which he would not allow to show on his face. Coyote rode with his right arm in a sling. Colored Beads had been "bullet-creased'' along the left side of his skull. Only by the will of Yosen had he survived. Others of the warriors had sustained more minor wounds and injuries. Hardly one of them was not marked in one way or another.

Cut Lip had been left behind. He had been gut shot and could not ride. They propped him up against a rock and left his weapons with him to await the Yaqui scouts of the Mexicans. Thus Cut Lip became *Nah-welh'-coht Kah-el-keh— The wounded warrior, crippled in battle, who cannot get away*—governed by the code that he must sacrifice his life in order for the other members of the band to escape.

The terrain south and east of the malpais country and Muerte Springs was rolling, like waves frozen in position so that moving objects seen at a distance might be visible for a time only to vanish, then reappear again like distant, slowly operating jack-in-the-boxes. The moon was rising. In time the landscape would be almost day-bright. The skein of fine dust trailing high behind the herd then could be seen for many miles.

Alec rode miles ahead of the herd on a faltering horse. He and Baishan, the least wounded, rode as advance scouts. As it was, there were hardly enough warriors and novices left to handle the large herd. Alec had tried to talk Baishan into abandoning the herd and striking out for the Big Mountain. Baishan would have none of it. The victory had been too costly. Some profit had to be shown for it. Alec had argued that the repeating carbines and revolvers should be enough profit. It had been of no use. Despite his intensive study of the Chiricahuas, he had not yet penetrated the intangible subtleness of the Chiricahua mind. Baishan had agreed to have the herd held in a shallow valley until he and Alec scouted Muerte Springs. It was a dangerous business riding on such a scout. It should have been done afoot. There was no time.

Alec saw nothing but the barren rolling terrain. It was almost as though he had ridden off the face of the earth onto a lunar landscape upon which he was the only living person. Far ahead, just faintly discernible in the growing moonlight, were the humped shades of the malpais country. The Chiricahua Mountains, far beyond the malpais, were nothing but indistinct suggestions of peaks.

Ben Truitt had been trying to locate his ten Scouts. He was sure they had ''gone over the hill.'' He was some miles south of Muerte Springs when he caught an indistinct movement out of the corner of his eye. Dismounting, he tethered his bay in a hollow, took his field glasses, hit the dirt, and bellied up to the rim of the hollow. He focused the glasses on the lone rider approaching. It might be one of the Scouts. The powerful glasses aided by the growing moonlight identified the rider as a tall Apache. Ben studied him. To a skilled and experienced horseman like Ben Truitt there were notable differences in the riding styles of Americans, Mexicans, and Apaches. The approaching horseman might possibly be part Mexican, or perhaps a Mexican *captiva* raised as an Apache. The rider came closer, moving more slowly now, quartering back and forth in wide sweeps, as though intent on looking for tracks. Ben was sure now that the buck rode like a white man, and a cavalryman to boot. Alec was with the raiding Chiricahuas according to the man who called himself Captain Crozier. Ben knew he'd have to take a gamble, with the stakes of life or death. The rider had slowed to a walk.

Ben unbuckled his gunbelt and placed it to one side. He slid his double-barreled derringer up under the tight wristband of his left sleeve. He stood up in full view and raised his arms. There was an instant reaction from the Apache. He slid over on the far side of the horse. A rifle was thrust over the saddle to cover Ben. All Ben could see was a thick mane of hair bound by a headband and a pair of moccasined legs showing under the barrel of the horse. The horse was almost done. Its legs were splayed and his head hung low. Its hide glistened with sweat which ran down to cut wavy runnels through the dust. Gummy yellowish strings of foam hung from its mouth.

Ben knew a little Apache tongue. ''Friend!'' he called out. ''I'm a friend of the white man Never Still! Do you know of him? I'm a friend!'' He lowered his voice. ''Goddamn you,'' he added in good old Anglo-Saxon.

The warrior circled around his horse and came toward Ben, treading noiselessly like a two-legged hunting panther. His rifle was at hip level, and aimed at Ben. As he came nearer his dusty sweat-stained calico headband could be distinguished. His white face paint had run and streaked down his face. His filthy red and white checked shirt was ripped from one side of his lean belly to the other and was stained black with dried blood. Ben's bowels and bladder weakened. He was sure now that he had made a fatal mistake. This sonofabitch was the true article—a real rimrock Apache. He was certain of it when he caught the body stench of stale sweat and dried blood mingled with the acrid horse odor that had permeated the buck's clothing.

The warrior stopped fifteen feet from Ben and surveyed him. "You loco, goddamned Rebel," he said in a thirst-hoarse voice. "Just what the hell are you doing out here alone in Chiricahua country?" He grinned, cracking the dust and paint on his face.

Ben grinned faintly back as he lowered his arms he felt a warm dribbling down his left leg. "Jesus," he blurted hoarsely. "You put the fear of God and sudden death into me with that getup, Alec."

"You didn't answer my question, Ben."

"Are you with them Los Padres raiders?"

Alec nodded. "Those *gambrusinos* won't ever kill or scalp anyone anymore. I killed Chico Diaz." Alec lifted his ripped shirt to show the thin line of dried blood across his belly. He grinned faintly, showing his white teeth. "I should have scalped that damned animal."

Ben was uneasy. Was this the once-cultured graduate of the Military Academy, the consummate cavalry officer? He looked beyond Alec. There was no one else to be seen.

"You still haven't answered my question," Alec said.

"Are you heading for Muerte Springs?" Ben asked.

"Where else? We've got a big herd of horses and mules back some miles. We lost warriors at Los Padres. We're riding short-handed on blown horses. Almost all of the warriors have been wounded or injured. We'd never be able to make the Big Mountain without the water. To top it, Mexican cavalry with Yaqui scouts are somewhere behind us and moving fast. So it's Muerte Springs for certain.''

Ben shook his head. "No chance, Alec.'' He swiftly told Alec of Trapnell's ambush at Muerte Springs. He told him too of Anne Sinclair and of how she had left the springs with the column.

"This Mexican officer you spoke about, Ben. Describe him,'' Alec requested. When Ben did so, Alec nodded. "No question about it. He is the man who calls himself Milo Chaffin.''

"You can't go to the springs now, Alec,'' Ben said quietly.

"We can't do otherwise. Don't worry, there will be no ambush.''

Ben studied him. "What do you intend to do? Surely you can't attack Trapnell? All he's got with him are a bunch of clerks and those damned coffee coolers, if they haven't skedaddled by now.'' Ben stopped talking as he saw the look on Alec's face. He suddenly realized he might have betrayed his trust to a man who had seemed to have become Chiricahua not only in appearance but in character as well. This was a man Ben thought he knew, but there was something alien about him now. A horrifying feeling came over Ben that this educated white man, this professional soldier, had truly become a renegade.

Alec pointed toward the malpais hills. "Go back, Ben. Tell Trapnell to leave at once. I can't stop the Chiricahuas from going there. I'll try to stall them for a time. In any case, they won't approach the springs while the moon is still up.''

"And if he refuses to leave?'' Ben asked.

Alec looked at him. "If he is still there after moonset, the Chiricahuas will move in on him in the dark, run off his horses, and kill every man. My advice to you personally is to warn Trapnell and get the hell out of there.''

Ben studied Alec. "And what will be your part in this? Just who are you, Kershaw? What role are you playing?''

Alec looked away from him. "You haven't much time,'' he said.

Ben buckled his gunbelt. "I have no use for Trapnell and

his bluebellied soldiers, but I'm honor bound to fight with them if he decides to stay."

"It'll be your death warrant, Ben."

"Would you come in and parley if he agrees?"

Alec shook his head. "I'm not in command of the Chiricahuas. Baishan is the war chief. He makes the decisions; he gives the orders." He smiled grimly. "Even if I were allowed to parley, Trapnell would try to kill me on sight."

"Why not? You're the enemy now."

"And you? What am I to *you*? Friend or enemy?"

Ben picked up his carbine and walked to his horse. He turned. "You know how I really feel about those red niggers you're with. As long as you are with them, you are nothing to me. *You don't exist*."

They stood there for a moment, two men who had once been close friends, perhaps brothers in a sense. Then Ben mounted and rode toward the distant springs. He turned and looked back.

Alec was gazing toward the rising moon. He fingered his four-stranded medicine cord. He dipped the fingers of his right hand into a pouch and then chanted in slurring Chiricahua. When he was done chanting, he flicked out his fingers to throw a fine spray of yellowish powder. "*Ek!*" he cried sharply. He was praying to the moon.

CHAPTER 28

MUERTE SPRINGS SEEMED DESERTED WHEN BEN returned. Trapnell had done a comparatively good job of concealing the traces of the recent presence of the column. It was sufficient for *him*, at least. There were also no clues of the ambushers.

Ben led his horse into the shadowed mouth of the pass. He stopped short when he heard the faint clicking of a weapon being cocked.

Colonel Trapnell appeared out of the shadows with a pistol

in his hand. He smiled. "You see, Truitt? Look how well
I've planned." He looked beyond Ben out past the springs to
the distant vista of rolling terrain. "What have you learned?
Where are my Scouts?"

"There *are* Chiricahuas out there, Colonel," Ben replied.
"Your Scouts have vanished. Did any of them return here?"

Trapnell shook his head.

Ben shrugged. "They're gone for sure, then. Pulled foot.
Skedadled. I knew they would."

"You don't seem to have much control over them," Trapnell said coldly.

"You were warned about them, Colonel. Apaches are
guerrilla fighters. Their tactics are hit and run. They don't
fight on defense unless absolutely forced to do so."

Trapnell waved his pistol to indicate the unseen positions
of his men. "This is *not* to be a defensive fight, Truitt. It's
an ambush. My Scouts up there must learn how to fight like
white men. It's the only way the Apaches will eventually be
defeated."

Ben couldn't believe him. "Have you any idea why General Crook started recruiting Apache Scouts? Not to fight like
white men, but to show white troops how the Apaches can
be found and defeated on their own ground. Without them,
the Apaches can never be defeated."

Trapnell stared at him. "I find that incredible! However,
there is not time to discuss the matter. You say the Chiricahuas are out there? Did you actually see any of them?"

Ben shook his head. "No."

"Then how can you be certain?"

"A man gets a *feeling* for them, Colonel. I have that feeling," Ben replied. "Colonel, you must give up this ambush.
The Chiricahuas are sure to come here. You can't depend on
your Apache Scouts. The name Chiricahua can stampede
them faster than a prairie fire. Once darkness comes, they'll
vanish just like that bunch out there supposedly scouting for
you. Your headquarters clerks will be absolutely useless.
You'll all be throwing your lives away. For God's sake, sir,
this is not the way to fight Apaches!"

"My decision stands," insisted Trapnell.

"Remember what Crozier told you. These Chiricahuas will be armed to the teeth with Spencer repeaters and Colt revolvers. Your men are still armed with Sharps single-shot carbines."

Trapnell nodded. "Ah, but we have the advantage of surprise!" he cried. "In any case, if the ambush is not successful, we can at least deny them the use of the springs. Then they'll either have to withdraw or surrender. Do you see my point, Truitt?"

It was hopeless. Ben shrugged.

Trapnell looked out toward the moonlit terrain to the south. He seemed to lapse into deep thought. "This is my great chance," he mused.

Later, after Ben had picketed his horse in a deep draw off the pass, Trapnell showed him the disposition of the soldiers and Apache Scouts. It was well thought out, Ben figured, except for the fact that it would not be successful against the Chiricahuas.

Ben couldn't read the expressions of the Scouts, but he was sure of what they must be thinking. They knew by now that Scouts who had been with Ben had vanished. As long as the moon revealed them, they couldn't make their move. But after moonset . . . There were no enigmatical expressions on the taut white faces of the clerks of Trapnell's headquarters section. Most of these men were fairly well educated for Regular Army soldiers. As clerks they were mostly capable and efficient; as field soldiers they were absolute novices. Their noncommissioned officer was Corporal Sam Pettis. He had fifteen years' service. He had served throughout the Civil War as a clerk at Jefferson Barracks, Missouri. He had risen to sergeant a few times, until demon drink demoted him. He was living proof of the saying, "If there were no drunks, there would be no clerks in the army."

Pettis drew Ben aside when Trapnell was well out of earshot. "For God's sake, Truitt," he whispered hoarsely, "what can we do? This is hopeless. My section and I are not field soldiers. All of us without exception have fired only familiarization courses with the Sharps carbine. Not one of us ever qualified for marksman. Is it true that the Chiricahuas have repeating carbines?''

"That's what that greaser officer said," Ben replied.

Pettis looked around the position. "Well, maybe if we're under cover, we can give a good account of ourselves."

"They won't be around until after dark, Pettis," Ben said.

Pettis stared at him. "But even so, surely *our* Scouts will alert us?"

Ben hated to do it, but he had begun to realize that if he couldn't get Trapnell to leave, he could at least see to it that the men had a chance to save their lives. It would be desertion in the face of the enemy, at least in Trapnell's point of view. But if the headquarters section remained behind, they'd be doomed. The chances against Trapnell surviving if he went on with this madness were monumental. In case of his death the headquarters section would not be held responsible for desertion, providing they kept their mouths shut about what actually happened, and stuck to their own story.

"Truitt?" Pettis asked nervously.

Ben looked at him. "Once it's dark, Pettis, the Scouts will be gone. Desertion doesn't mean a goddamned thing to *them*. They only signed up to get a nice gun, a horse, three squares a day, and pay at the end of the month. They didn't sign the payroll to be patriots and fight for their country."

"You're sure they'll leave?" demanded the noncom.

Ben nodded. "You can copper that bet."

"What should we do? Leave here on our own after moonset?"

Ben walked away. He turned. "It's not for me to say."

"Are you staying?"

"For a time," Ben replied. "For a time . . ."

Pettis looked at the men closest to him. He glanced from one to the other of them. They all nodded.

The moon was reaching its zenith.

The herd was restless. The Chiricahuas were getting nervous. Somewhere to the south Mexican troops with Yaqui scouts were slowly moving toward them, feeling their way carefully for fear of an Apache ambush. Baishan had sent back his own scouts to keep contact with the Mexican soldiers.

"We'll have to go to Muerte Springs during moonlight," Corn Flower said.

"Too dangerous," Hair Rope said. "Not until after dark."

Keen Sighted was inspecting the bullet wound in his thigh. It was already exuding pus. "Some of us are wounded. Is the herd worth the risk of losing more warriors? Let them go. Let's go home!"

Baishan and Alec stood apart from them. "What do you think?" Baishan asked.

Alec looked out across the rolling terrain to the distant malpais hills. "I say we should scout the springs first."

Baishan studied him. "If the Mexicans are not there yet, we still have a good chance of getting in and out of there before they arrive. You were nearer the springs than I. Is there any reason we can't go in? We can send in scouts first. If they are lost, at least the rest will be warned. That is, my brother, if there is anyone there waiting for us."

It was almost as though the astute Chiricahua were reading Alec's mind. Alec did not look at him. There would be little chance that Trapnell would know the springs were being scouted by one or two Apaches. In that way, Baishan would learn about the ambush and avoid it. That is, unless he planned to move in after moonset and kill off the ambushers.

Baishan put his hand on Alec's shoulder. "Is there something you know, Never Still?'" he asked quietly.

Alec turned and walked to his horse. "I'll go first," he said over his shoulder.

"Never Still!" Baishan called out sharply.

Alec turned. "Yes?"

"You are not going alone, " the chief said firmly.

"I'll go with him," Black Bear said.

Baishan shook his head. "It is my duty to go," he said.

Alec could not refuse him. They rode together toward the springs.

The moon was far on the wane when Milo Chaffin returned to the cave where he had left Anne. He squatted beside her and studied her from head to toe. Jesus, but she was a piece of goods! What to do? What to do? He was almost sure Trapnell would not survive the ambush. The damned fool didn't know the Apache. This forced Milo into a dilemma. He had Trapnell's woman. Trapnell was wealthy. If he survived the ambush, he'd want his woman back. He'd have to pay a great deal for that privilege. On the other hand, if Trapnell did *not* survive the ambush, Milo would be stuck with the woman. There was a possibility, of course, that someone else might pay ransom to have her returned, but that was far too risky. The deal would have to be made quickly, giving Milo time to split-ass out of the country. He looked toward the cave entrance. The canyon was already forming shadows. The Chiricahuas might very well be moving in by now. He would have to make damned hasty tracks away from Muerte Springs as soon as it was dark.

Anne moved a little. Milo eyed her fine figure and the full breasts straining against the material of her shirt. He made up his mind—a bird in the hand, and all the rest of that bullshit. . . . He drew his thin-bladed Mexican *cuchillo* and cut through the bonds around her ankles, allowing her to straighten out. He reached out and ripped her shirt from throat to waist, then sliced through the straps of her camisole. The luscious cherry-tipped fruit spilled out into his dirty, grasping hands. He didn't have much time for foreplay. He yanked off her boots, cut through her belt, and peeled off her breeches and underthings. *Jesus*, he thought, it's a damned shame he couldn't take her with him.

Milo stood up, dropped his gunbelt, and unbuttoned his trousers. He grinned. "It isn't exactly a whore's bed, lady," he said, "but it'll have to do. Now, just play along, don't struggle, and you won't get hurt." He held up the slim-bladed knife. "Otherwise, you'll have to be persuaded? You understand?"

Anne looked beyond him. A shadow had darkened the cave entrance. She could dimly make out what appeared to be a tall figure standing there. A cold feeling came over her. *Apache!* Then, as her eyes became accustomed to the dimness, she saw the warrior place a finger to his lips, then step aside out of sight.

Milo was busy forcing her legs apart. One of the horses whinnied sharply. He looked quickly toward the entrance.

The horse whinnied again.

Milo walked cautiously to the entrance and looked out. He saw nothing and turned to go back to Anne.

"Captain Chaffin, I believe," a quiet voice said out of the shadows.

Milo whirled and in a split-second of action threw the *cuchillo* in a full overhand cast. The blade flashed in the dying moonlight as it was aimed directly for the intruder's throat.

Alec instinctively raised his left arm to shield his throat and face. The tip of the knife struck his forearm and penetrated to the bone. He staggered. The shock and pain sickened him. Chaffin whirled and sprinted away. Alec yanked the knife free and ran after him. He could not shoot. A gun report would be heard by the ambushers at the springs.

Chaffin ran through the shallow canyon toward the open desert. He looked back over his shoulder to see the tall lean Apache loping after him. The moonlight glistened on the bloody knife held in his pursuer's right hand. Blood dripped from his left forearm. He was gaining rapidly. Chaffin whirled and clawed for his Colt. It was not there, but still in his gunbelt in the cave. He turned to run again. It was too late. The Apache closed in and drove the knife up under Chaffin's left shoulder blade and into the heart. He left it there.

Alec jumped back. "*Yahtatsan!*" he said.

Anne sat with her back against the cave wall, her hands resting in her lap. She looked up at Alec as he came into the cave. He was gripping his left forearm with his right hand. Blood leaked and dripped through his finger. He cut through her wrist bonds with his own knife and drew her to her feet. They clung together in the dimness. She sobbed convulsively. He stepped back, picked up her torn clothing, and held it out to her, then returned to the mouth of the cave while she hurriedly dressed as best she could. He bound his wound while he waited.

He turned as she came to him. "Why in God's name did you return here?" he asked bluntly.

"I had heard you were with the Chiricahuas," she replied.

He shook his head. "The odds of your finding me here were a million to one, Anne."

She smiled a little. "But I *did* find you!"

He rolled his eyes upward. "Christ," he said. "The only reason I came here was to find out where Trapnell had hidden his horses. The moon is almost gone. The Chiricahuas will be here before too long."

"Can't we leave now?" she asked.

He hesitated for a moment. "I can't," he finally replied.

"But why?" she demanded. "Is it because of your loyalty to those savages?"

He looked down at her. "Partly."

"And what else, Alec?"

"It's Trapnell. He's still planning to carry out his ambush. He hasn't a chance. His Scouts and probably his soldiers will pull out of there as soon as it's dark enough. Then the Chiricahuas will move in. That will be the end of him unless I can save him."

She studied him. "He means nothing to you, Alec. If he had the chance, he'd not do it for you. For God's sake, let us leave here now!"

He raised his head. "Wait," he whispered. He padded outside. There was some movement in the gathering darkness near the horse herd. "Stay here," he said over his shoulder, then he was gone.

She waited tensely. She picked up her Spencer and levered a round into the chamber.

Minutes passed slowly.

Alec whistled softly from outside. He came into the cave. "It's the first of Trapnell's Scouts," he whispered. "They're starting to pull out."

They waited in the darkness. After a time it was quiet again.

"Can't we leave now?" she pleaded again.

He clamped a dirty, bloodstained hand over her mouth.

"Shut up!" he hissed close to her ear. "If they see me, it'll be the end of me!"

Later, when the darkness was thicker, Alec went toward the herd again. In a little while he was back. "Keep quiet. Don't move," he whispered.

Then she heard the sound of muffled hoofbeats and the low voices of men mingled with the creaking of saddle leather. She felt rather than saw the horsemen pass the entrance to the cave and ride through the shallow canyon leading to the desert beyond. Then it was quiet again.

Alec left the cave. When he returned, he drew her close. "Those were Trapnell's soldiers. The Scouts must have left just ahead of them but by another way."

"Then we can leave now?" she asked.

He shook his head. "There isn't a horse left in the canyon," he replied quietly.

A wolf howled from a hill above the canyon.

"That's Baishan," Alec whispered. "I'll have to go. Stay here. Sit tight. I'll get back as soon as I can." He started for the cave entrance.

"Alec!" she called.

He turned.

"What if you don't get back?" she asked.

He did not reply. He left the cave. A moment later she heard him give a perfect imitation of a wolf howl.

CHAPTER 29

THE MOON WAS LONG GONE. BEN TRUITT LAY IN A SHALlow depression overlooking the springs. Now and again he had heard vague sounds in the darkness as the moonlight had first faded out and then died altogether. After a time it had become deathly quiet.

"Truitt?" Trapnell called softly.

"Here," Ben replied.

The colonel came through the darkness and crouched beside Ben. "Have you changed the position of any of the men?" he asked.

Ben shook his head.

"Then where are they?" demanded Trapnell.

Ben hesitated for a moment. "I told you they'd pull foot, Colonel. You won't find a damned one of them."

"But my soldiers? Surely they're still here?"

"Not a one, Colonel," Ben replied dryly.

"You're certain?"

"Positive. I'm all you've got left, Colonel."

"I'll track them down, damn them!" Trapnell cried.

"Not a chance. Colonel, for Christ's sake! Take a warning! Maybe it's not too late. Get the hell out of here!"

"We've seen no Chiricahuas yet."

Ben shook his head in disgust. "You won't *ever* see them. Colonel, let me go back and see if I can find a couple of horses for us at least."

Trapnell stared into the darkness. Finally, he nodded his head. "All right, Truitt, but we'll use them only if necessary."

Ben stared at him. "You still plan to stay here?" He looked closely at Trapnell, and the slow realization came to him that the man was deathly frightened. Perhaps it wasn't that the colonel wanted to stay at the springs, but instead was more frightened to leave them and risk the unknown dangers of the desert and the dark night.

Ben took his Spencer and crawled through the tumbled chaos of the malpais until he could descend into the pass. He headed for the draw where he had left his bay.

Baishan crouched in a declivity beside Alec. "You say the soldiers and the Scouts have all left?" he asked.

"I showed you the place where the horses were kept," Alec replied. Maybe he could convince Baishan to have the captured herd brought in for watering. Then, hopefully, if Trapnell was still in the area, he would have enough sense to lay low, keep his presence unknown, and leave after the Chiricahuas were gone. It would be a gamble. The cost might just be Trapnell's life, and possibly that of Ben Truitt unless he too had taken French leave along with the Scouts and soldiers.

"We'd better get back to the herd and move them here," Alec said.

Baishan said nothing.

"Do you hear me, brother?" asked Alec. "Time is running out. Those damned Mexicans might be closer than we think. We'll either have to get water or run for the Big Mountain without it."

Baishan was fingering his medicine cord and muttering to himself. It was almost as though he were alone.

"Baishan?" Alec hissed. "Make a decision! *Now!*"

The Chiricahua looked at him. "This is not a good place, Never Still," he said fearfully.

"I know that! Whoever said it was?"

"It's worse at night," Baishan continued. "It is then that the spirits of the dead return here to wait for vengeance on the living."

Alec heaved a sigh. "That's not true," he said.

Baishan drew him close. "That's because you are a White-Eye! What do you know? White men are blind. They see nothing except that which is solid and easily seen. They know nothing of the spirit world! You who dress and act like one of The People are still a White-Eye! You know nothing!"

"Look, my brother," Alec said in a low tense voice. "What will you do now? There are no ambushers left at the springs. The Mexicans have not come. Now is your chance! But you've got to move!"

Baishan looked up at the sky. "We must wait until dawn," he said firmly.

"This is madness! What about the Mexicans?" demanded Alec.

Baishan shrugged. "Better to risk the Mexicans than the spirits of the dead. We can kill Mexicans with rocks. Who can kill those already dead?"

It was no use. They must wait until dawn.

Ben could not find his bay. He stood there in the darkness trying to make a decision. He knew he'd never make it out of the malpais and across the desert afoot. He also knew that if he'd returned to Trapnell, he'd never convince him to leave, and Ben didn't want to die with the damned fool. His only alternative was to seek a hiding place not too far from the springs and sit tight until it was all over. If he could help Trapnell, he'd do it. If not, he had a good chance of surviving this madness.

Baishan left to return to his warriors, leaving Alec on watch. The Chiricahua planned to instruct Black Bear, who was his second-in-command, to wait until the first traces of the false dawn appeared, then to move in on the springs. If, however, the Mexicans appeared, Black Bear was to abandon the herd and head back to the Big Mountain. Baishan and Alec would follow later.

Alec returned to Anne. He guided her back to the pass and into a place of hiding closer to the springs. He had decided that if the Chiricahuas successfully watered their herd, or instead returned to the Big Mountain, he would leave them and take Anne back to safety. If, however, the Mexicans arrived and gave battle, that would be another matter.

Alec moved in toward the springs. Somewhere in the darkness Trapnell was hiding, and perhaps Brazos as well.

"Stay where you are, Kershaw," a voice said from behind him.

Alec turned. "You're damned good at this business, Rebel," he said quietly.

"I had a good teacher. Raise your hands!" Ben ordered.

Alec raised his hands. "Now that you have me, what are you going to do with me?" he asked.

Ben shrugged. "How the hell do I know? All I want to do is keep Trapnell from getting an Apache knife in his back. Maybe yours."

"I wasn't planning to kill him," Alec said. "Which is probably different than what he has in mind for me."

"The man is all alone now. All he's got is me. Alec, he's frightened half to death. He doesn't want to stay and he can't run. Christ, if you only knew how badly *I* want to run!"

"You've got until dawn to get him out of here. The Chiricahuas won't come in here until then. They're scared of the spirits of the dead. They don't fear the Mexicans as much.''

Ben tilted his head to one side and studied Alec. ''Ah, but I've got *you*. How much are *you* worth to the Chiricahuas? Maybe I can make a deal with Baishan.''

Alec shook his head. ''It won't work.''

''Why not? He's your brother, ain't he? That should be worth something.''

Alec thought about Cut Lip, gut shot and unable to ride, propped up against a rock with his weapons in the path of the Mexican troops. ''*Nah-welh'-coht Kah-el-keh,*'' Alec said, almost as though to himself.

''What kind of gibberish is that?'' demanded Ben.

''A code, Ben. You wouldn't understand. You're the enemy. Not mine, but theirs. As long as I ride as one of them, I am bound by their code of conduct.''

Ben stared at him. ''You've gone loco for sure.''

There was faint movement behind Ben. Christ, thought Alec, if that's Baishan . . .

Anne spoke out of the darkness. ''Drop the gun, Ben,'' she said quietly.

Ben began to turn toward her. Alec moved in three plunging strides, yanked Ben's right shoulder back, and hit him with a jolting right cross that staggered him and put him down. Alec caught his Spencer before it hit the ground.

They worked fast. Alec bound Ben's wrists together, then hoisted him onto his shoulders. He trotted beside Anne through the darkness back to the cave where he had left her. Then he gagged Ben and tied his ankles together.

''Where's Burton?'' Anne whispered.

Alec shook his head. ''Keep an eye on this one. Don't give him a chance. He might kill you if he gets an opening. I doubt it, but if he's desperate enough, he might try.'' He kissed her and turned to leave.

''Where are you going now?''

''To try to find Trapnell,'' he said dryly. ''If he's still around by dawn, he won't live to see the sunrise.'' He vanished into the shadows.

The faintest trace of dawn light was in the eastern sky when Baishan returned. He looked at the bloodstained bandage on Alec's left forearm. "That looks fresh," he said.

Alec nodded. "I fell on a sharp rock," he explained.

Baishan was satisfied. "We'll go to the springs now, brother. The herd will soon be on the way."

They walked together through the pass toward Muerte Springs.

It was tomb-quiet around the springs. Nothing moved. There was no wind. The scattered skulls and bones shone dimly in the growing pale light. Baishan fingered his medicine cord. He scattered *hoddentin* in preparation for praying to the dawn. They stood with their backs to one of the burned-out adobe huts.

"Kershaw," a cold voice said from behind them.

Alec and Baishan whirled. Trapnell stood in the doorway of the hut, not twenty feet away, pistol in hand, and aimed directly at Alec's face. There was a set look to Trapnell's face, and his teeth showed between his tightly drawn lips. He cocked the pistol.

Baishan moved fast. He raised his carbine for a clear and easy shot at Trapnell. Alec thrust out his left arm under the carbine barrel and forced it upward. Both guns cracked simultaneously. The carbine bullet whined thinly through the air. The .44 caliber slug hit Baishan just below the rib cage with the sound of a stick being whipped into thick mud. His eyes were wide with surprise as he looked at Alec, then he fell heavily back into the shallow pool.

Trapnell darted sideways, cocked his pistol, and aimed at Alec. Alec dropped flat, rolled over, came up on his feet, and closed in on Trapnell. The pistol cracked. The slug plucked at the slack in Alec's shirt. That was Trapnell's last chance. At the last possible second Alec closed his fists and hit Trapnell with a vicious one-two, sending him flat on his back. The colonel did not try to rise.

Alec stood there for a few seconds, then dragged Baishan from the bloodstained water. He ripped open Baishan's shirt and wadded his own headband over the wound to stop the flow of blood.

There was hardly any time left. Alec picked up Trapnell and placed him across his shoulders. He trotted into the shadowed pass and carried the colonel to the hiding place of Anne and Ben. Alec dumped him on the ground. He cut Ben loose and grabbed him by the shirt front. "Listen, you Rebel sonofabitch!" he snarled. "I'm giving the both of you a chance to live. Keep him quiet when he wakes up. The Chiricahuas will soon be here, but only long enough to water their horses. There are Mexican troops heading this way. You can turn yourselves over to them."

"What about Anne?" Ben asked.

"Take her with you."

She shook her head. "Not on your life, Alec. I've found you again and I'm not going to lose you. I'm staying with you."

"How the hell am I going to explain you?" Alec demanded.

She smiled sweetly. "You'll think of something. Besides, Baishan invited me to the Big Mountain, as well as you, remember?"

"She's got you there, Alec," Ben said dryly. "Will you shake my hand?"

They gripped hands and looked into each other's eyes. All was well between them again.

Anne and Alec were attending to Baishan when the first of the Chiricahuas showed up at the springs. They stared uncomprehendingly at the unconscious Baishan and at Anne. Alec quickly explained that soldiers had been at the springs and had left because of the approach of the Chiricahuas. One of the soldiers had lagged behind, and had attacked and wounded Baishan. The soldier had then made good his escape. The woman had become separated from the retreating party in the confusion and had been left behind. By coincidence she was Alec's woman. The Runner verified that fact.

Keen Sighted was in an ugly mood because of his wound. "What will you do with her, Never Still?" he asked truculently.

"Why, take her with us," Alec replied coolly.

The Apache shook his head. "She'll slow us down too much. Kill her now and have done with it!"

"She rides with us," Alec said flatly.

Keen Sighted dropped his hand to the haft of his knife. He and Alec locked eyes. The rest of the warriors watched them closely.

The Runner stepped in between them. "Enough! This woman was with Never Still when he saved my life at Muerte Canyon. She helped him. Without the both of them I would have died of the black poison sickness. She rides with us!"

The tension was was broken by the arrival of Hair Rope on his dying horse. "The Mexicans are only a few miles away!" he shouted. "They are approaching slowly for fear of an ambush! Get on with the watering!"

The Mexican's Yaqui Scouts reached the south side of the malpais just as the last of the horse herd was driven by the Chiricahuas into the pass leading to the north and safety.

C H A P T E R 30

IT WAS LATE AFTERNOON. THE SEASON WAS EARTH IS Reddish Brown, the late fall. Already Ghost Face, winter, was making his chill presence felt on the Big Mountain. Soon it would be time for the Chiricahuas to leave for the foothills. That thought was in Alec Kershaw's mind as he sat in the wickiup of Baishan beside the chief's pallet. Baishan had not uttered a word since being wounded at Muerte Springs. Only his eyes could express his feelings, and they were enigmatical. It was out of Alec's "power" to do anything for him. The Chiricahuas knew of Never Still's power, of course. Had he not saved The Runner from death by the always fatal black poisoning? Not even that last resort, the Ghost Dance, had ever done that. The bullet was still embedded in Baishan's chest, close to his heart. Alec could not probe for it. The odds of Baishan surviving a probing were insurmountable. Alec knew Baishan would soon die, and he knew that Baishan was aware of it as well. Baishan and he had both seen far too much battle and death not to be aware of the fate of one wounded in this fashion.

Alec had been in constant attendance on the chief in the weeks since they had returned to the rancheria. True, the *diyis* of the band were there as well. Black Wind had gone up the mountain to pray for Baishan's recovery. Olgigah, The Singer, a *diyi* of another band said to have remarkable curing powers for such wounds, had been sent for to aid in the effort. He was cousin to Baishan. The Runner had succeeded Looking Glass, his first mentor. Since her loss he had become assistant to Black Wind. Though young in years, The Runner had gained much prestige by surviving the black poison sickness as well as the savage massacre at San Tiburcio. He had performed notably at Los Padres and on the return march to the Big Mountain. Baishan had not spoken to any of them since his wounding.

Baishan was in one of his deep comas. Alec expected him to die every time he drifted off this way. Only the two of them knew the real truth of Baishan's wounding. The shocked and uncomprehending look on the Apache's face when he had fallen from Trapnell's bullet was with Alec constantly during his waking hours and in his dreams while asleep. Night after night Alec woke up during the recurring dream of the event at Muerte Springs. Anne had been awakened too. He had not told her the truth for fear of frightening her about what might happen to him and her probable fate as well if the story got out. Alec would be killed. Anne would probably be claimed by some warrior. There would be no marriage. She would become the abject slave to his wife, or wives, hounded and beaten by them, a life of perpetual hell from which there could be no escape.

The puzzle that engrossed Alec was whether or not Baishan was truly incapable of speech or if he was remaining silent by his own will.

In moments of weakness Alec thought of escaping from the rancheria. He was almost sure he could make it alone; he knew he'd not succeed if he took Anne with him. He must bring her along if he did leave, though, no matter the odds.

It had become a tormenting dilemma for him. Was he thinking only of his own skin? The truth evaded him or perhaps,
in a deeper sense, he was subconsciously evading it.

The Runner came into the wickiup to relieve Alec and
looked intently at him.

Alec shook his head. "No change," he said quietly.

"Do you think there will be?"

"I don't know," Alec replied.

The Runner touched the stump of his left arm. "Are you
sure? You had the power to save me from the black poison
sickness. Such great power should be able to save my brother's life as well." He studied Alec with his large expressive
eyes.

Alec wondered uneasily just how much The Runner actually knew. Perhaps he had guessed the truth and only his
loyalty to Alec had kept him quiet. Was it possible that he
truly believed Alec could save Baishan and therefore would
not speak out?

"My grandfather Black Wind is still up on the mountain
praying," The Runner said. "He has been up there three days
and three nights. He has no food or water and no shelter. If
he doesn't come down soon, he'll die up there."

Alec shrugged. "Perhaps that's the way he wants it," he
said, a little cruelly perhaps. What good would all the old
man's praying and fasting do now? Baishan was doomed.

The Runner looked at Baishan. "Where does he go when
he sleeps, Never Still? Does he slide down the sand hill to the
underworld? Does he meet the figure with no face who en-
tices him with fruit to stay in that dark place?"

Alec shook his head. "If he does meet the figure, he must
be refusing the fruit, for he always awakens here."

The Runner looked sideways at Alec. "I think he refuses
the fruit and returns here to our world for some powerful reason of his own," he said thoughtfully.

Alec did not look at him. "Such as?"

"I don't know. Perhaps it is *you* who knows."

Alec stood up, bending to avoid the low roof. He went to
the door and looked back. "No, I don't," he replied shortly.
He left the wickiup.

The rancheria, usually so full of life when the people went about their everyday chores and business and the children played, was always quiet now. It was an eerie quietness. It was as though someone or something invisible but there all the same were haunting the silent woods or the brooding mountaintop where Black Wind kept his lonely vigil in the cold wind, watching and waiting, *always waiting.* . . .

Throughout the rancheria were the rounded blackened places of burned wickiups, mute testimony to those people massacred at San Tiburcio and those who had died at Los Padres. All their possessions had been burned as well. Their horses had been killed. Their families mourned for thirty days and nights, morning, noon, and night. The names of the dead would never be spoken again.

Anne was seated on her pallet with an old Mexican serape draped around her shoulders. A fire was dying in the fire pit. She looked questioningly at Alec as he entered and dropped the rawhide door covering into place.

He sat down beside her. "No change," he said.

"You can do nothing?"

He shook his head. "The finest surgeons in the world using the latest techniques couldn't save him now. I doubt if ever they could have. He's doomed."

"What happens now?"

"I don't know. Black Wind is still up on the mountain praying."

"What good can that blind and decrepit old man do up there?" she asked.

Alec shrugged. "When and if he comes down, he'll likely call for the Curing, or Ghost Dance. It's the last shot in the locker, the last possible resort. I think everyone knows that and are but waiting for him to come down from the mountain and make it official."

She shook her head. "I can't believe these people. Do they really think that by wearing weird costumes, dancing, singing, and chanting they can save a person who is obviously dying?"

He looked into the strange, elusive shadows moving across

the thick bed of deep red embers in the fire pot. "It worked for me," he said quietly.

"I can't believe you! An educated man and with medical training to boot, thinking such a thing!" she cried.

"This is not our world. These are not our people. I truly believe that primitive peoples are closer to nature and its great mysteries than we so-called civilized people will ever know. Perhaps earlier in our civilization we might have had those same senses, but they are lost now, overlaid and buried by what we term our culture."

She studied him. "You surprise me."

"They surprise *me*! I've seen things here for which there is no possible scientific explanation. Yet I am positive they happened."

"Such as your so-called miraculous cure after you were wounded at Los Padres?" she asked skeptically.

Alec nodded. "They brought me here badly wounded and did all they could for me with their native medical knowledge. When that failed they called for the Curing Dance. Somehow, God alone knows, it healed me."

"I can't imagine you accepting that."

"I'm here, aren't I?" he asked sharply.

"Perhaps you would have survived in any case," she persisted.

Alec was silent for a time. After a while he looked sideways at her. "Ah, but we don't really *know* that, do we?" he asked quietly.

Anne had no answer.

It was nearing dusk when Black Wind came down from the mountain. One moment the steep trail was empty of life and in the next an indistinct figure evolved, seemingly more shadow than substance. The old shaman moved as noiselessly as a wraith of drifting smoke. The people gathered on the wide circular area of barren hardpacked earth that was the dancing ground. Alec and Anne waited there with the rest of the band. A breeze bearing a chill crept through the treetops, rustling the leaves and fluttering the loose clothing of the people.

Black Wind walked slowly into the center of the dancing

ground. He wore his buckskin medicine shirt, the front and back of which were joined only at the shoulders. The shirt was painted with symbolic designs of the butterfly, medicine gods, the sun, a moon mask, three crescent moons, and a wavy snake design. His skull-shaped medicine cap was made of the skin of a nearly grown fawn which had been captured alive and strangled. It was decorated with eagle feathers, abalone shell, and chalchihuitl stone. It was painted with symbols of the clouds, a rainbow, hail, the morning star, the God of Wind, the Mountain Spirits, and the sun. A big rattlesnake rattle had been fastened upright at the apex of the cap. The tail of the hat represented the centipede, an important animal god of the Apaches. The hat was very old, soiled with dirt, and begrimed with soot.

Anne stood half behind a tree watching the ancient *diyi* as he moved around the center of the dancing area giving instructions to the Singer and The Runner, as well as the rest of his people. She had never seen the old man before. She looked curiously at Alec.

"Black Wind," Alec whispered. "He's been totally blind for perhaps forty years. His medicine hat is the most sacred of his possessions. The hat gives him life and strength and enables him to peer into the future. With it he can tell who has stolen horses, foresee the approach of enemies, and aid in curing the sick. Those figures you see on his hat and medicine shirt are all symbolic and can be prayed to in time of need." Alec paused for a moment. "As you see him now, he has ceased to be a man, but instead has become the 'power' he represents, in this instance the power of healing the sick."

"You sound almost as though you believe it," Anne said.

Alec shook his head. "It's not quite a question of belief or disbelief. You'll never see anything for the rest of your life to match what you will witness tonight. These people believe that evil spirits are the cause of sickness. Their treatment is designed to drive the spirit, or the sickness, which are one and the same, away from the patient. It consists mostly of dancing. It is always performed at night. The real significance of what you will see is known only to the Apaches, and

even then, only the medicine men know the full portent of
it.''

Five fires had been kindled on the dancing ground. One
stood at each of the cardinal points of the compass. The center fire represented the zenith. A lone drummer was to be the
musician. His instrument was a large iron kettle partially
filled with water over which had been stretched a well-soaped
cloth. His single drumstick was a hooped stick which he
struck from side to side on the drum head.

All was ready. The people spoke in low tones or whispers,
glancing uneasily over their shoulders into the dark woods,
and in the direction of the stream that ran along one side of
the canyon. Baishan had been carried from his wickiup and
placed facing to the east on a pallet beside the central fire.
Alec and Anne stood at the end of the line of people. Anne
was behind a bifurcated tree trunk looking through the V-
shaped gap. It wasn't much shelter, but it helped a little bit,
at least psychologically.

It became very quiet, except for the subdued crackling of
the fires and the whisper of the chill wind in the treetops.

Anne suddenly became aware of a distant rhythmical
buzzing sound emanating from the dark woods in the direction of the stream. The buzzing gradually became louder.
Then, through the mingled shadows and drifting fire smoke
a grotesque black-hooded man-figure appeared in the firelight. A U-shaped framework rose above his head with an arc
of wooden slats above it. The slats were painted in primary
colors. In the center of the arc rose the form of a four-barred
cross. He wore a buckskin *himper* from waist to knees and
the typical *n'deh b'keh* desert moccasins on his legs. The
himper and moccasins were painted in various colors and designs. He wore a girdle of spruce branches around his waist.
His bare torso was painted white with black dots. His hood
was crested in front by the feathers of a large turkey tail di-
vided into two parts, one on each side of the head so that they
appeared like two large donkey ears. He held a forked stick
in his left hand. It was similar to the trident of the sea god,
Neptune. In his right hand he held a long cord to which was
attached a flat rectangular piece of wood painted front and

back with wavy lines. He twirled this with great dexterity around his head front to rear, creating the buzzing sound.

Alec drew Anne close to him. "He is the Clown of the Mountain Spirits. The thing he whirls over his head is a rhombus, or bull-roarer. The top is carved like a human head representing the Wind God. The wavy lines on the front depict his entrails, those on the back are his hair. The wood is pine or fir, from a tree struck by lightning. It is called *tziditinde,* or the 'sounding wood.' His torso is painted white with black spots to represent a young deer which is his invisible steed. You'll see him ride the deer at one time or another."

The Clown crow-hopped into the dancing circle. Black Wind covered his face with his hands and began to chant. The drumbeat began. The people started a monotonous singsong cadence, led by Black Wind, The Singer, and The Runner. The Clown hopped about, sometimes shrieking or whooping, and occasionally gobbling like a turkey.

"Look!" Anne whispered to Alec.

Four torches had appeared in the woods. They moved toward the dancing ground. Then the four Gan, or Mountain Spirit impersonators, appeared. Their masks held spread turkey tails rather than parted ones like that of the Clown. Each of the Gan had a thunderbolt painted on his arms from wrist to shoulder and a crescent moon painted on his chest. There were white dots on their torsos instead of the Clown's black spots. They too wore girdles of spruce branches and carried a wand in each hand. The wands were about two inches wide and three feet long. A thunderbolt was drawn on each side. Four feathers, two to a side, were suspended from each wand. They entered the circle from the southwest.

"The Men of the Mountain. The white dots on their torsos indicate they are pure of heart," Alec whispered to Anne. "It is dangerous to imitate a Mountain Spirit unless one is pure of heart."

The Gan circled the dance area, moving closer and closer to Baishan. They constantly put their heads near the ground as though smelling for something. They clucked, sputtered, and gobbled while strutting like giant turkeys and waving their wands in imitation of flying birds.

The Gan came closer to Baishan, halted suddenly as though surprised at his presence, then danced backward several yards. They strutted back and forth seven times, gobbling and waving their wands. It was remarkable mimicry. Anne half-closed her eyes and watched them through the mingled smoke and rising dust, and it almost seemed to her that these were indeed giant turkeys. Meanwhile the Clown performed his antics by himself, rolling on the ground, somersaulting, and generally making a fool of himself in order to amuse the crowd. Suddenly, as though at an unheard command, the drumming and singing stopped short. Buckskin Shaker, the oldest squaw in the rancheria and "godmother" to the medicine men, hobbled into the dancing area, sprinkled *hodden-tin* on the dancers, and blew her breath on them. They instantly left for the dark shelter of the woods.

Anne leaned close to Alec. "Is that all?"

Alec shook his head. "Only the beginning. You've a long night ahead of you, Annie girl. The ceremony lasts until dawn."

The singing and chanting began to increase. The Gan and Clown reentered the circle from the southwest. The Gan formed a single line column facing west. Baishan was turned to face them. The only motion about him was the rising and falling of his chest and the slight movement of his eyes, from which the firelight reflected like dark rubies. The Clown went through his antics. The Gan danced for a long time in single file. They approached Baishan once more, then backed away. They repeated this action over and over again, each time getting nearer to the chief. They seemed to be in no hurry. Each movement and gesture must be performed exactly so. After what seemed a long time, the leading Gan finally reached Baishan. He placed his crossed wands in the four cardinal directions on Baishan's head, back, lower extremities, and chest. Then the Gan danced backward, raised the crossed wands toward the northeastern heavens, and abruptly parted them with a sweeping motion while emitting a hissing sound from his mouth.

Alec shook Anne gently. "He's scattering the 'sick,' " he explained. She seemed half-asleep. Her head snapped up and her eyes widened as the lead dancer emitted a piercing howl and cantered off into the darkness as though mounted on a steed. One after the other of the remaining dancers and the Clown performed the same act. The Clown concluded his performance by sweeping his wand over Baishan as though collecting something, then stabbing repeatedly at the wand with his trident.

"He's spearing the 'sick,' which he's captured on his wand," Alec whispered.

The Gan and the Clown reappeared three more times. The first time Baishan was turned to face the southeast and the dancers approached from that direction. The second time he was faced southwest while the dancers approached from the northeast. The third time he turned to the northwest and the dancers came from the southeast. Then there came a long pause before the reappearance of the Gan. The Clown dashed about, waking up the sleeping, poking the drowsy with his trident, and forcing them to their feet. One time he cantered back and forth, suddenly darted toward Anne's protective tree, and poked the trident through the fork to wake her up. The drowsy people swayed and sometimes staggered in their dancing in their effort to stay awake. The singing never wavered or stopped.

Hour after hour; incessant pounding of the drum; slap and shuffle of moccasined feet; never ceasing singing and chanting.

Alec supported Anne as they shuffled back and forth. "Do you feel the *power*?" he whispered.

She forced her eyes open. "I feel nothing but exhaustion," she mumbled. "How many times must they do this? How much longer does this go on?"

"It's done thirteen times—lucky or unlucky."

She yawned prodigiously. "Which one is this?"

He shrugged. "Nine or ten. I've lost count."

"My God! It'll soon be dawn!"

Alec nodded. "That's the whole purpose."

"What happens then?"

He hesitated. "He either recovers or he dies," he quietly replied.

In the darkest hours before dawn an intensity seemed to gather around the people, the dancers, and Baishan. It was nothing palpable, yet it was there. It was almost as though the area had been transported to another dimension, a limbo between heaven and earth, belonging to both and yet to neither.

The Clown dashed about with redoubled energy. Everyone must dance, or the spell might lose power and be broken—*dance, dance, dance*.

The faintest tinge of gray appeared in the eastern sky. The chanting increased and became louder. The people began to screech like owls. The dancing became more intense. Black Wind, The Singer, and The Runner ran around, sprinkling everyone with *hoddentin*. The drumbeat cadence changed into a peculiar sort of rhythm. The chanting and owl-screeching became ear-grating.

"The last final effort, Anne," Alec Shouted. "Dance! Dance! *Dance!* Sing! Sing! *Sing!*"

Anne looked sideways at him, and it was almost as though his face had changed, as though this were not the man she knew but a person of another, alien world. It was at once both fascinating and frightening.

Incessant pounding of the drum; slap and shuffle of moccasined feet; chanting, screeching, singing at what seemed an impossible pitch.

The Gan dancers approached Baishan. The people changed into the Wheel Dance. The din was horrendous, echoing from the canyon walls and the mountain. The excitement was intense. It was fever pitch. The Gan closed in. The *diyis* raised Baishan to his feet and supported him. His head hung, he wobbled and staggered, but he *danced*. . . .

"It's impossible!" cried Anne.

"But there it is!" shouted Alec.

The lead dancer of the Gan came to Baishan. The sky was lighter now. The Gan hopped and strutted, bent low, then arose in exact imitation of a giant tom turkey. The sun was almost due up. He motioned the *diyis* aside. They released

Baishan. The Gan thrust his wands into Baishan's hands and danced backward. Baishan stumbled around, then raised his wands high toward the respective homes of the gods of heaven and swayed violently. It seemed impossible that he could stay on his feet.

The sunrise exploded silently in the eastern sky.

Baishan fell heavily. One of the wands snapped under the weight of his body. He did not move. He did not rise.

The drumming, singing, and dancing stopped instantly. The sudden unbroken silence was eerie to an extreme. Black Wind slowly approached his grandson. He knelt beside him for a moment, then rose stiffly. Gone were the incredibly agile movements of the night's dancing.

Black Wind raised his skinny arms toward the rising sun. *"Hio esken eskingo boyonsidda!* he cried in the strong voice of his full manhood. *"Where is the child this morning?"* He paused, bowed his head for a moment, then raised it again. *"Where will he be the day after tomorrow? We don't know! His soul has gone into the air. . . ."* It was the cry from a broken heart. He knelt and covered Baishan's face with a cloth. The Gan and Clown vanished swiftly into the woods. The Singer and The Runner scattered earth and ashes around Baishan. Then the mournful death chant rose from all the people.

"He's gone," Alec whispered to Anne.

Her face was taut and ashen white. "How did he dance like that in his condition?" she asked slowly.

"The power," Alec replied simply.

"Is that all?" she asked.

Alec shrugged. "Is there any other explanation?"

She studied him closely. "Alec, for God's sake, tell me! Was he still alive when he danced there at the end?"

Alec turned away from her without a word and walked into the shadowed woods.

CHAPTER 31

BAISHAN WAS LAID OUT IN HIS WICKIUP. HE HAD BEEN stripped and cleaned. His thick hair had been washed, parted, and brushed until smooth and glossy. He was attired in his ceremonial clothing and moccasins. He wrists were covered with bracelets and beads. His four-stranded medicine cord, adorned with stones, beads, feathers, and fetishes, was around his neck. His wives had removed everything from the wickiup except his personal belongings. They had removed everything red from their clothing and possessions and destroyed it. The cloth and hide covering of the wickiup was removed and an opening made in the north side so that it might be entered from there rather than from the customary eastern side.

All the people filed through the wickiup to see him. When the last of them had passed through the lodge, Baishan was wrapped in a blanket shroud with his most intimate possessions. He was carried from the lodge and placed on a litter. The wickiup was set afire. Gunshots from the direction of the corrals punctuated the dismal coyotelike howlings of the chanting that had never ceased since his death. One would have sworn that the chanters were joined by the real howling of wolves and coyotes, as though they had gathered to mourn the passing of the chief–Baishan.

Anne was startled by the shooting. "What's that, Alec?" she asked.

"They are killing his horses," Alec replied.

"How long does this chanting go on? It's beginning to drive me mad," she said tensely.

"Thirty days, morning, noon, and night," he replied.

At sunrise the warriors carried Baishan up the mountain. The day before they had pried a huge boulder from the earth and enlarged the cavity. The body was cramped into sitting position facing the rising sun. The three *diyis* sprinkled ashes and *hoddentin* around the grave site starting from the southwest corner. They uttered prayers so that Baishan's soul would enter *O'zho*, or Heaven. The grave was packed with earth and stones. The boulder was laboriously levered back into position. Rocks were piled around the base to keep out the wolves and coyotes. The mourners filed silently down the long steep trail to the canyon far below. Soon only Black Wind and Alec were left at the grave site.

The old man sat with his back against the boulder facing the rising sun. He was motionless. His breathing was hardly noticeable. He looked across the vast panorama of the Chiricahuas as though he could truly see them as he had seen them forty years past before he had been blinded.

The band had suffered a grievous loss, far greater than that of an older person whose death was ordained. The death of any young warrior was a blow to the band, whose numbers diminished every year, but the passing of Baishan, a great war leader in his prime, was almost akin to a mortal blow.

Black Wind turned and looked directly at Alec, who was standing fifty feet away. Alec had not spoken during or after the burial. "You will be leaving the Big Mountain now, Never Still," Black Wind said quietly. It was not a question, but a statement of fact. How had Black Wind known he was there at all and had remained behind after the others had left? Was it pure guesswork?

Alec walked closer to Black Wind. "That is true, Grandfather," he replied.

Black Wind nodded. "You can't stay with these people. This is not the place for you. You must leave. . . ."

Alec stared incredulously at him. It was the same voice he thought he had heard seemingly so long ago in Looking Glass's wickiup. Yet the old man had been up on the mountain then. Coincidence? Yes, that was it! Alec slowly shook his head. And yet . . .

"If you ever return," the old man continued, "will it be as friend or enemy."

Again, it was not a question.

"Hopefully, as a friend," Alec said.

Black Wind shook his head. "If you return to being a soldier, it will have to be on the terms of your war leader. We both know that it will be as an enemy.''

"I don't know if I will return to being a soldier.''

Black Wind nodded. "You will. That is your true life, Never Still. Do you remember how we talked in the *yoshti* before our people crossed the canyon at San Tiburcio? You said the Americans were like the leaves of the trees. They are strong and well armed. They think of all this vast land as only theirs. You said there was no way The People could defeat them. Do you remember?''

"Yes I do, Grandfather, but none of you believed me.''

There was a long pause. "*I* did,'' Black Wind said quietly. "I know the Americans are like the leaves of summer—the Time of Many Leaves. Our people are like the leaves during Ghost Face. There are only a few left, clinging stubbornly to the branches until they too are blown off and fall to the ground. Nothing will save us. If we bend to the will of the White-Eyes and try to become farmers like the Papagos and the Pimas, then they will be satisfied, for a time at least. Where will we be told to live? On barren land where nothing will grow. In the sickly bottomlands of the desert. There The People will die, not bravely as in battle, when they are young and strong, but slowly, one by one, of the white man's sickness, and more than that because they will not have the freedom we have here on the Big Mountain.'' He paused and looked east again, as though savoring the full glory of the rising sun despite the physical blindness. "Nothing can save The People,'' he continued at last. "Perhaps a great Ghost Dance might do it. A ceremony attended by all of The People—Chiricahuas, Mimbrenos, Tontos, White Mountain, *all*, *all* . . . Would that not save us, Never Still?''

"It could not save your grandson yesterday, Grandfather.''

There came a long silence. It seemed as though the old *diyi* were asleep. Alec turned to leave. He started for the head of the trail.

"What really happened at Muerte Springs?'' Black Wind called after him.

Alec stopped short. He turned slowly. "What do you mean?" he asked quietly.

"I know now. I can tell by the way you spoke, " Black Wind said.

The old man had him there, Alec thought.

"My grandson The Runner told me he saw the way his brother looked at you, but never said a word. Why did he not speak, Never Still?"

"He could not speak, Grandfather."

Black Wind shook his head. "Do you mean he *would* not speak? Was there something he could not say for fear of betraying his friend and blood brother Never Still?"

The old man was a devil! The memory of Muerte Springs came flooding back into Alec's mind. He remembered all too well the look on Baishan's face as Alec had struck up his carbine, thus saving Trapnell's life.

"There is no answer," Black Wind said at last. "You cannot live in two worlds, Never Still. It is only by the will of Yosen you have survived here as long as you have. You knew that long ago, yet you stayed. Why?"

Alec suddenly felt completely exhausted mentally, and he realized what a terrible tension he had been under these past few weeks. "I'm not sure myself, Grandfather," he admitted at last.

Minutes drifted past. "Many things in our lives cannot be changed," Black Wind said, almost as though he were thinking aloud. "The seasons, night and day, and whether we are born of The People, or as Americans or Mexicans. If you are born one way, you must remain that way the remainder of your life and perhaps after death as well. We here on Big Mountain are of The People. You belong to the world of the White-Eyes. You must return to them. You must dedicate yourself to their way of life." He paused, then turned to look directly at Alec. "However, there may be a difference in you. Perhaps you understand us better than most of your people do. To that end, perhaps it *is* better that you return to being a soldier. In so doing, you might be of help to The People when eventually we are defeated. That is a certainty. Perhaps it is the will of Yosen you will be there to help us at that time when we must live and die as the White-Eyes will us to.'' He nodded. "Yes, that is it. *Enju*—it is good.'' His voice died away. He bowed his head.

Alec waited. The wind had suddenly grown chilly. It was very quiet. The birdcalls were hushed. The wind-rustled leaves could hardly be heard. The old man sat as though carved from part of the boulder against which his back rested.

Alec at last walked to Black Wind. He bent and looked up into the deeply lined face with its sightless eyes. The eyes were wide open. He was no longer breathing. He was gone forever. He had "crossed the canyon" to be with his grandson.

Alec left him there. He walked down to where the trail made a turn. Once past the turn he would no longer be able to see the grave site. The sun shone brightly on the boulder. "*Yadalanh,*" Alec said quietly. "Farewell, Grandfather. Farewell, my brother."

He continued down the trail. Several times he thought he saw an indistinct and shadowy movement in the dark woods as though someone or *something* were keeping noiseless pace with him. A wolf? Perhaps it was a mountain lion. The words of Looking Glass came back to him: "There are many ghosts in our lives. There are many ghosts in these woods and on the ⸱ Mountain.''

The Runner rode with Anne and Alec to the rim of Muerte Canyon. Alec had said farewell to all the people—gruff Black Bear, smiling Corn Flower, quiet and introspective Hair Rope, and all the others with whom he had lived and fought against the *gambrusinos*. They all seemed to know he would not return, at least not as one of *them*.

Alec knew the Big Mountain now almost as well as the Chiricahuas and as no white man had ever known it. He knew most of the secret trails—many of the places of ingress and egress, most of the secret hiding places—but not all. Now he would never be shown them. They reined in their horses and dismounted.

The Runner was short on years, but now long on wisdom and experience. Young as he was, he had succeeded Black Wind as head *diyi*.

Alec looked at him. "Will we ever meet again as friends and brothers?"

"Only Yosen knows that," The Runner replied.

Alec smiled a little. "That is so, and he won't tell."

They gripped each other's shoulders. The Runner led his horse to the turn of the trail where he had once said good-bye to Alec and Ben, hoping in his heart that Alec would not leave. His prayers and hopes had been realized at that time. This time, he knew, would not be the same. He turned, raised his arm, and called out strongly, "*Yadalanh*, Never Still!" Then he was gone.

Anne looked back along the trail. "What will happen to these people?"

Alec shrugged. "It's only a matter of time. There never have been very many of them. Their numbers get fewer every years because of their incessant warfare. Like most Indians, the Apaches have never learned to cooperate with each other as a whole."

"And there can be no Ghost Dance as the last possible resort."

Alec nodded. "You're learning, Anne. The Ghost Dance is their greatest power. Sometimes it succeeds. More often it fails. No power on earth can save these people in their present life-style."

She looked up at him. In the past week or so she had begun to notice a deep-seated melancholy in his eyes. He was no longer the man she had remembered at Muerte Canyon and Fort Bowie. He was changed forever. "Yet, if you return to the Service, you might be ordered to lead troops against them. It might be a fight to the death."

He picked up the reins of his horse and looked through the deep-shadowed woods. "Perhaps it's possible I can do more good as a friend in the ranks of their greatest enemy than if I did not return to the Service." He smiled a little grimly. "That is, if I *can* return to the Service. If so, I plan to dedicate my future career to helping The People as best I can." He looked down at her. "With your help, of course."

They led their horses along the steep, precipitous trail down into the canyon depths. Overhead a golden eagle soared

powerfully higher, as though to disappear into the eye of Holos, The Sun. Perhaps it was the spirit of Baishan. It was just
as well. He could not have survived the inevitable defeat and
final degradation of The People.

Hi-dicho—It is finished.

AUTHOR NOTE

MY RESEARCH FOR *The Ghost Dancers* has been compiled for the past forty-five years. All of the sources are far too numerous to note here, but special mention should be made of the following: *The Apache Scouts: A Chiricahua Appraisal*, by Eve Ball; *Medicine Men of the Apache* and *On the Border with Crook*, by Lieutenant (later Captain) J. G. Bourke; *The First Hundred Years of Nino Cochise*, by Ciyé "Nino" Cochise, as told to A. Kinney Griffith; *Life Among The Apaches*, by John C. Cremony; *The Apache Indians*, by Frank Lockwood; *The People Called Apache*, by Thomas E. Mails; *An Apache Life Way, Myths and Tales of the Chiricahua Apaches*, by Dr. Morris E. Opler, and *The Raid and War-Path Language of the Chiricahua Apache*, by Dr. Morris E. Opler and Harry Hoijer; *The Trails of Pete Kitchen* and *TUCSON TUBAC TUMACACORI TOHELL*, by Colonel Gil Proctor; *The Conquest of Apacheria*, by Dan L. Thrapp; *The Apaches, Eagles of the Southwest*, by Donald E. Worcester.

There are many dialectical variations in Apache words, so I chose one version and used it throughout the novel. The Ghost Dance scenes are a compilation of various descriptions of the ceremony, no two of which are exactly alike.

During the past thirty years I have visited all of the major scenes depicted in the novel—the Chiricahua Mountains, Fort Bowie, Tumacacori, Tucson, and along the Mexican border on both sides. In particular I knew Pete Kitchen's ranch quite well. At the time I stayed there, the ranch was owned by Colonel Gil Proctor, soldier, writer, historian, and master storyteller of the legends from both sides of the border. I drank many a cold *cerveza* with him in his study at the ranch while listening to his fabulous tales. I slept in a bedroom, the outer walls of which were pocked with Apache bullet holes and arrow points. The ranch was already a place of legend during Pete Kitchen's time and remains so today.

The final surrender of the Apaches led by Geronimo took place at Skeleton Canyon, September 1886, about fourteen years after the fictional death of Baishan. A small band of Chiricahuas did not surrender, but instead fled back into Mexico and their hideout in the inner fastnesses of the Sierra Madre Occidental. Their names were never again mentioned by the Apaches who did surrender; they were referred to only as ''The Nameless Ones.'' In 1927 a Mexican rancher, Francisco Fimbres, was attacked by these hostile Apaches. His wife and son were killed. Fimbres dedicated his life to exterminating the savages. He led eleven expeditions into the Sierra Madre between 1927 and 1933. In 1933 the Mexicans killed twenty-four of The Nameless Ones and captured three small children. This wiped out the band that had existed, virtually unknown, for almost fifty years after the supposed surrender of *all* hostile Apaches.

Vaya,

Gordon D. Shirreffs
Granada Hills, California